Midnight on F

Keira Willis was born in Manchester in 1986 and decided quite early on that she was going to grow up to be both a writer and a barrister (Reader, this did not happen). She graduated with a degree in English Literature, followed by studying for an MEd at Queens' College, Cambridge while teaching English and Drama at a secondary school. She eventually decided that it was time to get back to writing stories.

Midnight on Hanging Bridge is the third instalment in the *Tib Street Ballroom* series. Despite the title of the series, there is still (regrettably) no real dancing contained within - though there is a single occurrence of shimmying on '80s nightclub dance floors in this one!

MIDNIGHT ON HANGING BRIDGE

KEIRA WILLIS

MARMALADE PRESS

Published by Marmalade Press
www.marmaladepress.co.uk

First published 2025

A CIP catalogue record for this book
is available from the British Library

Printed and bound in Great Britain by
Clays Ltd, Elcograf S.p.A.

Typeset in Adobe Garamond Pro and Futura by Spike-E

ISBN 978-1-9997645-5-5

To Sam
with love

ONE

Detective Inspector Andrew Joyce was about to commit murder in broad daylight, and there was nothing anybody could do about it.

He tightened his fingers around the cold metal in his right hand and slowly exhaled through his nose, trying to block out the relentless wailing that had been feverishly spinning his fraying patience into what was beginning to look like an increasingly tempting garrotte.

Andrew could still see the smug expression at the corner of his vision, needling him as the seconds passed with a mocking sluggishness; those beady little eyes nestled behind cheap plastic spectacles stared at him, unblinking, and the slight curl to the thin lips was like a personalised invitation to Andrew's mounting need for vengeance.

The wail sounded again – closer now – and as the pitch crawled higher with a gasping intake of breath, Andrew finally snapped.

He spun around to unleash the projectile on its intended target, entirely ready to wipe that self-satisfied grin away for good.

'Sorry, sir!'

Andrew paused in surprise at the shout; hand still raised above his shoulder. His nose twitched as Detective Constable Lloyd Parker materialised in front of him, clutching a stack of white and green paper bags.

'Are you alright there, boss?' Lloyd asked slowly as his apologetic expression crept towards baffled concern. The frown deepened when he looked quickly between Andrew's face and the can of fizzy Vimto still being held threateningly at chin-height. 'What did I miss?'

Andrew pursed his lips and slowly returned his arm to his side. 'Nothing.'

Lloyd turned his head, scanning their surroundings for anything out of the ordinary. He raised his eyebrows. 'Sir, were you about to deck that plastic Santa with a can of pop?'

Andrew decided that it would probably be best to avoid answering Lloyd's question. He kept his eyes averted from the five-foot Father Christmas, with its stupid rictus sneer still in place. 'What took you so bloody long?'

Lloyd, fully aware that he'd deduced Andrew's planned course of action correctly, shrugged in response. 'They didn't have any of the turkey and cranberry ones made up, and you know what the boss would be like if I came back without three of them for him.'

To his eternal chagrin, Andrew *did* know what DCI Higson would be like if Lloyd returned without his specified lunch order.

'Oh, and they'd run out of their own stuffing as well,' Lloyd continued, 'so I had to wait because one of the girls had just nipped up to Safeway to get more of that one that comes in the box. You know, the one you just add water to? Mum refuses to buy it – she says it's tasteless – even though *her* stuffing is like cardboard. Anyway, it wasn't finished in the oven.'

Andrew was still trying to process Lloyd's rambling explanation when the godawful shrieking rallied with renewed vigour.

'Christ.' Lloyd winced, nodding towards the bawling toddler who, by then, was prostrate on the ground. 'I thought kids loved all this Christmas stuff.'

Andrew glanced up at the heavily decorated tree towering over the heaving mass of shoppers navigating the Arndale Centre and shook his head. 'Apparently not at all of them.'

To a degree, Andrew could relate. He could pinpoint the exact moment that *he* had decided that he hated Christmas: It had been July 1963, and his mother – unusually lucid that day – had asked him what he wanted for Christmas that year. He'd stared at her, confused that she'd brought up Christmas in the middle of summer, and even more confused that she'd asked him such a question in the first place. He'd been unable to recall a single other occurrence of that same inquiry in the decade since his birth.

Agatha hadn't seemed fazed by her son's silence; she'd just taken a sip of her tea and leant back in her chair to patiently await a response.

'I don't know,' is all Andrew had eventually been able to offer quietly. It hadn't been quite the truth, of course. The truth had been that he hadn't given two hoots about Christmas – or much else for that matter – since his older brother Rob's sudden death the year before, but he had been certain that his mother wouldn't appreciate that answer.

Agatha hadn't actually appreciated the answer he'd given either. She'd slammed her mug down on the small kitchen table and stone-cold milky tea had violently sloshed up the sides and over the lip.

Andrew had watched as the chalky liquid had crept towards the edge of the table. When the first drop had hit the vinyl tile with a barely audible splash, Agatha had risen slowly to her feet and pressed her palms flat to the stained tabletop. She'd leant down towards her son, with greasy strands of unkempt hair falling like mismatched curtains either side of her reddened eyes, shaking her head in obvious disappointment.

'Then you'll get nothing from me,' she'd sneered. 'Which is all you deserve.'

Andrew had known better than to answer back, and so he'd remained mute and motionless, with his head bowed, letting his mother hiss furious accusations at him until she'd abruptly left the room.

Later that afternoon, Nana Joyce had arrived and helped

Andrew pack his belongings into his granddad's war-battered duffle bag. The house had still been simmering in strained silence when they'd left together, but Agatha had been nowhere to be seen.

By the time Christmas had arrived five months later, Agatha had made no attempt to see her son. As promised, Andrew hadn't received a single thing from her that December.

'Should we go, boss?'

Andrew blinked away the lingering traces of his mother's bitter words and rolled his eyes at Lloyd. 'You're never this keen to get back to work.'

Lloyd raised his eyebrows and gestured towards his watch. 'It's already nearly half-twelve. Higson'll kill me if there's not lunch on his desk when he comes in!'

Andrew couldn't argue with that assessment, so he just turned and headed for the exit without further comment.

On a personal note, he wasn't actually raring to get back to Tib Street. Back in the beginning, when he'd first been transferred to the Ballroom, he couldn't have imagined there ever being a day when he'd willingly choose to be there; that had all changed, of course, but for months now he'd been trudging through the tedious, *entirely pointless* cases that Higson had been handing out to them, and he was really starting to wonder just how much longer he could stay there without dropping dead from sheer boredom.

The case they'd finally cracked that morning was as perfect an example of the problem as Andrew would be able to find: the sudden disappearance of Alan Jermyn, a man who'd spent the sixties selling exotic animals to rich idiots who'd thought that crocodiles and leopards would make great pets. Jermyn had apparently left his shop in January 1972 to deliver a puma to a customer – Angelica Fortnum – out in Bowdon. Mrs Fortnum had been rather put out when Jermyn didn't arrive as promised

4

and had called the police the next morning to complain that Jermyn had taken her money but not delivered the promised big cat. By all accounts, Jermyn had never returned to his shop, and disappeared off the face of the earth, along with Angelica Fortnum's puma and a significant wad of cash.

When Andrew had called her earlier that week, a snappish Mrs Fortnum had been very keen for him to understand just how disappointed her guests had been when they'd arrived on the evening of Jermyn's disappearance and there'd been no lovely new animal for them to coo over after pudding. Andrew had been the very picture of professionalism and had refrained from asking why the hell anyone would *want* a puma to come to dinner in the first place, nor had he questioned just why you'd still be quite so bitter about the whole thing fifteen years later. If Andrew had learned anything at all since moving to the Ballroom, it was that extremely rich people often had significantly more money than sense. He'd seen very little evidence to suggest that this problem wasn't endemic in the upper echelons of society, with only *very specific* exceptions aside.

Although Mrs Fortnum had been entirely useless to Andrew's investigation, and despite Lloyd's fortnight-long campaign to convince his colleagues that Jermyn had clearly been eaten by the puma – which, incidentally, in Lloyd's argument, had somehow relocated itself to the South West to begin its new career as the Beast of Exmoor after offing Jermyn – they had eventually happened upon the truth of the matter that morning when the Ballroom had received a tearful phone call from the missing man himself.

Thankfully, the Ballroom's resident pragmatist, DS Jen Cusack, had been the one to answer the phone and listen to the entire snivelling story, because Andrew's soul-deep lack of patience for hysteria would have entirely failed to cope with it.

According to his sergeant's summary, Jermyn had copped to

the fact that there'd never actually been a puma in his possession, and he'd simply buggered off to Benidorm with Angelica Fortnum's money, in order to open a bar with a woman he'd met on holiday the year before.

'Why's he admitting to it now?' Lloyd had asked, his bewilderment overshadowed by abject disappointment that his Beast of Exmoor theory hadn't played out.

Jen had shrugged. 'Apparently, he found God after his wife filed for divorce last year, and he felt *compelled* to tell us the truth as part of atoning for his past sins. One of his mates has known where he's been the whole time, and when they told Jermyn we'd been asking after him again he decided to call us and confess.'

'Which friend?' Andrew had asked tersely, desperately hoping that they could at least go and do something about whichever one of Jermyn's associates had been withholding key information from the Ballroom's investigation.

'He wouldn't say,' Jen had winced. 'Apparently, Jesus wouldn't want him to dob his mates in.'

'Do we get to go to Spain?' Lloyd had asked hopefully, already immersed in a daydream of winter sun.

Jen had rolled her eyes. 'Doubt it. Apparently, he's coming back to Manchester for Christmas – he's given me his flight details and everything.'

'He's given you his flight details?' Andrew had asked blankly.

Jen had nodded with yet another shrug. 'Yeah. He says he lands on the twenty-fourth, and he'll be expecting us at the airport.'

'It's a Christmas miracle, sir,' Lloyd had guffawed, and Andrew had only barely restrained himself from throwing something at the younger man.

'We can't even be sure it's him,' Andrew had argued instead. 'Anyone could have made that call!'

'I guess we'll find out next Thursday,' Jen had concluded as she'd turned away to write up the call.

And that, really, had been that.

Higson had told them that he bloody well wouldn't be going to the airport on Christmas Eve, and that they could argue amongst themselves over who was going to make up the welcome party for Jermyn's possible return. He'd then grumpily announced that he was going out, and that he'd be expecting lunch on his desk when he got back.

Even knowing that there were few worse places to be than a shopping centre the week before Christmas, Andrew had offered to go and buy sandwiches with Lloyd because somehow staying in the Ballroom without anything to do had seemed an even less attractive option. The whole trip, however, had only confirmed what Andrew already knew – that he was genuinely down to his last nerve, and something fundamental needed to change.

'Boss?' Lloyd asked with uncharacteristic hesitance as they turned the corner at Debenhams and found themselves back on Tib Street.

'Yeah?'

'Do you think it's weird that all the cases we've had recently are a bit...' Lloyd trailed off and twisted his lips.

A bit shit, Andrew thought. 'A bit pedestrian?' is what he voiced aloud.

'Well, I was going to say, 'a bit shit', to be honest,' Lloyd admitted as the Ballroom came into view further up the street. 'But, yeah, *pedestrian.*'

'It can't always be murders and gangs, Lloyd,' Andrew replied, hoping that his own frustration was imperceptible.

'Yeah, I know that,' Lloyd agreed begrudgingly, 'but it's been months since we've had anything even a bit interesting. I mean, when was the last time Peggy agreed to come in and take a look at something?'

Andrew knew *exactly* how long it had been since they'd had to call Peggy Swan in – five whole months. Handing Lloyd that precise answer felt a bit like giving away more than he'd like though, so he offered a one-shouldered shrug instead. 'Couple of months?'

Lloyd shook his head as they reached the battered door and awkwardly fished around in his pockets for his keys, all the while trying not to drop Higson's hefty lunch order. 'It's way longer than that. Come on, it was the summer, surely.'

Andrew didn't answer. Instead, he feigned an interest in the continually baffling *Cheryl Richard Dance Studio* plaque that hung on the exterior wall. He'd been at Tib Street for just over eighteen months, and he *still* hadn't the foggiest about the Ballroom's history beyond the most basic of explanations he'd received on his first day.

Lloyd kicked the bottom left of the door and then threw his shoulder against the centre until it scraped open with a sound too akin to nails on a chalkboard for Andrew's liking. He'd drenched the whole thing with WD-40 in the summer, but it didn't seem to have made the slightest difference.

Andrew nipped past while Lloyd reversed the same steps to close the door again and took the stairs as quickly as he could without breaking into an actual run. Dolly's particular blend of cigarette smoke and bleach was lingering in the air, and Andrew had no desire whatsoever to find himself face to face with their terrifying cleaning lady and her enigmatic pronouncements about life or her more specifically pointed criticisms of Andrew and his appearance.

'I was about to send out a search party!' Jen exclaimed as Andrew dropped despondently into his chair and proffered the carrier bag of fizzy pop cans towards her.

'It's mental in that place,' Lloyd muttered as he handed one paper bag to Jen and another to Andrew. He then turned and placed the remainder on Higson's desk. 'Boss not back yet?'

'No,' Jen confirmed as she carefully unwrapped her lunch.

'Where'd he go anyway?' Lloyd asked around a mouthful of sandwich.

'Don't talk when you're eating,' Jen chastised her younger colleague. 'As for Higson, I have no idea. He can't have gone far though.'

'How'd you figure that one?' Lloyd asked, mouth blessedly empty again.

'Car keys are still on his desk.' Jen nodded towards the DCI's corner of the room.

Andrew was fairly certain that Higson was propping up a bar somewhere in the vicinity of Tib Street and he'd no doubt appear when his stomach told him it was lunchtime. 'He'll be back in a minute.'

A minute passed, and there was no sign of Higson.

Nor was there any sign of Higson when Andrew pushed his chair back and stood up an hour later.

'Right, I need to do something,' he said, pressing his fingertips to his temples. 'We're not getting any further with Jermyn until Christmas Eve, but I can't just sit here and wait for that.'

Lloyd looked at him as though he'd sprouted an extra head. 'But Higson's not here.'

'So? I think I'm perfectly capable of going to the archive room and picking up a case file.'

Lloyd blanched. 'You really wanna go in there? Even after what Peggy said?'

No, Andrew could safely say that he really didn't want to go into the archive room. After his own slightly odd experience earlier in the year, he hadn't been thrilled to hear that Peggy had experienced something unsettling enough to send her fleeing from the building.

'There's nothing there, Lloyd,' Andrew replied as steadily as he could manage. 'It's just a boring room full of files.'

'Sir, I'm not sure this is a very good idea,' Jen added. 'DCI Higson did say that he didn't want any of us going in there, and that he'd pick out the cases.'

'Well, he's not here right now,' Andrew replied, backing towards the double doors. 'Look, I'll just go and grab whatever he's left on the top of the pile. No matter how bloody dull it is, it's got to be better than sitting here waiting for him to come back for lunch.'

Jen grimaced and then sighed in what Andrew would take as tacit agreement for his plan. Lloyd continued to look troubled with just a smidge of eagerness but given that was Lloyd's default expression whenever anything remotely ghost-adjacent was brought up, Andrew assumed he had the younger man's backing too. He snatched up the heavy keyring from Higson's desk and left the room before either of his colleagues could invent another protest.

Andrew jogged down the staircase to the lower landing, spurred on by an almost childish sense of freedom, but his steps slowed dramatically as he actually approached the door to the first archive room.

A shiver tried to fight its way up his spine, but he shrugged it off with a quiet rumble of disdain. It was just a bloody boring room, filled to the brim with what were apparently the world's most bloody boring files.

He turned the key in the lock, surprised by how loud the click sounded in the otherwise silent hallway.

Armed with the disappointing knowledge that ghosts were, unfortunately, something he should be concerned about, Andrew steeled himself and pushed down on the handle.

Absolutely nothing of note happened, and the door swung open easily. There was no immediate sense of being watched, nor any hint of a threat lurking in the furthest shadowy corners.

Tension bled from his shoulders, and he stepped into the room with a sigh of relief.

Andrew kicked the doorstop into place to counteract the sloping floor of the room and switched on the light.

Any relief was immediately replaced with a sense of dawning disgust as the buttery glow of the single, naked bulb above his head revealed the chaotic, grimy mess that the archive room had become.

He wrinkled his nose as his eyes trailed over the numerous mugs on the small table in the centre of the room; none had been drained completely, and the varying quantities of remaining rancid coffee were scarring the air with a sour tang that tickled the back of Andrew's throat as he stepped closer.

There were two overflowing ashtrays on the old carpet, and a third was perched precariously at the very edge of the table, right next to a tall stack of files.

Andrew assumed that these were the cases that Higson had already pulled for the team to work on. With a brief but potent yearning for a pair of gloves, he gingerly picked up the top file and opened it.

'Oh, for fuck's sake,' he muttered to himself as he despondently scanned the file. Higson couldn't really want them to look into a spate of break-ins at Italian restaurants in the fifties, could he?

He knew that he'd told the others that he was just going to bring back the first case he found, but he'd rather submit himself to the mercy of rabid Christmas shoppers on Market Street than go back upstairs with *that*.

'Oops,' he said dryly as he carelessly pushed the remaining files onto the floor, dropping the folder in his hand into the sliding mass. He picked another case at random.

Surely this way, he'd have plausible deniability if Higson questioned him on why he hadn't taken the Italian restaurant case. If Andrew had entered the archive to discover that the files had all fallen on the floor, then it really couldn't be his fault if he selected a different file instead, could it?

He knew how immature he was being, but if Higson was going to treat them all like idiots for reasons unknown, then Andrew figured that he could allow himself to act the prat on this occasion.

'Please, Christ, be something better,' Andrew hissed as he opened the new case file. The words 'Theft' and 'Lord Mayor' jumped out at him, and for just a second, he thought that he might be onto something.

Andrew's triumph was felled a moment later when he scanned the initial incident report and saw that the date was in the forties.

According to the brief, neatly typed sheet of paper, the Lord Mayor's hotel room had been broken into while he was attending a function, and he'd returned to discover that some of his belongings had been taken. The valuables stolen included gold-plated cufflinks and a pair of socks that he'd worn to every ceremonial occasion during his tenure.

Andrew growled in frustration. Higson was obviously taking the complete piss, and Andrew couldn't for the life of him understand why.

Initially, when the cases had turned towards the pointless, Andrew had been content to assume that it was because Peggy had been increasingly declining to consult on investigations after the *Lady Bancroft* debacle and so Higson had been focusing on finding cases that the Ballroom could investigate without the need for any ghostly intervention. That excuse had worn thin as the summer had dwindled, and now it was nearly Christmas, and a missing pair of novelty socks turned out to be the straw that finally broke the camel's back.

Andrew crouched down to pick up an armful of files, fully intending to unceremoniously drop them on Higson's desk when he returned, while also asking for an explanation for what the hell was actually going on.

As he reached out to retrieve some papers that had ended up

under the table, Andrew paused when something caught his eye. For a split second he wasn't sure what it was that had snared his attention, and a sense of apprehension twisted in his gut, but he relaxed as he turned his head.

There, on the seat of the rickety chair that had been tucked beneath the table, was a single case folder. Unlike the sparsely filled ones that now littered the floor, this one looked to be bursting with paper, and even from his awkward vantage point, Andrew could see that the file was stained and well-worn. It was an obvious anomaly, and Andrew was instantly drawn to it.

He staggered to his feet and pulled the chair back so that he could pick up the case file.

The cover was emblazoned with a smudged Manchester City Police stamp, which suggested that it was an original file, and not the usual sort of copy produced for the Ballroom. A vertical groove ran down the middle, and another indent bisected the file from left to right, as though the whole thing been quite savagely folded in half in both directions on multiple occasions in its past.

Admittedly, the date on the smudged stamp was December 1967, but even the fact that it was a twenty-year-old case wasn't enough to dent Andrew's curiosity.

Inside, the margins of a handwritten incident report were covered in Higson's distinctive, spidery scrawl; the ink was more faded in some places than others, which suggested that Higson had been making notes on this case for *years*.

He'd barely read to the end of the first paragraph when he remembered that he was on borrowed time. He needed to get this file out of the archive room and in front of Jen and Lloyd before Higson got back, otherwise he could kiss goodbye to any chance he had of finding out more.

He snapped the file closed, gave the coffee mugs one final horrified glance and made for the door.

Listening carefully for any hint that Higson had made it back to the building, Andrew removed the doorstop and hurried out of the room towards the staircase.

His right foot had just hit the upper landing when an awful realisation brought him up short:

The archive room door hadn't closed behind him.

He vividly remembered the last time that had happened, and it was with more than a smidge of trepidation that he warily turned his head to look back over his shoulder.

Sure enough, the door was wide open, but nothing held it in place.

Andrew swallowed heavily and waited, almost holding his breath for fear he might disturb something. He stared at the door, not entirely sure whether he wanted it to move or not.

Just as he'd convinced himself that holding a staring contest with an inanimate object wasn't the best use of his time and that he should really go back and close the door, a car backfired noisily out on Tib Street.

Andrew jolted in surprise at the blast of sound, clutching the file tighter to his chest.

The archive room door lazily swung towards the landing, as though it had nothing better to do than give Andrew a heart attack, before closing with the softest of clicks.

Andrew knew a dismissal when he saw one, so he turned on his heel and bolted up the staircase.

TWO

Convincing his colleagues that he'd found the perfect case was dispiritingly more difficult than Andrew had anticipated.

As he'd prepared to read out the case summary, he'd had to fight the gleeful smile that was trying to claw its way onto his face. After all, it wasn't as though Andrew thought that suspicious disappearances were *funny*, and he certainly didn't want anyone to think that he did. He'd schooled his features and tried to make the circumstances surrounding the vanishing of seventeen-year-old Lily Woodhouse and one PC Davy Nash sound as mundane as possible.

Yet, when he eventually looked up from the conclusion of the cover page, Andrew had the feeling that he might not have been as successful in containing his enthusiasm as he'd hoped.

'This is really the next one the boss was going to give us?' Lloyd asked in obvious surprise. He then did something complicated with his eyebrows that made him look even more astonished. 'You're sure?'

Andrew made a noncommittal sound in the back of his throat and averted his eyes from the other man. Unfortunately, this meant that he managed to catch Jen's shrewd gaze instead. She didn't look surprised at all; no, Jen looked downright unconvinced.

Andrew cleared his throat and turned back to Lloyd. 'It's an unsolved case from twenty years ago. That's what we're supposed to be working on here, isn't it?'

'Well, yeah, but a missing girl and a missing copper?' Lloyd's eyebrows finally disappeared beneath his messy hair. 'Bit heavy, isn't it?'

'Sir?' Jen interjected before Andrew could remind Lloyd that he'd been the one complaining about the trivial nature of their recent cases. 'I've been in that archive room hundreds of times in the past five years, pulling out all sorts of cases.'

'And?'

'*And,* I've never seen that case file before.' Jen shook her head vehemently. 'I don't remember the boss ever mentioning it, but you're saying that he's been looking into it for years?'

'His notes are all over it,' Andrew replied, holding up the file so that Jen could see Higson's scribbles.

'I think we should wait until he gets back,' Jen replied steadily, nodding towards Higson's still-empty chair.

Andrew sighed. It wasn't often that he disagreed with Jen. He understood where her hesitation came from, but he was going to lose the plot entirely if they didn't get on with something new. It was even less often that he pulled rank, but desperate times and all that. He shook his head. 'We're on this until we're given a good reason why we shouldn't be.'

Jen's eyes narrowed marginally, but eventually she nodded her acceptance and reached for her notebook and biro. 'Alright, where do we start?'

'We need to work out how everyone in this case is connected,' Andrew replied, relieved that he hadn't needed to argue the point any further. 'Given all the notes in here, I reckon Higson's done most of the legwork already.'

'What year did you say it was?' Lloyd asked.

'Sixty-seven,' Andrew replied, checking the stamp again.

'Wasn't Higson *here* in the sixties? Part of the Ballroom, I mean.'

Andrew didn't know the answer to that, so he looked to Jen, who always seemed to have knowledge about their boss that he and Lloyd weren't privy to.

Jen nodded. 'He was. Not the whole time though. He went back to A Division for a few years after his first stint here.'

Andrew scanned the list of people who'd given statements as

part of the investigation and then paused in surprise. 'Hang on.'

'What?' Lloyd asked.

Andrew tapped the page. '*Higson* is listed as a witness.'

'What, really?' Lloyd hopped off the edge of his desk and went to look over Andrew's shoulder. 'Oh, yeah, look. DS William Higson, A Division. God, it's weird to think about the boss being young, isn't it?'

Andrew ignored him.

'DC Richard Chambers?' Jen squinted in surprise as she read the name of Andrew's former boss. 'Case Re-examination Division. Wait, Chambers was part of the Ballroom?'

Andrew thought back to the day he'd been transferred from CID to Tib Street; to the Case Re-examination Division, to give it its proper name, or to the Graveyard, if he wanted to use his former colleagues' nickname for the place instead. DCI Chambers, as he was by now, had mentioned that he'd been at the Ballroom in the sixties, but as Andrew had been filled with despair at the very idea of the weird department he was being unwillingly moved to, he hadn't really given Chambers' comments much thought. 'Yeah, he told me that.'

He ran his finger down the list of names, and another jumped out at Andrew. 'Here, look: DCI James Prentice. Chambers mentioned him when he sent me here. I think there might have been a bit of hero-worship there.'

Lloyd grimaced. 'And knowing what we know about Chambers these days, does that tell us anything about this Prentice character?'

'Speculation, Lloyd,' Andrew replied, but he'd be lying if he hadn't thought the same thing. Chambers certainly wasn't to be trusted, so it wasn't a huge leap of logic to imagine that he'd learned the ropes from his own DCI back in the sixties.

Jen's forehead creased. 'Sir, *really*, don't you think we should wait for DCI Higson?'

There was no chance of that. Andrew was rapidly concluding that they were never supposed to have seen this file, and he didn't want Higson to try and take it away from them until Andrew had enough of an argument for why they should definitely investigate a case that their boss had apparently been secretly looking into for two decades.

'Where is he, anyway?' Lloyd asked for what felt like the hundredth time that afternoon.

'Look,' Andrew said, ignoring Lloyd as he spread the file open on his desk. 'Let's just get the basic facts of it all straight before he gets here, and then we'll see what happens.'

'*We'll see what happens* usually means 'no chance' when my Mum says it,' muttered Lloyd grumpily.

Andrew ignored him again. 'Jen, can you get this down?'

Jen nodded and primed her pen as she took a seat across from him.

Andrew looked down at the file, re-reading quickly as he pulled out facts to relay to Jen. 'Okay, Lily Woodhouse. Seventeen at the time of her disappearance. She lived with her parents in Heaton Moor; in the house she grew up in. Left school at fifteen and found work as a cleaner. She appeared on television in the spring before she disappeared.'

'What? She was famous?' Lloyd asked.

Andrew shook his head. 'No, I don't think so. Not really, anyway. It says here that she was on something called *Saturday Spotlight*, whatever that is.'

'Oh, I remember that,' Jen interjected. 'It was a talent show. I suppose it was a bit like *Opportunity Knocks*, but it had a lot more novelty acts on. I used to watch it with my cousins.'

Andrew couldn't recall ever seeing an episode, but as he'd spent his teenaged Saturdays either with his mother, who'd banned TV, or with his grandparents, who only watched *The Two Ronnies* and, oddly, *Z Cars*, that wasn't entirely surprising.

'Do you remember seeing this Lily Woodhouse girl?' Lloyd asked Jen.

Jen shook her head. 'It was twenty-years ago, Lloyd. They used to have loads of people on each episode. I can't even remember how the competition worked. I think there *might* have been an overall winner at the end?'

'Lily won her year,' Andrew said, checking the file to confirm. 'Trophy and a cash prize, apparently.'

'What was her act?' Lloyd was obviously intrigued.

'Doesn't say here,' Andrew replied. He flicked through a few more pages until he found Lily's expanded background information. Born in March 1950, *blah blah blah*, described by her former teachers as very bright but easily bored. *Ah*, applied to be on *Saturday Spotlight* to showcase her supposed extraordinary talent of –'

Andrew choked on his own saliva with sudden, violent regret for picking up the file in the first place.

'What is it, sir?' Lloyd asked.

Without then waiting for Andrew to stop coughing and reply, Lloyd just reached over to pluck the paper from his boss's hand and read aloud. 'Lily applied to be on *Saturday Spotlight* to showcase her supposed extraordinary talent of psychic divination'.

Lloyd's head snapped up, his expression full of wonder. 'She could read minds! That's what that means, right?'

As he slapped his chest with his palm, Andrew noticed that Jen was doing an extremely poor job of pretending that she wasn't laughing at him.

'Nobody can read anybody else's mind,' Andrew spluttered eventually. 'It's a party trick.'

Lloyd, as expected, looked entirely unconvinced by Andrew's argument. 'That would be one hell of a motive to make someone disappear though, wouldn't it? If Lily knew something that she shouldn't have done?'

Andrew raised his eyebrows as he took the paper back.

'Sorry, sir,' Lloyd added, abashed as he returned to the other side of Andrew's desk. 'Just an idea.'

'Maybe save the ideas until we've actually read the case file, yeah?' Andrew looked back down at Lily's information. 'So, she won *Saturday Spotlight* in April sixty-seven, and it looks like she became a bit of a fixture in town after that. Her parents seemed to think that she spent most of the year staying with various friends as she wasn't at home much after she appeared on TV.'

Jen frowned. 'They *think* she was staying with friends? She'd only just turned seventeen.'

'Plenty of seventeen-year-olds can fend for themselves,' Andrew reasoned.

'Doesn't mean that people shouldn't care where they are,' Jen countered immediately, eyes flashing.

Personally, Andrew would have been much happier if his mother had never had a clue where he'd been, but he wasn't going to say that when this situation had clearly struck a nerve with Jen.

'Either way, her parents are the ones that reported her missing,' Andrew continued reading.

'When?' Jen asked, pen poised once more, although she still looked troubled.

'Fourth of December. A Monday. Apparently, her employer called her parents that morning because Lily hadn't turned up for work on Friday night but then hadn't arrived on Monday morning either.' Andrew ran his finger down the page until he found the date he'd seen earlier. 'The last sighting of her was on the previous Thursday night – the thirtieth of November.'

'Seen by her parents?' Lloyd asked.

Andrew shook his head. 'No. Multiple witnesses saw her at the Free Trade Hall. There was a ballet on, and she was seen 'laughing in the foyer' during the interval, in the company of a young man, later identified as PC Davy Nash.'

'The other missing person,' Lloyd said slowly.

'Were they in a relationship?' Jen asked. 'Or did they just happen to meet at the Free Trade Hall?'

'Lily's parents seemed to think that she was in a relationship at the time, but they had no actual proof of that,' Andrew said, paraphrasing Mrs Woodhouse's captured words. 'As for Davy Nash; his personnel file says that he was married and had two young children.'

'An affair?' Lloyd offered.

Andrew sighed as he scanned a couple of short statements and then his eyes widened. 'At least two witnesses are claiming that Lily and Nash looked very cosy together. But then there's this.'

Andrew turned the file around so the other two could see it clearly. He pointed first at a sentence that had been transcribed as part of a statement by a witness named as Barbara Jackson.

'They were definitely there together,' Jen read aloud. 'They couldn't stop smiling at each other and he kept putting his arm around her. It was obvious to me that it was all very new. You notice these things when you've been married for years.'

'Right, but then...' Andrew swept his finger over to the corresponding handwritten note from Higson. It was succinct, if nothing else.

'*Bullshit. Bridge,*' Lloyd read. 'So, the boss doesn't agree with that version of events?'

'Doesn't look like it, does it?' Andrew replied, sensing that his colleagues had finally clambered aboard his train of thought. 'Higson's own statement says he'd been at the same pub as Davy Nash earlier that evening, but that Davy had left, saying that he was meeting someone at the Free Trade Hall.'

Andrew held up the signed paper that amounted to Higson's three-sentence witness statement.

'And what's this bridge he's on about?' Lloyd asked.

Andrew shrugged.

'Alright.' Jen twisted her lips in thought as she nodded. 'It's interesting, I'll give you that.'

Andrew felt slightly less thrilled about this acceptance than he had done before the whole 'psychic' revelation, but his grandmother had always told him to never look a gift horse in the mouth, and having Lloyd *and* Jen onside for when Higson returned would only help his case.

'Let's split everything between us,' Andrew said, pulling out stacks of paper, ready to divide the research up. 'We need links between anyone and everyone in that file, and we need basic facts. Let's leave Higson's notes out of it for now.'

'Why?' Lloyd asked as he picked up a sheaf of paper. 'Don't you think they're relevant?'

'I think they're probably the most relevant things in there,' Andrew replied truthfully, 'but we need to start from scratch with it. There's no point reopening a case with a half-formed idea of what happened; nothing good would come of that.'

As someone who had definitely entered into some previous investigations with exactly that mindset, Andrew knew the real truth to his words. This case was obviously important to Higson, and, by default, that made this case important to the Ballroom as a whole. He was even willing to lay the whole 'psychic' thing aside for now and ignore it, rather than openly declare it to be utter nonsense.

Well, Andrew thought as he picked up a pen and settled down to read his portion of the case file, *at least there aren't any ghosts in this one.*

THREE

Thursday morning dawned with a leaden gloom. Heavy clouds and an unseasonably mild breeze had swaddled Gatley in an unnatural hush, and Andrew found his eyes closing as he slouched at the bus stop around the corner from his house.

A sharp jangle of glass on glass startled him. His eyes snapped open, and he blinked furiously to try and rouse himself back to full alertness as a figure shambled towards him in the darkness.

'Alright?' the milkman greeted him gruffly, keeping his head bowed as he waddled past, basket in hand.

Andrew still hadn't managed to muster up a reply by the time the milkman climbed back into the waiting milk float and set off towards the centre of Gatley.

It was his own fault, really. Despite Jen's protestations, Andrew had taken the Woodhouse-Nash file home with him the night before to make sure that he could read the whole thing in detail before Higson inevitably kicked off about the fact that his DI had liberated the file from the archive room. In the fading light of the Ballroom, Andrew had seen Higson's continued absence as a blessing, allowing him to get up to speed on the first case that had caught his attention in the best part of six months, but as he'd read over the file while the evening had ticked away around him at home, Andrew had found himself wishing that he could ask Higson questions about the case and the notes that had been scribbled throughout the file.

Two beams of light wobbled into view at the end of the main road, and Andrew sighed loudly as he rolled his shoulders and reached down to pick up the satchel resting against his feet.

It had been six weeks since he'd coaxed his spluttering and groaning Vauxhall Belmont into a parking space outside Luke Warner's garage in Heald Green. Warner had initially reassured him that it was an easy fix (*'Couple of days, mate!'*), and even though Andrew was a natural-born cynic, he'd been compelled to believe in this assessment entirely because the thought of taking the lethargic, creaking, disappointingly *humid* bus to town every day was enough to make him shudder.

The 'easy fix' label had been ripped off within twenty-four hours, when Warner had called Andrew at work to tell him that it was a more serious issue than first thought. The 'couple of days' had become a 'couple of weeks' (*'I'll have to order the parts in, yeah?'*) and now it was mid-December and the car was nothing more than an inconvenient ornament, abandoned forlornly outside his house until such time that Andrew decided whether or not he was going to pay Warner to fix it, or just get rid of the damn thing.

The bus doors opened with a tired hiss that Andrew could relate to. He climbed aboard and made it to an empty seat with minimal interaction, which was the best he could hope for. He leaned his head against the window and glumly watched as Gatley blurred into Northenden.

As the bus and its ever-increasing collection of passengers suffered through the absurdly slow, stop-start journey up Palatine Road towards the city centre, Andrew closed his eyes and locked his arms over the satchel on his lap. He had no intention of actually sleeping, but the illusion would mean that nobody should try and engage him in conversation.

Jen had offered to drive him to and from work when she'd learned that the Belmont was out of action, but Andrew had politely declined. He hadn't intended for anyone to find out about the car, but Jen had answered one of Warner's calls to the Ballroom when Andrew hadn't been quick enough, and she'd taken the message about just how much the repairs were going to cost.

It wasn't that Andrew hadn't appreciated Jen's offer – he really had – but neither Jen nor Lloyd had tried particularly hard to hide the fact that they were concerned about him and his general wellbeing over the preceding nine months. And, alright, *fine*, maybe he'd declined a few social invitations from them, but that was only because he wanted to go back to his blessedly quiet house and pass his evenings with a sense of peace that he'd thought he'd lost forever - nothing else. He still went to the pub with them sometimes, but from the pitying looks and upbeat chivvying, you'd have thought Andrew had become a hermit.

Admittedly, he'd generally only accepted invitations at the point when Charlie Swan had involved himself in the situation. It was always better to agree to go for a quick pint than it was to squirm through whatever scene Charlie would no doubt cause if Andrew continued to refuse. He'd learned the hard way that it was impossible to become a total recluse when Charlie knew you existed and also knew where you lived.

At least they'd all eventually stopped trying to talk to Andrew about Peggy. And there was nothing to talk about there anyway, was there?

The bus hit a pothole and Andrew's temple collided heavily with the window. He winced, rubbing his face with a grumble as the bus paused at another set of traffic lights, idling next to Whitworth Park.

It was still lamentably dark outside, and Andrew longed for the brighter early mornings that were still months and months away from making a reappearance. Brighter early mornings he wanted to experience from the sanctuary of his own car, where he didn't have a smoker's cough erupting behind him, or have to feel the sharp, beady glares of elderly women who judged him on sight if he didn't fold his long legs out of their way quickly enough so that they could slink into the seat next to him.

He slouched further down in his uncomfortable orange perch, fingers itching to snap the satchel open and get the file out. He wouldn't do that though. He may have taken the file home to read, but he wasn't stupid enough to get it out on public transport; not when Higson would genuinely kill him if he lost it, and not when Andrew was fairly certain of what conclusion his DCI's own investigations over the years seemed to have reached.

Whatever had happened to Lily Woodhouse and PC Davy Nash, it hadn't been a disappearance spurred on by an illicit affair. Higson was certain about that, and so Andrew now felt entirely comfortable with that being his starting point, even if he didn't yet know how or why his boss had reached that conclusion. Hopefully Higson would actually provide some context when he showed his face in the Ballroom that morning.

Eventually, the bus reached Piccadilly Gardens, and Andrew stood to make it politely obvious that he needed his grumpy seatmate to move out of the way to let him pass. She obviously didn't appreciate the request and tutted loudly when she eventually rose to her feet with zero haste and deigned to allow Andrew to shuffle out into the aisle.

He hopped off the bus with a hasty thanks to the driver – *See? Polite* – and found himself glancing up at the darkened windows of Lewis's department store just like he had every weekday morning in recent memory.

He hadn't set foot through the shop's doors since they'd investigated Marnie Driscoll's murder during his very first week on Tib Street, and not even the most festive window display would ever be enough to erase the memories of the utter shitshow that whole debacle had been. He still felt the irrational need to duck for cover any time he caught the scent of a strong, floral perfume.

He turned away and headed for Tib Street, foregoing the buttons on the new wool overcoat his grandparents had pressed into his hands as 'an early Christmas present' after Sunday lunch the week before. Considering most of his belongings had been destroyed in his mother's last act of vengeance, he'd been very grateful to them, even if the unseasonably warm weather hadn't quite given him the right use for the coat yet.

The fleeting idea of a quick cup of tea and a bacon sandwich at Howth's was dashed almost immediately. There was always the fear that he'd find Charlie in there, elbows propped on the Formica counter, shovelling breakfast into his face as a greasy antidote to whatever terrible decisions he'd no doubt made the night before.

He could always pop back out to get something later. What he really wanted anyway was a large mug of black coffee, which was always readily available at the Ballroom and, these days at least, came without the threat of an overly exuberant aristocrat in the vicinity.

Tib Street was quiet in that particularly unnerving way it only ever managed to be during the hours surrounding daybreak, but after six weeks of early arrivals Andrew had finally developed enough of a resistance to it that he no longer felt the need to walk more quickly than he normally would.

Halfway to the Ballroom, Andrew drew to a surprised stop when he heard the distinctive scraping sound of the door to the Cheryl Richard Dance Studio being pulled open.

There was nobody on the pavement in front of the building.

Before Andrew's mind could jump straight towards the horrifying but plausible idea that perhaps there *was* someone there and he just couldn't see them, a figure stepped out of the building and onto Tib Street.

At first, he didn't recognise the man – it was neither Higson nor Lloyd – and it was only when the figure partially turned his head towards Andrew's end of the street that his identity clicked into place: Neil Fallon, Andrew's former CID colleague.

Fallon was a jumped-up little arse who thought he was God's gift to the earth and, more worryingly for Andrew in that moment, was generally considered to be his old DCI's general dogsbody.

Andrew couldn't come up with a single good reason for why Fallon would be on Tib Street if he wasn't there to ruin Andrew's day in some capacity.

Andrew was just about to shout and ask Fallon how the hell he'd managed to get into the building in the first place, when a familiar, bulky mass lumbered out of the door, cigarette already firmly clamped between his lips as he stopped to talk to Fallon.

Higson.

What in Christ's name was Higson doing at the Ballroom so early? And, more to the point, what was Higson doing having a casual chat with someone like Neil bloody Fallon?

Whatever the reason, Andrew instinctively knew that it wouldn't do for him to be seen by either of them. He crept backwards, grateful for the fact that he could conceal himself in the doorway to Affleck's Palace. The shopping arcade was still closed, so he wasn't worried about anyone opening the door behind him, but Andrew still had to carefully step over discarded bottles to avoid making a sound. He chose not to look too carefully at what else he might be sharing the doorway with.

He leant back around the corner, careful not to overbalance and end up sprawled on the pavement, which would render his little foray into espionage useless.

Higson was listening as Fallon spoke quickly, and for the most part he looked fairly passive. Well, as passive as a hulking great bear of a man could ever look, Andrew supposed. That was, of course, until Fallon leaned closer and said something that suddenly had Higson grabbing the slightly younger man by the shirtfront and shoving him until his back hit the driver's door of a white car that was parked outside the building.

Whatever was going on, Andrew couldn't be expected to stay out of it when it looked like his boss was only a split-second away from thumping a fellow police officer – albeit an absolute dickhead – and he almost stepped out from his hiding place to intervene.

But then, Fallon shook his head slowly and angrily shrugged out of Higson's loosened grasp.

Higson didn't move beyond raising his hand to his face to take his cigarette and tap a shower of ash directly on to Fallon's poorly shined shoes.

Fallon, who'd apparently developed a couple of brain cells since Andrew had last seen him, didn't react, other than to open the very car door his spine had been so recently acquainted with, and then climb in.

Andrew whipped himself back out of sight as Fallon started reversing, with Higson, all the while, standing motionless as he watched the manoeuvring unmarked Ford Capri.

As the sound of the car faded into the distance, Andrew stayed hidden. When he eventually heard the door to the building clang closed, he slowly counted to thirty. He wanted to ensure that he gave Higson enough time to get back up into the Ballroom and make it seem as though Andrew had only just arrived on Tib Street.

Andrew fully intended to find out what had occurred between his boss and Fallon, but he was hoping that Higson would tell him the story unprompted. If he didn't, then Andrew knew that he was going to have to ask outright, whether he wanted to or not.

Deciding that enough time had passed, Andrew stepped back down onto the pavement and headed for the Ballroom, readying himself for the fact that he was also going to have to speak to Higson about the Woodhouse-Nash investigation.

He immediately realised his mistake. He hadn't heard the door closing behind Higson as he'd made his way back into their building; instead, it had been the sound of Higson pulling the door closed before striding off up the road.

Andrew just about caught sight of Higson's back before it vanished around the corner in the distance.

'Shit!' Andrew hissed, running up the road.

He barely paused at the kerb when he had to cross Church Street. Thankfully there wasn't much in the way of traffic as it was still so early, but he still had to leap out of the way of a street sweeper.

As he approached the corner where he'd seen Higson disappear, Andrew slowed. He was fairly certain that his boss hadn't spotted him, but if Higson thought he was being followed by someone he could easily be waiting to pounce just out of sight; Andrew had no desire to get thumped by Higson before he'd even had a coffee.

Andrew hesitantly looked around the corner, but the pavement was deserted of cantankerous DCIs.

Frowning, he jogged to the other end of the short road that connected Tib Street to the much busier Oldham Street and looked both ways in bewilderment.

Where the hell had Higson disappeared to?

Andrew turned back to look in the direction he'd just come from. Beyond the general grime and detritus that was somehow even worse this end of Tib Street, there was nothing out of place.

There was, however, a pub on the corner.

The Cross Keys was in darkness, as it should have been, but Andrew wasn't entirely sure that something as banal as opening hours or licensing laws would stop Higson from making himself at home if he fancied it.

Feeling only a bit ridiculous, Andrew knocked on the door. Small flecks of red paint peeled from the door and peppered the ground around his feet when his knuckles hit the wood. The place had clearly seen much better days.

When the third knock remained unanswered, Andrew had to admit defeat. Irritated, he trudged back to the Ballroom, frustrated that he was going to have to wait even longer to question Higson about a growing list of things that weren't quite adding up.

Andrew had to slam his shoulder against the exterior door twice before it budged just enough that he could slowly push it open the rest of the way.

The building was quiet and seemed as empty as he was sure it could ever be, so he headed straight to the small kitchen tucked away behind the staircase to make a coffee.

He was safe in the knowledge that Dolly wasn't yet in the vicinity, but he didn't want to run the risk of bumping into her by waiting for the coffee machine to wake up and get going, so he passed over the box of paper filters and instead opened the rickety cupboard above the counter.

The usual jar of Maxwell House had been replaced by Nescafé – Lloyd had clearly been won over by those bloody inescapable TV adverts – but Andrew was neither fussy nor brand-loyal when it wasn't even eight o'clock, so he dumped a heaped spoon of the instant coffee into a mug and switched on the kettle.

He tapped his fingertips against the small window that overlooked the junk-filled storage yard as he waited for the water to boil. The window barely allowed any daylight in at the best of times, but with an overcast December sky it might as well have been bricked up for all the good it was doing. Maybe Alan Jermyn's disappearance to Benidorm made a bit more sense to him on mornings like this one.

The kettle finally came to the boil and Andrew sighed in relief. He hastily poured the water into his mug and left the dank kitchen.

He was still stirring the coffee granules to get them to dissolve when he reached his desk, to find a scrawled note from Higson waiting for him:

Joyce! Where the fuck is MY file?

Ah.

A noisy clang from downstairs surprised Andrew enough that he nearly spilled his coffee. He put the mug down in readiness and shrugged off his coat, before retrieving the file from the satchel and clutching it to his chest.

Higson wasn't getting it back without a fight; not when the note he'd left on Andrew's desk all but confirmed that the DCI had been purposefully hiding the case from his team, and not when Higson was skulking around the Ballroom with someone like Fallon.

The doors opened and Andrew's fingers tightened around the sheaf of paper.

Lloyd frowned, took a bite of his sandwich, and then asked, 'You alright there, boss?'

Andrew sagged in a combination of relief and annoyance, just as Jen followed Lloyd into the room.

'Morning, sir,' she greeted him brightly, but her brow creased immediately when she saw Andrew's expression. 'What? What is it?'

'Was there any sign of Higson when you came in?' Andrew asked shortly.

'No.'

'Higson in at this time?' Lloyd raised an eyebrow. 'Are you mental?'

'He was in here half an hour ago,' Andrew replied, watching as his colleagues looked instantly taken aback. 'Well, actually he was outside again by the time I saw him.'

'Did you ask him why he was here so early?' Jen was visibly puzzled as she approached Andrew's desk.

Andrew shrugged. 'Didn't get the chance. He was too busy having some kind of argument with that twat Fallon from CID, and then h-'

'What?' Jen asked again, and now she sounded more concerned than confused. 'An argument?'

'Yeah.' Andrew nodded. 'Then Fallon drove off by himself. By the time I realised that Higson hadn't actually come back in here, he was too far ahead for me to catch up with him.'

'Where did he go?' Lloyd asked. He'd finished his sandwich and was untwisting a packet of chocolate digestives.

'I lost him on Oldham Street,' Andrew replied tersely. 'I don't know where he went after that.'

'Do you know what the argument was about?' Jen asked.

'They were too far away.'

Jen nodded her acceptance, but her disappointment was apparent.

'Look, let's just wait and see what Higson has to say when he gets in,' Andrew suggested. 'If he won't tell us, I could call someone at CID and quietly find out if they know why Fallon would be hanging around here.'

'You can't call that lot!' Lloyd argued, forgetting all about his biscuits in his obvious horror.

'Lloyd, for the millionth time, we can't work under the assumption that everyone at CID is bent,' Andrew replied as reasonably as he could, even though he was personally inclined to agree with Lloyd's concern. 'Besides, I meant Mike anyway.'

'Mike from the Railway, Mike?' Lloyd asked. 'Football Mike?'

Over time, Andrew had come to understand that Lloyd knew an awful lot of people socially, and therefore labelled his acquaintances based on the location he usually interacted with them (generally tagged with a pub or club) or based on a specific fact he remembered about them. Thus, DS Mike Lawson – one of Andrew's few contacts outside of work – had been shelved in Lloyd's mind with the details that he frequented Andrew's local in Gatley, and that he was the coach of the five-a-side football team that Andrew had been harangued into rejoining in September.

He rolled his eyes. 'DS Mike Lawson. You remember him, Jen?'

'Yeah, him,' Lloyd agreed, looking significantly less apprehensive. 'He's sound.'

Jen, however, did *not* look any less apprehensive. She was staring at the note that Higson had left about the Woodhouse/Nash file.

'Come on, he'll be in soon,' Andrew said, wondering if he could casually get the note out of Jen's eyeline without looking too desperate about it. 'I want to go over everything I read last night with both of you before he gets back.'

Jen looked between the note and Andrew a few times. 'Alright,' she agreed slowly, 'but if he tells us to drop it, we have to drop it.'

Andrew made a movement that was as noncommittal as he could manage, being neither quite a shrug, but certainly not a nod either. He knew that once he revealed Higson's suspicions about what had happened to Lily Woodhouse and Davy Nash, both Jen and Lloyd would see just how important it was for them to investigate their disappearances, but he needed to get all of the information laid out for them before Higson could interfere.

'Right,' Andrew began as his colleagues sat down, 'let's start at the beginning: January 1967.'

FOUR

'I still think those ones next to your head need to be further to the right.'

Peggy Swan turned to glare down at her brother. The stepladder wobbled slightly as she shifted her weight, and she reached out to wrap her free hand around the staircase next to her. 'Do you want to come up here and do it yourself?'

Charlie's lip curled at the stepladder, and he shuddered, 'No, thanks.'

'Then maybe you should stay out of it and just let me get on.'

'You asked for my opinion!' Charlie argued, putting his hands on his hips.

'No, I didn't,' Peggy replied with a sigh. She held the box of decorations against her hip with one hand and carefully stepped down until she had both feet firmly on the ground. 'I asked you to hand me the next set of baubles.'

'Same thing.'

Peggy rolled her eyes and looked up at the gargantuan Christmas tree that stretched up towards the galleried landing, the branches reaching out as though trying to grasp the staircase that curved around it. 'Couldn't you have picked out a smaller tree?'

'Why would I do that?' Charlie looked genuinely aghast at the idea.

'Because we don't need a twelve-foot Christmas tree, Charlie!' Peggy shook her head. 'Even if I lean over the stairs, I'm still not going to be anywhere near being able to reach the top.'

'The Dans will do it, just like they always used to,' Charlie replied, as though Peggy was entirely dense for not having considered this.

Dan Moss and Dan Turner – collectively known to the Swan

siblings as 'the Dans' because they'd always seemed to appear together – had worked on the Butterton Estate for as long as Peggy could remember. For much of her childhood, the two men had been the ones drafted in to decorate the numerous Christmas trees her mother had insisted upon installing throughout the house.

'Charlie, it must have taken them hours just to get the lights on this thing yesterday. I'm sure they both have better things to do these days than faff about with an absurdly tall Christmas tree.'

Charlie grinned triumphantly. 'Actually, no, they don't. They're the ones who suggested it when they brought the tree up here. I think they'd quite enjoy the creative process, to be honest. They won't have Mother screeching at them this time around, will they? Which is always a bonus!'

Peggy couldn't argue with that. They hadn't seen the former Countess of Acresfield since she'd swept out of the Court Theatre's auditorium back in March, threatening to ruin all their lives, as though she hadn't already been doing that for decades.

'Oh, that looks nice!'

Charlie's flinch at the sound of the new voice was barely noticeable, but Peggy still heard him swear under his breath.

Her brother dealt with Marnie's sudden appearances with significantly more grace these days, and long gone were the times when he would jump three feet in the air and accuse Marnie of trying to frighten him to death. Privately, Peggy didn't think Charlie's newfound tolerance would apply if he ever knowingly encountered another particularly lively ghost in the future. For this reason – and a significant number of others, if she were to be completely honest about it – Peggy was eternally grateful that Marnie really did seem to be one of a kind.

'Don't you think there are a few too many decorations on the left?' Charlie asked, tilting his head and narrowing his eyes critically, as though he were inspecting a revered artistic masterpiece and not a half-decorated Christmas tree.

Marnie surveyed the scene with an equal intensity and eventually shook her head. 'No, I like it.'

Peggy shot Charlie a triumphant smirk.

'Well, I suppose there's no accounting for taste, is there?' Charlie muttered as he checked his watch. 'Anyway, don't spend too much longer on this. Father has been droning on about yields, or interest, or something or other for *hours*, so I finally told him that I had very important business to attend to elsewhere. I don't, *obviously*, but I was thinking that if we left in the next half an hour or so, we'd have plenty of time to go for dinner before we have to meet the others.'

Peggy frowned. 'What are you talking about?'

'Oh, come on Peg, if Father knows I'm still in the house, he'll only send Timothy after me and make me go back to his study.' Charlie made another face of distaste. 'I don't know why he won't just talk to *you* about all this estate nonsense anyway.'

Peggy knew exactly why her father wouldn't talk to her about it – as did Charlie – but that wasn't really the focus of her concern just then. 'No, I meant what did you mean about 'meeting the others?'

'Christmas party,' Charlie and Marnie replied in perfect unison.

Comprehension dawned and Peggy snorted in outrage. 'I am *not* going out with you, Charlie. I told you weeks ago.'

Charlie's eyes sparkled with a dangerous mirth. 'Yes, I do remember you telling me that you couldn't possibly come out because you were already busy on the seventeenth.'

'I *am* busy,' Peggy retorted, clutching the box of old baubles more tightly. 'I'm decorating the tree.'

'No, you're not, the Dans are.' Charlie shook his head. 'Look, you haven't come to town in months. Come on, it'll be fun. You know it will!'

Peggy knew no such thing, and she said as much.

'Please?' Charlie pleaded as he plucked the box from his sister's grasp. 'It can be your Christmas present to me.'

'You know full well that I've already bought you a Christmas present,' Peggy replied brusquely. 'Plus, I'm expecting Albany to call tonight.'

'He can call back tomorrow!' Charlie argued. 'Even acclaimed directors have regular access to telephones in New York, you know.'

'Yes, well, I agreed to speak to him tonight.' Peggy frowned. 'He's very busy with his new production.'

Charlie made a face. 'And *you're* very busy going out for the evening. Look, I've already told everyone that you're coming.'

'So, *un*-tell them,' Peggy replied, far more harshly than she'd really meant to.

'Right, and you don't think that might seem a bit churlish on your part?'

Peggy raised her eyebrows. '*Churlish?*'

'Peg, do you know how many times you've complained that you haven't been called into consult for the Ballroom recently?' Charlie seemed genuinely bewildered. 'Come on, if nothing else this will give you the perfect excuse to ask what all that was about.'

'Like you don't already know,' Peggy replied, shaking her head. Charlie had been out with Lloyd as regularly as he always had, and Peggy knew that Jen, and even Andrew, had been with them on occasion. She didn't doubt that the subject of her absence had cropped up at least once in that time.

Charlie rolled his eyes. 'Well, not to burst your bubble or anything, but you haven't been central to our conversations.'

Peggy had to fight the urge to stick her tongue out at him.

'It'll be fun, Peggy,' Marnie interjected, obviously sensing that things between the Swan siblings were about to go downhill at speed. 'We're not going to see you for weeks once you go away, and you've spent ages locked in that library with all that boring paperwork.'

'*That boring paperwork* keeps this place going, you know,' Peggy replied, even though she'd been bored to tears with it all after the first afternoon of filing.

'Come on!' Marnie added in what she clearly thought was a persuasive tone. 'It's Christmas, Peggy, and I actually want to enjoy it this year. You know how difficult the last one was for me. Please?'

Peggy wrinkled her nose at the obvious underhanded tactics. The problem, though, was that she *did* remember how difficult the previous Christmas had been for Marnie. It had been the first December since Marnie had been murdered by Athena Hughes in a jealous rage, and Marnie had not coped with the festive period well.

First, she'd been devastated that she wouldn't be choosing a Christmas tree with her dad, or shopping for gifts with her mum. Then, as they'd moved closer to the twenty-fifth, the daily tantrums about her former fiancé, Rex Hughes, had increased in regularity as she'd been reminded that she would never get the wedding she'd dreamed about, or any of the life with Rex and their hypothetical children that she'd had all planned out.

By Christmas Eve, Marnie had been inconsolable, and Peggy and Charlie had spent the entire night awake trying to get her back towards the peace she'd found over the preceding months.

Peggy had understood, of course, and if she was honest, she'd been expecting a rerun of the same events this year. So far, though, Marnie had been distinctly more chipper than she had the year before, and the substantial difference in attitude was actually making Peggy a little bit edgy.

This time of year was always going to be difficult for Marnie and, as her friend, Peggy would do whatever she could to minimise Marnie's distress. None of that should diminish the fact that Peggy had her own reasons for not wanting to spend her evening socialising though.

Peggy was well aware that it had been her own idea to put some distance between herself and the Ballroom – a decision she still stood by, because it had given her the space to work through some things in her own time – but even back then when things had been difficult, she hadn't thought that it would become an enduring exile.

In August, Higson had called her, wanting her insight on some odd, historic arson attacks. Peggy had been delighted to get back to the Ballroom, even if her enthusiasm had been tempered somewhat by her own awkwardness, and by Andrew's blatantly cautious interactions with her on the few occasions they'd found themselves alone together.

She'd hoped – perhaps more desperately than she'd even admitted to herself at the time – that it would be the beginning of things returning to way that they had been before the *Lady Bancroft* case. But Higson had been oddly agitated for reasons that she still hadn't fathomed by the time they'd closed the Carmichael case, and the days of radio silence had stretched to weeks, and then months. Suddenly, it was almost the end of the year and Peggy couldn't help but feel like her time at the Ballroom had come to a permanent end.

'Peggy, they want to see you,' Charlie began, in another attempt to cajole his sister. 'Besides, it's not just the Ballroom lot. Fiona's coming – you remember Lloyd's girlfriend, right? You liked her – and one of Fiona's friends too. Look, Sonic Youth's rumoured to be playing tonight so the place will be rammed, and you can always just hide in a dark corner if you want to, but *please* come out with us.'

Peggy didn't want to go out.

Saying that, Peggy didn't actually want to stay in and wait by the phone for another call from a harried Albany Cohen either though – he'd inevitably ask her about her travel plans again, and it was a conversation that she was putting off for as long as possible. She had enough self-awareness to know that while she might have worked through *some* things in the previous six months, she definitely hadn't come to terms with *everything*. She certainly didn't feel quite ready to throw herself wholeheartedly into a transatlantic love affair.

'Please,' Charlie repeated, halting Peggy's thoughts before they went in a direction she'd be unhappy with. 'Everyone's expecting you. You don't even have to stay for very long if you don't want to. Promise.'

'Hey, I'll even ditch that lot and come back here with you if it's a dud,' Marnie added with a solemn nod.

Sensing that she was never going to hear the end of it if she didn't go, Peggy sighed long and loud. 'Oh, Jesus, *fine*, but I'm only staying for one drink.'

Marnie cheered and Charlie looked far more relieved than Peggy was comfortable with. She wasn't actually a hermit, no matter what her brother believed.

Peggy shoved the box of baubles into Charlie's hands, pleased with the surprised *oomph* it elicited when the corner hit him in the chest. 'I'm going to get ready, so you can tidy up out here. Timothy will have a fit if you don't.'

'Eurgh, *fine*,' Charlie agreed with obvious reluctance. 'Be quick though. If Timothy catches me, I'll get him to tell you all about the drinks reception that Father is apparently planning.'

Peggy's foot paused in mid-air at the bottom of the staircase. 'What drinks reception? When?'

'No idea,' Charlie replied disdainfully. 'I stopped listening almost immediately. Anyway, I can't imagine it will ever happen. Father would rather drop dead than spend time with anyone socially, wouldn't he? However, I am to understand that Timothy is *enthusiastic* about the plans, and I'm sure he would find great pleasure in regaling you with the guest list.'

Peggy shuddered and hurried up the stairs before Charlie's threats could come to pass.

* * *

Andrew threw his pen down onto his desk in frustration. 'Where the hell is he?'

'I think it might be time to actually go and look for him,' Jen proposed. She'd been worried all day, but her expression had become noticeably more pinched as the afternoon had bled slowly into twilight.

Andrew had been about to voice the same suggestion, so he immediately nodded his agreement.

Lloyd stood up and reached for the parka draped over the back of his chair. 'If we divvy up his usual haunts between the three of us, we should be able to cover most of them pretty quickly.'

'Agreed,' Andrew said as he pulled on his own coat. 'Jen, do you want t-'

The finer details of Andrew's plan of action were sent scattering as a car door slammed loudly, followed by the awfully familiar sound of an engine being strangled.

Andrew nearly vaulted over his desk to pelt towards the wall of windows that looked down over the street below.

Sure enough, there was Higson's battered red car, executing a typically clumsy three-point turn behind an equally shabby white van.

Swearing loudly, Andrew turned from the view and ran towards the double doors, yanking them open as soon as his fingers closed over the handles.

He barrelled down the staircase, with at least one set of footsteps clattering behind him. There wasn't a chance that he was letting Higson bugger off into the sunset without answering at least *one* question about what the hell was going on.

As always, the door to the street was entirely uncooperative and it took longer than it should have done to wrench it open. So, by the time Andrew hurtled onto the pavement, Higson's car had already reached the far end of Tib Street.

To Andrew, it felt like a depressing repeat of that morning; only this time it wasn't Higson's hulking figure shrinking into the distance, but his brake lights fading into the dusk as the car trundled off towards Ancoats.

'Bollocks!' Andrew yelled at nothing in particular as he skidded to a halt.

'Well,' said Lloyd, somewhat breathlessly, as he paused, 'at least we sort of know where he is.'

'I think that's our cue to call it a day, sir,' Jen added. She still looked perturbed, but no longer as downright anxious as she had since lunchtime.

Andrew would have preferred not to have reached the same conclusion himself, but there wasn't really any point waiting around in the Ballroom; Higson clearly wouldn't be making any further appearances that evening. 'Yeah, alright. I want both of you in early tomorrow though, just in case Higson gets in at the bloody crack of dawn again.'

Lloyd nodded his agreement and then beamed.

Andrew frowned.

'Right, so if we're done here, do you want to head straight to the pub and get some food there before we move on?' Lloyd asked.

Andrew's nose wrinkled in confusion. What was Lloyd on about now?

'Or we could get a takeaway if that's easier?' Lloyd added, which didn't really make things any clearer.

'What?' Andrew had to ask.

'Christmas party!' Lloyd grinned, but then he frowned. 'You didn't forget did you, boss?'

Andrew *had* forgotten.

When Lloyd had first mooted the idea weeks ago, Andrew had thought that he'd have plenty of time to come up with an excuse to avoid the outing; it would have needed to be something last minute, so as to not provoke suspicion, but he feared that he may have whizzed right past 'last-minute' without meaning to, and was now left only with on-the-spot lying available to him.

'No, I hadn't forgotten,' Andrew started, 'but I j-'

'Boss, you *can't* bail on me!' Lloyd hissed in alarm. 'Fi's bringing Julie, and we've already told her all about you.'

'Why the hell did you do that?' Andrew asked, outraged.

'Sir, *please* don't do this to me!' Lloyd practically shrieked. 'Fi will kill me.'

'Not really my problem,' Andrew replied, turning and heading back to the Ballroom with every intention of picking up his things and catching the next bus back to Gatley.

'Sir, you really should come out with us,' Jen said as she climbed up the stairs behind him. 'I think it'd be a real shame for you to miss out. We've not had much to celebrate recently, have we?'

'What would we be celebrating tonight then?' Andrew asked as they reached the landing.

Jen shrugged again. 'Making it through another year, mostly in one piece?'

'Boss, please!' Lloyd called plaintively as he scurried up the stairs, cutting off any reply that Andrew might have had for Jen. 'Julie's really nice, I promise. Please!'

Andrew didn't want to go out and make small talk with Fiona's friend.

Andrew didn't want to go home and stare at the four walls

either though – there'd been enough of that recently.

'At least come for one drink,' Jen suggested quietly. 'It's Christmas after all, sir.'

'Oh, fine,' he sighed. 'One drink and then I'm going home.

'Thank fuck.' Lloyd sagged in relief. 'Thanks, mate.'

Andrew couldn't even be bothered to chastise him for that. He just slumped back into his desk chair and unknotted his tie with a sigh, utterly resigned to his fate.

FIVE

The Troubadour had never been Peggy's favourite place to spend an evening in town. She enjoyed the music, but she'd outgrown any longing to spend her nights in places with sticky floors and dim lighting.

The same couldn't be said for Charlie and Marnie. They both revered the decaying club as a sacred space, where all ills could be exorcised, at least temporarily, at the altar of fuzzy guitar riffs and cheap vodka.

Peggy was putting the cloakroom ticket for her coat in her handbag when Marnie suddenly appeared by her side.

'Marnie, for Christ's sake, you should have waited until we were somewhere less busy,' Peggy complained sharply, pulling open the door that led towards the smoky bar. 'It's bad enough that we could bump into someone you used to know as it is.'

Recently, Marnie had been getting too cavalier about when and where she chose to appear, but every time Peggy suggested that her friend might want to employ a little more subtlety, Marnie laughed it off.

As expected, Marnie just grinned. 'Oh, come on, nobody would believe their eyes anyway. I didn't drop dead in my pyjamas, Peggy. I want to go out!'

Peggy didn't have time to reply as Charlie bounded over, shouting over the din of the live band to tell them that he'd secured a good table.

They crossed the packed dance floor and Marnie sat down at the table Charlie indicated. Peggy took the seat beside her.

'I'll go and see if the others are here yet,' Charlie suggested. 'I'll get drinks on the way back. The usual?'

Marnie nodded. 'Could you get a couple of bags of crisps too?'

Charlie arched an eyebrow. 'But you can't eat them.'

'Really?' Marnie asked, the very picture of aghast. 'I hadn't noticed!'

Charlie had also got better at ignoring Marnie's dramatised sarcasm and left without even rolling his eyes.

'I just like holding the packet,' Marnie muttered gloomily, tucking her permanently shoeless feet beneath her chair.

That was something else that Marnie had been doing more often; complaining about small, specific things that she missed about being alive and then disappearing for days at a time. Peggy was keeping a close eye on this behaviour, but as she was neither Marnie's mother, nor her keeper, she would continue to keep her thoughts to herself for the time being.

A few minutes passed, with Marnie fidgeting slightly as she obviously tried to work her way up to saying something.

'Are you really going to go to New York?' Marnie asked eventually, bobbing her head to the beat as the band launched into a Smiths cover.

Peggy frowned. 'Well, like I said, I haven't entirely made up my mind yet. We'll see.'

'You know, for most people 'we'll see' would definitely mean 'no',' Marnie replied, a shrewd tilt to her head. 'If I asked my mum if I could do something when I was younger and she said, 'we'll see', I knew that was the kiss of death for any plans I'd made. With you though, I'm really not so sure.'

'Does it really matter either way?' Peggy asked tiredly.

'Well, yeah, course it does.' Marnie instantly stopped nodding to the song. She looked unnervingly serious. 'Because, what happens to me if you're not here?'

Peggy opened her mouth, but an answer wasn't immediately forthcoming.

She was saved by the return of her brother, waving his hand in the air like a tour guide.

'Look who I found at the bar!' Charlie announced loudly, gesturing theatrically towards the three people trailing behind him.

'Peggy!' Jen Cusack smiled widely but sounded far too surprised for Peggy's liking.

A little alarm bell began to gently ring in Peggy's mind.

'Your brother didn't say you were coming too!' Lloyd Parker added with a friendly wave as he put his pint glass down on the table as Charlie disappeared again.

The alarm bell became a clamour.

'Hiya, Marnie!' Lloyd grinned

Peggy still didn't know how Marnie could sit there so publicly and not be petrified that someone else would recognise her. If it were Peggy in her shoes, she'd probably never leave the damn house.

'Did you hear Sonic Youth's supposed to be in later?' Lloyd asked cheerfully, oblivious to all of Peggy's unease.

'Yeah!' Marnie replied eagerly, all anxieties of only moments earlier apparently evaporating in an instant.

'The boss doesn't even know who they are,' Lloyd stage whispered.

'Oh, leave him alone, Lloyd,' a short, pretty woman Peggy had briefly met before chimed in and nudged Lloyd in the ribs. 'Not everyone's obsessed like you are.'

'It's not obsession, Fi!' Lloyd protested, but he was laughing. 'It's basic stuff everyone should know.'

'Would you excuse me for one second, please?' Peggy gave her best impression of a smile as she stood up and shuffled around the table. 'I just need to speak to Charlie.'

I just need to kill *Charlie*, is what she meant.

Her brother's argument had revolved around the fact that he'd already told everyone that Peggy would be with him and therefore she might look somewhat petulant if she didn't show up. Now it was apparent that she hadn't been expected at all.

She headed for the bar, slipping through gaps in the crowd, which was pressing closer and closer to the stage, buoyed forward by the rumours of who might be on next. She toyed with the idea of making her way back to the cloakroom and heading home but that *would* make her look petulant. Besides, Marnie would only follow her anyway.

'Ooh, sorry!' A woman in a spectacular silver dress stopped short in front of her, the two drinks in her hands only an inch away from colliding with Peggy.

'Not your fault!' Peggy assured her as pleasantly as she could muster as she tried to duck past. It was the truth, after all. The Troubadour was busier than Peggy had seen it in a long time.

'Peggy?'

Peggy turned, startled. Standing behind the woman who'd just apologised to her was Andrew Joyce. Andrew looked surprised, but not as astonished by her presence as Jen and Lloyd had been, so Peggy could only assume that her brother had given him the heads-up at the bar.

'Oh, hi,' Peggy replied eventually, giving him a curt nod. 'I'm looking for Charlie.'

'He's just coming back,' Andrew replied, tipping his head back towards the bar behind him. Unexpectedly, he held out the shorter of the two glasses he was holding. 'He said this was for you.'

'Oh, right, thanks.' Peggy awkwardly took the drink as Andrew held it out over the shoulder of the woman who'd just apologised to Peggy.

'So, you're Peggy,' the woman said, smiling widely.

Peggy was indeed Peggy, but she had no idea how this woman knew that.

The woman laughed. 'Sorry, no, listen to me sounding like a right weirdo! I've heard a lot about you from Lloyd. I'm Julie, Fiona's friend. They didn't say you were coming out tonight.'

'Yes,' Peggy replied slowly, 'I think there might have been a bit of miscommunication.'

'Well, the more the merrier in my book!' Julie beamed at her. 'Let's go sit before we get stuck over here for the rest of the night.'

Peggy caught sight of Charlie heading towards them. He didn't even have the good grace to look sheepish about the fact that he'd lied to his sister. Instead, he had a terribly supercilious look on his face that Peggy was more than familiar with.

'Oh, don't give me that look, Peg,' Charlie chirped breezily as he strode past, drinks in hand, and with at least four packets of crisps held to his chest with his elbows.

Actually, Peggy *would* be giving him that look for the foreseeable future, and she was definitely going to kill him as soon as there were fewer witnesses.

'Everything alright?' Andrew asked, which Peggy appreciated, even if it sounded like the question went against his better judgement.

'Fine,' Peggy replied. 'Thanks.'

'Shall we?' Andrew nodded in the direction that Charlie and Julie had disappeared.

Peggy turned on her heel and squeezed her way back onto the dance floor, trying to forge a path back to the table. She gave up saying 'excuse me' after the first three people ignored her, and she weaved her way through the excited crowd shoulder first, with Andrew right behind her.

By the time they reached the others, Lloyd and Fiona were squashed in together where Peggy had been sitting earlier, and Charlie was perched on the very edge of the other end of the bench next to Marnie. Someone had found a couple of extra chairs in Peggy's absence, leaving Julie and Jen bookending a pair of empty seats between them.

Peggy dropped into the chair beside Jen, thankful to be as far away from her meddling brother as possible.

'How've you been?' Jen asked, tapping her glass of wine against Peggy's Campari and tonic.

'Oh, you know.' Peggy shrugged. 'Fine, really, thanks.'

'Marnie's just told us about your travel plans,' Jen added smiling widely once more.

'Oh, has she?' Peggy asked, fighting the urge to turn and glare at where Marnie was no doubt eavesdropping. 'Well, nothing's really decided yet. There's a lot of paperwork for the estate that needs sorting by January, so I probably shouldn't be hopping on a flight to New York just before then.'

'New York!' Fiona exclaimed from across the table, her eyes wide and wondering. 'Oh, I'd *love* to go. You're so lucky! I've told Lloyd a hundred times that we should save up for a little holiday there. It sounds so exciting!'

'Do you know how expensive flights to New York are, Fi?' Lloyd looked disgusted at the thought. 'And then we'd have to, you know, actually *be* there.'

Fiona rolled her eyes. 'I don't know why you hate the idea so much. I think you'd love it. Ask Julie, she went a couple of years ago. Didn't you, Julie?'

'Didn't I what?' Julie called from the other end of the table, leaning past Andrew, with whom she'd previously been in quiet conversation.

'Go to New York,' Fiona explained.

'Yeah,' Julie nodded, brightening. 'My cousins live in New Jersey, so we had a couple of days in New York before I flew home. Why? You haven't got Lloyd to agree to take you, have you?'

Fiona laughed. 'Fat chance. No, Peggy's going next week.'

Peggy, who had definitely not made that decision yet, opened her mouth to refute that statement, but she was cut off as the stage plunged into darkness behind her and the band disappeared with a final smash of cymbals.

As the crowd roared, Lloyd practically fell over Fiona as he tried to scramble to his feet and get out towards the stage. 'We need to get near the front now that lot are off!'

'Jesus, Lloyd!' Fiona yelped, pushing Lloyd back onto his seat. 'Just bloody wait for me to move, yeah?'

Peggy couldn't help but laugh at the awfully wounded expression on Lloyd's face as he waited for his girlfriend to let him pass.

'Well, come on then!' Lloyd said, turning back to the table, horrified that nobody else was moving. 'It might be them!'

Fiona rolled her eyes. 'Alright, fine.'

Marnie pushed Charlie up. 'Come on, you've been going on about it all day. Peggy? Jen?'

'No, thanks,' Jen said, picking up her wine. 'Perfectly happy where I am.'

'Same,' agreed Peggy.

Julie took a large sip of her drink as she stood. 'Wait for me! Andrew?'

'Er, no, you're alright,' Andrew replied with a quick smile. 'I don't actually know who Sonic Boom are.'

Lloyd threw his hands up in disgust and stalked off towards the dance floor.

Peggy raised her eyebrows at Andrew. 'I can't tell if you're just winding him up or not.'

Andrew shrugged with one shoulder but then snorted into his pint.

'Sir,' Jen chastised him, but she was grinning.

Peggy watched as Lloyd made a series of hand gestures that didn't seem to make any sense to the group of people who'd followed him to the dance floor. Charlie, in particular, looked completely baffled.

'How's the Ballroom?' Peggy asked eventually, because it was probably her turn to ask a question and not make this whole encounter awkward. She kept her eyes on the table, not quite sure that she wanted to hear the answer.

'It's fine,' Andrew replied quickly.

Out of the corner of her eye, Peggy saw Jen turn towards Andrew, eyebrows raised high enough to disappear beneath her fringe.

'Oh, well, that's good,' Peggy replied when nothing further was added. She traced a drop of condensation on her glass with her finger. She hadn't expected them to tell her that the place had fallen apart without her, of course, but she'd wondered what had happened to the cases where they might have previously called Peggy in to consult on. She could admit to herself that she'd spent hours in the midnight darkness of her bedroom staring at nothing and wondering if they'd found someone to replace her. *It's fine* didn't really tell her much, but she wasn't sure that she could expect more details these days.

'How's Butterton?' Andrew asked because, apparently, they really were going to have a paint-by-numbers conversation.

'Oh, you know, it's busy,' Peggy lied fluidly.

Andrew tapped his knuckles on the tabletop. 'Well, that's good. Yeah.'

It was excruciating, and Peggy thought that following the others towards the stage might actually be a good idea after all.

Jen was still frowning at Andrew as she got to her feet. 'Right, I'll go get another round in. There'll be no queue at the bar just now, so I might as well take advantage. The usual?'

Peggy wanted to offer to go instead because she didn't actually want to be left behind to make uncomfortable small talk with somebody she had apparently forgotten how to speak to. Jen, however, didn't even wait for an answer to her question before she disappeared into the crowd.

Disgruntled, Peggy picked up her glass and swirled the red liquid around until the ice cubes clinked merrily against each other, wondering how long it would take for either Jen to get back or for the next band to take the stage.

'Actually, it's a bit shit,' Andrew said suddenly.

Peggy turned in surprise, but the detective wasn't looking at her.

'The Ballroom, I mean,' Andrew clarified, staring into his pint glass as though it offered the answers to the universe. 'Technically that's actually Lloyd's conclusion, but I wouldn't disagree with him.'

'But you said th-'

'I know what I said,' Andrew cut her off with a self-deprecating grimace. 'Higson won't let us near anything interesting.'

'Why not?' Peggy put her drink down and gave Andrew her full attention.

Andrew shrugged as he finally looked at Peggy. 'Not too sure about that yet. I suppose some of it must be that he doesn't think we can do much with the ones you've declined to consult on.'

Peggy shook her head, trying to make sense of that statement. 'What?'

Andrew looked immediately contrite as he misinterpreted her expression. 'No, I didn't mean it like that. I know you've been busy. I'm not trying to blame you for th-'

'I haven't declined anything. Higson hasn't called me since the Carmichael case.'

Andrew looked taken aback. 'What?'

'What?' Peggy repeated.

For a long moment they just surveyed each other warily.

'Higson hasn't called you?' Andrew asked slowly. 'At all?'

'Not since August,' Peggy confirmed. 'I thought he'd decided that you didn't need my help anymore, and that maybe you'd found someone else.'

It was Andrew's turn to shake his head. 'Since the summer,

we've had nothing more challenging than a spate of historical bike thefts, a handful of attempted burglaries from ten years ago, a pair of stolen socks, and *one* missing person.'

'A missing person?' Peggy asked, thinking that at least that one sounded like something that Andrew would feel compelled to investigate. She thought it best not to ask about the stolen socks.

Andrew sighed loudly, full of obvious disappointment. 'He's been living the good life in Spain for fifteen years. He actually called Tib Street and gave himself up yesterday.'

'He gave himself up? After fifteen years?'

'He's given us his *flight details* for when he lands in Manchester next week, Peggy,' Andrew replied flatly.

Peggy couldn't help chuckling at Andrew's disheartened expression and she turned away to hide her smile.

Andrew rubbed his hands over his face. 'What the hell is he up to?'

'Who? The no-longer-missing man?'

'Higson.' Andrew's expression morphed into clear apology. 'Sorry, you don't want to hear any of this.'

'No, I do,' Peggy said quickly. She smoothed imaginary wrinkles out of her dress with her palms before looking back over to Andrew. 'Truth be told, I've missed it all. I'm not sure I've ever been quite so bored.'

Andrew looked surprised again. 'But you said t-'

'I know what I said,' Peggy interjected in a perfect echo of Andrew's own earlier statement.

'So, you would have come back if Higson had asked you to help?'

'Of course,' Peggy replied, leaning back in her chair. 'I meant it when I said that I needed to have something else in my life, but I also meant it when I said that I wasn't leaving.'

Not leaving yet, is what she'd actually said to him, but that 'yet' had gone skittering further and further into the distance with every second she'd felt like she was missing out on doing something useful with her life.

'Maybe I should have called.' Peggy folded her arms and sighed again.

Andrew leant towards her, looking incredibly serious. 'Peggy, Higson told us more than once that you were turning cases down after the Carmichael investigation. Why would he lie about that?'

Peggy's stomach dropped. 'Andrew, I swear I'm telling the truth. I wouldn't have said an-'

'Peggy, stop!' Andrew held his hand up, cutting her denial short. 'I'm not doubting you at all. I'm *asking* you why you think Higson would lie about that.'

Peggy didn't have an answer for him.

Andrew looked back over his shoulder, clearly checking that nobody could overhear them, and dropped his voice to a murmur. 'Higson's up to something. This morning, I saw him coming out of the Ballroom with someone from CID; someone I used to have the unfortunate experience of working with.'

Peggy's eyes widened. She could still vividly remember a moment only days into their acquaintance, when Andrew had been so keen to spirit her away from a hospital corridor so that she wouldn't have to speak to anyone from his former division. That had been the moment that she'd realised that she might have read Andrew and his integrity entirely incorrectly. 'I thought Higson had the same opinion of CID as you.'

'So did I. I tried to follow him this morning, but I lost him at the end of Tib Street. He didn't come back to the Ballroom. Then, on top of all that, I went into the archive room yesterday and found a case that Higson seems to have been keeping tabs on since the late sixties. I think it's fair to say that he's been hiding it from us.'

'What sort of case?' Peggy asked even as she wondered if Andrew would share the specifics with someone who was now outside of the Ballroom team.

'A seventeen-year-old girl disappeared around the same time as a young police officer,' Andrew explained without hesitation. 'They were apparently seen together before their disappearances.'

'Together how? Professionally or personally?'

'Personally,' Andrew confirmed, though he looked unconvinced. 'Higson's named as a witness, but he doesn't seem to believe a word of most of it. Another supposed witness is Higson's former DCI from when he was first at Tib Street, and Chambers too: *my* old DCI.'

Oh, Peggy knew who DCI Chambers was. She'd never met Andrew's former boss, but she'd gathered enough to know that he wasn't someone Andrew trusted in the slightest.

A sudden roar from the crowd startled them both, and the stage lights came up as the bulbs above Peggy and Andrew dimmed to almost nothing.

'Perfect timing!' Jen announced loudly as she appeared and carefully set down the three drinks she had tightly clamped between her hands.

'Thanks,' Peggy said.

'Everything alright?' Jen looked warily between Peggy and Andrew as she took a seat on the opposite side of the table.

'I was just telling Peggy about today,' Andrew shouted, just as a crash of cymbals kicked off the first notes of a bass line that Peggy could feel in her chest.

'Oh, good,' Jen replied, looking relieved. 'You know, I thi-'

Whatever Jen was going to say next was cut off by Lloyd slumping into the seat beside Jen and grumpily folding his arms.

'I thought you were waiting for this lot!' Andrew yelled, pointing towards the stage where another band had finally appeared.

'*That* isn't Sonic Youth,' Lloyd grumbled loudly, looking even more disgusted than he had earlier. '*That* is the Twats.'

Andrew looked rightfully alarmed. 'There's no way that's a real band name.'

'It's not,' Lloyd confirmed morosely. 'But I went to school with two of them, so trust me when I tell you it's accurate. Worse though, is that they're actually shit.'

Andrew pushed Lloyd's previously abandoned beer towards him. 'Drink that, it'll make it sound better.'

Peggy laughed and turned towards the dance floor. Charlie and Marnie, buoyed along by the rippling crowd, didn't seem too bothered that the rumours hadn't panned out. Julie and Fiona were laughing and dancing beside them as though they didn't have a care in the world.

God, Peggy missed feeling like that.

Charlie caught her eye and made a wild beckoning motion.

Peggy shook her head vehemently and pointed at the table.

Charlie rolled his eyes and went back to flailing his arms in time to the beat.

'He's a terrible dancer,' Andrew said right by Peggy's ear, startling her slightly.

'Utterly, *utterly* terrible,' Peggy agreed, grinning as her brother tried to execute a sort of pirouette which resulted in Julie and Marnie shrieking with laughter.

'Come on, pick up your glasses,' Jen instructed, looking around the table. 'A toast.'

'To what?' Lloyd asked dejectedly.

Jen rolled her eyes and nudged Lloyd with her elbow. 'Oh, cheer up. Like I said earlier, we're all still here, and all in one piece. Happy Christmas!'

Peggy added her drink to the clink of glasses above the table, feeling marginally lighter than she had when she'd walked into the Troubadour. 'Happy Christmas.'

SIX

By the time Andrew switched on the coffee machine on Friday morning, the throbbing headache that had briefly left him incapacitated on the Ballroom's ratty blue sofa had faded to a dull but persistent rumble.

Just as he had the day before, Andrew chucked an unholy amount of instant coffee into a chipped mug and leant back against the peeling counter while he waited for the kettle to boil.

He ran his tongue along his gums and grimaced. Despite brushing his teeth twice before he'd ventured downstairs, he still had that unpleasant woolly mouth sensation that came from drinking too much cheap beer and even cheaper spirits.

Some might say he only had himself to blame, but Andrew was placing the fault squarely on Lloyd and Charlie's terrible influence.

He didn't know what time they'd left the Troubadour, but it had felt late enough – or perhaps *early* enough – that Andrew had decided that it wasn't worth travelling all the way back to Gatley.

Jen had taken charge of getting Lloyd, Fiona and Julie into a taxi with her as they were all heading in the same direction, and Andrew had waved them off as he'd turned to walk to Tib Street.

Unsurprisingly, Peggy had then informed Andrew that if he was going to pigheadedly refuse to go home, then at least he could get into her taxi so that it could drop him on Tib Street on the way out of the city.

Even with vodka sloshing through his veins, Andrew had known that arguing with her would be futile, and so he'd allowed himself to be pulled into a car, only to practically fall out if it again five minutes later when it had stopped outside the Ballroom.

With a dull *click*, the kettle announced that it had done its job, and Andrew poured the water over the coffee granules. He then switched on the coffee machine, knowing that the others would probably need some caffeine as soon as they got in.

He'd almost reached the door when he turned back and unceremoniously dumped a heaped teaspoon of sugar into his mug. That would help.

The building had been still and silent since Andrew had woken just before six, but he'd been on tenterhooks since the haze of his hangover had started to clear, knowing that if Higson was holding another clandestine meeting at the Ballroom, it was likely to be at this godforsaken time of day.

Back upstairs, Andrew rested his forehead against a window. There was no sign of movement on the street, and Higson's car hadn't made an appearance.

He trudged over to his desk and sat, wrapping his fingers around the steaming mug. The Woodhouse file was open in front of him, his own notes laid out neatly, ready for his attempt to reasonably present his thoughts to Higson before his DCI laid into him for taking the file in the first place.

The sky gradually lightened, but the sun remained behind a thick curtain of cloud, softly diffusing the light before it hit the windows and stretched towards where Andrew sat.

Jen arrived an hour later, bearing an apple and a small pot of yoghurt, which she deposited on Andrew's desk. 'Breakfast, sir.'

'Thanks, Jen,' Andrew said gratefully, pressing his palms into his cheeks. He picked up the yoghurt and raised an eyebrow. 'Strawberry Munch Bunch?'

Jen grinned. 'My nieces stayed at the weekend, and they left a couple of those behind. They're not too bad.'

Andrew shrugged. He peeled back the foil lid and plucked the spoon from his long-empty coffee mug.

'No sign of DCI Higson?' Jen asked as she hung her coat over the back of her chair.

Andrew shook his head as he shovelled yoghurt into his mouth. Jen was right – it wasn't too bad at all.

'Hmm.' Jen was beginning to look concerned again. 'Do you want a coffee?'

'I'll get them,' Andrew offered, standing up and stretching his back out of the slouch it had settled into. 'Listen, as soon as Lloyd gets in, I'm going to pop over to Bootle Street for a quick shower. If Higson turns up while I'm out, don't let him leave, and have Lloyd come and get me.'

Jen nodded her agreement, and Andrew made his way back down to the kitchen.

Just as he reached for the coffee pot, Andrew heard the unmistakeable sound of a shoulder hitting the front door from the other side.

He hurried back out into the entrance hall, hoping that it was Higson, and praying that it wasn't Dolly.

'Morning, boss,' a very bleary-eyed Lloyd greeted him, squinting into the darkness.

'Coffee?' Andrew offered.

'God, yes, please.'

Andrew almost laughed at the desperate gratitude on Lloyd's face.

'Is he in yet?' Lloyd asked as he traipsed towards the staircase.

'Not yet.'

'He's got to be in soon, surely?' Lloyd asked, and now Andrew could hear the thread of worry beneath Lloyd's weariness.

'Surely,' Andrew agreed with as much confidence as he could dredge up, which could be described as 'minimal' at best.

That confidence just about survived the time it took Andrew to finish his coffee, run to Bootle Street nick to throw himself in the shower, and then race back to Tib Street to find that the Ballroom was still as Higson-less as when he'd left.

It had disappeared entirely by the time lunchtime came and

went without a single sighting of his DCI.

At two o'clock Andrew's watch beeped to alert him to the time, and he felt something in the increasingly strained atmosphere snap.

He snatched up the phone from his desk and pulled his notebook towards him, flipping back to the first page where he had the home phone numbers of the whole team scribbled down in case of an emergency. He only had Higson's number because Jen had given it to him.

'What are you doing?' Lloyd asked. He was still bundled up in his parka and on at least his fifth coffee of the day.

'Calling Higson's house,' Andrew replied, double checking the number as he dialled.

The call rang out.

Jen, who apparently had as much faith in Andrew's phone call plan as he did, was already buttoning up her coat by the time Andrew put the receiver down.

'He's probably just in the pub, right?' Lloyd asked, not sounding confident at all.

'Yeah,' Andrew replied, though it felt like a lie. 'Okay, Lloyd, I want you to stay here. Give it ten minutes, then call Higson's house again. Keep calling until Jen and I get back.'

He pulled his own overcoat on and headed for the double doors. 'Jen, you go down as far as the Peveril and check everywhere between there and Tib Street on the way back.'

'Sir.'

'I'll check the Pelican first, just in case, and then I'll go as far as the Crown and back,' Andrew added as they reached the ground floor. 'Be as quick as you can, because if he's not there and Lloyd can't get hold of him, we're going to have to come up with a better plan, and quickly.'

Jen nodded seriously as Andrew wrenched open the door and then she took off towards Market Street at a run.

Andrew gave the cars on the street a cursory scan, but there was no sign of Higson's little red rust bucket. This didn't give him high hopes that Higson would be in the Pelican; the pub was within easy walking distance of the Ballroom so there'd be no reason for Higson to park anywhere but Tib Street, especially with the nightmare that was the constant parade of roadworks in the city centre.

Andrew hurried down the road after Jen and then took a sharp right as he exited Tib Street.

When he opened the door to the old pub a minute later, he instantly knew that he was out of luck. The pub was virtually empty, with only a couple of regulars sitting on stools at the bar, each bearing a pint and an overflowing ashtray.

He jogged over to where the barman was restocking the crisps, and without preamble asked, 'Have you seen Higson today?'

The barman, as Andrew suspected, knew exactly who he was talking about. 'Nah, not today.'

'Alright, thanks.'

'He ain't been in for days,' the barman added as Andrew headed for the door. 'I thought summat terrible must've happened.'

The barman laughed at his own attempt at a joke, but Andrew yanked open the door and stepped back out onto the street without reply.

If Higson wasn't in the Pelican but he'd come up this way from Tib Street, he was unlikely to go further than the Crown on Deansgate. Higson thought a lot of the pubs in the centre were now, in his words, 'full of poncy arses', and wouldn't patronise them any longer. At least that narrowed down the number of establishments Andrew would have to try and check before they shut at three.

As he hurried through the city towards the river, Andrew tried to work out just when Higson had first started behaving strangely. Lying about Peggy's willingness to help out since the summer hadn't been the start of it, had it? Higson had been acting out of character months before that. Back when they'd been investigating that supposedly cursed bloody play, Higson had been making trips to Tib Street over the weekend – which was unheard of before that point – and he'd been in the archive rooms *searching* for something, hadn't he?

Andrew sped up again as the Crown came into view in the distance.

As it was, he still hadn't forgiven himself for his own conduct back then, and it was unlikely that he'd change his stance on that any time soon. The Ballroom had almost lost Peggy because of him and his idiotic behaviour. Perhaps now, after speaking to her for the first time in months, he might be able to allow himself to think that she might come back to consult on cases. Andrew just needed to keep his mouth shut and never, *ever* mention the conversation they'd had on Tib Street the day after they'd closed the *Lady Bancroft* case, and then maybe – *just maybe* – they could go back to how they'd been before he'd acted like a total moron and tied himself into knots with the boundaries of their relationship.

He shook his head at himself. *Enough.* Now wasn't the time to run through a litany of his past mistakes; not when he knew he'd have plenty of time for that when he was inevitably lying awake in the dead of night again.

Right then he had one job, and that was to track down Higson.

Unfortunately, the Crown was also devoid of the Ballroom's DCI. Andrew noted that there were a few more suited men than there had been last time he'd been in, so he wondered if Higson had already struck this place from his list of acceptable drinking establishments.

It was the same story in every pub Andrew tried on his way back to the Ballroom. He even detoured down Oldham Street to take him in a full circle and popped into the place he'd tried the day before: the Cross Keys. The inside was somehow dingier than he'd even imagined, and right on the dot of three o'clock he was swept right back out of there by a man who assured him, in a quiet, rasping voice, that Higson hadn't set foot on their shabby carpet in years.

Dismayed, Andrew walked briskly back towards the Ballroom as drizzle began to mist the air, hoping that Higson had arrived in his absence, or that Jen or Lloyd had located him.

As he rounded the corner onto Tib Street itself, he drew up short in surprise. Higson's car was parked almost directly in front of him, tucked in neatly behind the same white van as the day before. Andrew put his hand on the bonnet; the metal was cold, so the car couldn't have been driven recently.

With the angle and size of the van, it would likely have been impossible to see the car from the Ballroom's doorway. This, coupled with the fact that Andrew had begun his search at the opposite end of the street and had headed towards the city centre, meant that he couldn't be certain about how long Higson's car had been parked there.

He jogged back to the Ballroom, shouldered his way through the door and then sprinted up the stairs.

As Andrew reappeared, Lloyd looked over in hopeful surprise; he still had the phone to his ear.

'Anything?' Andrew asked, unable to hide his frustration.

Lloyd shook his head. 'I've called four times since you left. I suppose Mrs H could be out.'

Andrew knew that his boss was married, yet the mention of *Mrs* Higson still surprised him enough that it took him a good few seconds to recalibrate.

Jen burst through the doors behind him. 'Anything?'

Andrew shook his head and ran a hand over his face. 'His car's at the end of the street.'

'So, he's nearby?' Jen looked a shade more reassured. 'Maybe there's somewhere we missed.'

Andrew shook his head. 'No, I don't like this. Last night, Peggy told me that Higson hasn't offered her a case to consult on since the summer.'

'No, that's not right,' Lloyd said slowly as he put the phone down again. 'It can't have been more than two weeks since the last time the boss said she'd turned him down.'

'Do you think Peggy's lying?' Andrew asked evenly.

'No, course not,' Lloyd replied immediately, hands held up in surrender.

'So, what then?'

Jen looked between her colleagues. 'Why would he do that? Don't get me wrong, sir, I completely believe what Peggy said to you, but what reason would DCI Higson have for lying?'

'I don't know,' Andrew replied, heading back to his desk. 'Look, I doubt Higson's home address is going to be on file anywhere in this building. I suppose we could check with Division; surely they'd have it somewhere.'

'No.' Jen shook her head.

'Jen, I don't want to involve anyone else either, but w-'

'No,' Jen interrupted more firmly. 'I mean you don't need to call them. I know where he lives.'

Andrew wanted to ask her how she could possibly have that information when Higson guarded his privacy like a bad-tempered lion with a sore head, but there wasn't time. For now, he'd just have to add it to his list of the many, many things he still didn't know about Jen.

'I'll head over there now,' Jen offered.

'No, let's all go,' Andrew suggested instead. He didn't add 'just in case', but they all heard it clearly anyway.

As Jen and Lloyd headed downstairs, Andrew picked up the Woodhouse file and was careful to tuck his notes inside before shoving everything back into the satchel.

He swung the strap of the bag over his shoulder and headed for the door.

As Andrew passed by Higson's desk, he heard what sounded like gently rustling paper. He spun in a complete circle, but he could see nothing out of the ordinary.

He shook his head at himself, but as he turned towards the door his eyes landed on the heavy bunch of keys for the building's rooms in the middle of Higson's desk, half-concealed beneath discarded files. He wouldn't have been able to swear it, but he was fairly certain that he hadn't seen the keys there earlier.

He nodded slowly and reached over to hesitantly pick up the keyring.

A few seconds passed and Andrew held his breath.

The sound of the door to the street scraping open shattered the stillness and Andrew strode out of the room, careful to lock the double doors behind him.

* * *

With Jen driving slightly faster than she normally would, it only took them quarter of an hour to reach Withington.

As they passed the imposing red frontage of the public baths, Andrew looked over and saw that Jen's knuckles were stark white against the steering wheel.

In the backseat, Lloyd looked worried, but this hadn't stopped him from producing a bag of Jelly Babies from his coat minutes after they'd left Tib Street.

'It's just up here,' Jen said quietly, keeping her eyes straight ahead as she turned off the main road.

A minute later, Andrew climbed out of the car to find himself looking up at a 1930s semi-detached house that strongly reminded him of his own home. The planting in the front garden was chaotic, and the porch had seen better days, but it was obvious from the polished house number and the winter pansies sitting in pots by the doorstep that this was a much-loved home. A cheerfully decorated Christmas tree was visible in the bay window and if he hadn't had more on his mind, Andrew probably would have found the image of surly Higson stringing a tree with fairy lights hilarious in its absurdity.

Andrew briskly walked to the front door and rapped his knuckles on the glass pane. He waited a few seconds and then repeated the action.

'Jen, can you check if next door's seen anything?' Andrew pointed to the adjoining house. 'No need to panic anyone though. We could have read the whole thing wrong and we're about to get bollocked for harassing Higson while he's laid up with flu.'

Jen nodded and made her way back towards the pavement.

'What do you want me to do, boss?' Lloyd asked.

'Go round the back and have a look through the windows if you can. See if anyone's inside.'

Lloyd gave him a small salute and traipsed up the side of the house to a garden gate that opened easily when he pushed it.

Andrew flipped up the letterbox cover and peered into the hallway. There were no lights on inside, and the doors were all closed, leaving Andrew with no line of sight into any other rooms.

He stepped back from the door with a sigh and looked around. There was a small rockery section by the step. Would Higson have hidden a spare key there? He'd hope that his boss had a better sense of security than that, but Andrew could count on one hand the number of people he knew who *hadn't* hidden a spare key within spitting distance of their front door.

By the time Andrew had turned over a fourth rock, his plan had progressed to considering whether it was going to be necessary to attempt to break into the house.

He was contemplating the large piece of limestone in his hand when a stern voice shouted from behind him:

'What on *earth* do you think you're bloody well doing?'

Andrew dropped the rock in alarm, hopping backwards as it narrowly missed his foot.

A tall, slim woman wearing a bright blue raincoat and a dark scowl was standing on the drive with her hands on his hips. '*Well?*'

Andrew reached for his identification and held it out to her. 'Detective Inspector Andrew Joyce, Greater Manchester Police.'

The woman's face softened immediately, and she looked at him with almost motherly concern. 'Oh, Andrew, love, is everything alright?'

'Pardon?' Andrew asked stupidly as the woman stepped towards him and lightly grasped his arm.

'My Bill's told me all about you,' the woman continued. 'I've heard all about that terrible business with your haunted house.'

Andrew was fairly sure he was gawping as his mind cartwheeled from '*Andrew, love*' to '*my Bill*' and back again. *This* was Mrs Higson?

Thankfully, Jen returned at that moment. 'Annie!'

The woman turned in surprise. 'Jenny, what's going on?'

'We're not sure,' Jen replied gently, not seeming at all surprised that she'd just been called *Jenny*. 'It might be nothing at all. Can we come in for a bit, please?'

'Course,' Annie agreed and went to unlock the door.

Andrew had just about followed Annie and Jen into the entrance hall when Lloyd appeared at his shoulder.

'Did you find a key then?' Lloyd asked.

'They found me, love,' Annie replied loudly as she marched towards the kitchen. 'I expect you're Lloyd?'

'Er, that's right!' Lloyd called back, and then whispered to Andrew, 'Is that Mrs H?'

Andrew didn't answer because he was too busy looking at the bookshelves that ran along the wall from the front door to, what Andrew assumed, was the living room; there seemed to be an eclectic mix of everything from children's books to mystery novels, but also what looked like hefty mathematics texts.

Jen caught him looking at the books. 'Annie's a maths lecturer at the university.'

Even the surprise of this information was nothing, however, compared to the sheer bewilderment that washed over Andrew a second later when he saw the harp beneath the stairs. He stopped so suddenly that Lloyd walked right into his back.

Annie Higson looked amused as she glanced back from the kitchen. 'It's mine, Andrew, and it was my mother's before that. Don't worry, you haven't missed anything; Bill couldn't play the spoons if he'd been born with them for hands.'

Lloyd lightly shoved Andrew forwards with a quiet 'sorry, sir'.

Andrew stumbled into the kitchen, which was neat as a pin, and headed towards where Annie was filling the kettle at the tap.

'Let me do that,' Andrew offered, gently taking the kettle from her grip.

Annie nodded gratefully and took a seat at the small kitchen table. She then gestured that Lloyd and Jen should do the same.

'Has something happened to Bill?' Annie asked, and Andrew could hear the real fear beneath her straightforward enquiry.

'We have no reason to think so,' Jen explained calmly, 'but we're not quite sure where Bill is right now, or how we can get hold of him.'

Andrew had never heard Jen refer to their boss so casually before, and he almost went cross-eyed in surprise.

As he flicked the kettle's switch, his brain registered the small travel bag that was now resting by Annie's feet; she'd had it next to her on the driveway, but he hadn't thought to question it in his initial surprise.

'Have you been away, Mrs Higson?' Andrew asked as he located the teapot.

'Please call me, Annie, love,' she replied gently. 'I've been at my sister's house in Buxton for a few days. Bill suggested that I go and stay for the full week, but I came back early. Unfortunately, I wasn't blessed with the patience of a saint.'

Andrew found that difficult to believe but kept that thought to himself. He set the teapot down in the middle of the table.

'Mugs are in the cupboard behind you,' Annie directed him. 'Sugar's on the side, and there should be milk in the fridge.'

Andrew gathered everything and then took the final empty seat at the table.

'Annie, when was the last time you saw your husband?' Andrew asked carefully.

'Monday morning when he dropped me to the train station,' Annie replied.

'Did he speak to you at all while you were in Buxton?'

Annie shook her head. 'No. Bill finds Sarah – that's my sister – impossible; always has. He'd only call the house if he really needed to speak to me about something. When was he last in work?'

'I saw him yesterday morning,' Andrew replied, jabbing at the teabags in the teapot with a spoon. 'He was on Tib Street, speaking to another police officer; someone who had no business being at the Ballroom.'

Annie frowned. 'And did Bill tell you why he was meeting this other person?'

Andrew shook his head. 'He didn't actually know I'd spotted him, and then I lost him at the other end of the street. We haven't seen him since.'

'No, we saw his car leave Tib Street last night,' Lloyd corrected. 'Remember? And then you said it was back on Tib Street today, boss.'

'Yes, we saw his *car*,' Andrew replied, 'but we can't be one-hundred percent certain about who the driver was either time.'

Truth be told, Andrew had spent quite a lot of time that afternoon thinking about the protracted three-point turn of the night before: it had been loud and drawn-out enough to ensure that it would be noticed by anyone up in the Ballroom, but there'd be plenty of time to drive off down the road even if someone had sprinted down the stairs just as Andrew had, because the bloody front door would always put a stop to any burst of speed.

Lloyd looked unconvinced, but Andrew could only shrug in reply as he picked up the teapot to pour a cup for their host. 'Annie, how much did he tell you about cases he was working on?' he asked carefully.

'Oh, I know all about what you do on Tib Street,' Annie confirmed as she took her tea gratefully and added a generous splash of milk. 'Bill and I have kept very few secrets from each other. He wouldn't always tell me the full details of a case – out of respect for those involved – but I generally had a good idea.'

'Has he mentioned any cases at all over the past few weeks, or months, even?' Andrew finished pouring tea for the others and then himself. 'Has he mentioned any names? Or talked about any particular investigations that he might have kept an eye on over the years? Maybe one that had originally been opened when he was at A Division?'

Annie's gaze whipped back towards Andrew. She suddenly looked ashen in the weak afternoon sunlight. 'Not poor Davy Nash? And that lovely little girl?'

Andrew's mouth fell open. 'You know what I'm talking about?'

Annie wrapped both hands around her mug of tea as though in prayer. 'Until this year, Bill hadn't spoken about them in such a long time, but then recently…'

She trailed off, and Andrew let the silence settle around them, knowing that Annie would continue when she was ready.

Eventually, Annie looked directly at Andrew again. 'I think he always felt a terrible sense of guilt over what had happened, particularly about Davy. They were friends, did you know that?'

Andrew shook his head. He'd read that file ten times from back to front and back again, and at no point had he found any hint of a close relationship between Higson and Davy Nash; only that curt statement that they'd both been in the same pub.

Annie swallowed heavily. 'Davy was a good ten years younger than him, and they never worked together, what with Bill being at Tib Street and then back at A Division while Davy was in uniform. Chris – Chris Benson – knew Davy from outside of work though, and he introduced him to Bill.

'Unless one of them was working a night shift, the three of them used to meet up at the Hanging Bridge pub every week.' Annie took a long drink of her tea. 'Thursday was darts night, and for a few years – once they had Davy on their team – nary a week went by when they didn't win their bar tab back, and then some.'

Bridge, Andrew thought. *Hanging Bridge*. Is that what Higson had been referring to in his notes?

Annie laughed slightly, unaware of Andrew's wheeling thoughts. 'Our two boys loved Fridays, because they knew their dad would always come back with a present for each of them. Just something small he'd pick up from the market with whatever was left over from the previous night's winnings. It was usually some tatty old book or a jigsaw puzzle missing a piece or two, but to the boys it was like he'd brought home treasure.'

Despite his best attempt, Andrew knew that he hadn't managed to keep the stark astonishment from his expression, because Annie gave him a knowing look even if she very graciously chose not to comment on it.

'One Thursday, Bill didn't come home.' Annie pushed her mug away from her and curled her fingers together on her lap. 'I wasn't worried. I thought that something must have come up at work and he'd been pulled in overnight. It wouldn't have been the first time that had happened, but when he still wasn't back by Friday evening, I started to get worried.

'It was Sunday morning before he came home.' Annie shook her head as though trying to rid herself of the memory. 'He was so quiet. He barely said hello to us. He just went upstairs and shut himself in the bedroom.'

Jen reached over and squeezed Annie's hand.

'Later that night, once the boys were in bed, he told me *some* of what had happened,' Annie added softly. 'He said that he and Benson had gone for a pie like always, and then they'd met up with Davy in the Hanging Bridge just after eight-thirty. Almost immediately, Davy realised that he'd left his keys and his beer money at the station when he'd clocked off; he'd finished a bit later than usual and had left in a hurry to meet the lads at the pub.

'Bill told him not to worry and that he'd cover his beer and bus fare home, but Davy wouldn't have any of it.' Annie sighed loudly. 'His wife, Beth, hadn't been doing too well. She'd had twins earlier in the year, and it had all been a bit of a traumatic business for her. They had a little terraced house in Hulme, on the same street they'd grown up on – childhood sweethearts, they were – and Beth's mum still lived a few doors down. Even with Beth's mum there to help, Davy had wanted to be at home every hour he could get away from work. It was the first time in months that he'd made it to a darts night, and he didn't want to disturb Beth or wake the babies by knocking on the door when he finally got home. So, off he went to get his things, promising that he'd be back for darts kick-off at nine, and that it'd be his turn to get a round in.'

Annie lapsed back into silence.

'But he didn't come back?' Andrew hazarded a guess.

'No, he didn't.' Annie pinched the bridge of her nose. 'When he hadn't come back after an hour, Bill thought that he must have just decided to go home anyway. He didn't think anything *bad* could have happened to him.'

Everything that Andrew had thought he'd learned about the case had been slowly throwing itself out of the window as he'd listened to Annie speak. None of this had been in the file. This Thursday evening that Annie Higson was describing, was the very night that Davy Nash and Lily Woodhouse had supposedly been seen by multiple, apparently *credible*, witnesses in the bar at the Free Trade Hall. Higson had given a statement to the same effect himself, for Christ's sake.

'Bill and Chris stayed to play darts. They didn't win, of course,' Annie explained. 'They went their separate ways at closing time. Bill stopped for a smoke outside the pub, and a few minutes later he saw something that proved that Lily and Davy hadn't just run off together.'

Andrew hadn't realised that he'd been leaning further forwards as Annie spoke. 'What did he see?'

Annie closed her eyes as she shook her head again. '*That*, Andrew, love, is one of the very few secrets that exists between us. Whatever it was, Bill was terribly agitated about it. He thought it was too dangerous for me to know. I kept on at him about it, and in the end, he just walked out of the house. In all the years we've been married, it's the only time he's ever behaved like that.'

For a long moment Andrew could hear nothing but his own heartbeat. He glanced around the table and saw the obvious confusion on Jen and Lloyd's faces. He shook himself out of his stupor; he now had two varying accounts of the same night and thought he might be even further away from understanding any of it than he had been when he'd walked into the kitchen.

'Annie,' he said slowly, 'I've got the original case file here, and there's a signed statement from DCI Higson that asserts that Davy Nash told him that he was going to meet someone at the Free Trade Hall.'

'Which I think you already know is a bloody lie,' Annie replied vehemently. 'I know you haven't known my husband for very long, but I've known him since we were teenagers, and I would swear on my own life - and the life of my boys - that Bill is not a liar, so he would only have made that statement if he'd been *compelled* to.'

Annie was correct about the fact that Andrew hadn't known Higson for very long in the scheme of things, but he thought that he knew his boss well enough to be certain that Higson did actually abhor liars.

Andrew nodded his agreement. 'So, you knew about the witness statement?'

'I did, but Bill wouldn't tell me *why* he'd done that, even though I could see that it was eating away at him,' Annie confirmed. 'I've always thought it must have been what spurred him on to help Beth and her babies.'

Andrew frowned; he could feel his headache coming back. 'What do you mean?'

'Do you know what they started saying about Davy, and about that poor Woodhouse girl after they disappeared?' Annie asked. 'Was that in the file?'

Andrew had read it again just that morning. 'That Lily was a communist sympathiser, and that she'd got Davy caught up in her beliefs?'

'Yes, that.' Annie shook her head. 'It was a load of rubbish, of course, but there were people turning up outside poor Beth Nash's house at all hours of the day, painting awful words on her front door. Then there was the press asking her questions about her husband having an affair with a teenage girl, and even her own neighbours calling her and Davy all sorts of names. She was terrified, poor lass.'

None of that had been mentioned in the original investigation either.

'Bill couldn't stand seeing it,' Annie continued. 'About six weeks after Davy vanished, Bill had his sister come round to look after the boys, and he took me over to see Beth. I thought we were just going to check in on her and the twins, but when we arrived, Beth was waiting with two packed bags and a baby on each hip. You know, I think we could do with some more tea.'

'I'll do it, Annie,' Jen offered before Annie could leave the table.

Annie shook her head. 'Jenny, y-'

'You just stay there and tell Inspector Joyce everything you know, alright?' Jen said, cutting her off with a gentle firmness.

Annie sighed loudly, and it was obvious to Andrew that here sat someone else who knew when it was futile to argue with Jen.

'We all got straight back into Bill's car,' Annie added softly. 'I had little Julia on my lap; she was such a calm baby. Beth kept hold of Anthony – he was fussier than his sister – and he cried for such a long time.'

'Where did you go?' Andrew asked quietly. He was worried that at any moment, Annie was going to stop talking and he'd have no idea what to do next.

Annie took a deep breath. 'You know, I swore to Bill that I'd never tell anyone where we took Beth and the kids that night. He made me promise.'

Clasping his own hands together, Andrew prepared himself for an argument.

It wasn't necessary.

'We took them up to the Lakes,' Annie stated decisively. 'To a tiny little place just south of Keswick. Bill knew it well, because his Mum's lot were from up that way. He'd sorted it all out with some cousin of his – a farmer – who'd agreed to let Beth and the kids stay in an old workers' cottage until they could get themselves back on their feet. He'd been planning it for weeks, apparently, and the only other person who knew about it until that night was Beth herself.'

Annie paused and pressed her fingers to her lips. 'She looked so scared when we drove away. She was barely more than a girl herself, and we just left her there in the dark. She couldn't even tell her own mother where she'd gone.'

'Why not?' Andrew asked quickly. 'If this was to just get her away from harassment then why all the secrecy with her family?'

Annie closed her eyes for a long moment. 'It was only after we left that Bill told me that nobody was to ever know what we'd done; that Beth could be in real danger if anyone ever found out where she'd gone.'

Andrew fought the urge to put his head in his hands. 'Did you ever see Beth Nash after that night?'

Annie shook her head. 'I don't know if Bill did. The following year, we got a Christmas card in the post. It was signed from Beth, Julie and Anthony Gower.'

'Gower,' Andrew repeated.

'Yes, I don't know why,' Annie replied. 'It wasn't her maiden name, but she'd obviously been told not to use 'Nash' for anything.'

Jen put the refilled teapot down in the middle of the table.

'Was she still in the cottage, do you know?' Andrew asked.

'No. She'd written her new address on the inside of the card. Bill saw it and got all agitated about it. He thought it would be best if nobody knew where she was, not even him.'

Andrew thought he might already know the answer to his next question, but he asked it anyway. 'Any chance you still have the card?'

Annie sighed loudly. 'Bill threw it in the fire that night. I've always thought that Bill must have the address somewhere. He'd want to know where Beth was, wouldn't he? In case Davy turned up.'

Andrew actually thought that everything about his DCI's behaviour back in sixty-seven heavily suggested that Higson knew, or at least strongly suspected, that Davy Nash was actually dead, and he'd never be called upon to reunite the Nash family. As it wouldn't help to distress Annie any further, he kept this to himself.

'Do you remember any of the address at all?' Jen asked as she poured Annie another cup of tea.

'It was nearly twenty-years ago, Jenny!'

'I know,' Jen replied soothingly. 'But *anything* might help us, Annie. Do you know if she was still up in the Lake District?'

'The only word I remember was Staveshead.' Annie shook her head, obviously dissatisfied with her memory. 'No, it could have been Staves*mere*. I don't know. It might have been a village or a town, but it could have been the name of a road, or a house. I'm sorry.'

'Don't apologise, Annie. We'd know none of this without you,' Jen said.

Andrew had to brace himself for the next part. 'Annie, if he wanted to hide himself away for some reason, do you have any idea where he'd go?'

'Once upon a time I would have said he'd have gone to Chris,' Annie replied, worrying her hands. She didn't need to reiterate the fact that Chris Benson had been dead for almost two years. 'Do you think something bad's happened to Bill?'

'I think the fact that he wanted you to go to your sister's house suggests that he didn't want you at home this week,' Andrew replied, diplomatically dodging the question. 'I think that means that he was either worried about something happening here, or that he was planning on making himself scarce for a few days and didn't want to worry you.'

Annie nodded slowly. 'But you think it's directly related to Davy and Lily Woodhouse?'

'Honestly? I don't know for certain, but I'd be willing to bet on it,' Andrew replied. 'I don't particularly like coincidences.'

'Neither does Bill,' Annie replied. 'It's one of the reasons he likes you so much.'

Andrew was startled enough that he twitched, his elbow slipping off the tabletop.

'Don't look so surprised, love,' Annie added, with the ghost of a smile.

'Um…' Andrew cleared his throat. 'Annie, you said that this case came up again earlier this year. Do you know why that was? What could have brought it up again?'

Annie looked up at the ceiling for a second, clearly thinking hard. 'It was after Frank Jackson's funeral, I think.'

Frank Jackson. Andrew recognised that name. He tried to think back to the notes he'd made over the past couple of days. 'He was at Tib Street in the sixties, wasn't he?'

Annie's face darkened. 'He was.'

'Why did Bill leave Tib Street, Annie?' Jen asked carefully. 'He's never said.'

For a long moment, Annie said nothing, but her face twisted into a scowl before she said, 'Bill loved working at the Ballroom, until his boss retired, and they brought in Jimmy Prentice as acting DCI.

'Prentice had no interest in investigating old cases. He just wanted somewhere where he could foster his own little gang of thugs, right in the heart of the city,' Annie clenched her hands into fists. 'Bill couldn't stay there, and as soon as an opportunity presented itself, he went back to A Division. He was convinced that Prentice was a 'fixer' for the city's gangsters. Prentice used to swan about in his Jag, with his lackeys – Frank Jackson and an arrogant little git called Sean Kelly. They cosied up to all the rich nonces who worked on King Street, parading around at fancy parties with beautiful girls hanging off their arms; always at the kinds of places, and with the kind of people, that police officers should have no business with.'

'Shit,' Lloyd breathed, and Andrew didn't have the heart to reprimand him for it.

'Bill could never prove any wrongdoing,' Annie continued, patting Lloyd on the hand. 'He stayed at Division until Prentice left the force for Spain in the seventies. Jackson and Kelly left fairly shortly after that, and Bill's been at the Ballroom ever since.'

Off the top of his head, Andrew couldn't remember whether Sean Kelly had been on the list of witnesses, but he definitely remembered someone else who had been.

'What about Chambers?' Andrew asked. 'He would have been DC Chambers back then.'

'Dickie Chambers?' Annie asked, and at Andrew's nod, continued, 'I know that he was at the Ballroom when Bill wasn't. I think he was Prentice's office errand boy; he wasn't really part of the mob as far as I could tell. I always got the impression that Jimmy and co thought he was a bit of a joke. He was your DCI, wasn't he?'

'He was,' Andrew confirmed, feeling unpleasantness rise up in his chest again.

'He'll have been at Jackson's funeral, I'm sure of it,' Annie added. 'Bill wouldn't have gone to it unless he'd had to. In fact, *yes*, I was right earlier; it was definitely *after* the funeral that Davy came up in conversation for the first time in years.'

Andrew nodded. 'When would the funeral have been?'

'February.' Annie pursed her lips in thought. 'No, March, I think.'

March had been the *Lady Bancroft* investigation; exactly when Higson's uncharacteristic early morning and weekend visits to the Ballroom had begun, at least as far as Andrew was aware of them.

Annie looked around the kitchen suddenly, as though realising something. 'I see you're still one short in number.'

'Pardon?' Andrew asked, puzzled.

'Well, all that business with your Miss Swan. Sorry, I mean, Miss *Jones*,' Annie clarified with a wave of her hand that suggested that Andrew should *obviously* be fully aware of what on earth that was supposed to mean.

Andrew sat up straighter and blinked hard, feeling like the conversation was about to upend everything he thought he knew for at least the third time that afternoon. 'What?'

'Well, Bill's just been so worried about her for months now, hasn't he?' Annie was now looking at Andrew as though she thought that he might actually be significantly denser than she'd assumed. 'I suppose that all started around the same time too, didn't it?'

Andrew just about suppressed the urge to ask 'what' again. He looked up to find both Jen and Lloyd looking at him quizzically. His own bafflement made a sharp left towards alarm as everything he'd just heard lined up into a neat, yet horrifying, little row of facts in his mind:

A twenty-year-old missing persons case, Peggy's lengthy absence from the Ballroom, Fallon's visit to Tib Street, and now Higson's disappearance.

They were all connected, Andrew was now certain about it.

The problem, of course, was that he didn't have a bloody clue how.

SEVEN

Charlie Swan was almost *dangerously* bored.

He'd been rudely woken that morning by Timothy knocking on his bedroom door with his signature brand of aggressive politeness. Such a disagreeable start to his day had been a frequent feature of his teenage years, so it had taken an embarrassing amount of time for Charlie to dispel the haze of sleep and realise that he was no longer fifteen and just home for the school holidays.

Once Charlie had staggered over to unlock the door, the ancient butler had graced him with his usual judgemental once-over, and then brusquely informed Charlie that his father required his presence without delay.

As much as Charlie would have enjoyed sauntering into his father's wing of the house still wearing last night's clothes, reeking of both stale cigarette smoke and the snakebite and black that Julie had spilled all over him, he knew that it would only end in a lengthy lecture. Charlie had always liked to keep contact with the Earl to the bare minimum, but that had been getting harder since he'd turned thirty-one earlier in the year and his father had harshly informed him that it was 'bloody well time to grow up'.

Charlie, of course, had no intention of fulfilling his father's wish – he'd spent three decades disappointing the man thus far, so he saw no reason to stop any time soon – but he'd known that a shower and a change of clothes would improve his prospects of a speedy release from his father's study.

If Charlie had known why his father had wanted to see him, he would have ignored Timothy's knock, drawn the duvet over his head, and gone straight back to sleep. As he hadn't been blessed with the gift of precognition, he'd walked into a room full of suited estate staff without so much as a single drop of coffee for protection from the inevitable tedium. It had been an update on everything from the estate's game and wildlife management strategy to the future renovation of certain outbuildings.

In the three hours it took to escape, Charlie hadn't been spoken to directly even once. It had been a real hoot.

After a detour to the kitchen to make a sandwich, he'd locked himself in the library because it would be the last place that either his father or Timothy would think to look for him. He would have just gone out entirely, but he was still being haunted by his hangover.

He'd seen Peggy's small car trundling down the driveway about an hour into his captivity that morning, which was unusual now that she didn't ever seem to be at the Ballroom anymore.

Charlie had no idea what that was about. He really hadn't been lying the night before - when it came to socialising with the Ballroom lot, Peggy had been designated an off-limits topic beyond the most basic polite enquiries.

The sound of an approaching car had Charlie loping towards the window, hoping his boredom was about to lift.

He frowned, folding his arms as he pressed his nose closer to the glass to squint into the distance. The car passing the lake didn't belong to his sister, but he couldn't make out the driver.

It was only when the car approached the house that Charlie realised that it was Jen driving, and that she had both Joycie and Lloyd in the car with her.

Charlie's dire boredom was violently run through with a bolt of excitement. There was no way that this was a social call. The Ballroom team had never made it a habit to drive out to Butterton House unless a situation desperately warranted it, so that meant that something interesting was finally going on. Thank Christ for that!

He hurried out of the library in an attempt to reach the door before Timothy was even aware that there were guests approaching the house. Charlie skidded to a halt as his socked feet slid over the polished floor, and he opened the door before anyone outside could do anything as daft as knock and immediately conjure a cantankerous butler in the entrance hall.

The smile slid from his face as soon as he laid eyes on the matching expressions the three visitors wore. Andrew Joyce with a sombre expression wasn't anything particularly out of the ordinary, and Jen was always professional when she was working, but even *Lloyd* looked a bit green around the gills, so Charlie's excitement dimmed with alarming speed.

'What's going on?' he asked brusquely.

'Can we come in, Charlie?' Jen asked.

Charlie pulled the door wide. 'Library. Be quick about it.'

Once the three detectives had disappeared from view, Charlie closed the front door as quietly as he could and then jogged after them.

'Where's Peggy?' Andrew asked as he took a seat in the chair by the fireplace.

'Out,' Charlie replied, flopping back down into the armchair he'd previously been ensconced in. 'No, I don't know where she went. No, I don't know when she'll be back.'

'Now's not the time to be flippant, Charlie,' Andrew retorted, and Charlie raised an eyebrow.

'You could have called ahead,' Charlie replied evenly.

Whatever Andrew was planning to say to that was derailed by the sudden appearance of Marnie right next to Lloyd, who shrieked in surprise as he stumbled sideways.

'Oh, relax.' Marnie rolled her eyes as he she leant back against the window. 'What's going on?'

'We need to speak to Peggy,' Jen replied. As answers went, it wasn't particularly informative.

'Well, where is she?' Marnie asked, looking around.

'She went out a few hours ago,' Charlie offered, 'but that's all I know.'

'Typical.' Marnie sighed loudly as she turned to look at the far wall. 'Any ideas, Emmy?'

Emmy – Very Great Aunt Emmeline, to be more precise – was one of the resident ghosts of Butterton House. Charlie had never been able to see her, but he'd been aware of her presence since Peggy first told him about her when they were children. Marnie and Emmeline had bonded over their shared love of *Neighbours* and fashion magazines. The fact that they were also both dead probably had something to do with it.

While Charlie was now at ease with the concept of Emmeline being in the room with them, Andrew clearly wasn't, and Charlie had to suppress a laugh at the look of poorly controlled unease on the detective's face.

Marnie screwed up her face as though listening intently but not quite understanding what she was hearing. 'Holiday gentleman? What do you mean? With the…? Oh! You mean a *travel agent*?'

Marnie turned back to the rest of them. 'Emmy thinks that Peggy's gone to see a travel agent.'

'Oh, for New York?' Lloyd asked, obviously fully recovered from his fright.

Charlie highly doubted that, given Peggy's reluctance to actually commit to accepting Cohen's invitation to visit. She'd originally been invited out there over the summer, but had declined, telling Cohen that she was too busy with cases. He'd then invited her for Thanksgiving, but that had turned into early December; and now, as far as Charlie understood it, the invitation was to spend New Year in the Big Apple. Charlie would happily bet half his fortune that his sister wasn't currently booking a flight to New York so much as rooting around for another excuse to delay the trip again.

But Charlie wasn't meddling, was he? So, he wasn't going to

ask, nor was he going to speculate on why Peggy was repeatedly dodging Cohen's declarations of interest, even though he had a bloody good idea!

Well, he wasn't going to speculate *out loud*.

Charlie slapped his knees with his palms. 'Well, I'm sure she'll be back shortly. Does anyone want a cup of tea? I could probably get to the kitchen and back without Timothy noticing.'

'Charlie, this is serious,' Andrew snapped, and *blimey* he did actually look disturbingly serious.

Charlie's concern intensified. 'What's going on?'

Jen and Andrew looked at each other quickly and had what appeared to be a significant conversation in silence, because a few seconds later Jen nodded shortly and turned to face Charlie.

'Has Peggy said anything to you about the last time she spoke to DCI Higson?' Jen asked carefully. She then looked to Marnie. 'To either of you?'

Charlie shrugged. 'No. She helped on that weird arson case as asked, and that was it.'

'Carmichael,' Jen confirmed. 'But nothing since then? At all? Higson didn't give her any sort of message once we'd closed that case?'

Charlie's brows knitted. 'What sort of message?'

'Anything.'

'I don't remember her mentioning anything,' Charlie replied, and Marnie only shrugged in agreement. 'Well, nothing besides wondering why nobody ever called her back in.'

Jen looked surprisingly deflated. 'Alright, thanks Charlie.'

Marnie nodded towards the window. 'It's alright. You can ask her yourself.'

Sure enough, Peggy's car was making its way back up the driveway. She obviously spotted Jen's car, because instead of driving to the garages as expected, she parked and almost ran for the front door.

Charlie hurried over to the library door and opened it, waiting for his sister to appear in the entrance hall. 'Peg!'

'What's going on?' Peggy asked as she hurried towards him. 'Is that Jen's car outside? Is everyone alright?'

'In here.'

Charlie locked the door behind them and didn't say a word when Peggy sat down in the armchair he'd just vacated.

'What's wrong?' Peggy's apprehension was evident on her face as she looked around the room.

'We don't know where Higson is.' Andrew clasped his hands together. 'I already told you that he's been acting oddly for days – *months*, really – and now…'

Peggy's mouth dropped open in horror as Andrew trailed off. 'You don't think he's…'

'No!' Andrew waved his hand vehemently. 'No, not that. That's not why we're here. It's just…'

Charlie, concerned that they were about to enter into a lengthy period of unfinished sentences – an activity for which those two had form – cleared his throat loudly. 'Could someone please tell us what any of this has to do with us?'

Andrew looked, as usual, as though he were about to argue, but he only sighed loudly and began to explain.

For the majority of the story, Charlie listened intently – he'd learned the hard way that any interruption would inevitably lead to him being excluded from further discussion – but upon learning of the team's trip to Withington that morning, he couldn't help exclaiming, 'Mrs Higson! What's she like?'

Lloyd looked like he was about to launch into an enthusiastic description, but Jen shushed them both immediately. Honestly, it was like being back at school.

Peggy, for her part, sat silently throughout the entire recap, eyes never leaving Andrew as he laid out the facts as they currently understood them.

'What is it you want me to do?' Peggy asked when Andrew had finished explaining that Higson's weird behaviour seemed to have started after somebody or other's funeral earlier in the year. Charlie thought this was an entirely fair question, because he had no idea where Joycie was going with any of it.

'Last night you told me that Higson hadn't called you at all since August,' Andrew replied slowly, 'and that even before that it hadn't been as often as before.'

'Correct.'

'This morning, Annie told us that Higson's been worried about you for months,' Andrew continued, 'and I think that worry is what's been keeping him from calling you back to Tib Street.'

Peggy shook her head slowly. 'I don't understand. Why would Higson be worried about me?'

'The girl who went missing back in sixty-seven had been on a television talent show months before she disappeared,' Andrew replied. 'Apparently she was psychic.'

Charlie nearly snorted with laughter at the constipated look on Andrew's face at the mere thought of anyone being psychic. 'And, what? You think she was actually talking to ghosts like Peg?'

Andrew glared ferociously and Charlie thought he looked caught out. 'No, I don't.'

'You don't?' Charlie raised his eyebrows in disbelief. Joycie was a terrible liar. 'Really?'

'What was the girl's name?' Peggy asked, recapturing Andrew's attention.

'Lily Woodhouse,' Lloyd piped up.

Charlie wasn't sure whether he was the one who made the shrill noise of surprise, or if it had been Peggy. Actually, it could easily have been both of them.

'Lily Woodhouse?' Peggy repeated sharply.

'You know who she is?' Andrew asked, nose wrinkled in puzzlement.

Peggy folded her arms, and she scowled at Charlie. 'You explain.'

Right, so she was still pissed off about all of that then.

Charlie sighed loudly. 'We were teenagers when Lily Woodhouse was on that show. Peggy was at school in Switzerland by then, so knew nothing about it. This was a few years after I'd made the *miscalculation* of telling a friend that Peggy could speak to the dead.'

Charlie magnanimously ignored both Marnie's muttered, 'Idiot!' and Andrew's slow, judgemental shake of his head.

'Anyway,' he continued loudly, 'that summer, Peggy was supposed to come back home for the first time in ages and, *well,* let's just say that our father caught wind of people making jokes about how Peg was coming home to try her luck on TV now that someone as 'crazy' as her had found her fifteen minutes of fame. Needless to say, Peg didn't come home until Christmas.'

Even distracted by the shame that always reared up to choke him a bit when he was reminded of his youthful stupidity, Charlie couldn't miss the fleeting glance Joycie gave Peggy, loaded to the brim with blatant concern.

Peggy looked down at her feet. 'I still don't understand what this has to do with me.'

'Whatever the reason, Higson wanted to keep you away from the Ballroom,' Andrew explained, and he was obviously choosing his words very carefully, 'but we need someone to come to Tib Street and see if we can get anything useful from Benson.'

'Of course,' Peggy agreed immediately. 'Now?'

Andrew looked pained enough that Charlie braced himself for whatever was coming next.

'It can't be you, Peggy,' Andrew stated quietly but firmly. 'Not this time.'

Peggy's face twitched in surprise. 'So, you came all the way out here to tell me that you don't need me?'

'No.' Andrew took a deep breath and refocussed his attention elsewhere. 'Marnie, we need you to come to Tib Street.'

'What?' Marnie cried as Charlie only blinked in astonishment. 'Me?'

'Yes, you,' Andrew replied, and it sounded like it was taking every ounce of his energy to force himself through this entire exchange. 'Benson's known Higson for decades and was around when Nash and Lily disappeared. He could have an inkling about where Higson's gone. Plus, he might know why CID officers are showing up at the Ballroom for out-of-hours meetings.'

Marnie was looking at Peggy, clearly torn between loyalty to her friend and assisting the very people who'd helped solve her own murder.

Andrew barrelled on regardless, 'Marnie, we also need you to stay at the Ballroom over the weekend, just in case anyone who shouldn't be there tries to come in, or if Higson makes a reappearance.'

Marnie apparently took umbrage at that. 'I'm not a bloody guard dog! Why can't one of you stay there? It's not like you weren't living there when you were too scared to go home, is it?'

Andrew pursed his lips. 'We can't, Marnie. We're going to try and track down Beth Nash and her kids this weekend. If we can find her, then maybe we can try and understand what Higson's got himself into.'

'You don't know he's got himself into anything!' Marnie protested. 'It's only been a day since you saw him. It's not like he's a missing child.'

'Marnie, you should go with them.'

Everyone turned in surprise as Peggy spoke. His sister's voice had been perfectly level, but Charlie could tell that it was masking injury.

And that, after everything that Peggy had done – had *risked* – for the Ballroom and the people in it, just wouldn't do. He decided that he might put his 'not meddling' resolution back into its box for a while.

'Where in the Lake District are you going?' Charlie asked as innocently as he could, directing his question at Lloyd.

'Staveshead,' Lloyd replied immediately, just as Charlie had hoped he would. 'Or maybe Stavesmere.'

'Lloyd!' Andrew barked sharply, but the damage had been done.

'Well, they're quite close to each other,' Charlie offered with a smile. 'Easy to mix up. I've done it myself.'

'Whatever you're planning, stop right now,' Andrew warned.

'You're so suspicious, Joycie,' Charlie replied evenly, shaking his head. 'I'm not planning anything.'

Andrew narrowed his eyes, but didn't say anything else.

'Alright,' Jen said loudly, standing up. 'I think we should probably get back into town. The Ballroom's been empty for hours as it is.'

'Just hold your horses there one second!' Charlie called. 'Has it really not crossed your mind that Lily Woodhouse wasn't psychic?'

Andrew bristled immediately. 'Of course she wasn't psychic! Nobody is psychic!'

Charlie scoffed. 'Nice to see you've really opened your mind.'

'We're leaving,' Andrew snapped.

Charlie held out his hands as though about to deliver a thought-provoking sermon. 'Just give me one second.'

Andrew looked ready to walk out anyway, but then he glanced at a visibly disgruntled Peggy and changed his mind with a twist of his lips. He growled in annoyance. 'Fine. *What?*'

'Well, you don't know what happened to this girl, or the policeman she was with, right?' Charlie continued anyway. 'They could very easily be dead, couldn't they?'

'Charlie!' Peggy and Jen scolded him in unison.

Charlie saw the exact moment when Andrew obviously twigged where Charlie's argument was heading. 'Got there, Joycie?'

'Could you recap for the rest of us?' Marnie grumbled.

'What if you find this woman in the Lake District and she knows nothing?' Charlie added. 'But what if she has her own personal ghost and just doesn't know it? What if her husband died twenty years ago and he decided to spend his afterlife following his poor wife and kids around? What if you could ask *him* what happened on the night he disappeared, and how Higson fits into everything?'

'They're *massive* 'what ifs',' Andrew replied, shaking his head.

Jen was wavering. 'They are, sir, yeah, but Charlie might actually have a point.'

'Look, it's all very simple,' Charlie carried on, not giving anyone else the opportunity to interject, 'Peggy could just take a quick peek, couldn't she?'

'I am actually right here!' Peggy snapped crossly.

'Marnie can take a look, and then go back to the Ballroom,' Andrew countered.

'Hey! I'm *also* right here!' Marnie argued loudly. 'And, *no*, actually, I don't know if I'd be able to easily get between the Ballroom and the Lake District. I have no connection to the place, and Peggy wouldn't be there.'

'See?' Charlie said again. God, he loved being right.

'If you turn up in the Lake District, I'll have you arrested,' Andrew threatened Charlie.

Charlie snorted. 'Oh? On what grounds, Joycie? I'd love to know!'

'Stop it, both of you!' Peggy admonished them. 'Andrew, I understand you not wanting me at Tib Street right now but, as much as it pains me to say this, Charlie's actually correct. I might be able to help if you track down Beth Nash.'

Andrew looked ready to argue again.

'*And*, if Higson thought it necessary to actually *hide* this woman and her children, then don't you think it might raise suspicion if three police officers suddenly turn up asking questions about her?' Peggy continued. 'It's not like being in the middle of Manchester. These are small places. People will notice, and people will talk.'

'So, what are you suggesting?' Andrew asked, and Charlie noted that Joycie was being much more pleasant with Peggy than with him, even if the detective still looked appalled. 'That we don't go?'

Peggy shook her head. 'I'm suggesting that perhaps you should take a more subtle approach. You know, don't all three of you go checking into a little B&B telling everyone that you're from Greater Manchester Police. You could be putting Beth Nash in real danger.'

Joycie was wavering. Charlie could see it plain as day.

'What do we do then, boss?' Lloyd asked Andrew. 'The Lake District and talking to Benson are the only leads we have.'

Andrew sighed in frustration and turned back to Charlie. 'Oh, for Christ's sake, just say whatever it is that you've been saving up for your grand finale.'

Charlie beamed. 'Well, I just so happen to have a house that's right near Stavesmere *and* Staveshead.'

'Of course you bloody do,' Andrew grumbled, closing his eyes as he pinched the bridge of his nose.

'It's not your house yet, Charlie,' Peggy sighed tiredly.

'Close enough, Peg.' Charlie grinned. 'Close enough.'

EIGHT

Andrew had always hated sitting in the back of the car.

By the time he reached Jen's car, though, Marnie was already perched in the passenger seat with a look on her face that was just daring him to start an argument.

He knew he hadn't imagined the disappointment in her eyes when he simply opened the door behind Jen and climbed in without comment. He made sure to close the door slightly harder than necessary though; he was only human after all.

Not for the first time, Andrew had walked into a room, fully equipped with a plan to proceed with an investigation, only to watch in dismay while his strategy was dismantled by one Swan sibling or the other. It had happened the very first time he'd set foot in Butterton House so it really shouldn't surprise him anymore.

Still, at least he'd held firm on one part of his original plan, and he would need to be content with that, even if said part of the plan had just turned around in her seat to glare at him.

'What?' he asked sharply.

'You should have called,' Marnie replied, as Jen started the engine.

'We came straight from Withing-'

'*Before* today,' Marnie snapped. 'Higson isn't the only one with Peggy's number, you know.'

Andrew couldn't argue with that. Honestly, he'd been waiting for Marnie to give him grief for it when they'd been at the Troubadour the night before; he'd given himself enough grief about it for months as it was.

That aside, he couldn't bring himself to give Marnie the satisfaction of agreeing with her aloud. Instead, he matched her glower and gave the barest nod.

Marnie's eyes narrowed calculatingly as he held her gaze. God, Andrew hated it when she did things like that, because it never failed to make made him wonder if she could somehow really see through him, and whether or not that was a skill she'd possessed when she'd been alive.

'Jelly Baby?' Lloyd asked with a mild air of desperation, shoving the half-empty bag into the space between Andrew and Marnie.

Raising her chin imperiously, Marnie leant back slightly before she broke eye contact and reached for a sweet.

Andrew would take it for the declaration of a truce that he thought it might be.

'Red ones were always my favourites,' Marnie added quietly as she turned back to face the direction they were driving, keeping the sweet pinched between her thumb and forefinger.

'Boss?' Lloyd prompted, crinkling the bag noisily.

'Thanks,' Andrew sighed and took a sweet.

He curled his lip when he saw that he'd picked a green one – categorically the worst Jelly Baby – but he shoved it in his mouth and chewed anyway.

'So, are you going to tell me why I had to come with you in the car, and not just pop into the Ballroom?' Marnie asked as they drove through the village on the way back to the main road. 'Why the big production?'

Andrew was glad that Marnie had waited until they'd left the Swans behind before she'd asked that question. He had the distinct feeling that they wouldn't have been any happier with the answer than Marnie was, no doubt, about to be.

'Because we can't actually be sure that the Ballroom's not being watched right now,' Andrew replied tiredly.

'Watched?' Marnie asked incredulously.

'There's a white van on Tib Street,' Lloyd explained. 'It might just be a white van, but it's been outside all week taking up loads of space. I've had to park round the corner more than once because of it. We were talking about it on the way over, and we just think it's a bit weird. Like I said, though, it might be nothing.'

Lloyd was correct, it might be nothing at all, but Andrew couldn't ignore the gut-feeling that something was awry.

'Why would anyone be watching though?' Marnie's scepticism was obvious.

Andrew shrugged. 'To see if Higson comes back? To see if we know where he's gone? To find out more about Peggy? Take your pick.'

'Has Higson *really* been keeping Peggy away because he's worried about her?' Marnie asked doubtfully as she stared out of her window.

'Yes,' Andrew replied, certain that Annie wouldn't have lied about that. 'And all of *this* isn't just about keeping Peggy away from Tib Street. I need anyone who might be watching the Ballroom to think that you're Peggy. Well, not Peggy, exactly, but *Miss Jones*.'

Marnie's head whipped back instantly. 'Are you using me as *bait*?'

Well, Andrew wouldn't have put it quite like that.

'Well, you and Peggy look nothing like each other,' Jen explained evenly, and Andrew was inordinately grateful for his sergeant once again. 'That might help to keep Peggy's identity hidden, just in case. We don't really know what sort of threat we're facing here, Marnie, if there's even a threat at all.'

'But you still want me to sit in the Ballroom and wait for these people – whoever they might be – to come in after me?' Marnie asked in horror.

Andrew really didn't want to be the one to have to point out that it wasn't like anyone could kill Marnie *again*. He thought it unlikely that he'd survive a comment like that.

Seemingly, nobody else wanted to point that out either and the silence in the car thickened as the unuttered truth festered between them.

Marnie laughed harshly a long moment later as the unescapable realisation dawned. 'Oh. Right.'

'Look,' Andrew replied wearily, 'back when we first started looking into your case, it didn't even occur to me to give Peggy an alias to use when she was in Lewis's, because I didn't think there was any need for one. I thought she'd be out of there within the day, and that would be the end of it. Obviously, I was wrong.'

'How surprising,' Marnie muttered darkly.

Andrew chose to ignore that comment. He had a much more pressing concern. 'Because of that, it means that there are more people out there who know how and why Peggy is connected to the Ballroom than I'm comfortable with. So, Marnie, I need to ask you something, and it's very important that you think carefully about it before you answer, alright?'

Marnie looked at him as though that would not be alright at all, thanks, but she eventually shrugged one shoulder.

Andrew steeled himself. 'Do you think that Rex would ever have told anybody about Peggy's involvement with the Ballroom?'

Marnie looked so stricken at the mention of her ex-fiancé, Andrew was worried that she was about to disappear right before his eyes.

'What?' Lloyd asked in surprise from beside him. 'What's Rex Hughes got to do with this?'

'Hopefully nothing,' Andrew replied as steadily as was possible when talking about the man who'd nearly got Peggy killed. He'd known Marnie was going to be particularly touchy about this conversation, and it was one he'd rather not be having, but the idea had begun to bother him on the drive to Butterton, and he'd been unable to ignore it.

'You can't possibly think that Rex has anything to do with this!' Marnie hissed, utterly appalled.

'Can you just answer the question?' Andrew replied sharply, aware of Jen's troubled glances towards him in the mirror. 'Please.'

Marnie shook her head, lips pursed. 'No, he wouldn't do that.'

'Are you sure?'

'As sure as I can be,' Marnie snapped. 'You know what happened to Athena when she kept going on about seeing ghosts in her cell. I know that Rex wouldn't want that to happen to him, so why would he mention Peggy?'

Andrew was fully aware of Athena Hughes' transfer away from the area a few months earlier, once she'd been deemed as 'disturbed'. Marnie's regular visits to the woman who'd murdered her had caused enough fuss that Athena had been relocated down south. He was also fully aware that it really would be better for Rex to never mention Peggy's involvement; she'd wanted her name kept out of the whole situation, and Rex wasn't going to argue about not facing kidnapping charges on top of everything else, was he?

Still, Andrew hadn't trusted Rex Hughes from the first moment he'd encountered him, and he knew that Hughes had garnered a collection of friends in high places, and in CID itself. Admittedly, those friends hadn't jumped at the chance to help him when his drug empire had gone up in flames after Marnie's murder, but Higson's apparent concern for Peggy's safety, and the appearance of Fallon on Tib Street brought everything far too close to CID, and to Chambers, for Andrew to be comfortable with.

On every case following Marnie's, Peggy had requested that she be known only as Peggy Jones, and Andrew was now immensely grateful for that fact. The fewer people with the name Peggy Swan on their lips, the better.

The only other person outside of the Ballroom who knew Peggy's real name and her true association with the team was the director of the play they'd investigated earlier in the year, Albany

Cohen. Peggy had gone as Peggy Jones during the case, but she'd obviously revealed her true identity on one of the – no doubt – many dates she'd been on with Cohen since March. Andrew would rather Cohen hadn't that information at all, but it wasn't up to him in the slightest, was it? Peggy was free to conduct her personal life however she wished, and with whomever she chose.

'You alright there, boss?' Lloyd asked. 'You look a bit green.'

Andrew shook himself. 'Fine.'

Marnie was still glaring at him, but that wasn't exactly unusual.

'I wouldn't have asked if I didn't think I needed to,' Andrew muttered eventually. 'And I wouldn't be asking you to do *this* either.'

It took a good long while, but eventually Marnie gave another one-shouldered shrug and turned her face away, effectively ending the conversation.

Andrew caught Jen's eyes in the mirror and wondered if he looked as on edge as his sergeant did.

The tense silence remained in place the entire way back to the city centre.

Just before they reached the turning to Tib Street, Andrew asked Jen to stop the car.

'Marnie, can you give us five minutes, and then come and knock on the door please?' Andrew asked. Under the circumstances, he'd have preferred to give an order than make a polite request, but he had enough experience to know that it wouldn't be the correct tactic when it came to Marnie.

'Whatever,' Marnie replied snottily before she opened the door, climbed out, and then slammed it hard enough to make the car shake.

'Fuck me, she's scary when she wants to be,' Lloyd muttered.

'Lloyd,' Andrew warned.

'Sorry, boss.'

Jen navigated the car onto Tib Street, and they all made sure to avert their eyes from the white van, which didn't appear to have moved since that morning, while she parked.

'Not a word until we get upstairs,' Andrew muttered as he got out of the car and went to unlock the main door.

As he stepped into the hallway, Andrew was immediately punched by the smell of cigarette smoke – stronger than the usual lingering scent – and it may actually have been the first time he was pleased to know that Dolly was around. He'd been concerned that they'd been away from the building too long, and that if anyone was looking for an opportunity to get inside, they'd given them one between their trips to Withington and Butterton House. If anyone had tried to gain entrance, Andrew was certain that Dolly would have given them what for and then hexed them for their troubles.

'What are we going to do when Marnie gets here?' Lloyd asked as they all trooped up the stairs.

'Jen, when she knocks, I want you to go down and let her in,' Andrew explained as he unlocked the Ballroom doors. 'Make as big a fuss over it being Miss Jones as you reckon you can get away with.'

'Sir,' Jen agreed.

'Then, when we all leave later, Marnie can walk off around the corner before getting herself back in here unseen,' Andrew added as he sat down at his desk. 'That way anyone outside will think the building's empty over the weekend, even though Marnie will actually still be here.'

'Our woman on the inside,' Lloyd said, nodding with enthusiasm. 'She'll be like a spy. She'll probably enjoy it all when she realises that!'

'I bloody doubt it,' Andrew muttered with a sigh. Marnie would do exactly as she liked, and Andrew could only hope that, just this once, it would be what he'd had asked her to do.

* * *

When Peggy had left the Troubadour the night before, she'd experienced a feeling of lightness that had less to do with the final round of drinks that Lloyd had presented the table with, and more with the fact that she'd genuinely enjoyed herself.

When she'd then easily managed to convince Andrew and his stubbornness to share a taxi to Tib Street, Peggy had felt as though the tide was turning and that things were heading back to the way that they'd been before March.

But to hear Andrew tell her that afternoon that she wasn't needed this time around – that she *couldn't* be needed – had felt like a slap in the face.

'Peg?'

Peggy looked up in surprise and immediately caught the side of her index finger in the zip of the old leather weekend bag she'd been packing. She hissed in pain, frantically rubbing the spot that was already forming an impressive blood blister.

'Peg?' Charlie called again from the other side of the bedroom door. 'Can I come in?'

Peggy stalked across the room, shaking her hand as she did so. She yanked open the door. 'What, Charlie?'

Charlie looked slightly taken aback by his sister's immediate hostility.

Peggy closed her eyes and took a breath. 'Sorry. Sorry, I just hurt myself. Come in.'

With Marnie absent, Charlie took the opportunity to perch in the window seat, plumping the cushions until they were arranged just so. He finally settled back and clasped his hands together. 'Are you alright?'

The inquiry was more hesitant than Peggy had been

expecting, and she didn't think it was entirely down to the way she'd snapped at her brother moments earlier.

'I'm fine,' she replied while she zipped up the bag without further incident and then sank onto the bed next to it.

'I heard you on the phone to Marnie,' Charlie continued quietly. 'You didn't sound thrilled.'

Peggy sighed and stared at her feet as she replayed the snippy phone call she'd received an hour or so earlier. 'Marnie's not delighted about being forced to stay in the Ballroom all weekend. Apparently, she had *plans*.'

'What plans?' Charlie asked, wrinkling her nose.

'I have no idea. I mentioned it to Emmeline, assuming that I should tell her that Marnie wouldn't be around to do whatever it was that they had arranged, but Emmy said that she didn't know what Marnie was talking about.' Peggy exhaled loudly. 'You remember what she was like last December, don't you?'

Charlie shuddered at the memory. 'She seems better this year though, don't you think?'

Peggy shrugged and glanced at her bedside clock. 'Was there anything specific you wanted, Charlie? I want to wash my hair before bed now that we're leaving so early.'

Charlie made another face of disgust. 'What time does Joycie want us to pick him up now?'

'Five,' Peggy replied. 'So, we need to leave here at half-four.'

'*Half-four?*' Charlie recoiled as though he'd been physically struck.

'Oh, come off it, you're still awake at that time half the week!' Peggy argued, armed with many memories of her brother stumbling up the staircase, only just home again, while the sun rose in the windows behind him.

'Yes, but normally I'm heading *towards* bed at that time, not away from it!'

'Look, Charlie, if you want to argue with Andrew about it

then, please, go ahead,' Peggy replied wearily.

'I thought you'd be happier about finally getting involved with a case, you know.'

Peggy had thought the same. 'Well, the circumstances don't exactly warrant much enthusiasm. We're only going at all because you made such a fuss about it. It's not like they actually wanted my help, is it?'

'Peggy...' Charlie trailed off and he sounded terribly unhappy. 'I don't think that's entirely fair.'

Peggy was well aware that it wasn't entirely fair, but there was something sharply humiliating about the fact that her inclusion on the trip north was mostly due to her brother's meddling, rather than any sort of genuine request for her help. She thought that she should probably force a beggars can't be choosers attitude on herself – after all, the only thing she'd wanted for months had been a chance to get back into the Ballroom – but Andrew's hesitance and Marnie's tetchiness needled away at any sense of excitement that she might have otherwise had.

'Oh, I spoke to Mrs Laycock,' Charlie added eventually, obviously trying to steer his sister away from the introspection that was likely broadcasting clearly from her face. 'She promised to make sure that the fridge is stocked, and the house will be warm by the time we arrive.'

'She really doesn't have to go to any trouble, Charlie,' Peggy said, uneasy that they were now getting someone else involved in the scheme. Andrew would likely be displeased about that fact.

Charlie rolled his eyes. 'When has that ever stopped her before? Look, if we'd turned up tomorrow without warning, you know that she'd only find any excuse under the sun to invite herself in for tea, and then we'd be stuffed, wouldn't we?'

'What did you say to her? You didn't mention the investigation, surely?'

'Of course I didn't! I just said that we'd had a last-minute change to our plans, so we'd decided to head up for the weekend with some friends,' Charlie replied. 'She seemed delighted, to be honest.'

Peggy groaned. She liked Mrs Laycock a lot – she always had – but the woman was a lethal combination of supremely nosy and terrifyingly eagle-eyed.

'Joycie's the one I'm concerned about,' Charlie continued, twisting his lips. 'Lloyd and Jen know how to behave like normal, sociable human beings, but Joycie is very, well, *Joycie.*'

'That's not very fair, Charlie,' Peggy argued, feeling the need to defend Andrew against such a slight, even if she was still a bit pissed off with him for a number of reasons.

'Well, you would say that, wouldn't you?' Charlie muttered.

It was Peggy's turn to roll her eyes that time. 'Go on, get out, I need to get sorted for tomorrow.'

Charlie sighed loudly and rose to his feet. 'Are you *sure* we can't take something more fun than the Rangie?'

'No, Charlie! For God's sake, we're not going over this again,' Peggy grumbled, pushing her brother towards the door. 'That's the car we're taking, and *I* am driving.'

'Well, I'm not going to argue with you about the driving part,' Charlie replied, raising his hands in surrender before opening the bedroom door. 'I'll be perfectly content to pass out in the backseat, and you and Joycie can get on with having all those hushed little secret tête-à-têtes that you're both so fond of.'

Just for that, Peggy decided that she wasn't going to bother bringing any car snacks for her brother.

'Goodnight, Charlie,' she said snippily, shutting the door in his face as he laughed at her.

'See you at half-four!' he called from the other side, obviously still highly amused by himself.

Peggy took a deep breath and then very slowly released it through her nose, trying to tamp down the war between irritation and apprehension that she'd already been fighting before Charlie's interruption.

Back at the very beginning of all this, when Peggy had first met the Ballroom team, she'd had to prove her worth to both them and to the investigation, and now there was a genuine nervousness thrumming through her veins at the realisation that she was going to have fight her way back in again.

She just really hoped that the door was still open.

NINE

Peggy nervously tapped her finger against her lips while her other hand drummed an anxious counterpoint on the steering wheel. Beyond checking her watch, her attention hadn't strayed from the wing mirror since she'd pulled up across the road from the south entrance to Hollyhedge Park a quarter of an hour earlier, but there hadn't been a hint of movement. Where the hell was Andrew? It was gone ten past five, and it wasn't like him to be late.

Charlie's head appeared next to her left shoulder as he leant forward and yawned loudly. 'I'm sure he's just being slow, Peg. It's a godawful time of night.'

Peggy nodded silently and pulled her coat more tightly around her. It had been a cold, almost moonless night, and there wasn't even the hint of an approaching dawn. She'd killed the engine when they'd parked, and the interior of the car had cooled rapidly without the hot air blowing from the vents. She rubbed her palms together in an attempt to manufacture a bit of warmth.

A flicker of something shifting in the gloom caught Peggy's attention. 'Hang on. I think I can see someone in the park.'

Moments later, Andrew arrived at the short railings at the edge of the park and Peggy flicked the headlights back on to alert him to their location. Andrew looked over in surprise, clearly on alert, and Peggy switched on the interior light so that he could see her.

Andrew's shoulders relaxed immediately, and he gave her a short nod before he dropped a rucksack over the railings onto the pavement before following the same path himself.

He jogged to the car, giving it a suspicious once over before heading round to the passenger door. Peggy could only be glad that she'd argued Charlie down to the Range Rover.

'Morning,' Peggy greeted Andrew quietly as he climbed in.

'Barely,' Andrew replied as he scrubbed his hands over his face before fastening his seatbelt. He winced apologetically. 'Sorry. Morning.'

Peggy waved away the apology, turning the key in the ignition.

Andrew retrieved a paper file from his backpack, tucked it between his seat and the door, and then passed the bag over his shoulder to Charlie.

'Seatbelt, Charlie,' Peggy pointedly instructed her brother's reflection.

Charlie grumbled, but the loud click a couple of seconds later told Peggy that he'd complied.

Andrew was intently checking the mirror as Peggy pulled the car away from the kerb.

'Did anyone see you?' Andrew asked.

Peggy shook her head. 'We've barely seen a soul since we left Butterton, and nobody at all since we got here.'

'Because it's the middle of the night,' Charlie complained.

'You didn't have to come,' Peggy retorted.

'Well, middle of the night or not, there was someone watching my house,' Andrew added as they headed for the motorway.

'What?' Peggy asked sharply. 'Who was it?'

Andrew shrugged. 'I don't know. They were too far away. They'd parked about four houses up on the other side of the road, nowhere near a streetlight. Same car was parked just up from the bus stop when I got back last night. I've got the number plate so we can check it later.'

'Do they know you saw them?' Charlie asked.

'No chance,' Andrew replied confidently. 'I didn't switch on any lights, and I went out the back door, over the fence and straight into the park, so as far as they're concerned, I'm still in the house.'

Peggy glanced at Andrew out of the corner of her eye. 'Did you speak to Marnie last night?'

'Yeah, she didn't say much beyond the fact that the van was still outside, and Benson hadn't made an appearance,' Andrew replied, folding his arms and clamping his hands under his armpits. He was obviously cold after his traipse through the park.

Peggy flipped the direction of the farthest heating vent so that it was pointed at Andrew. 'There's a flask of tea in the footwell.'

'Thanks,' Andrew said gratefully, reaching down for it.

'Do you think anyone will have been watching Jen and Lloyd?' Peggy asked as Andrew carefully poured tea into the lid.

Andrew shrugged again. 'Jen was babysitting at her sister's last night, which will have hopefully thrown off anyone looking for her anyway, but she's smart enough to check. Lloyd was going out last night and then crashing at a friend's. I doubt *anyone* could manage to follow him for a whole night out anyway; he always wants to go somewhere else the second a song he hates gets played.'

Peggy almost laughed at the hint of long-suffering in Andrew's explanation.

'I still don't understand why *I* was banned from going out last night,' Charlie complained.

'Because you have even less of a bloody clue about subtlety than Lloyd,' Andrew replied, awkwardly replacing the cap on the flask before holding the filled lid out towards Peggy. 'Tea?'

'Thanks.' Peggy took the tea clumsily but managed not to spill it before taking a drink and handing it back.

Andrew settled back in his seat, his hands wrapped tightly around the lid between sips.

'No, I'm fine. I actually don't want tea right now,' Charlie muttered petulantly, 'thanks so much for asking.'

Peggy was glad to see that Andrew ignored her brother entirely. It was far too early for childish bickering, and they had a two-hour drive ahead of them.

'Have you heard from Higson?' Peggy asked before Charlie could add further dramatics.

Andrew shook his head. 'I called Annie at her sister's last night and she hadn't heard anything either. I've given her the number of your house up north, so she can get hold of us if she needs to.'

'Good idea. Marnie's promised to check in regularly too, somewhat begrudgingly,' Peggy explained. She still wasn't sure that Charlie's reasoning for Marnie's mood the night before was correct. She was even less sure when she caught the shift in Andrew's expression.

'Look, I didn't want to bring it up any more than she did, but with everything going on right now I needed to check,' Andrew protested, holding the tea out to Peggy again. 'I don't understand how she can still think that utter bastard possesses even a shred of decency after everything he did!'

'What?' Peggy's hand wobbled in surprise, and she had to quickly reassert her grip on the tea.

'What?' Andrew repeated, eyes wide as he rescued the lid from Peggy. 'She didn't mention anything to you?'

Peggy shook her head.

'What's *he* got to do with any of this?' Charlie asked icily, clearly leaping to the same conclusion about the identity of 'that utter bastard' as Peggy had.

Andrew looked like he'd been caught red-handed. He'd obviously assumed that Peggy had been informed of whatever he and Marnie had spoken about. He also looked like he was trying incredibly hard to work out how to backtrack on what he'd just said, and that just wasn't going to cut it.

'Andrew, *why* were you talking to Marnie about Rex?' Peggy's brows knitted in concern.

Andrew mumbled his way through his misgivings about Rex's knowledge of Peggy's association with the Ballroom, and Rex's apparent connections to certain officers from CID.

Charlie remained silent, but Peggy could feel the rage radiating from the back seat. She hoped to God that there was never an occasion where Charlie and Rex Hughes found themselves together in a locked room.

'Marnie's convinced that Rex won't have said anything,' Andrew concluded. 'Given that he seemed happy to keep his mouth shut about any involvement with you back when he was arrested, I'd say she's probably correct.'

Peggy held out her hand for the tea and then took a deep breath, steeling herself. 'I think Marnie's been visiting Rex.'

'What?'

Peggy winced as the shout came from both directions. 'I don't know for certain.'

'Have you asked her?' Andrew demanded.

'Since when?' Charlie snapped a split second later.

'Of course I've asked her,' Peggy sighed, 'and she's denied it every time. As for when, she first started disappearing for a couple of days at a time back in March. Whenever she reappeared, she just seemed...off.'

'Why didn't you say anything?' Andrew asked, and he was obviously trying not to sound too accusatory. Peggy fleetingly wondered if this was something he'd been actively working on in her absence.

'Because I wasn't certain that I was right. Plus, we were in the middle of a case back then,' she replied evenly, keeping her eyes on the road ahead. 'After that, it seemed like she was back to her normal self. It's only started again in the last couple of months.'

'What makes you think it's something to do with Hughes?' Andrew reached for the flask as he spoke.

'Marnie was miserable every time she came back,' Peggy explained. 'Not just sad or unhappy, but downright wretched. It was like she'd had her heart broken all over again; I could almost feel it, which doesn't happen that often.'

Andrew shivered and Peggy knew it wasn't because he was cold. He poured more tea and took a large gulp.

'Wouldn't there be a record of Rex's interviews though? You'd know if he'd ever mentioned…' Peggy trailed off, really not wanting to make herself the focus even as she was trying to pull Andrew back to the investigation.

'It's a good idea, but everything to do with Marnie's case, apart from the copy of the original file at the Ballroom, is over at CID.' Andrew curled his lips in distaste. 'I don't want to risk drawing attention to anything by requesting it. Though I suppose…'

Charlie growled in annoyance. 'You're both doing it again, and it's bloody annoying. Finish a sentence, for Christ's sake.'

Andrew turned to glare at Charlie. 'I was going to say that I could ask Mike to try and get us a copy.'

'Mike?' Peggy asked, wrinkling her nose as she tried to put a face to the single name.

'He means Mike from the pub,' Charlie supplied uselessly.

Peggy wrinkled her nose. 'That doesn't help.'

'Mike Lawson, a DS from CID,' Andrew clarified. 'I've asked him to drive past Higson's house a few times this weekend and let us know if he sees any movement inside. He's trying to find out if there's any chat about why Fallon was at the Ballroom the other day.'

'You trust him?' Peggy asked.

'I do,' Andrew replied seriously, passing over the tea again. 'I've known him for a long time, and I wouldn't have asked him to help out if I had any reason to doubt him.'

The car settled into silence, broken only by the occasional yawn, and they were north of Manchester before Andrew spoke quietly again:

'I went to the library on my way home last night. I wanted to see if I could find anything else on Lily Woodhouse.'

Peggy's eyes flicked up to the rearview mirror, confirming that her brother had dozed off, slouched in the corner of the backseat with his mouth hanging open like a congested toddler. Andrew was nothing if not predictable; he'd obviously clocked Charlie's departure from the conversation and was taking the opportunity to talk about the case without the risk of any 'helpful' comments from the younger Swan.

'She was in the papers a lot,' Andrew continued as he picked up the file he'd stowed earlier and rested it on his knees. 'It looks like she became quite the fixture of the city's social circle after she appeared on TV. I found loads of photographs of her at parties, or at events with footballers and musicians, so the fact that she was supposedly at the ballet on the night she disappeared wouldn't raise any questions by itself. Davy Nash, though, was about as far removed from Lily's usual crowd as you could get, so even if I believed that they were both at the Free Trade Hall, I'd still have questions about *why* they were together, and how they'd formed an acquaintance in the first place.'

'How certain are you that they *weren't* at the Free Trade Hall?' Peggy asked as she steered the car onto the slip road that would take them further north towards Preston.

'Lily might reasonably have been there, but if she was, I'm certain that it wasn't with Davy Nash,' Andrew replied. 'Ignoring his official statement, Higson's own notes call bullshit on it, and Annie's story is the same. That's without even considering the fact that the majority of witnesses that claim to have seen Lily and Nash together are linked to police officers, if not police officers themselves.'

'And you don't think that Higson is just covering for his friend?' Peggy asked carefully. 'Davy Nash wouldn't be the first man to stray from his marriage, would he?'

'No, he wouldn't,' Andrew agreed, 'but I just don't see it. Annie said that Davy and his wife were childhood sweethearts, and that he'd been spending as much time with his kids as he could.'

Peggy nodded slowly. 'Why were multiple people so keen to say that they were seen together then? If something terrible really did happen to both Lily and Davy on the same night and, as Higson's investigation strongly suggests, police officers were involved in covering up what really happened, why publicly link the disappearances in the first place? Why couldn't Lily have just been another teenage runaway, and Davy Nash a man who walked out on his family, *independently* of each other?'

Andrew raised his eyebrows and gave her an approving look.

'What?'

'It's probably not too late to pack in your life of luxury and become a detective, you know.' Andrew shot her a fleeting grin before he sobered again. 'That's exactly what I've been asking myself for the last two days, and exactly what I want to ask Higson.'

'What else did you find out about Lily?' Peggy asked, glancing over as Andrew opened the file. Photocopies of news articles gave Peggy a glimpse of an impeccably dressed young woman smiling coyly at something off camera, doe eyes wide and knowing. Even in poorly reproduced black and white, Lily Woodhouse sparkled right off the page; the photos reminded Peggy of those Yardley adverts with Jean Shrimpton that had been everywhere when Peggy had been a teenager herself.

'Well,' Andrew replied, looking quickly over his right shoulder, 'Charlie's theory about how Lily was getting the information to put on her psychic act might actually have some credence. It turns out, that eight years before Lily's stint on television, her twin sister, Violet, drowned on a family holiday in

North Wales.'

Peggy felt another pang of sympathy for the missing girl, and even though her attention was on the road, she could feel Andrew's eyes on her. Lily would only have been nine when her sister died, which was the same age Andrew had been when his older brother had been killed in an accident. For almost twenty-five years, Andrew hadn't known that Rob had returned to the house he'd grown up in – the very house Andrew still lived in – but that had all changed during their first case, when Peggy had seen Rob on Acacia Road. Andrew might still be the most sceptical person Peggy had ever encountered, but she knew that the circumstances would still lend him a natural inclination to follow this line of investigation, which meant that Peggy expected that she was about to wrong-foot the detective entirely.

'We can't know that for certain though,' she said.

Andrew, as expected, twitched in surprise. 'You don't think Lily could have been speaking to her sister?'

'Of course she could have been,' Peggy sighed, 'but it doesn't mean that she actually was, does it? How many people claim to be psychics, Andrew? And do you think every one of them can see ghosts?'

The expression of disbelief remained on Andrew's face, though it shifted marginally towards thoughtfulness.

'I was fourteen when Lily was on TV and, like Charlie said, I knew nothing about her at all until I got a call at school on behalf of my father,' Peggy explained hesitantly, not thrilled to be dredging up a period of her life she tried to avoid thinking about.

Andrew made a face and shook his head, but he remained silent.

'I was advised that it would be in everyone's best interests if I stayed on in Switzerland instead of coming home as planned,' Peggy continued, hitting the indicator slightly more viciously than required as she overtook a lorry. 'I spoke to Charlie on the phone a few times that summer, and he told me all about the jokes everyone was making about me and this girl who'd been on television. He felt guilty about it all, of course, but I'm sure if it hadn't been the 'ghost' thing that ostracised me from the social circle my father expected us to be part of, it would have been something else in the end.

'By then, it had been a good few years since Charlie had told his friend about me but even almost a thousand miles away, I still hadn't managed to get away from it. I doubt I ever even considered the possibility that Lily could see ghosts, because I wouldn't have been able to understand how someone could so confidently and happily share that supposed 'gift' with the world, even dressing it up as being 'psychic'. I suppose I still don't understand it, even now. I mean, do you know how many people I've actually *told* about what I can do?'

'Not many,' Andrew offered.

'Charlie and my mother,' Peggy replied with a scathing little laugh. 'That's it. I never spoke to my father about it, and I never – thank God – shared it with Edgar. Charlie told Lloyd, who, in turn, told you. Then, any time we've been on a case, and someone's needed to know the specifics of what exactly I'm doing there, *you* are the one who's explained it.'

Andrew's eyes widened, and he looked like he was about to launch into an apology, and so Peggy waved towards him before he could start; she neither needed nor wanted one.

'I just mean that I don't know how a teenage girl could want anyone knowing just how *different* she was.' Peggy shot Andrew a self-deprecating smile. 'Then again, maybe that just says more about me than anyone else.'

'I'm supposed to be the cynical one,' Andrew said quietly. His lips quirked faintly, but Peggy could tell that he wasn't really joking. 'You could be right. Maybe Lily was just a pretty, young con artist, and maybe she tried it on with the wrong person, but there's one thing you're not considering here, Peggy.'

'What?'

'Higson.' Andrew shrugged.

Peggy frowned in confusion. 'What do you mean?'

'Do you remember what he was like when he first met you? He was delighted!' Andrew replied. 'When you first turned down the plan to go into Lewis's, he made me run after you and get you to agree.'

'Really?'

Andrew nodded. 'He told me I was going straight back to CID in the morning if I couldn't convince you to stay. I'm sure I told you that at the time.'

'You did, but I thought you were just being dramatic to try and get me to feel sorry for you.'

Andrew chuckled. 'No, he really had put me in my place. He did the same again after the *Lady Bancroft* case.'

Peggy readjusted her grip on the steering wheel as nonchalantly as possible; she'd hoped that that case, and everything surrounding it, was off limits. 'Right?'

Andrew pursed his lips. 'I suppose what I'm trying to say is that Higson has always wanted you at the Ballroom, and I can't think of a single good reason for him to keep you away, other than if he really thought that you could be in danger. He stopped calling you at the exact same time he went back to looking at a twenty-year old case. That sounds an awful lot like Higson had reason to be worried that whatever happened to Lily Woodhouse might have something to do with how she apparently just *knew* things; and, that he had the knowledge – or at least a strong suspicion – that Lily had disappeared because she was like you. I can't see how it all makes sense otherwise.'

'It could just be a coincidence.'

'You know I feel about coincidences, Peggy.'

That was true, and because she knew *that*, a realisation dawned, sure and startling in its clarity. Frowning, she turned her head until she could see Andrew's face. 'Which means that you were already convinced that Lily's entire psychic act came down to her speaking to ghosts *before* you found out about her twin sister's death. If that's true, why didn't you say that when you first came to Butterton yesterday? Why did you deny it when Charlie voiced the idea?'

Andrew looked out the window for a long moment before he replied. 'Because, at the end of the day, it doesn't really matter whether Lily could speak to the dead or not; what matters is that Higson was worried enough about you to lie to all of us, and now he's disappeared.

'We came to Butterton because we needed to try and talk to Benson, and asking Marnie was the only idea I could come up with that didn't involve *you* going to the Ballroom. Besides, I wasn't convinced that Lily was like you. I actually thought that I might be overthinking it – now, don't look quite so surprised, I do occasionally have some self-awareness – but then Charlie came out with exactly what I'd been theorising on the drive over. Never tell him I said this, but he does have an infuriating habit of being right about these sorts of things.'

Peggy checked the mirror again, but Charlie would have crowed loudly about it if he'd heard what Andrew had said. 'I know.'

'Also, Marnie's pissed off with me again,' Andrew added.

Marnie's pissed off with everyone right now, Peggy thought petulantly. 'Because of Rex?'

'No. Because Higson didn't call you, but neither did I.'

Peggy tried very hard not to scowl at Marnie's interference.

'She's actually right about this one, Peggy,' Andrew continued, his hands held up in obvious remorse. 'And I *am* sorry.'

Peggy shook her head vehemently. 'There's nothing to be sorry for. Really.'

'Peggy, I still s-'

'Andrew, it's fine.' It came out a bit harsher than she'd intended, but as it immediately got Andrew to stop talking, she was okay with it. She didn't want to hear that he'd been guilt-tripped into giving an apology or an explanation, lest her feelings be hurt otherwise. She didn't want to hear that she was being *permitted* to come along out of some misplaced guilt. 'Look, there was no reason for me to be at the Ballroom for the past few months, but maybe I can actually be useful this weekend.'

Andrew, annoyingly, didn't look like he'd be easily diverted from whatever course of regretful rationalisation he'd set himself on, and Peggy just hadn't had enough tea to even begin to deal with that.

'Tell me about Beth Nash,' she instructed bluntly, hoping that a hard swerve in topic would kill the current thread. 'And Davy too. You said yesterday that he and Higson were friends, didn't you?'

Andrew narrowed his eyes, and for just a second, Peggy thought that he was going to call out her obvious deviation, but he just sighed unhappily and reached for the flask. 'Yeah, they were friends for a few years. Annie said they used to meet up with Benson for darts every Thursday night. Well, every Thursday night until a few months before Davy and Lily disappeared.'

Andrew paused and held out the newly filled lid to Peggy.

She accepted the tea with a quiet *thanks*, and then lapsed back into silence, letting Andrew talk until they'd driven well beyond Preston.

TEN

They'd left the monotonous gloom of the motorway behind them as they'd approached the final thirty miles of their journey north, but any sprawling view of the fells or sheer expanse of sky that should have been afforded to them had been smothered beneath a heavy shroud of fog. Wisps of cloud had swirled lazily in the beams of their headlights, dancing hypnotically as the car wound towards the south shore of Ullswater, and Andrew hadn't been able to avoid recalling the stories that Grandpa Joyce used to tell about spirits that would hide in the mist, waiting to lure unsuspecting travellers into danger.

When they'd eventually reached Briersthwaite, Peggy had sighed loudly in relief as they'd passed the sign welcoming them to the village. The white-knuckled grip she'd had on the steering wheel as she'd navigated the car through the winding roads north of Windermere remained, however, until she'd driven through an open set of wrought iron gates and drawn the car to a halt on a gravelled stretch of driveway.

Andrew had tiredly climbed out of the Range Rover and looked up at the house – St. Sunday's Grange, according to the sign on the gatepost – and had been struck by how it looked like a tiny, less-polished version of Butterton House. He'd meant 'tiny' in a relative sense, of course, as the frontage of the house still had more windows on its ground floor than Andrew's home had in total, and outbuildings stretched in both directions for as far as Andrew could see.

He'd silently followed Peggy through the front door and down a long corridor, stopping only once to peer into a comfortable-looking room where a fire had been crackling in the hearth. Lamps and wall sconces had been switched on, and their bulbs dimmed low enough to illuminate their route with a warm golden glow.

Charlie had appeared behind them only moments after they'd reached the kitchen, and he'd immediately directed both Andrew and Peggy straight back out of the room again, with an instruction to go and sit down while he made a pot of tea.

Before he'd complied, Andrew noted that the fridge had been stocked with not just bottles of fresh milk, but what looked like enough food to feed a small army for a few days. A tall Victoria sponge took centre stage on the kitchen table, covered by a glass cloche that barely contained its lofty layers.

When Andrew had made his way back to the room he'd peeked into, Peggy had already folded herself into one of the large armchairs by the fire, eyes closed, and feet tucked up beneath her. She'd briefly cracked open one eye and gestured with a nod that Andrew could take the other chair and then resettled into stillness.

The nearly unnatural tranquillity had remained intact, even through Charlie's return with a trayful of tea and toast, and Andrew would almost have described himself as 'content' when an hour had ticked by without further interruption; *well*, as content as it was possible to be when your boss was missing, you had a twenty-year old case to investigate, and you were still trying to work out how to find a woman with a last known address from two decades earlier.

A shrill ringing cut through the peace, and Andrew's eyes snapped open in surprise. Blinking away ribbons of drowsiness, he realised that the sky beyond the large windows had lightened considerably; he must have dozed off.

As Charlie traipsed out of the room to answer the door, Andrew stood slowly, raising his arms high above his head, trying to stretch out his shoulders and force himself back to full alertness.

Peggy was still curled up in the armchair, and Andrew only briefly hesitated before he reached over and gently shook her shoulder. 'Peggy? I think Jen and Lloyd might be here.'

She made a soft noise of profound unhappiness but nodded slowly to let him know that she'd understood.

Andrew straightened up again with a quiet snort of fond amusement and was immediately struck dumb by the view through the window. A perfectly manicured lawn, wet with dew, rolled gently down to a wide band of gravel that itself blended seamlessly into the dark water lapping gently at the shoreline. A wooden dock stretched out into the water, and even with weathered edges, it still looked too sharp and incongruous against the backdrop of undulating fells on the far shore of the lake, that were still partially hidden by a blanket of fog.

'You should really see it when the sun's out.'

Andrew turned in surprise at Peggy's voice. While he'd been distracted by Ullswater, she'd soundlessly made her way to stand next to him.

No matter where they were, Peggy always seemed to run cold, so Andrew wasn't surprised to see that her arms were folded as she kept her coat wrapped firmly around herself, despite the warmth of the room. More than once, he'd wondered if it had anything to do with the fact that Peggy was almost caught between two worlds, but he'd never asked and, to be honest, it wasn't something he liked to dwell on.

With significantly less discretion than Peggy, Lloyd materialised to Andrew's left. 'Shit, look at that view! Morning, boss. Morning, Peggy.'

'Morning, Lloyd,' Peggy replied, clearly amused as she turned away. 'Hi, Jen. Was the drive alright?'

'Fine until we hit that fog,' Jen replied wearily, and Andrew was surprised to see his usually put-together sergeant looking worse for wear. 'We drove straight past the turn-off to Briersthwaite, and then did it again going back in the other direction trying to find it.'

'Sit by the fire, both of you,' Peggy suggested. She moved

towards the chairs that she and Andrew had vacated, turning them enough that they still benefited from the warmth, but so that anyone sitting there could converse with someone sitting on either of the two squashy-looking sofas further back in the room. 'Tea, Charlie, please?'

Charlie disappeared off to the kitchen without complaint as everyone sat down again.

'Did either of you notice anyone watching you last night or this morning?' Andrew asked the new arrivals bluntly. There wasn't any point dancing around the subject.

Jen wrinkled her nose. 'I can't be certain, but I think a car followed me from Tib Street out to my sister's house; if it was the same one, it was still there when Liz – that's my sister – and Dan went out, because I waved them off at the door with my nieces. It was nowhere to be seen this morning, though, and I circled back up the street twice before I went to get Lloyd; I didn't see anyone in a car, or even on the street.'

Andrew nodded, feeling relieved. 'How about you, Lloyd?'

Lloyd shook his head. 'I don't think so, but I did what you said and kept moving on after every drink or two anyway. Fi nearly lamped me for it, but I didn't notice anyone after us.'

'That's good,' Andrew confirmed, folding his arms and leaning forwards, 'because someone was definitely watching my house this morning.'

'Bloody hell, really?' Lloyd's eyes were wide and alarmed. 'Who was it?'

'I couldn't see them,' Andrew replied, and then recounted how he'd made his way through the park to meet the Swans.

'Bloody hell,' Lloyd repeated. 'What's going on?'

Andrew would have loved to have had an answer for that question. 'We need to do whatever we can to track down Beth Nash. If we can, we might be able to work out what's so important about this case that Higson spent twenty years going back to it. If nothing else, we'd at least know whether Higson has been in contact with her this whole time, or if she's seen him recently.'

Lloyd's eyes lit up as Charlie returned with another trayful of breakfast things, and he immediately hopped out of his chair and made a beeline for the large cafetière.

'How far are we from where Annie thought Beth Nash might be?' Jen asked, gratefully accepting the cup of tea and plate of buttered toast that Charlie passed to her. 'Either place.'

'We're about halfway between both towns,' Charlie replied as he flopped down into the middle of the empty sofa opposite Peggy and Andrew. 'Stavesmere is about fifteen miles south, back near Ambleside, and Staveshead is the same distance, but north towards Keswick. It's half an hour or so to each from here. Did Mrs Higson lean more towards one than the other?'

Andrew shook his head. 'She said Staveshead first, but almost immediately thought it could be Stavesmere. She did say that Higson had originally taken Beth and the kids to a place near Keswick though, didn't she?'

Jen nodded. 'She did, but she also couldn't be sure that she was remembering anything else accurately.'

'It's still the only lead we have right now,' Andrew replied. 'I think our best bet is to split up, try both places, and hope that one of them pans out.'

'Why don't Lloyd and I take Stavesmere then?' Jen suggested. 'We've already driven that road to come up here, so we should be able to find it easily enough.'

'Peggy, can you drive us to Staveshead then?' Andrew asked.

Peggy looked surprised, and Andrew frowned. Had she been expecting to be cut out of the investigation now that she'd delivered Andrew to the Lake District? He'd talked to her about the case in the car, but he obviously hadn't done a good enough job of letting her know that they all still saw her as an integral part of the

Ballroom team.

'Peggy?' Andrew prompted.

'Sure, that's fine,' Peggy agreed eventually, shaking herself.

Charlie opened his mouth, no doubt ready to announce what job he'd given himself, so Andrew held up his hand to pause any forthcoming declaration. 'Charlie, you need to stay here.'

Unsurprisingly, Charlie looked outraged at being sidelined. 'What? Why?'

'Because Marnie, Annie Higson and Mike all have the telephone number for here, and I'm expecting calls from all three of them this morning,' Andrew replied evenly. 'Someone needs to be here to answer the phone.'

'But…' Charlie trailed off with a loud sigh. 'Oh, *fine.*'

'Jen, if you and Lloyd manage to locate Beth Nash – and remember, she's more likely to be going by Beth Gower these days – I want one of you to stay with her while the other comes back here to wait for us, alright?' Andrew looked seriously between Jen and Lloyd. 'Same goes for if you learn anything about where Higson might be.'

Andrew checked his watch. 'Right, it's quarter past nine. Follow up on anything, even if it seems insignificant, and be back here for half-twelve. Subtlety, Lloyd, yeah?'

'Got it, boss,' Lloyd replied before gulping down his coffee. 'I'll drive if you want, Jen. You did the whole way here.'

'Ready to go?' Andrew asked, turning to Peggy and covering his mouth as he yawned.

Peggy gave her own yawn in reply, narrowing her eyes judgementally.

'Sorry,' Andrew chuckled lightly, rubbing his cheeks vigorously as he stood up. He turned to Charlie. 'When the phone rings write down everything you're told, alright?'

'I do actually know how to take a message, Joycie.'

'Mrs Laycock's likely to pop in, Charlie,' Peggy said, as she opened her handbag for the keys. 'She's left the one cake already, but you know what she's like when you're here. Don't you dare tell her what's actually going on though.'

'Who's this now?' Andrew asked, alert again.

'Mrs Laycock,' Peggy replied. 'She's a neighbour, but also the pseudo-housekeeper for this place. Charlie called her yesterday to let her know we were coming early this morning, which is why we have a fridge full of food and the house was actually warm when we arrived. She's entirely lovely, has four adult daughters, and wants to adopt Charlie; she thinks he's far too skinny and has been trying to fatten him up with cake since we were kids. She's no doubt got a table full of teacakes and muffins ready to bring round for him. This is all part of her plan to get Charlie to fall in love with one of her daughters, so that she'll get to keep him as her son-in law.'

Andrew snorted when Charlie's face fell.

Peggy shuddered. 'God forbid if she finds out you're here as well. *Four* daughters, Andrew. She'll have a lemon drizzle with your name on it within the hour.'

Andrew sobered immediately and Peggy grinned at him before leaving the room.

'Peg's not joking,' Charlie warned. 'Mrs Laycock is desperate for a wedding.'

'You can't tell anyone what we're doing here,' Andrew warned, deciding it was safer to not to dwell on anything either Swan sibling had just said.

'Yes, thank you, I'm well aware. I told Mrs L that we were coming up with some friends for the weekend. Is there any chance you could tone down the, well, *you-ness* of you?'

Andrew frowned. 'What's that supposed to mean?'

'Well, you do have a tendency to look at everyone new you meet as though they're a suspect in a murder, don't you, Joycie?'

'No, I don't.'

Charlie rolled his eyes and then shook his head pityingly. 'No, of course you don't. Silly me.'

Andrew pursed his lips. 'Answer the phone and don't move until we get back.'

With a dramatic sigh, Charlie flopped back down on the sofa.

Andrew decided that this didn't warrant further reply and left the room without another word.

As he reached the open front door, he nearly walked straight into Peggy as she hurried in from outside.

'Oh! Sorry,' she said, taking a step back. 'I was just coming to see if you were ready to go.'

Andrew nodded, pulling the door closed behind them. 'Do you want me to drive? You'll have to tell me where to go. I've only ever been to Windermere, and that was when I was about twelve.'

Peggy shook her head as she reached the car. 'Charlie knows it far better than me. He spent summers up here as a teenager, so he's the one with the bus timetable and taxi routes to every pub or party venue in the area seared into his brain. I don't mind driving, but you're in charge of directions.'

Andrew looked down as Peggy held out a battered leather-bound road atlas.

He took the book and opened the cover, raising his eyebrows. 'Peggy, this is twenty-five years old.'

Peggy shrugged. 'It's either that, or I stay here so that Charlie can direct you.'

'Not a chance,' Andrew replied, immediately heading for the passenger seat. 'Let's just try not to get lost.'

* * *

Despite two fairly hairy instances with junctions that didn't exist in the road atlas, they actually managed to find Staveshead with surprising ease.

The small town was postcard-pretty, but in a more unassuming way than the well-known shoreline towns and villages with their dramatic views over the water. Peggy could easily imagine it teeming with tourists on a summer's day, but in mid-December it was devoid of visitors and Peggy easily parked the Range Rover in a space halfway up the main street.

She and Andrew climbed out of the car, and Peggy took a moment to get her bearings. A teashop appeared shuttered for the winter, and the kitschy souvenirs in the darkened window of the shop next door were gathering dust. She could hear high-pitched shrieking and laughing from somewhere nearby, so assumed they must be near a primary school. A butcher across the street seemed to be doing a roaring trade, with a queue stretching from the counter to the open door.

'Where to?' Peggy asked as Andrew surveyed the stone-faced shopfronts.

'Post office,' Andrew replied, nodding towards a red door across the street from where they'd parked. 'They might recognise Beth's name.'

They crossed the road together and entered the post office to find a short queue where the average age seemed to be about eighty-five.

A short woman with wiry, white hair and enormous, purple-rimmed glasses turned to unashamedly stare at the newcomers as they joined the line behind her.

'Alright?' she asked pointedly, making no attempt to hide the fact that she was clearly giving them a once-over.

Peggy felt Andrew tense and decided to head off any snappish comment by smiling toothily at the woman. 'Yes, thanks. Oh, are they your Christmas cards?'

Peggy pointed at the thick bundle of red envelopes the woman was clutching in her hands and shook her head. 'I meant to send mine last week, but I keep forgetting to bring them out with me.'

The woman nodded. 'Aye, I've popped in because I want the Christmas stamps. I didn't like last year's ones. Have ye seen this year's?'

Peggy shook her head once more. 'I haven't.'

'Much nicer for the kiddies this year,' the woman added sagely. She narrowed her eyes. 'Not from round here, are ye?'

'No, just visiting family before Christmas.' Peggy increased the wattage of her smile. 'We've actually just come in here because I'm trying to find an old family friend I haven't seen in, *gosh*, twenty years. I hoped someone might know where to find her.'

Peggy briefly worried that the 'gosh' had been a step too far, but then her new friend's face cleared of suspicion and was replaced by an expression of self-assurance.

'I've lived in Staveshead for twenty-five years. What's yer friend called? I'm sure I'll know her if she's still about.'

Bingo. Peggy did her best to convey innocence, just in case this woman was preparing to call her out for being a big fat liar. 'Beth. Beth Gower.'

An increasingly deepening frown was the only response Peggy received for a long moment, and she was about ready to back off and let Andrew try a different tactic when suddenly the woman's face cleared.

'There might've been a Beth Gower at the pub while ago,' she said, nodding at her own memory. '"Hind the bar, of course.'

'Of course,' Peggy agreed mildly. 'Which pub would that be?'

The woman cackled. 'The only one we've got, duck. Staveshead Arms. It'll be closed 'til half-eleven. Saying that, they've got a few rooms upstairs, so someone might be in now. Terry himself, maybe. Dunno if he'd know yer friend though.'

'No, that's brilliant, thank you so much for your help,' Peggy replied, laying it on thick as she surreptitiously pressed her hand against Andrew's forearm in a silent signal that it was time to leave, and began to back away. 'We'll head over there now.'

'Oh, yeah, thanks!' Andrew added far too brightly when the woman turned her sharpened gaze on him.

Peggy yanked him out of the Post Office before anyone had time to ask more questions.

Andrew stumbled to a halt, putting his hand out against the wall to steady himself. 'Jesus, Peggy, what was that for?'

'She was definitely about to start asking us more questions about Beth,' Peggy replied, straightening her coat, and entirely ignoring the assessing look Andrew was giving her. 'Look, if the pub turns out to be a dead end we can always come back here and see if anyone else knows Beth.'

'Alright. Let's try the pub and hope someone's there. This place isn't exactly rammed with either locals or tourists right now though, is it?'

At the far end of the main street, a windswept sign for the Staveshead Arms was hanging over the pavement, swinging gently in the breeze.

'That was a good idea back there,' Andrew said, shoving his hands into his coat pockets as they started towards the pub together.

Peggy shrugged. 'It's true what I said about people talking in places like this; if they get even the slightest hint that you're a detective, I doubt they'll talk to us.'

She expected some form of argument from Andrew but, astonishingly, he only gave another nod of agreement.

When they arrived in front of the Staveshead Arms, Peggy wasn't surprised to find the heavy black door of the pub firmly closed.

'Cross your fingers,' Andrew muttered to her as he reached up to rap on the door with his knuckles.

To their dual amazement, the door swung open only a moment later, and a man with a beaming smile appeared. The smile slid from his face and was replaced immediately by a puzzled expression. 'You're not Carly.'

'No,' Andrew replied. 'Sorry.'

The man shrugged. 'It's alright. I'm sure she'll be along in a bit.'

'Yeah, I'm sure she will,' Andrew agreed easily, despite clearly having no clue who Carly was, and Peggy nearly laughed out loud at the absurdity. 'Sorry, is this your pub?'

'Yeah. Terry Lonsdale.' The man held his hand out for Andrew to shake.

'Andy,' Andrew replied, noticeably careful to leave out his surname and also use the shortened version of his name that Peggy knew he normally avoided. 'This is Margaret. We're just trying to track down a family friend we haven't seen in a while, and we think she used to work here'

To their surprise, Terry laughed loudly. 'Must be the week for it!'

Andrew tensed again, and Peggy hoped this didn't mean he was about to launch into an interrogation.

'Oh, really?' Andrew asked in what Peggy assumed was supposed to be a casual manner.

Terry nodded, folding his arms and leaning against the doorframe, apparently unaware that the man he was talking to was about to bombard him with rapid fire questions. 'Yeah. We had a bloke in t'other night looking for someone as well. Couldn't help him though. Who is it you're lookin' for?'

'Beth Gower,' Peggy supplied, hoping that she was doing a better job of friendly and relaxed than Andrew's ever-narrowing eyes.

It didn't matter, because the minute Terry heard the name he stopped smiling and scowled darkly. 'That's who *he* was lookin' for too. What's goin' on? Who are you?'

To Peggy's complete astonishment, Andrew didn't immediately identify himself as a police officer, but instead he laughed loudly as though he were thoroughly relieved about something.

'It's going to be Uncle Bill, isn't it?' Andrew chuckled, shaking his head and turning to Peggy. 'I told him last week that we were fine looking for Beth without him. He never listens, does he?'

'No?' Peggy replied hesitantly.

'Big guy, right?' Andrew held his hands apart to emphasise his point and then gave Peggy what she thought was supposed to be a meaningful look. 'Beard, glasses. Likes a pint, or seven.'

Oh. Higson. Peggy nearly kicked herself for being so slow on the uptake. The doze she'd had in front of the fire at St Sunday's hadn't been nearly enough to offset the early start and long drive.

Terry looked less suspicious, but equally baffled. 'Yeah, that sounds like him.'

'I'm so sorry,' Andrew said, still shaking his head as he turned his palms out towards Terry. 'Bill can get a bit carried away. Did he cause you any trouble?'

Terry's face suddenly cleared, and he grinned. 'Nah, you're alright. Worst he did was call John Parish a twat.'

Andrew looked ready to apologise again, but Terry waved it away. 'No, John Parish *is* a twat, so he were right about that. I think Murray might've even bought him a pint for it. You don't look anything like your uncle, you know.'

'Thank Christ!' Andrew laughed. 'No, I look like my dad, and Uncle Bill's the other side of the family.'

Terry accepted the fact with a bob of his head. 'Well, like I told your uncle, I don't remember this girl. She must've been before my time.'

Andrew smiled again, though it was tinged with obvious disappointment. 'Alright, well thanks for your help, Terry. Oh! Actually, what night was Bill in? Was it Thursday?'

'Yeah, it would've been,' Terry replied, his nod gaining speed. 'He came in early and stayed just the one night. Left after Carly made him breakfast yesterday mornin'. Do you not really talk to him, or what?'

Andrew gave a one-shouldered shrug as he backed away. 'Uncle Bill's not a big one for having a chat. He likes to go off by himself; thinks he knows better than the rest of us, you know?'

Peggy knew that the bitterness in that response wasn't feigned in the slightest; Andrew was terrible at trusting people, but he was obviously sore that Higson had chosen to keep this whole investigation from him.

Andrew held up a hand in a gesture of farewell as he turned away. Peggy gave Terry one final smile and then hurried off after Andrew, who was already striding back down the main street.

He stopped so suddenly that Peggy almost ran past him.

'What the fuck is he up to?' Andrew asked harshly, scrubbing both hands through his hair in frustration.

Peggy had already gathered that Andrew was concerned about Higson, but this was the first time he'd shown real anger about the whole situation. 'Andrew, at least we know Higson was here.'

'Yeah, on Thursday!' Andrew snapped. 'The same night we apparently saw him driving away from Tib Street in his car! He must have had someone move that car to throw us off. *Why?*'

Peggy knew he wasn't angry with her, but she wasn't going to stand there and let him yell at her because Higson wasn't available. She crossed her arms and pointedly stared at him in silence.

Andrew deflated and sighed softly as he pinched the bridge of his nose. 'Sorry. It's not your fault.'

Peggy nudged him with her shoulder. 'Come on, let's see if we can find anyone else who might know where Beth is.'

Andrew didn't look entirely convinced, but then his eyes widened. 'Er, Peggy, your friend from earlier is staring at us.'

Peggy followed Andrew's gaze and saw the woman in the purple glasses gesturing towards them from outside the post office standing beside an equally elderly man in a brown trilby.

'I think they might want us to go over there,' Peggy whispered as the pair by the post office began waving.

She turned to Andrew askance when he didn't immediately move. 'I'm not going by myself!'

Andrew rolled his eyes but followed her anyway.

'Do you think we're about to be yelled at for lying about knowing Beth Gower?' Andrew asked out of the corner of his mouth as he smiled at the pensioners they were approaching.

'No idea.'

'These two were looking for their friend,' the woman in purple glasses announced as Peggy and Andrew stopped a few feet away. She pointed at the man next to her as though he might otherwise not be seen. 'Graham here thinks he knows the girl you're after.'

Graham smiled at Peggy and tipped the brim of his hat with a gnarled hand. 'She were a lovely young lass, Beth Gower. Two little kiddies, that's right, isn't it?'

'Yes,' Peggy replied eagerly. 'Twins.'

'She worked at the Arms for a year or so, but she got poached by Judith Brown, you know, over at the hotel. I expect she got paid much better.'

'Which hotel?' Andrew asked with a hint of impatience.

Graham looked at Andrew as though the younger man had asked a very stupid question. The woman in the purple glasses tutted and shook her head pityingly.

'This is Staveshead, son, not Keswick,' Graham replied gravely, with a curl of distaste at the mention of the larger town. 'Besides the rooms above the Arms, we've only got the one real hotel.'

He then politely tipped his hat at Peggy one more time and shuffled away without another word.

Peggy and Andrew were subjected to one final piercing ogle from behind purple frames, before the woman followed in Graham's wake.

'Thank you!' Peggy called, but neither of them turned around.

'I don't like this place at all,' Andrew muttered, and Peggy had to laugh at how unnerved he sounded.

'Where do you reckon the hotel is?' Peggy asked, looking around but not spotting any obvious signage on the main street. 'I suppose we could ask in the post office.'

Andrew shook his head. 'We don't need to.'

Peggy sighed loudly. 'Are you doing that thing that men do, where you just really hate asking for directions so you pretend that you don't need to? Charlie always does it, and so did my father; it drives me mad.'

Andrew initially looked so horrified at the suggestion that Peggy almost apologised, but then he snorted in amusement and pointed over Peggy's right shoulder. 'No, there's a great big flag on top of a building behind this street, so I'm taking a guess that we might need to go that way.'

'Oh,' Peggy replied primly, feeling terribly embarrassed. 'Well…'

Andrew grinned. 'I resent the fact that you would *ever* compare my behaviour to your brother's, by the way.'

Peggy scrunched up her nose. 'Alright, I might have been a bit unfair.'

'Then again…' Andrew trailed off as they turned off the main street and saw that the large green, white and blue Cumberland flag was indeed flying from a pole attached to the front wall of the Staveshead House Hotel.

'What?'

'I suppose I *could* just tell the manager I'm interested in buying the place,' Andrew replied as he opened the door and gestured for Peggy to go inside. 'It always seems to work when Charlie does it.'

'Please don't,' Peggy groaned as they headed for the reception desk, where a bored looking young man was flipping through a dog-eared copy of *Smash Hits* with Rick Astley on the cover.

The man looked up in surprise when he heard them approaching and quickly threw the magazine on the floor as though he thought that they might not have noticed him reading it. He smiled widely, looking positively delighted to see them. 'Good morning. Welcome to the Staveshead House Hotel!'

'Good morning,' Peggy replied, not quite able to muster the same stratospheric level of cheer. She glanced at the name badge clipped to the man's shirt. 'Dave.'

'Checking in?' Dave asked sunnily, but almost immediately frowned as he looked down at a large planner that was open on the desk. 'Though, I don't actually see any check-ins for today besides a coach party. There's not another sixteen of you outside, is there?'

'No.' Peggy shook her head. 'Sorry, not us.'

'Oh well, never mind,' Dave continued, cheerful once more as he tapped the planner with a red pen. 'We've actually still got two doubles free, so I can shift a couple of the coach party out of the nicest one on the top floor if you'd want that one.'

'Oh, God, no, please don't do that!' Peggy protested immediately as he looked poised to strike out the names next to room eighteen.

Dave looked up in surprise. 'Oh, it's alright. They're not here yet and they didn't specifically request the room, so they'll never know!'

'No, we don't need a room,' Andrew interjected.

Dave frowned and dropped the pen as he folded his arms. 'What do you want then?'

'Well–' Andrew began.

'Shit, you're not hotel inspectors, are you?' Dave asked, looking panicked. 'Shit, sorry, I shouldn't have said 'shit' at all, should I?'

Peggy held her hands up. 'It's alright, Dave. No, we're not inspectors. We're just looking for someone and hoped you might be able to help us.'

Dave's shoulders dropped the smallest amount as he relaxed. 'What, like you're the police?'

'No,' Peggy replied immediately, feeling like she, at least, wouldn't be lying.

'We're looking for my godmother,' Andrew supplied.

Peggy twitched slightly in surprise. They were now apparently on the third version of their story that morning; she supposed it would help muddy the waters if anyone else came asking after either Beth, or them for that matter. She forced a smile onto her face when Dave looked at her for confirmation. 'That's right.'

'Do you think she's staying here?' Dave asked, anxiously picking at the gold tinsel that had been sellotaped haphazardly along the top of the reception desk. 'Because I don't think I can just hand over that sort of information. Wait, can I?'

Andrew shook his head. 'No, you shouldn't really do that. Look, we've been told that she worked here at some point, and we're just trying to track her down before Christmas, that's all. She moved away when I was a teenager, and I haven't seen her since then. Her name's Beth Gower.'

Dave made an apologetic face. 'I don't remember a Beth ever working here, but I've only been here for a couple of years. I could ask my manager when she gets in though. Judith's family's had the hotel for nearly a century, so she might well know who you're looking for.'

'Thank you,' Andrew said, and the relief was genuine. Graham had mentioned someone called Judith giving Beth Gower a job at the hotel, so maybe they were finally onto something.

'Judith won't be in until after lunch,' Dave added. 'Do you want to come back in later, or I can call you if you're staying nearby? If you're not though, are you sure you don't need a room? It's a really nice place, honest.'

Peggy smiled kindly. 'Thanks Dave, but we're staying with family.'

Dave signed in resignation as he put a headed compliments slip on the desk. 'Alright, can you write your number on there?'

Peggy nodded and took the pen being offered to her.

'Whereabouts are you staying?' Dave asked Andrew while Peggy wrote down the number.

'Briersthwaite,' Andrew replied.

Dave looked impressed as Peggy handed the paper back. '*Oh*, very posh.'

Andrew shrugged. 'Yeah, it's alright.'

Dave looked down at the paper and picked up the pen. 'What's your name? So I can tell Judith who to call.'

'James McLeod,' Peggy replied before Andrew could even open his mouth. She was just as capable of amending the story as he was.

Dave accepted this information without looking up and scrawled the name next to the number. 'And your godmother was Beth Gower, you said, yeah?'

'That's it,' Andrew confirmed.

'Thanks, Dave.' Peggy smiled at him. 'You've been very helpful.'

'You'll tell Judith that right?'

'Of course,' Andrew replied with a serious nod.

They'd barely turned away from the desk before Dave had picked up the previously discarded *Smash Hits* again.

'Who's James McLeod?' Andrew asked as they headed back up towards Staveshead's main street once again.

'He's the gardener at St Sunday's,' Peggy replied, rubbing her hands together. The wind had picked up while they'd been in the hotel. 'He has a cottage behind the house, so if for any reason anyone did come to the village to check, they'd quickly find that he was a real person. He's also away for the whole winter, so he's perfectly safe. Plus, if anyone calls before we get back, Charlie should twig why someone from a hotel in Staveshead is looking for James.'

'That's smart.'

'Thanks.' Peggy shrugged away the praise with a wrinkle of her nose as the Range Rover came back into view. 'So, what now?'

Andrew checked his watch and then pointed towards where Terry Lonsdale was putting a sandwich board covered in white chalk out on the pavement in front of the Staveshead Arms. 'How about an early lunch and the chance to find someone else who saw Higson here the other night?'

Peggy made a face. 'Well, how could a girl possibly say no to that?'

ELEVEN

Although they'd practically been on the heels of Terry Lonsdale as he'd headed back into the Staveshead Arms, they weren't actually the first customers in there. Seven or eight people – more than likely locals – were already seated in the main bar area, even though Andrew's watch told him that it was significantly closer to eleven o'clock than it was to half-past. He had more important things to be worrying about than Terry Lonsdale's loose interpretation of licensing laws.

The majority of customers already had drinks, and a few were lazily flipping through the plastic-covered pages of the food menus. Andrew was pleased that nobody paid much heed to them as they tucked themselves away on a small table in the back corner of the pub, right beside a jauntily decorated Christmas tree.

Terry gave them a quick wave as he headed back behind the bar to chat to a cheerful middle-aged woman in a bright yellow jumper embroidered with bees and daisies.

Andrew handed a menu to Peggy and nodded his head towards the bar. 'Do you think that's Carly?'

Peggy shrugged off her coat as she looked over in time to see Terry disappear through a door that had been semi-disguised by a curtain of long beaded cords that had been pinned to the top of the frame. 'Could be.'

'I'll go up and order. See if I can get anything useful about Higson before Terry comes back,' Andrew suggested.

'Uncle Bill, you mean,' Peggy corrected him with a wry smile as she slid the menu back to him. 'Soup and a ham sandwich, please. Oh, and a Coke.'

He checked that he'd remembered to put his wallet in his coat pocket and headed over to the bar. The woman who might have been the last person to see Higson in Staveshead smiled widely at Andrew as he approached.

'What can I get for you?'

Andrew repeated Peggy's lunch order and then decided on the same for himself.

'That everything, love?' the woman asked tapping a biro against the small notepad in her hand.

'Yes,' Andrew replied, opening his wallet and pausing. 'Actually, no. Could I get some chips as well, please?'

'Two portions?'

Andrew shook his head as he handed over a five-pound note, considering how he was going to bring up the subject of Higson. 'Just the one, thanks. We'll share.'

As she silently counted Andrew's change back into his hand, the woman added, 'Terry tells me we had your uncle in.'

Andrew hoped that his face wasn't broadcasting just how much he couldn't quite believe his luck. 'Yeah, Bill.'

'You don't look much like him.'

For the second time that morning, Andrew laughed off that comment. 'So I've been told.'

'He puts away his breakfast, doesn't he?' The woman grinned again as she turned to reach for two half pint glasses. 'He was pleased to hear I always do a proper fry up when we've got guests in.'

So, this *was* Carly then. 'I bet he was!'

'We don't get much in the way of guests this time of year,' Carly continued, 'it's usually too cold. We'll perk up a bit between Christmas and New Year when people have family up. Sorry, you don't need to know any of that, but the point is that Terry had just about enough for one big breakfast in the fridge yesterday morning. I still had to pop back out to the shop before your uncle was done, mind, because he wanted more bacon.'

Andrew rolled his eyes before he could stop himself. Apparently, Higson behaved exactly the same outside of the Ballroom as is in it; Annie Higson must have the patience of a saint, no matter what she said to the contrary. 'Sorry about that.'

Carly laughed, batting away the apology with a wave of her hand as she reached down beneath the bar and produced two glass bottles of Coke. 'He was more than happy to offer to pay for all the extras, so don't you go worrying yourself about it.'

Andrew certainly wasn't going to worry about it; not when he was far too busy thinking about every single time Higson 'forgot' his wallet and the others had to chip in for his lunch, and yet here he'd apparently been *offering* to pay extra.

'You from up this way yourself then, or just your uncle's lot?' Carly asked as she rang a small brass call bell perched behind the bar and tore the page with Andrew's order out of her notepad.

Andrew shook his head. 'No, my parents met in Manchester. I've been up here for holidays, but I've never lived here.'

Carly accepted the story with a nod as she set the bottles down in front of Andrew. 'Mellswater, he said, did he? Where he grew up?'

Andrew nodded swiftly, hoping that this was the place that Higson had actually told Carly, and that she wouldn't suddenly correct herself and make him look like the complete liar he was. 'Yeah. He often comes up at Christmastime. We're up for a few days to see the family too.' He nodded over to where Peggy was idly looking through the menu again, though Andrew knew her well enough to be sure that she was listening to everything being said at the bar.

'Terry said you were still looking for your friend?' Carly asked. She popped the caps off the Coke bottles just as a sullen-looking teenage girl fought her way through the beaded curtain and held her hand out for the paper in Carly's hand, cutting off any reply that Andrew might have had.

'Jer says to tell you that he hasn't got any mince pies left, and there were none in the shop this mornin',' the girl grumbled to Carly, peering at Andrew and then quickly averting her eyes. 'An' he's not got much in the way of frozen peas either.'

'Alright.' Carly sighed loudly She gestured round at the pub, where another small group of new arrivals was settling in beneath the large crown glass window. 'Well, look, I can't go out now. Have you asked your dad if he could go instead?'

The girl stomped back through the curtain.

'Take that order to Jer first!' Carly called after her. She turned back to Andrew and shook her head. 'Sorry about that. Teenagers, eh?'

Andrew made a face that he hoped conveyed agreement even though he was mostly just annoyed that he couldn't see how to focus the conversation back on Higson or Beth without raising any kind of suspicion.

'Terry's daughter, Lauren,' Carly added, pointing in the direction of where the teenager could now be heard yelling for her father from somewhere in the back. 'Lovely girl usually, but she's just had her heart broken by a boy at school. She's done the crying bit and moved onto the being angry at the world part. I'm hoping she's over it more by next week because I'm having her and her dad round for Christmas dinner!'

Andrew was struck by just how freely people in Staveshead seemed to give up information about their personal lives. He wasn't entirely sure whether it was just because he wasn't in Manchester anymore, or simply because he was wearing jeans and a jumper and hadn't once mentioned being a police officer. He preferred the first theory, but Peggy had posited more than once that even people with nothing to hide were probably inclined to tell *Andrew* something more readily than they might inform Detective Inspector Joyce.

Terry Lonsdale came through the beaded curtain at a speed

that suggested he might be running for his life. He shook his head gravely at Carly as a door slammed upstairs.

'What did you say to her now?' Carly asked, accusation clear as day as she put her hands on her hips.

'Nothin'!' Terry held up his hands. 'I just told her that I'd give that little shit a piece of my mind if he so much as shows his face in here again, and that I'd bar both him and his dad for life. What's wrong with that? Oh, hiya, Andy. Havin' some lunch?'

Carly looked at the ceiling as though wishing for divine intervention.

To Andrew's surprise, it actually arrived.

'Everything okay?' Peggy smiled at everyone as she appeared at Andrew's shoulder.

'I was getting a bit lonely over there,' she added with a laugh as she leant her elbows on the bar next to the Coke bottles.

'Sorry, sweetheart,' Carly replied with a smile. 'That was me keeping him talking, and then Terry's come along, proving he doesn't know the first thing about women.'

Peggy laughed again as Terry's indignation grew in the face of Carly's teasing.

'Now, you're definitely not from around here, are you, duck?' Carly asked, pushing a glass towards Peggy.

Peggy shook her head with an easy smile as she poured most of the Coke from the bottle. 'No. Just visiting for a few days and hoping to track down an old friend of Andy's family while we're here.'

'Yeah, his uncle told me about her.' Carly grimaced sympathetically. 'Such a shame. Her moving away so suddenly and not leaving a forwarding address, I mean. Though I understand why she'd do that after going through everything your man, Bill, told me.'

Andrew frowned. What was that supposed to mean? More

importantly, how the hell was he supposed to ask when he should already rightly know why Beth Gower had apparently left the area. There was no way Higson would have told this woman the truth, was there?

'It was awful, wasn't it?' Peggy agreed quietly, and Andrew had to make himself stand still and not spin around in surprise. *What was she doing?*

Carly patted the back of Peggy's hand. 'She sounds like such a brave girl, though I suppose she knew she had to get those kiddies away from a terrible man like that.'

Andrew took a moment to wonder if his consciousness had entirely switched off for a moment and he'd somehow missed half a conversation.

'I suppose you didn't know her at all,' Carly said, shaking her head at Peggy.

'No, I didn't,' Peggy confirmed. 'I've heard a lot about her though.'

'Well, like I said to your uncle, I'm a blow-in, so I wouldn't know her from Adam, I'm afraid,' Carly added, 'though you can bet I'd give that husband of hers a sound hiding if I met him. Is he still around?'

'Nobody's seen Beth's husband in years,' Andrew replied, finally finding a tiny fleck of truth in the midst of all the fabrications, even if that truth didn't quite align with the picture Higson had painted for Carly. Andrew would admit that if Higson had told Beth to use the cover story of running from a bad marriage it had been a clever move. As long as Beth had cemented herself as part of the local community, it would likely have afforded her an extra layer of protection if anyone ever came looking for her. The only problem was that nobody around here seemed to actually know Beth, and at no point had Andrew had any sense that he was being lied to by people trying to protect a friend.

'Good riddance,' Carly concluded firmly, and Terry nodded his agreement.

'Would you be ab-' Peggy started but then cut herself off with a loud sigh. 'No, never mind.'

Carly patted Peggy's hand sympathetically again. 'No, duck, you look troubled. What is it?'

Peggy actually did look troubled, and Andrew was entirely wrong-footed because he wasn't certain whether she was still playing a part or not.

'Well,' Peggy answered hesitantly, 'I was hoping you could tell us whether or not Bill seemed alright when he left here.'

Carly tilted her head questioningly. 'Alright?'

'It's just that he can get himself into a bit of a mood if things aren't quite going his way.' Peggy glanced at Andrew with just the faintest glimmer of humour in her eyes. 'Family trait.'

'Seemed fine t'me,' Terry replied with a shrug.

Carly nodded but then almost immediately frowned. 'Though, I suppose he did give John Parish what for on Thursday night, didn't he, Terry?'

'Yeah, I told 'em that already,' Terry said, gesturing towards Andrew. 'Though as I said earlier, your uncle weren't wrong about John, and he isn't the first person to have ended up in an argument with him after a few scoops.'

Peggy smiled, radiating a sense of self-deprecation. 'Sorry, it's just me getting a bit het up about it. We worry about Bill. I'm sure you know how it is. He doesn't really like asking for help.'

'Another family trait?' Carly asked, raising her eyebrows as she nodded towards Andrew.

'Something like that,' Peggy agreed, and Andrew was starting to feel slightly victimised now that they'd reached the second comparison between his character and Higson's. 'Bill and his wife were close to Beth and the children, so I think there's some guilt about not knowing what's happened to her since she left.'

It was a bit like watching Charlie charm his way into someone's good graces, only with significantly more tact and a complete lack of hereditary titles peppering the conversation, and Andrew would be lying again if he said he wasn't fascinated.

'He seemed fine, love, honestly,' Carly said, giving Peggy an encouraging smile.

'Well, thank you, you've set my mind at ease,' Peggy replied with yet another one of those indecipherable smiles.

Terry shrugged again, folding his arms. 'He paid his bill and then last thing he did was ask me about the bus to Carlisle to catch the train. I had to tell him that he'd be hours waiting for it, so I called Pete Tiller for him – he runs taxis round here in the summer, but not so much in the winter unless it's as a favour to one of us. Anyway, your uncle went off to the station with him. Pete didn't have anything particular to say about him when he came in for a pint last night.'

Andrew's eyes narrowed in suspicion when he saw Carly glance at Terry in bewilderment before she looked at Peggy with a resurgence of concern.

Peggy noticed too, Andrew was sure of it, but she didn't give any reaction beyond sipping her Coke.

A bell rang from somewhere in the back.

'I don't think Lauren's coming down to help,' Carly said pointedly to Terry.

Terry sighed loudly. 'Yeah, alright, I'll deal with it. Who's ordered food?'

'Sheila and Geoff,' Carly replied, pointing to a couple who seemed to be ignoring each other entirely. 'Toasties, the usual. The Bowling Club have all ordered, but they're waiting for June and Charlotte to arrive, so I've asked Jer to hold off cooking anything until they get here. Oh, and these two are waiting for soup.'

'Reckon that'll be the toasties then,' Terry replied. 'I'll go get them.'

As Terry left, Peggy yawned widely as she stood up straight and shot Carly an apologetic smile. 'So sorry, one last thing; could you just tell me where the loo is please?'

Carly pointed to the other end of the bar. 'Just through the door over there.'

'Thanks,' Peggy replied before heading off in the direction Carly had indicated.

As Peggy reached the other end of the bar, Carly still looked perturbed, but Andrew didn't feel he was quite in a position to ask her outright what the issue was; not without sounding like DI Joyce had entered the building.

'Lovely girl,' Carly said approvingly when Peggy ducked out of sight.

Andrew didn't know whether he was allowed to agree with that statement or not, so instead he just gave Carly a quick smile and reached for the glasses and bottles, trying to figure out how he was going to carry it all in one trip. 'I'd better let you both get on. Thanks.'

'Your food won't be too long,' Carly said, and then batted his hands away. 'You take the glasses, and I'll bring the rest.'

Carly was only a few steps behind when Andrew reached the table, and he moved out of the way so that she could put the two bottles down.

'Look,' said Carly, somewhat awkwardly as Andrew sat down, 'I didn't want to say anything back there because your lovely girl looked so worried about your uncle.'

There was so much wrong with the second half of that statement that Andrew had to force himself to ignore it and focus on not spilling any of the drink he was pouring when he looked up at Carly. 'Didn't want to say what?'

Carly made a face. 'It's probably nothing, but it's just that what Terry said doesn't really make sense, and it just made me think, that's all.'

'About what?' Andrew asked, caught somewhere between reticence and impatience. He thought he might finally understand why Charlie often got so annoyed with unfinished sentences.

'When I left to go and buy the extra bacon yesterday morning, your uncle was eating the rest of his breakfast. Funnily enough, he was sitting exactly where you are now,' Carly said, shaking her head in mild wonder. 'When I came back a few minutes later – the shop's just up the other end of the street, you see – he wasn't here.'

Andrew shook his head slowly, unsure where Carly was going with this. 'Where was he?'

'He was in the back,' Carly replied, wrinkling her nose. 'Through the curtain there, and he was talking to someone on the phone. That's fine – Terry always tells guests they can use the phone if they need to, and your uncle left some coins to cover the call, not that he really needed to – but he hung up quickly when I came into the corridor on the way to the kitchen.'

'Right?'

'He told me that he'd just been calling a taxi to pick him up once he'd checked out,' Carly replied, shifting from one foot to the other. 'I didn't think anything of it at the time because I saw him leave with Pete Tiller an hour later, but now Terry's said that *he's* the one that called Pete. That does seem a bit, well, *unusual*, doesn't it?'

'Unusual' was certainly one word for it.

'A bit odd,' Andrew replied as evenly as he could. 'Sometimes there's no real accounting for the things Uncle Bill does.'

Carly looked unconvinced, but before she could remark any further, Terry appeared with two bowls of soup.

'I was wrong about the toasties,' he said, placing the bowls down. 'I'll be back with your sandwiches in a sec.'

'And chips!' Carly called after him, before turning back to

Andrew, clearly readying herself to ask another question. She took a deep breath, but then her eyes widened, and she pasted on a strained smile.

Andrew's confusion was alleviated almost instantly when it became clear that Peggy was only a few feet from the table.

'Sorry, excuse me,' Peggy said, as she shuffled past Carly and sat down opposite Andrew.

'Two ham sandwiches and one portion of chips,' Terry announced as he reappeared behind Carly and deposited the rest of their lunch on the table. 'Enjoy. Come on, Carly, leave them be to eat their lunch.'

Carly gave Andrew one final quizzical look before nodding and following Terry back towards the bar.

'Good shout on the chips,' Peggy said as she reached over with her fork to spear one from the bowl, blowing lightly to cool it. 'So, did you find out what it was that Carly didn't want to say in front of me?'

Andrew grinned as he shook his head. 'I *knew* you'd caught that look she gave you.'

One corner of Peggy's mouth lifted the tiniest amount. 'I have actually been paying attention to how you do things, you know. Well?'

Andrew sobered and repeated what Carly had just told him.

'Who could he have been calling?' Peggy asked, pushing the bowl of chips towards Andrew. 'Annie, maybe?'

Andrew shook his head, chewing thoughtfully. 'Can't have been. We were already at the house when she got back from Buxton, and this would have been first thing yesterday morning. Carly said he was speaking, so it wasn't like he was waiting for someone to pick up.'

'He could have been leaving a message,' Peggy countered.

'He could,' Andrew agreed, 'but if he was, it wasn't for Annie. They don't have an answering machine; I asked her yesterday.

There was no message at the Ballroom, and nothing for any of the rest of us at home either.'

While Andrew had been listing all of the people that Higson *hadn't* called, his disappointment with his own progress had reared its head again. They'd come all the way to the Lake District and, so far, all they'd discovered was that Beth Gower might once have worked in the hotel, that Higson had behaved like a bit of a nuisance, and that he'd made a furtive phone call to an unidentified person before he'd left Staveshead for the train station in Carlisle. He said as much to Peggy.

'No. You also know that wherever Higson is, and whatever is going on with him, has got something to do with Davy Nash and Lily Woodhouse,' Peggy offered. 'You were right.'

Andrew knew that Peggy was trying to get him to see the positive side of things, but it didn't really help when he still had no idea what had happened in 1967, nor why Higson's interest in the case had been reignited earlier that year.

He picked at the crust of his sandwich gloomily. 'It doesn't sound like Higson managed to track Beth down though, does it?'

'Not really.'

'Which means that he didn't have a clue where she's been for most of the past two decades, and we still don't know why he was so desperate to find her that he risked alerting other people to her presence,' Andrew continued with a sigh. 'And so much for hoping that if we found her, she might've been able to tell us where we could find *Higson*.'

Peggy picked up her spoon and hovered it over the surface of the steaming soup for a moment without actually touching the liquid. Eventually, she huffed out a breath, looking pensive as she put her spoon down again. 'Do you think there's any chance that Davy is alive and well, and with Beth?'

'Without Higson knowing about it?' Andrew grimaced as he shook his head. 'I can't see how Nash would have known where to go without someone telling him that his wife and kids had been stashed away up here.'

'Stranger things have happened.'

Andrew couldn't really argue with that statement, but he still couldn't see how Davy Nash would have been able to track down Beth without help. Plus, all of that only applied if something terrible hadn't happened to him twenty years earlier anyway. Questions surrounding the nature of Lily Woodhouse's involvement in any of it also lingered without any hint of an answer; and still beneath that, Andrew was trying not to dwell on the fact that someone was going out of their way to keep eyes on the Ballroom team outside of work. *Oh*, and lest he forget, there was also the fact that Higson hadn't shared anything about his plan with anyone at the Ballroom – the very people who were supposed to be on his team.

'Why would he come up here? Does he think Beth is in danger?' Andrew mused as his appetite disappeared entirely.

'You never know,' Peggy added quietly as she picked up her soup spoon again, 'we might get back to the house and find out that Marnie or Mike has tracked Higson down, or even that he's been in contact with Annie. Then you could ask him yourself.'

Andrew didn't have the heart to tell Peggy that he couldn't bring himself to believe that.

He was quite certain that she didn't believe it either.

TWELVE

Their drive back to St Sunday's was largely quiet.

Andrew was brooding, staring out of the passenger window as the car rattled along. Peggy suspected that while some of this gloomy disposition could be explained away as general disappointment for not immediately tracking down Beth Gower, the majority was likely because all evidence suggested that Higson hadn't trusted the Ballroom team enough – not trusted *Andrew* enough – to share anything about his ongoing investigation. Despite her best efforts, Peggy hadn't been able to think of a single thing to say that might possibly have made him feel better, and so she'd kept her mouth shut and her eyes on the road the whole way back to Briersthwaite.

The driveway was otherwise empty when they arrived. Considering they'd returned later than Andrew's aim of twelve-thirty, Peggy was surprised that Jen and Lloyd hadn't beaten them back to the house.

She'd barely reached down to engage the handbrake when the front door burst open, and Charlie practically leapt onto the gravel. He was wearing a ridiculous, green velvet dressing gown over his clothes, and an expression of pure alarm.

Andrew tumbled out of the car, momentarily getting caught in the seatbelt as he tried to move as quickly as possible. 'What is it? What's happened?'

Peggy clambered out and strode towards her brother, who reached out with both hands to grasp her shoulders. 'Charlie?'

'Um,' said Charlie, eyes wide.

'Charlie!' Peggy snapped forcefully, generally satisfied that Charlie didn't look like he'd been harmed in any way. 'What's happened? Are you alright?'

'Come inside, both of you,' Charlie replied, shaking his head.

'It's almost one, and you need to hear this for yourselves.'

Peggy glanced at Andrew questioningly, only to find that he was staring straight back at her with the same astronomical level of bewilderment she could feel radiating from her own expression.

Peggy hastily followed Charlie, with Andrew barely a full step behind her as they hurried along the corridor.

When they reached the kitchen, Charlie threw himself into the chair at the head of the table and put his head in his hands. What looked like a half-eaten cheese sandwich lay on a plate near his elbow and, even from the doorway, Peggy could tell that the full mug of milky tea next to the plate had been allowed to grow cold.

'Charlie, you're scaring me a bit,' Peggy said honestly as she hesitantly approached her brother and crouched in front of him. 'What's happening?'

'Just listen. Just…' Charlie trailed off and he reached out to turn up the volume of the old radio he'd moved from the worktop to the table.

Peggy frowned and looked up and over her shoulder at Andrew in confusion. Why on earth was Charlie listening to Radio 4? Charlie *never* listened to Radio 4, and yet Peggy was entirely certain that she could hear Alan Coren on *The News Quiz* only scant centimetres from her brother's bowed head.

'I put the telly on earlier,' Charlie mumbled into his fingers, 'and they had one of those newsflash bulletin things. I didn't know how I was going to get hold of you, but I knew that the news would be on here at one.'

He looked up and pointed at the radio as the programme ended with an announcement that it was the last episode in the series, and then immediately made way for the one o'clock news.

'Charlie, *what* is going on?' Andrew snapped as the newsreader introduced the bulletin.

'Shut up!' Charlie retorted, significantly more aggressively than Peggy would have expected.

Andrew blinked in surprise and briefly held his hands up in surrender.

Peggy frowned as the newsreader continued her report in clipped tones:

'…*were called to the scene in Hale Barns just after seven o'clock this morning, when a neighbour reported hearing gunshots.*'

'What is this?' Peggy asked as she tried to catch Charlie's eyes, completely lost as to what her brother was trying to convey.

Charlie just shook his head silently.

'*The victim has been identified as former Greater Manchester Police office, Sean Kelly.*'

Andrew's breath caught loudly behind her, and it was obvious to Peggy that this name meant something to him. She wondered if Sean Kelly was someone Andrew had worked with at CID, but almost immediately discounted the idea because there was no way that Charlie would have known that, nor would it have inspired such a reaction from him even if he had.

'Who's Sean Kelly?' she asked Andrew, but he clearly wasn't listening to her, and his eyes were almost as wild as Charlie's.

'*Officers from GMP remain at the scene, and a cordon remains in place on Elmwood, with local traffic being diverted. Residents have been advised to remain in their homes as officers conduct door-to-door enquiries in their search for the alleged gunman.*

'*The force has already taken the unusual step of publicly identifying a person of interest at this early stage in their investigation. The public has been advised not to approach the man, identified in this morning's briefing as serving GMP Detective Chief Inspector, William Higson.*'

Peggy didn't hear anything else as the newsreader's voice seemed to collapse into unintelligible bursts of static in her ears. She lurched to her feet in a panic, stumbling backwards into Andrew as she tried to regain her balance.

Andrew caught Peggy's arm tightly as he steadied her, but when she turned to ask him to confirm that he couldn't possibly have just heard the same utter madness on the radio as she had, he looked as though he were a million miles away.

Charlie switched the radio off and looked up at his sister in trepidation.

Suddenly, Andrew let go of Peggy's elbow and marched out of the kitchen without explanation.

'Come on!' Peggy barked at Charlie as she turned and followed Andrew back to the living room.

Andrew was pacing around the room, obviously looking for something.

'What do you need?' Peggy asked.

Andrew waved his hand insistently. 'Remote? For the TV?'

Charlie quickly retrieved the remote from down the side of the sofa cushion where he'd been lounging earlier and threw it towards Andrew's open hands.

Andrew immediately switched on the TV, viciously stabbing at the remote until he managed to change the channel and turn the volume up.

The three of them stood in an almost perfect line watching the small screen in the corner of the room as it played drizzle-speckled footage of people standing at the edge of a taped cordon, with the upper floors of what looked to be expansive houses only just visible behind a range of walls, mature hedges, and wrought iron railings.

Seconds later the camera refocused on a news reporter that Peggy didn't recognise; his face was stoic, even as the drizzle developed into heavier rain.

'Mr Kelly retired from the police force in 1976 and, according to neighbours, he's lived here in the upscale village of Hale Barns for the past fifteen years,' the reporter said evenly as fat raindrops scarred his beige jacket with streaks of grey. 'By all accounts he was an active and well-liked member of the community, and there is a palpable sense of disbelief among local residents that such a violent act could occur on their doorstep.'

'Kelly was at the Ballroom in the sixties,' Andrew said quietly.

'During the Lily Woodhouse case?' Peggy asked, keeping her eyes on the screen as the reporter continued to describe the events of the morning.

Andrew nodded. 'Annie referred to him as one of Prentice's lackeys. He was there, along with Frank Jackson.'

'Frank Jackson,' Peggy repeated, thinking back over everything Andrew had told her about the case. 'It was his funeral that Higson went to earlier in the year, wasn't it?'

'Yeah, and it was after his funeral that Higson started talking to Annie about Davy Nash again, and also when Higson started behaving oddly.' Andrew's frown dipped towards concern as he turned to look directly at Peggy. 'And apparently when he started worrying about you.'

Peggy looked at her feet, hoping to dispel the spotlight that had been angled towards her once more.

'Holy shit!'

Charlie's exclamation of surprise was accompanied by a dramatic point towards the television, where a photo of Higson was staring right back at all of them. The photo was obviously a good decade out of date, but even though the man looked slimmer, tidier and younger than Peggy had ever known him, his eyes were as sharp and knowing as they had been the last time she'd seen him on Tib Street.

Higson's face faded as the scene switched to a shot of a semi-detached house with two uniformed police officers stationed by the front door.

Andrew groaned loudly, and he had his palms pressed to his face when Peggy looked over. 'That's Higson's house.'

The words had barely left Andrew's mouth, when the phone on the console table by the front door emitted a shrill ring that Peggy could have sworn sounded more urgent than usual.

Wanting to momentarily distance herself from the narrative playing out on the news, Peggy took the opportunity to leave the room and answer the phone.

'Hello?' she asked cautiously as she lifted the receiver to her ear.

There was silence on the other end of the line, eventually broken by a tremulous intake of breath.

'Hello?' Peggy tried again.

'I'm looking for Andrew Joyce,' a woman's voice replied. She spoke quietly, but steadier than Peggy had expected after the shaky sigh.

'Who is this?' Peggy asked. She was fairly certain she knew the caller's identity, but Andrew had drummed the need for caution and discretion into all of them the day before.

'Annie Higson,' the voice confirmed Peggy's suspicions. 'Is that you Peggy, love?'

The warmth in the question took Peggy by surprise, and initially she nodded dumbly in response, until she remembered that Annie couldn't see her.

'Yes, it's Peggy,' she blurted out eventually. 'Hello, Mrs Higson.'

'Annie, please, sweetheart. Have you heard from Bill?'

'Not yet,' Peggy replied, hoping that she sounded confident that they *would* hear from Higson eventually. 'Annie, have you seen the news?'

Annie sniffed loudly, and Peggy recognised the sound of a sob being stifled. 'I've just seen it. Why would they be saying something so awful about Bill? Who would lie like that?'

It struck Peggy then that she hadn't believed that Higson had killed Sean Kelly for even a second, but if she'd had any doubts whatsoever, the iron certainty in Annie's voice would have been enough to convince her of Higson's innocence. 'We don't know yet, Annie. Andrew will figure it out.'

'You need to be careful,' Annie replied. 'All of you. Bill was so worried about you, darling.'

'But, why?' Peggy asked in a whisper before she could stop herself.

Annie sighed again. 'I don't know, love, but whatever the reason, it kept him up at night.'

Peggy held the phone more tightly to her ear, grounding herself. Before she worked up the courage to ask anything else, Andrew appeared next to her. He didn't speak, but he stared pointedly at the phone in question.

'Annie, Andrew's here now, so I'll pass you over to him.' Peggy thrust the receiver towards Andrew, not wanting to hear any more warnings about her safety delivered with such genuine concern.

Andrew fumbled the phone, raising his eyebrows questioningly.

Peggy just shook her head silently and retreated to the kitchen, closing the door behind her and leaning back against it with an unsteady breath of her own.

Charlie had tidied up in her absence, so she filled the kettle before retrieving five clean mugs from the draining board, certain that Jen and Lloyd would surely be back soon.

Even though she felt sick to her stomach – the greasy chips sitting heavily after the jolt of horror that had shot right through her at the sight of the news bulletin – Peggy removed the cloche from Mrs Laycock's Victoria sponge and then set out a stack of side plates and forks beside the cake.

When she'd left Butterton that morning, Peggy had hoped that she was going to be of more use to the investigation than providing tea and cake, but she feared that without being the one to complete this small task, she was entirely surplus to requirements just then.

She opened the fridge to locate the milk and the pot of clotted cream she'd seen earlier, silently hoping that Annie wasn't in the process of reminding Andrew of Higson's worries. She immediately shook her head at herself in mild disgust at the self-indulgence of the thought – Annie Higson had far more important things to be worrying about than someone she'd never met. Peggy couldn't begin to imagine what that poor woman must be going through.

Peggy closed the fridge and paused when she heard footsteps on the stone slabs of the corridor, knowing that Andrew was about to appear.

The phone screeched again, and Peggy lurched in surprise. The footsteps stopped and were followed by a muffled curse before they started up again, this time heading away from the kitchen.

As the kettle boiled a minute later, the latch on the kitchen door was released with a loud clank and Charlie shuffled in.

'He's on the phone to Mike now, I think,' Charlie informed his sister, nodding back towards the hallway. 'Doesn't sound very happy.'

The distinctive sound of a car hitting the gravel driveway at speed startled them both, and with a quick glance at each other the Swan siblings hurried towards the front door.

Peggy caught Andrew's eye as she passed him, and it was obvious that Charlie had been correct: Andrew wasn't happy at all. His hair was sticking up at odd angles which meant he'd been pulling at it in frustration, and his frown was so deeply embedded in his forehead that Peggy though that it might be permanent by the time he hung up.

Charlie yanked open the door to find Jen and Lloyd just on the other side.

Lloyd yelped in alarm, but he didn't drop the bar of Kendal Mint Cake in his right hand.

Jen's face had paled enough to look entirely bloodless, and as she opened her mouth to speak, Peggy reached over and squeezed her arm.

'We know,' Peggy said quietly as Charlie closed the door again. 'We saw the news.'

'Come on.' Charlie put his arm around Jen's shoulders as he turned on his heel and began to lead them all further into the house.

Andrew looked worriedly at Jen as she walked by. He gave Lloyd a slight nod and mouthed 'Mike' at him so that he understood the nature of the phone call.

As they reached the kitchen, Jen and Lloyd silently sat down at the table with Charlie while Peggy finished making the tea.

'I don't understand,' Jen murmured.

Peggy added an extra spoon of sugar to a mug of milky tea and pushed it towards Jen. 'Maybe Mike's telling Andrew a bit more about it all right now.'

'Did you at least manage to find anything out in Staveshead?' Lloyd asked Peggy as he tapped his teaspoon against his palm in a nervous tic. 'We got absolutely nothing from Stavesmere.'

'We did,' Peggy confirmed.

The kitchen door opened again, and Andrew walked in looking even more solemn than he had earlier.

'Boss,' Lloyd greeted him with a nod as Andrew claimed the empty seat next to Peggy. 'Peggy was just about to tell us what you found out.'

Peggy glanced at Andrew questioningly. There had been a time where she wouldn't have hesitated to take the lead in explaining something to the others, but it had been months since they'd worked together, and Peggy still wasn't quite sure where she stood.

Andrew remained silent though, so Peggy took that as tacit agreement to continue.

She walked them through the events that had led them to learning about Higson's brief stay in Stavesmere, and how they were hoping that the manager of the hotel would have something useful about Beth Nash for them if she called. Eventually, she reached the part of the story where Carly had told Andrew about Higson's phone call.

'Who could he have called?' Lloyd asked, chewing on his lip. 'Mrs H?'

Peggy looked to Andrew, content for him to be the one to answer any follow-up questions, and he leaned forward clasping his hands on the table. 'No, he definitely didn't call Annie. I asked her again earlier, just in case.'

'You've spoken to Annie?' Jen asked.

Andrew nodded. 'She called here just before you got back. She's still at her sister's, so hopefully that should buy her some time before anyone comes looking to ask questions. I've told her not to go home for the time being.'

'Is she alright?' Lloyd grimaced.

Andrew nodded even as he shrugged. 'She's doing her best. Totally convinced that Higson would never lay a finger on Sean Kelly, even if he'd made no secret of how much he despised him over the years.'

'And we're totally convinced of this ourselves too, aren't we?' Charlie asked haltingly.

A loud round of confirmation rang around the kitchen table, with varying degrees of colourful language.

'One of us had to ask!' Charlie held his hands up above his shoulders. 'Alright, *obviously,* we believe in Higson's innocence.'

'What did DS Lawson tell you, sir?' Jen asked quietly, still looking into her tea as though the mug might hold the answer to everything.

Peggy tensed when she saw Andrew's knuckles blanch as he tightened his fingers; whatever he was about to say, it couldn't possibly be good for them and their investigation.

'Chambers is leading the investigation,' Andrew said flatly. 'Mike's been called in. *Everyone's* been called in at CID. Given our connection to Higson, they're definitely going to be looking for us.'

Andrew unclasped his hands and pressed his fingertips against his brow bone. 'Mike detoured past my house on the way in, and there's already a couple of uniforms in a car right outside. I think it's fair to say they've worked out I'm not at home.'

Peggy winced. At least their subterfuge that morning meant that nobody should know that the Ballroom team was currently ensconced in a kitchen in the Lake District, even if the carefully executed illusion hadn't entirely paid off.

'What are we going to do, boss?' Lloyd asked. 'Should we go back? At least we can tell them that we don't have a bloody clue where Higson is.'

'The minute we leave here we're going to lose any chance we've got of tracking down Beth Nash,' Andrew replied. 'I'm not going to get through my front door before Chambers hauls me back to Chester House; I reckon it'll be the same for you and Jen.'

'But if we don't go back, surely they're going to be suspicious,' Jen suggested. She sounded as though she'd rather not be arguing this side of things. 'None of us are at home, and not one of us has made a call to CID to try and find out what's going on with our DCI. There's not a chance we could have all missed the news today, is there?'

Andrew shook his head slowly. 'No, not really, and you're right; it *does* look suspicious. But we know that Higson didn't kill Sean Kelly, and I'm almost one hundred percent certain that Chambers knows that too.'

Charlie made a face of distaste. 'Do you think Chambers is involved in this man's death?'

Andrew closed his eyes for a long moment as he clenched his jaw. 'Honestly, I don't know. I don't trust Chambers at all, but would he kill someone he used to work with and then frame Higson for it? If Chambers wanted to make life difficult for us, I don't think he'd need to try that hard.'

'But they announced Higson as a suspect!' Lloyd argued. 'That's a mental thing to do if they're not completely sure he's involved, or because someone really wants everyone to believe that he is.'

'I know,' Andrew sighed. 'I know that.'

'So, what are we going to do?' Jen asked, repeating Lloyd's earlier question.

'Mike's going to keep us updated,' Andrew replied and then he turned to Peggy. 'I'm a bit surprised that we haven't heard from Marnie. If someone really *is* looking for Higson, then I'd be surprised if they weren't on Tib Street by the end of the day.'

'I'll call her now,' Peggy said, pushing back her chair immediately. Reasonably, she knew that Marnie was perfectly safe and could either choose to keep herself hidden from anyone who entered the Ballroom, or take herself back to Butterton House, but it didn't make Peggy feel any better when she constantly carried around a responsibility for her friend. She was so used to having a vague awareness of Marnie being somewhat nearby, even if not in the same place, that it was peculiar to be far enough away that she had no sense of Marnie whatsoever.

Peggy dialled the familiar number and waited, twirling the cord of the phone through her fingers as she catalogued the changes to the décor in the hallway since her last visit. She'd spent precious little time in Briersthwaite in recent years, but she had always appreciated the silence that this house had afforded her. Unlike Butterton, St Sunday's was devoid of any hint of ghostly activity, so even though Peggy had learned how to keep ghostly intervention to a minimum – a necessity for the sake of her own sanity and for the ability to live a fairly normal life – it was still nice to have a rare chance to completely switch off from it all.

The call rang out and Peggy frowned. She was certain she'd dialled the correct number, and this was confirmed a moment later when the answerphone message kicked in. She pressed the switch on the cradle to end the call, keeping the receiver to her ear until the dial tone hummed once more. She redialled the number carefully, as though entering the number slower might somehow ensure the call would be answered the second time.

The call rang out again, and Peggy muttered a repeated plea for Marnie to pick up.

A click in her ear made her sigh in relief, but as she opened her mouth to ask Marnie just what on earth she was doing trying to give her a heart attack by not answering the phone, something icy and sharp twisted in Peggy's chest and she clamped her lips together before she could utter a sound.

There was silence on the other end, but if Peggy strained her ears, she was sure that she could hear someone breathing, and something rustling in the distance.

'Who is this?'

Peggy didn't recognise the cold voice, even when the question was repeated even more sharply.

A flash of movement in the corner of Peggy's eye alerted her to Andrew's reappearance from the kitchen, and she pressed a finger to her lips.

Andrew's forehead creased in confusion, and he nearly went cross-eyed when Peggy aggressively waved a hand towards him as he approached.

Still, he remained silent, so Peggy assumed that she'd telegraphed her wishes clearly enough.

Andrew raised his eyebrows, and Peggy turned the receiver to press it against Andrew's ear without explanation. He continued only to stare at Peggy in bewilderment as the silence stretched on.

The call disconnected and Andrew placed the receiver back in the cradle.

'Peggy, what happened?' Andrew asked in concern.

'A man answered the phone at the Ballroom,' Peggy explained, her voice shaking. 'I don't know who it was.'

'What did you say to him?'

'I didn't give us away, if that's what you meant,' Peggy replied as she folded her arms. It came out snappier than she'd meant it to, and Andrew looked slightly taken aback.

'That's not what I meant,' he replied, frowning. 'At all.'

'I called the Ballroom and there was no answer,' Peggy explained more evenly after she'd taken a very deep breath. 'I let it go to the machine and hung up. I called back again, hoping that Marnie would answer, but then that man picked up.'

'What did he say?' Andrew asked, crossing his own arms against his chest and leaning against the wall.

'Nothing at first,' Peggy replied, but when Andrew frowned again, she added, 'I knew there was something not quite right when the call was answered. Don't ask me how.'

Andrew shrugged. 'Trust your gut; it's an important part of what we do.'

'I could hear someone breathing,' Peggy explained, 'but I'm fairly sure that there was somebody else in the room; it sounded like they were moving things around, but the sound was too far away to be from the person holding the phone.'

Andrew nodded approvingly. 'That's good. Anything else?'

Peggy bit her lip, thinking back to the short call. 'There was nothing.'

'That's alright.'

'No,' Peggy added, shaking her head at herself for the misunderstanding. 'I mean there was *nothing* at all. Marnie's clever enough to know that I could still have heard her if she'd said anything at all, even if those in the Ballroom had no idea that she was there.'

'So, we know she's not there then?'

'Doesn't seem like it.' Peggy squinted at her shoes.

'Maybe she needed to go to Butterton for some reason,' Andrew said eventually.

Peggy sighed. 'Marnie's got the number for here; I left it at home for her as well, and made sure Timothy didn't have a hope in hell of finding it if he went snooping around my rooms. I'm sure she'll call when she has an update.'

Andrew didn't look entirely convinced by the positive viewpoint, but Peggy didn't feel all that convinced either by it either.

'I could call Butterton,' Peggy suggested eventually, even though she'd really rather not have made the offer. 'See if she's there.'

'God, no, don't do that,' Andrew said immediately, and with surprising vehemence. 'Timothy might answer, and then where will we be?'

Where indeed? Peggy thought.

The phone screeched shrilly again, and Peggy's hand flew to her chest in alarm. 'Jesus Christ!'

'I really hope it's not,' Andrew said, utterly deadpan, and Peggy was surprised at the panicked laugh that burst out of her.

Andrew apprehensively raised the receiver to his ear, obviously expecting the worst, and so it surprised Peggy when she saw his face clear a moment later.

'Yes, this is James McLeod,' he said into the phone, and it was quite obvious that this was for Peggy's benefit when he looked at her intently. 'Thank you so much for calling me, Ms Brown.'

'*Hotel?*' Peggy mouthed in question.

Andrew nodded at her and then returned his attention to the caller. 'Honestly, anything at all would be great. We're just so desperate to track her down before Christmas. I'm sure you know how these things are.'

Peggy had often wondered if Andrew was aware that he had a very specific way of speaking when he was trying to charm a witness or a suspect into telling him something useful. She suspected that he knew full well, because he wouldn't be a very good detective otherwise, would he?

'Oh, that would be fantastic,' Andrew said into the phone, before covering the mouthpiece and whispering to Peggy, 'Pen?'

Peggy opened the small drawer of the console table and retrieved a piece of paper. She was unhappy that it happened to have her father's insignia as a letterhead, but as she didn't have the luxury of time it would have to do. She dug out a biro and scribbled on the paper to make sure that it worked before she slid both items across the narrow slab of wood towards Andrew.

He picked up the pen and hurriedly wrote down whatever he was being told by Judith Brown, scrawling the words with far less care than he always took with paperwork. Peggy tilted her head, trying to read what he'd written.

'No, honestly, that's brilliant,' Andrew said enthusiastically, and it sounded genuine to Peggy. 'Thank you very much, Ms Brown. I will, absolutely. Merry Christmas to you too.'

'Well?' Peggy asked as the phone was replaced on the cradle.

'Well, I know where we need to go next.'

THIRTEEN

'I still don't understand why you want me to stay here again,' Charlie whined.

He was getting on Andrew's last nerve.

'Because the telephone can't answer itself,' Andrew replied, trying hard not to snap at him. Since he and Peggy had returned to the kitchen and explained what had happened, there had been a palpable – and volatile – mix of nerviness and anticipation in the room. The thought of unidentified people prowling around the Ballroom was an unpleasant thought, so instead they were all trying to focus on the fact that Judith Brown might have given them a lead.

Charlie, annoyingly, only brightened before abruptly leaving the room.

'So, do you think we'll actually find Beth Nash in Bowness, sir?' Lloyd asked as he stabbed another large slice of sponge cake with a fork. Apparently, the news that Beth had asked for her final payment from the hotel to be sent to her aunt via the post office in Bowness had been enough to restore his appetite.

'I don't know,' Andrew replied honestly. 'It was seventeen years ago, but it's the best we've got right now. There's nothing else we can do for Higson until we get back to Manchester, and we need to keep ourselves out of that whole shitshow for as long as we can. We need to follow this up.'

And hope for the best, he added silently.

'Where are we going to start though, sir?' Jen asked. She'd made a quick phone to call to Annie once everything had been explained, and Andrew was pleased to see that she was looking far less drawn than when she and Lloyd had first arrived back. 'The post office will definitely be closed by the time we get there.'

Andrew wasn't too upset about this fact; after that morning, he'd had enough of post offices. 'We have a name, and we've got to assume that this aunt is a real person, even if she's not an aunt at all.'

'Enid Wetherall,' Peggy said, reading the name from the paper Andrew had scribbled it on.

Andrew nodded. 'So, that's who we need to find.'

'And you don't think Beth really went to Harrogate like that hotel woman said she did?' Lloyd asked, frowning.

It was a good question. Judith Brown had been certain that Beth had told her that she abruptly needed to leave her employment at the hotel due to a family emergency back in Harrogate that would require her full attention for the foreseeable future. She'd apparently suggested that she might be back in Staveshead again in the following months, but Judith had never heard from her again. Yet, Annie Higson had told them all that Beth and Davy Nash had been childhood sweethearts and had still been living on the street they'd grown up on in Hulme when Davy had disappeared, and so Andrew was currently working under the assumption that there was no genuine connection to Harrogate.

'No, I don't think she went to Harrogate at all,' Andrew replied.

Charlie burst through the kitchen door, holding something grey and boxy in his right hand, with wires trailing from his palm to the floor.

'Christ, what the hell are you doing now?' Andrew asked.

'Answering machine!' Charlie triumphantly raised the box he was holding. 'I'll rerecord the message – nobody calling us wants to hear Timothy wittering on about my father's office hours – and set it back up again. See, the telephone *can* answer itself, after all!'

Andrew's eyes narrowed, but Peggy's fingers wrapped around his elbow, stopping the short-tempered retort that was building in his throat from actually escaping.

'Charlie, I don't think this is a good idea,' Peggy said, much more calmly than Andrew would have managed.

Charlie rolled his eyes so hard, Andrew was surprised that they didn't get stuck in the back of his head. 'No, of course you don't. Look, earlier today I had no way of getting in contact with any of you when the proverbial shit hit the proverbial fan, did I? So, me being here was more than a bit pointless. Anyway, Joycie, are you really telling me that you trust my message-taking skills over those of a purpose-built machine?'

Well, Andrew might be forced to concede that Charlie certainly had a point there.

'Come on, I'm great at talking to people,' Charlie added.

Annoyingly, he *also* had a point there. 'You're not so great at subtlety though, are you?'

Charlie shrugged off the ridiculous dressing gown and threw it over the back of one of the chairs. 'One day, you'll understand that the subtlety part is your downfall. If I look like I have nothing to hide, then people assume I am an entirely open book. They then proceed to tell me absolutely everything about their lives.'

Andrew met that smug grin with a glare. 'This isn't a game, Charlie.'

All trace of humour was wiped from Charlie's face immediately. 'I know. I can be useful.'

'Jesus, fine, but we're leaving in one minute, so bloody hurry up,' Andrew replied eventually, pointing at the answering machine.

Charlie nodded his head curtly. 'Look, I'll even let you drive my car.'

Andrew was left wondering how that was supposed to be in any way the compensation Charlie had clearly meant it to be as the other man practically ran from the room.

Peggy sighed loudly and removed her hand from Andrew's

arm now that any danger of him going rogue and thumping her brother had passed for the time being.

'Let's go then,' Andrew said, looking around at the others as they pulled their coats back on. He didn't think he'd ever felt quite so far away from how he'd imagined his career was going to pan out as he did in that moment; standing in the kitchen of a Lake District manor house, grasping at the smallest clues to the whereabouts of a woman he needed to find (even though he still didn't know *why* he needed to find her), all while his DCI was on the lam after being, if not outright accused, *heavily implicated* in the murder of a former police officer. Andrew could only be grateful for the fact that there still didn't seem to be anything paranormal to the case, so he was going to keep all thoughts of the supernatural locked firmly in the ever-expanding box inside his head until further notice.

Still, he wouldn't even bother trying to deny the fact that even without any ghostly intervention requiring Peggy's presence, he was immeasurably relieved to have her back as part of the team for this, particularly with how close to home it all was.

'You don't have to drive, you know,' Peggy said as they all trooped out to the driveway to wait for Charlie. 'I know how to get to Bowness.'

Andrew shook his head as Peggy stopped just outside the front door, house keys in hand. 'You've done more than enough ferrying me about today.'

Peggy shrugged and reached into her coat pocket for the car keys. 'Well, take these quickly before Charlie changes his mind, and we're all subjected to whatever old mix tape he's no doubt managed to find in his bedroom.'

He took the keys hurriedly and unlocked the car so that Jen and Lloyd could climb into the back. Just like Peggy, Jen needed a break from playing taxi soAndrew had suggested that they all travel together, for fear that Lloyd's notoriously slow driving behind the wheel of Jen's car would set them far behind schedule.

'It's nice in here,' Lloyd announced loudly, happily settling himself right in the middle of the bench seat as Andrew stood by the bonnet.

Charlie emerged from the house, strode across the gravel, and opened the passenger door.

'No!' Andrew barked at him.

Charlie paused, halfway towards sitting down, and unfolded himself back to standing. 'No?'

'No.' Andrew shook his head vehemently. 'Absolutely not.'

Charlie rolled his eyes for the hundredth time that morning but climbed into the back next to Lloyd with only minimal grumbling.

'Jen, please take the front seat,' Peggy called over as she locked up the house and headed towards the car.

'No, you're alright, Peggy,' Jen replied with a smile from behind the driver's seat before she closed the door.

Andrew would later blame a combination of stress and tiredness for his lapse in normal behaviour, but he found himself walking around the car with the intention of opening the passenger door for Peggy before he'd thought about just what the hell he was doing.

He realised just before his fingers curled over the handle and so he ended up sort of flapping his arm uselessly between himself and the car. Still, even that was probably better than actually opening the door for her.

Peggy, gracious as ever, kept all comments to herself and climbed into the car as though Andrew hadn't just behaved like a complete moron.

Silently berating himself for the horrible lapse in judgement, Andrew slouched into the driver's seat, avoiding all eye contact with any of his passengers.

He magnanimously chose to ignore Charlie's amused snort,

because if he didn't, Higson wasn't going to be the only of them under suspicion of murder before the day was out.

Andrew focused instead on situating himself in the car so that he could drive to Bowness. He groped around for the correct lever and eventually succeeded in pushing the seat back to compensate for the fact that his legs were much longer than Peggy's and there was no way that he could drive with his knees rammed under the steering wheel. 'Sorry, Jen. Just shout if I'm about to take your ankles out.'

'You're fine, sir,' Jen replied. 'Loads of room.'

Andrew noted that Peggy had the ancient road atlas on her lap, but she made no move to open it, even as she said, 'Head out of the village the same way we did this morning, only once we hit the main road you'll need to turn left instead, alright?'

'Alright,' Andrew agreed, and then he steered the bulky green car out of the driveway and onto the picturesque single street that seemed to make up the majority of Briersthwaite.

A woman wrapped in an oversized tartan shawl was walking towards them, and she peered curiously through the windscreen as they approached, raising her hand to wave with a wiggle of her fingers.

'Well, there goes any chance of keeping your existence a secret from Mrs Laycock,' Peggy muttered to Andrew out of the corner of her mouth while she smiled at their neighbour. 'She'll definitely make an excuse to pop over later.'

In his head, Andrew went back to that moment of introspection in the kitchen before they'd left and added the threat of the Swan's ad-hoc housekeeper attempting to play matchmaker while he was in the middle of an investigation to the list of oddities that his life and sanity were currently suffering from.

'What's the plan then?' Lloyd asked as they reached the main road, which was only marginally busier than it had been that morning.

'Well, the best places to get useful, local knowledge are going to be the same everywhere, aren't they?' Jen stated plainly, and not even for the first time that day, Andrew was glad to have someone so unshakeable on the team. 'Little shops, pubs, places like that.'

'Exactly,' Andrew agreed, unhappy to see that the mist of earlier seemed to be trying to make a comeback. 'We also know that Beth used to work in the hotel in Staveshead, so maybe she found a job in a hotel in Bowness without much trouble.'

'Bowness is a lot larger than Staveshead,' Peggy reminded them all, 'so even though we'll have more chances to potentially find Beth, it does mean we'll have significantly more ground to cover.'

'Well, there won't be much going on lakeside at this time of year,' Charlie added from the back. 'You're probably best parking in the middle of the main part of town, and then we can walk from there.'

'Are we asking after Beth, or just this Enid Wetherall?' Jen asked.

Andrew readjusted his hands on the steering wheel as he thought about how to answer that; he'd been weighing it up since they'd left St Sunday's. 'I think we should start with just Enid Wetherall. If Beth really did come here, then she very easily could have changed the name she was using. Sniffing around for information about one person might look suspicious enough as it is, but two might just be asking for trouble.'

'What should we say, boss?' Lloyd was eating something again, if the mangled question was anything to go by. 'When we're asking around, I mean?'

'You're looking for a family member, or a family friend,' Andrew replied. 'Be as vague as they'll let you get away with. With Beth, we at least knew how old she was and that she had two kids, which isn't much, but it's still significantly more information than we have about Enid Wetherall – she could be forty, but she could just as easily be ninety.'

'Or not a real person at all,' Charlie added, which, while entirely true, wasn't what anyone wanted to be reminded of.

The car lapsed back into silence, and Peggy switched on the radio. Andrew thought that she might have intentionally chosen a station with as little chat as possible to try and avoid hearing any news bulletins while they drove. He appreciated it.

It took over half an hour to reach Bowness, and Andrew was more than ready to get out and stretch his legs when he parked the Range Rover in the middle of the quiet car park that Peggy directed him to.

There was more of a breeze here than in even Stavesmere, and Andrew turned up the collar of his coat to keep the cold from the back of his neck.

'Right,' Charlie announced, clapping his hands together, 'we're about halfway up the main thoroughfare here, but there are plenty of little streets that lead off in all directions.'

'So, let's split up,' Andrew interjected before Charlie developed any notions about leading the investigation.

'How about Jen, Lloyd and I go that way?' Charlie suggested mildly, pointing to the right and then grinning at Andrew. 'You don't mind going the same way as Peg, do you Joycie?'

Andrew's eyes narrowed into a murderous glare, but before he could say anything, Peggy loudly announced that they should all just take a road or two each and meet back at the car in an hour, before she turned on her heel and practically bolted from the car park.

'What?' Charlie asked, in a wholly fraudulent protestation of innocence. 'What did I say?'

'Oh, fuck off, Charlie,' Andrew snarled, even less in the mood for Charlie's playground teasing than usual, and stomped off in the direction Peggy had already gone.

As Andrew reached the pavement, he looked up and down the main road and only just about caught sight of Peggy striding around the corner in the far distance, which was apparently par for the course for him this week.

'Well, that's just brilliant,' he growled to himself, as he crossed the road and headed for the greengrocers on the other side of the street. There was no chance of avoiding awkwardness between them now, was there?

He shook his head at himself again; he had a bloody job to do.

Peeking through the festively decorated shop window on his way to the door, he was pleased to see that a short queue had formed inside.

Good, he thought, when most of the customers turned to look at the new arrival as the brass bell tinkled above his head. He hoped that some of this nosiness would translate to helpful answers.

'Hi there,' Andrew said to the woman at the back of the queue as he conjured his most charming smile out of thin air. 'I'm really hoping that you might be able to help me.'

* * *

Twenty minutes after leaving the car park, Peggy was still berating herself for her mishandled exit from the situation. She was fully aware that she shouldn't be the one directing the order of things on an investigation but, Jesus Christ, *what on earth* had Charlie thought he was playing at back there?

Peggy had never spoken to Charlie about the conversation she'd had with Andrew on Tib Street after the *Lady Bancroft* case, but she was certain that her brother knew what had happened anyway; knew that Peggy had been forced to look her own jealousy in the face and confront what that meant for her ongoing work with the Ballroom team. Charlie and Marnie had made enough oblique references to Peggy's attachment to the team, with very particular emphasis on her relationship with

Andrew Joyce, that she was mortified about the whole thing any time she let herself think about it.

She was just going to have to hope that Andrew thought that Charlie was just being his usual obnoxious self, and that there was no real meaning lurking in that absolute bloody git's suggestive tone.

She sighed unhappily and looked around the street that she'd wandered onto. Bowness was a much larger tourist-trap than Staveshead at any time of year, but still many of the shops were closed, even though it was only just after three o'clock on a Saturday. From the darkened windows it was impossible to tell whether the closures were brief and unplanned, brought on by reduced footfall and a proximity to Christmas, or whether the businesses inside were fully shut up until spring came around again.

Unlike the shuttered ice-cream parlour next to where she'd paused, a chocolate shop a few units along appeared to be doing a roaring trade. Peggy decided that it was as a good a course of action as any, and so she made her way to the door and carefully pushed it open, mindful of the people crammed inside the relatively modest space.

Pleasantly, the shop was warmer than outside and smelled so wonderfully of rich chocolate and caramel that the air practically tasted of confectionary. Pre-packaged items were displayed on wall shelves to the left and right of the queueing customers, but the star attraction of the shop proved to be the large glass cabinet next to the till, where rows and rows of different handmade chocolates were displayed as a neat siren's call to anyone with even the remotest hint of a sweet tooth.

The people at the head of the queue were having something beautifully gift-wrapped in gold paper by the laughing young man behind the counter. He was wearing a smart navy apron over his shirt, which was somewhat at odds with the sparkly Christmas trees adorning the top of the deely boppers perched on his head.

As she watched the next customers joyfully choosing the perfect selection of chocolates from the case with the sort of precision that could only be displayed by regulars, Peggy was briefly visited by the vague notion that perhaps she should use the opportunity to buy a gift for Albany. Well, if she were to be completely honest, it was more that the notion actually concerned the fact that she hadn't thought of buying him a gift at all at any point, until confronted with the wrapping process at the counter.

Realising that she did actually need a reason to be in the queue, but not at all equipped with enough time to be selecting individual chocolates, she reached out and grabbed a box of chocolate snowflakes from the display to her left.

When Peggy finally reached the front, the smiling young man looked relieved when she confirmed that she really was just after the snowflakes, and he put the small silver tongs down with a comically large sigh at the reprieve.

'Do you want these gift-wrapped though?' he asked, waving the box gently and gesturing towards the array of coloured paper and ribbons displayed behind him.

She declined the offer politely and then immediately wondered if there was any significance lurking at the heart of that choice. She was almost certain that Marnie would have found something deep and meaningful to ascribe to it all if she were there, and likely would have informed Peggy that she was obviously further downgrading any of the already limited status she'd given to her and Albany's relationship – if you could even be so bold as to call it a relationship in the first place.

Peggy wondered whether she might be projecting her own thoughts onto an imaginary Marnie, and then abruptly realised that she'd been asked a question.

'Sorry,' Peggy said as airily as she could manage, while trying not to look like she'd lost the plot. 'I was somewhere else then for a second.'

'Wish I was,' the man laughed, which earned him an elbow to the ribs from the silver-haired woman who'd just appeared from a back room carrying a small, polished tray piled high with chocolate truffles.

'Oi, that's enough of your cheek,' the woman groused, but she was smiling.

'I asked if you were sure that was everything,' the man repeated to Peggy as he handed back her change.

'Oh, well, actually…Sorry, this might sound very odd, but I was just wondering if there was any chance you might know someone by the name of Enid Wetherall,' Peggy replied hesitantly.

'My mum worked here with Enid when they were just girls,' the woman behind the counter smiled warmly at Peggy, with no hint of reluctance or diversion in her voice. 'Enid showed her how to make macaroons. This place was a bakery back then, of course, and it was years before Enid began teaching.'

Peggy schooled her face into a smile of her own as she tried to tamp down the sudden rush of elation at finding a positive result while also trying to mentally calculate how old the woman in front of her was in order to craft a response accordingly. 'Oh, goodness, that's amazing.'

The woman continued to smile at Peggy. 'How do you know Enid?'

'She was a close friend of my grandmother a long time ago,' Peggy lied as fluently as she knew how. 'I was hoping to find Enid and put my grandmother in touch with her again. Is there any chance you'd be able to tell me where I could find her?'

The woman put down the tray of chocolates and reached over to squeeze Peggy's hand. 'Oh, sweetheart, you'll find Enid at St Martin's these days. I'm afraid she died about ten years ago.'

The blow of disenchantment hit hard and threw Peggy back down to earth at speed. 'Oh.'

'I'm sorry to have been the one to have to tell you that,' the woman said, and she sounded as though she really meant it. 'Are you alright?'

Peggy picked up her purchase and waved away the concern. 'I'm fine, honestly. Thank you. I just wasn't expecting that.'

'Do you want to sit down for a second?' the woman asked. 'Ernie here will get you a glass of water if you want.'

'No, you don't need to go to any trouble,' Peggy replied even though she did actually feel a bit nauseous. 'Thank you again.'

'Here, take a couple of these to see you on your way,' the woman said, picking up the tongs and throwing at least five truffles from the silver tray into a small cellophane bag and handed it over, ignoring Peggy's protestations. 'They'll see you right; they're absolutely soaked in rum. Exactly the sort of thing Enid would've loved.'

Realising that she was now holding up what was a fairly substantial queue, Peggy left her further thanks and took both her stash of chocolate and heavy burden of guilt back out into the blustery afternoon.

She supposed that she should probably go and try and find one of the others and let them know that she'd tracked down Enid Wetherall, but that unless she was available in the afterlife for a quick chat with Peggy, it was unlikely that she was going to be particularly helpful on the subject of Beth Nash.

Crestfallen, Peggy opened the small cellophane bag as she trudged back towards the main area of the town and shoved one of the pretty little truffles into her mouth whole before chewing dejectedly. Her eyes widened in surprise as the potent hit of lightly spiced alcohol hit the back of her throat. The woman in the shop hadn't been lying – the chocolate had been absolutely drenched in rum. It was so good, in fact, that Peggy thought that she might need to go back and buy a whole crate.

The sky was overcast, making it feel far later than it actually was, and Peggy tucked her chin down into the collar of her coat as she walked. As she passed the entrance to a small lane on her left, she turned her head to glance up the path and was surprised to see a church in the near distance. There was a small tourist sign above her head that pointed up the lane, informing her matter-of-factly that it was, indeed, St Martin's.

Even from where she stood, which was well outside the stone wall of the churchyard, Peggy could just about pick up the low murmur of mingling voices, and she closed her eyes with a small groan of displeasure. There weren't many things that Peggy disliked more than being in the vicinity of a church, but she was in Bowness as part of the Ballroom team, and it was her responsibility to check that she'd been told the truth about Enid Wetherall.

She took a deep breath, put the small bag of truffles into her pocket, and held the box of chocolate snowflakes to her chest as though they might somehow afford her a bit of protection from the onslaught she was expecting at any moment.

The voices grew louder but not any more coherent as she approached the boundary wall. The lychgate had been decorated with sprays of perfect white flowers, plaited together as they wound towards the roof, and the wind had blown clumps of pink and white confetti into the corners of the wooden structure. There must have been a wedding in the church earlier that day.

St Martin's was lit from within, and a honeyed glow spilled out through the open door, ready to welcome any visitors inside, but there was nobody in the churchyard. Well, nobody that anyone but Peggy would likely be aware of.

As she stepped through the gate, a clear voice rang out from inside the church itself, and Peggy recognised the opening verse of *Once in Royal David's City* being carried out into the churchyard. She wouldn't be able to explain to anyone else how she was certain that she was the only one who could hear the voice, but Peggy knew without a shadow of a doubt that the soloist in the church was no longer alive.

She was actually grateful to the unknown singer for providing a single voice for her to focus on and therefore more easily filter out the rest of the background noise.

She kept to the outer path of the churchyard, following the gentle curve of the wall. When she wasn't glancing quickly down each row of headstones for any sign of Enid Wetherall's name, Peggy trained her gaze on the uneven stones beneath her feet.

A handful of fairly well-defined outlines huddled together at the foot of the bell tower, and she didn't want to risk alerting any of them to the fact that she was aware of their presence. Peggy had learned early in life that ghosts were almost always unaware of her ability to converse with them as long as she avoided eye contact or direct communication.

Unlike the particular challenge that churches created for her, graveyards were often entirely devoid of spirits. Peggy, with her limited understanding of how the afterlife worked, had always assumed that this was because spirits seemed to be drawn to places – or, more rarely, people – that they were attached to in life, so, barring a couple of groundskeepers and one unbearably morose poet, Peggy had never really encountered anyone who wanted a quick chat amongst the headstones.

She was nearing the end of the rows when she finally spotted what she'd been looking for. A handsome slab of granite, engraved with a series of names and dates, dominated this corner of the churchyard, and the final line carved into the headstone brought Peggy to the end of her search:

ENID JOSEPHINE WETHERALL 1st June 1898 – 7th March 1978

A small ceramic pot of winter pansies was resting against the base of the memorial, the purple petals a bright and cheerful counterpoint to the cold stone behind them.

Peggy reached out and lightly pressed her fingertips to the top of the headstone. She'd obviously never met Enid, but she would still take a moment to pay her respects, even if it meant the end of the line for the investigation.

She took another deep breath, preparing to walk back past the church, but when she turned away from Enid's resting place, she was startled by a quiet voice behind her.

'Are you alright?'

Peggy reeled backwards in surprise, at first certain that the owner of the voice must be dead because she hadn't heard anyone approach, but when she looked up, she came face-to-face with an apologetic – and very much alive – man dressed entirely in black aside from the telltale flash of white at his collar.

'I'm so sorry,' he added, holding out his hands placatingly. 'I didn't mean to give you a fright.'

'No,' Peggy replied, with her free hand still pressed against where her heart was hammering behind her ribs. 'It's okay.'

'I'm Peter,' the man said, offering his hand. 'I'm the vicar here at St Martin's.'

'Margaret.'

'Pleasure to meet you. I don't recognise you from our congregation,' Peter continued, still smiling. 'Are you new to the area, or just visiting Bowness for Christmas?'

'I'm staying with family for a few days,' Peggy explained. 'We're closer to Ullswater, but I came to Bowness looking for someone. Enid Wetherall.'

The change in the vicar's expression was astonishing in its immediacy. At once, his open, pleasant countenance hardened, and Peggy saw suspicion ignite behind his eyes.

She fought to keep her expression neutral, even as she awaited the proverbial shoe to drop from above and smash her story to smithereens.

'I didn't realise that she'd passed away,' Peggy added steadily, as though she hadn't noticed any change in the vicar's mood. 'I was really hoping to speak to her.'

'Can I ask who you are, and exactly why you came here looking for Enid?'

There was no need to feign being taken aback by such an abrupt question when the sharpness of the inquiry provoked the response naturally. 'I beg your pardon?'

Peggy wished that she hadn't gone off without Andrew; he surely would have been able to invent some complete rubbish without any hint of hesitation that would, as always, be immediately believed when gifted alongside a charming smile.

Peter repeated his question with an equal level of mistrust.

'Enid was a close friend of my grandmother when they were young,' she offered as convincingly as she could.

When the vicar only raised his eyebrows, Peggy nearly groaned in frustration.

'They worked in a bakery together,' Peggy added, praying that the embellishment would help rather than hinder her story. 'It was where the chocolate shop is now. I was in there earlier buying a gift, which is how I found out that Enid had died. They lost touch years ago, but my grandmother still talks so fondly of Enid.'

Unfortunately for Peggy, none of this seemed to make a substantial dent in Peter's air of suspicion.

Think, she instructed herself firmly. What could she say to this man to convince him that she wasn't the complete fraud he believed her to be? The level of hostility seemed excessive, so, if nothing else, she needed to understand why this man's demeanour had transformed so rapidly at the mention of Enid's name.

She cast her eyes around quickly, looking for some form of inspiration. When her gaze flitted past the lychgate, it came to her: *confetti*.

'We were just really hoping to be able to find Enid and extend an invitation to our wedding,' Peggy said, trying to make the sad smile looked far less forced than it felt. 'It would have been a wonderful occasion to surprise my grandmother.'

She glanced back towards the lychgate, hoping that she looked wistful and sad, and then nearly swore loudly in alarm.

Andrew was passing the churchyard wall. All Peggy could do was hope that he walked by without noticing that she was there at all.

Because it was clearly not Peggy's day – and perhaps even, she thought wildly, because she was currently lying to a vicar – Andrew didn't continue on his way but instead looked over and caught her eye.

All of Peggy's attempts at telepathically telling Andrew that she'd really appreciate him just buggering off right now were redundant when the bloody idiot turned through the lychgate and started walking towards her and Peter.

'Excuse me just one second,' Peggy apologised hurriedly to Peter, before she all but sprinted towards the detective.

Andrew, as expected, looked baffled at whatever combination of expressions Peggy was wearing as she approached, and he frowned when she stopped in front of him. 'What's going on?'

'I really am very, *very* sorry about this,' Peggy said, hooking her arm around Andrew's elbow and all but pulling him to her side.

'Sorry about what?' Andrew hissed in concern as Peggy slowly steered them both towards where the vicar was waiting.

'Really cagey vicar, no idea why,' Peggy muttered out of the corner of her mouth. 'He was perfectly pleasant until I mentioned Enid and then he started interrogating me about who I was.'

'Why did you ask the vicar about Enid?' Andrew whispered. 'I thought you hated coming anywhere near churches.'

'Yes, well, I didn't really have a choice,' Peggy replied and then winced. 'Also, the vicar is going to think that you and I are getting married, alright?'

Andrew didn't actually squawk in outrage, but from the way he went completely rigid, Peggy knew that it was only a miracle that had stopped him from vocalising his exasperation.

'So sorry,' Peggy said as they rejoined Peter. 'I was just explaining how terribly sad my grandmother will be when she finds out that Enid has passed. Isn't that right, *Andy*?'

'Terribly sad,' Andrew wheezed eventually.

Ah, she probably should have mentioned the fact that she'd been in the churchyard looking for Enid's grave. To be fair, though, she'd been given very limited time to explain anything.

The vicar's reluctance seemed to have melted away at the sudden production of a purported fiancé. Whether this was because Peter somehow thought Andrew more genuine than Peggy, or just because he was a big fan of weddings, Peggy didn't actually care. She was thrilled to see him relax back into the friendliness he'd broadcast when he'd first spoken to her, even if she found the whole situation disheartening.

'Please forgive my hesitation to speak earlier,' Peter said, all smiles once again.

Peggy wouldn't have quite labelled it as 'hesitation', but she let it slide with a quirk of her lips to suggest that there were no hard feelings.

'It's just that things regarding Enid were complicated for a number of years,' Peter explained. 'With Enid never marrying or having children, there was quite a bit of nasty business regarding the apportioning of her estate between distant family members. Unfortunately, it continues to crop up every now and then. I sincerely apologise for my incorrect presumption, Margaret.'

Peggy let herself sag in relief; it was nice to know that she hadn't completely ballsed up the investigation. 'No, of course, that all sounds terrible. I'd really just hoped to be able to tell my grandmother something about Enid's life after they lost touch. I completely understand your position though. Thank you for your time.'

Shooting Peter a sad smile, Peggy turned away quickly, tugging Andrew along with her again.

'What are you doing?' Andrew whispered, agitation obvious.

'Behaving like my brother,' Peggy replied as they walked towards the gate. She was almost disappointed in herself.

'Excuse me!' Peter called suddenly from behind them. 'No, please wait!'

Peggy and Andrew turned their heads in perfect unison.

'Really, I'm so sorry,' Peter added loudly as he jogged towards them, now looking as flustered as Peggy had felt earlier.

The singer inside the church had moved onto *In the Bleak Midwinter* and Peggy shivered at the haunting melancholy that had crept into the voice.

'Are you alright?' Andrew asked quietly, upping Peggy's tally of people voicing that same question in the past half an hour to three.

Peggy nodded. 'Fine.'

Andrew looked as disbelieving as he always did when Peggy answered like that, but there was no time for any further explanation as Peter stopped in front of them, still apologising.

'I didn't know Enid hugely well,' Peter explained, wringing his hands. 'By the time I came to the parish, Enid wasn't as mobile as she'd obviously been in her younger years, and so while she came to a number of services, I wouldn't be able to call her a regular. Our conversations outside of St Martin's were limited to brief interactions at community events, or if we bumped into each other in the library or at the butcher's.

'Pam Moyes does the flowers for all our services, and I believe that she and Enid worked at the primary school together for many, many years. She lives on Rayrigg Brow these days; number thirty-two, I think, and I'm sure she'd be happy to talk to you about Enid. She'll also be here tomorrow morning before our eleven o'clock service if you wanted to try and catch her then.'

'Thank you,' Peggy replied, feeling marginally more generous towards Peter now that he'd given them some useful information.

'Oh, and there's always Jane Bell too!' Peter announced. 'She's a regular here. Jane cooked and cleaned for Enid for a good few years when her own children were very small, and they were often out together running errands. Jane might even have stayed in Enid's house for a while, if my memory serves me correctly. They were certainly very close.'

The spectre of elation at a possible real break in the case returned to hover again as Peter described Jane Bell, and Peggy could tell from the way Andrew's posture shifted slightly that he'd just had the same thought. Could Jane Bell really be Beth Nash by a different name?

'Do you know where we might find Ms Bell?' Andrew asked, the very picture of thankful courtesy. 'I know how much all of this means to Margaret and her family.'

Peter nodded. 'Jane lives above the chemist on Ash Street; it's just off the main road. Do you know it?'

'I'm sure we'll find it,' Andrew replied as he held out his hand for Peter to shake. 'Thank you again for your help.'

Andrew clasped Peggy's hand and gave a gentle tug that informed her in no uncertain terms that he wanted to get out of this situation before they had to enhance their story any further.

'Thank you!' Peggy smiled as they turned away. 'Merry Christmas!'

They passed under the flowers at the lychgate and almost crashed right into Charlie, who was wearing a particularly self-satisfied smile that Peggy was not a fan of.

'Oh, is there something you haven't told us?' he crowed gleefully as he pointedly looked at their joined hands and then at the church.

'Charlie!' Peggy yelped in horror.

'Didn't I already tell you to fuck off?' Andrew snapped at Charlie, wrenching his hand back from Peggy's as though he'd been burned.

Charlie held up his hands, but the smug smile didn't fade one iota under the twin murderous glares being shot in his direction. 'Christ, calm down. Now, do you want to know what I found out?'

Peggy got the feeling that Andrew would rather not have to listen to anything else Charlie had to say, but unfortunately, under the circumstances, he was going to have to.

'What is it?' Andrew asked, and Peggy could almost hear his teeth grinding together.

'Well,' Charlie started, and then grimaced, 'unfortunately, Enid Wetherall is dead.'

'We know,' Peggy replied, folding her arms.

'Oh.' Charlie deflated immediately, which Peggy was pleased about. 'Well, did you know that she used to teach at the primary school?'

'Yes.' Peggy shrugged. 'Is that all?'

'Well, yes…' Charlie trailed off, looking utterly disgruntled that his grand reveal hadn't worked out this time. 'Why? What else do *you* know?'

Once it became clear that Andrew had no intention of sharing any information with Charlie, Peggy rolled her eyes and quickly explained what they'd learned.

'So, Enid wasn't close with her family at all by the sounds of things?' Charlie asked, shaking his head. 'Yet, she knew Beth Nash well enough to let her forward her final payment from the hotel to her.'

'Sounds like it,' Peggy confirmed.

Charlie looked delighted. 'And you think this Jane Bell might be Beth Nash? We should go and speak to her straightaway.'

Andrew pressed his fist to his forehead in obvious irritation. '*You* aren't going anywhere near her.'

Charlie's joy slid towards outrage, but Peggy silenced him with a glower.

Andrew sighed loudly and pointed at Charlie. 'Saying that, I still need you to do something. Entirely, against my better judgement, mind!'

'What?' Charlie asked slowly.

'I need you to find Jen and Lloyd, and update them on everything,' Andrew replied grumpily, clearly wishing he was talking to *anyone* else. 'Tell them that a woman named Pam Moyes – she does the flowers at the church – used to teach at the primary school with Enid. She apparently lives on Rayrigg Brow; should be number thirty-two. Do you know where that is?'

Charlie shook his head. 'No, but I doubt it will be hard to find.'

'Tell Jen that I need her to pretend to be 'Margaret' for the purposes of any conversation she might have with Pam Moyes, and that the vicar of St Martin's gave her the address, alright?' Andrew continued firmly. 'I want to leave as little a trail as possible, just in case.'

Charlie nodded, and Peggy was relieved to see that her brother was obviously now taking this all more seriously. 'Do you think there's any point talking to this Pam Moyes woman if you think that Jane Bell might be Beth?'

Andrew shrugged. 'We could be wrong. Jane could very well just be Jane Bell, friend and home help to Enid Wetherall. If that's the case, then we'll need to talk to Pam Moyes anyway.'

'So, I suppose that means that you two are going to go and talk to Jane Bell then?' Charlie asked, barely refraining from rolling his eyes.

Honestly, Peggy wasn't sure she was going to be able to resist drowning him in Ullswater if he continued like this. Though, knowing her luck, he'd bloody well haunt her just to spite her, wouldn't he?

'Yes,' Andrew replied simply, thankfully not rising to Charlie's bait, 'and we're going to stop at the primary school on the way.'

'Why?' Charlie asked, wrinkling his nose. 'It's Saturday, there won't be anyone there.'

Andrew made a funny little face that Peggy couldn't quite interpret until he turned to her and said, 'Well, Enid Wetherall might be.'

FOURTEEN

Despite his hesitation to involve the younger Swan sibling, Andrew did actually know that Charlie would do precisely as he'd been asked, and that Jen was more than capable of keeping him in line should he even think about going off-piste.

He was actually less thrilled about the fact that he was going to have to take a backseat on the next part of the investigation, but he'd long since reconciled himself to the fact that if Peggy ever came back to the Ballroom, he was going to make it damn obvious that he trusted her implicitly; his failure to demonstrate that faith in the first place is what had nearly ended their partnership for good during the *Lady Bancroft* fiasco, and he wasn't inclined to risk that same outcome again.

'Do you know where the school is?' Peggy asked him as they left St Martin's behind them.

'I walked past it earlier. It's not too far away. Just up here and down to the right.'

Peggy pulled her coat more tightly around herself when another gust caught the street. 'I'm sorry about back there. I couldn't come up with any other story that I thought he might believe.'

'Don't worry about it.' Andrew cleared his throat. 'It was a good idea, and it worked. You have nothing to apologise for.'

Peggy wrinkled her nose but didn't say anything else, she just curled her fingers more tightly around whatever it was that she'd been holding in her hand when he'd found her in the churchyard.

'What is that anyway?' Andrew asked, gesturing towards the box.

'Hmm? *Oh*, I ended up in a chocolate shop; it's actually where I was when I found out that Enid had died,' Peggy explained. 'I needed to buy something so that I had a reason to be in the queue, so I just grabbed these off the shelf. In fact, that reminds me, can you hold them for a second, please?'

Peggy held out the box and Andrew took it, glancing down at the snowflake-shaped chocolates through the cellophane wrapping. He couldn't help but wonder if she'd had anyone specific in mind when she'd bought them.

Andrew had to then immediately tell himself off for wondering that in the first place.

Eventually, Peggy produced a small bag of what looked like even more chocolates from her coat pocket.

'Have one,' Peggy said, waving the bag towards him. 'You'll like them.'

Andrew took a chocolate and popped it into his mouth, coughing loudly when his teeth broke through the outer layer, and his tongue was doused in alcohol.

Peggy grinned at his obvious surprise. 'Sorry, I probably should have warned you about that.'

'Christ, that's good!' He laughed despite himself. 'Not sure I can legally drive now though, Peggy.'

His smile faded as they reached the school gates, and he watched Peggy's face fall.

'What is it?' he asked as Peggy looked away when her fingers wrapped around the ironwork of the gate.

'There's a little girl, right at the edge of the playground,' Peggy replied quietly.

Andrew turned automatically to look and realised a split-second too late what Peggy meant. The playground to him, of course, was only dusky and deserted.

'She's playing hopscotch by herself,' Peggy added, shaking her head with obvious sorrow. 'She can't be more than six.'

Andrew briefly closed his eyes. He really didn't want to be *that* guy, even if he needed to be. 'Peggy…'

'No, I know,' Peggy replied, shaking her head to recentre herself. 'I know, we have a job to do. Sorry.'

'Don't apologise.' Andrew shook his head. 'Is there anyone else here?'

'Yes,' Peggy replied, scanning the playground again. She momentarily released one finger from her grip on the gate to point. 'There's a woman over there, right next to the far door. Very faint, so I'm not sure how easy this will be.'

Andrew followed Peggy's gesture and found the correct spot. A greying stone slab marking the original girls' entrance to the building stood out against the red brick face of the Victorian school building.

'The gates are locked, so I'll have to call her over,' Peggy explained as she turned her head to look at him. Andrew thought that it might be less about asking permission to engage, and more about checking that he was alright with her bringing a ghost within a few feet of him.

Andrew gave the most encouraging nod he could manage. He'd known that this was a possible outcome when they'd left Manchester, but after that bizarre episode with the archive room door earlier in the week, not to mention the terror he'd experienced in his own home in the not-too-distant past, Andrew wasn't feeling fantastic about being anywhere near a ghost.

'Hello?' Peggy called, obviously trying to keep her voice down.

Andrew turned to face the street, ostensibly keeping an eye out for any passersby who might ask what on earth they were doing loitering near a closed school on a weekend. He was well aware that they both knew that he was also still unnerved by what was about to happen.

Neither of them mentioned that fact, of course.

'Hello,' Peggy said politely, significantly quieter than her initial salutation.

Andrew had to assume that the ghost had come closer. He did *not* shiver.

'My name's Margaret,' Peggy continued. 'Pardon? Yes, I really can see you. No, I'm not dead. Psychic? No, no, I don't think it's that.'

Andrew's entire career had been built on asking questions and subsequently lining up the answers so that he could reach for the truth within a problem, which meant that it was still off-putting to only hear one side of a conversation any time this happened. Lloyd had once asked him what it was specifically that made Andrew twitchy about it, because surely it was just like standing next to Peggy having a conversation on the telephone. It had been a sensible question, and all Andrew had been able to come up with as an answer was that the problem was that he knew it *wasn't* a one-sided conversation; he knew that there was a person right there beside him with expression and intonation in their responses. Between all that nuance was where you could learn so much about a person, and so much of that was lost in translation when you received a story second-hand; no matter how much you trusted the person relaying that story to you.

'I was wondering if I could ask you if you had ever worked with Enid Wetherall, or if yo–' Peggy cut herself off with a sharp, surprised intake of breath.

Andrew turned around so quickly he almost gave himself whiplash, nearly dropping the box of chocolates he was still holding. 'What?'

Peggy was still focussed on whoever it was that Andrew couldn't see. 'No, that's not it at all. It's – *no* – I'm – that's not why I'm here!'

'What?' Andrew asked again.

Peggy shook her head, but then she swallowed heavily as she went stock still, looking down towards the playground as her whole demeanour changed. Her lower lip trembled slightly, and

Andrew had the awful feeling that she was about to burst into tears.

'No, I'm not shouting at you,' Peggy said so quietly that Andrew almost missed it. 'My name's Peggy.'

His eyes widened in surprise when Peggy suddenly crouched down, sliding her hands further down on the gate to keep her steady.

'That's a very pretty name,' Peggy said with a watery smile. 'I'm glad to hear that Miss Wetherall was a nice lady.'

Oh God. Andrew's awful feeling sped away from thinking that Peggy was about to cry and arrived very firmly in the territory of understating *why*.

Peggy took another very deep breath. 'No, darling, I'm sorry, I haven't seen them. That's alright. You go and play.'

By the time she stood up, Peggy had a hand pressed to her mouth as if she were worried about what she might say if she let any words escape.

'Peg…' Andrew was at a loss of what to say beyond that.

The expression on Peggy's face was the same one that settled there any time Andrew had spoken about Rob in the past, and he knew that his suspicions were entirely correct.

'What's her name?' Andrew asked as he took a couple of steps backwards in a wordless suggestion that they leave the school.

'Sophie,' Peggy replied eventually.

'Come on,' Andrew said, tilting his head back towards the main street. 'Let's go and see Jane Bell. You can tell me what happened on the way.'

Peggy nodded with another great intake of air, which she blew out very slowly as they meandered back towards the centre of town.

'The teacher back there…' Peggy started a few minutes later, twisting her lips unhappily. 'She didn't want to speak to me; not when I asked about Enid. It was like when I mentioned her name to the vicar. You know, I don't think I've ever been accused of being a gold-digging relative before today, and now I've had it twice in one afternoon.'

Andrew shook his head, frustrated on Peggy's behalf, but also disappointed to have another path of investigation cut off before they'd barely looked at it. 'It's not your fault, Peggy.'

'That's the first time a ghost has ever outright refused to talk to me about something,' Peggy said, sounding a little like she couldn't quite believe it. She then laughed mirthlessly. 'Well, other than Marnie, obviously.'

'It happens to all of us Peggy,' Andrew said. At Peggy's incredulous eyebrow he added, 'I mean, I've had plenty of people refuse to answer questions for me, you know that.'

Peggy shrugged, missing offhand by a mile. 'Yes, but you can question someone *again*. Or you could send in Jen or Lloyd if you needed to take a different approach. If ghosts refuse to speak to me, then I'm of no use to the investigation.'

Andrew reached out and grasped Peggy's arm before he'd quite realised that he'd moved. 'Peggy, you've done tons for this investigation already, and none of it's really had the slightest thing to do with ghosts.'

His initial incredulity at finding that Peggy thought her only use was in speaking to ghosts lasted only a moment, before he was hit by a wave of guilt bearing the realisation that perhaps Peggy felt like that because *he* hadn't otherwise made it clear.

Peggy didn't look like she was about to agree with him any time soon, and Andrew had to stop himself from rolling his eyes at Peggy's ingrained inability to take any form of compliment; even though he'd mean it only with affection, he was certain that she wouldn't appreciate it just then.

'Ash Street,' Peggy said suddenly, changing the subject abruptly as she pointed at a street sign hanging high on a wall to their right. 'That's what the vicar said, isn't it?'

'Yeah,' Andrew replied, knowing that there was no point trying to bring the conversation back round to the previous topic. 'We need to find the chemist.'

They crossed the road together, checking each shop front carefully.

Andrew grimaced at the animatronic cobbler in the window of a shoe shop. The over-exaggerated features gave him the creeps, and the fact that it had been dressed to look like Father Christmas only seemed to make it more repulsive. *Surely*, Andrew thought as he cast the figure one final dark glance, *an elf costume would have been more appropriate.*

Beyond the shoe shop, the whole street had been cheerfully decorated, and in the growing duskiness of the late afternoon, the bright Christmas lights strung across the width of the street bathed the buildings in a kaleidoscopic scattering of merriment.

It was busier than it had been elsewhere in town, and a fair number of people were bustling around. Most were clutching a variety of shopping bags as they headed home or, for the lucky few, into one of the cafés or restaurants dotted along the route.

If it hadn't been for *absolutely everything else* going on in Andrew's life in that moment, he might actually have felt festive.

A particularly lurid flash of green suddenly caught his eye and Andrew spotted an illuminated cross in the window of a shop further up the street. 'I think I found the chemist.'

As they approached the shopfront, Andrew cast his eyes up and was pleased to see that lights were on in two of the three windows above the chemist. In itself, that didn't necessarily mean that anyone was home; Andrew knew that people left lamps switched on for all sorts of reasons when they left the house. However, the light in the window on the left flickered with a subtle colour change every few seconds or so, which made Andrew almost certain that there was a television on in that room; *that* would make it far more likely that the flat was currently occupied.

The entrance to the flat was a nondescript brown door with a plain rectangular window above it. It was to the left of the chemist and set back ever so slightly enough from the shop frontage to almost camouflage it from the casual glances of passersby. There was a brass forty-two screwed to the wall, and beneath that, someone had carefully written the name 'BELL' on a piece of card that had been taped inside the clear plastic base of the doorbell.

'Come and stand here, right next to the door,' Andrew instructed, stepping to the side so that Peggy could wedge into the narrow space beside him. 'Just in case this is who we're looking for, I don't want them to glance out of the window up there and decide that they're not answering the door to a pair of strangers.'

'Good idea,' Peggy agreed.

'Ready?'

On Peggy's nod, Andrew pressed the doorbell once and waited.

Almost immediately, another light was switched on inside and the window above the door glowed brighter.

A couple of seconds after that, the door was opened to reveal a smiling woman on the other side.

Andrew blinked hard, fighting the urge to shake his head and check that his eyes weren't playing tricks on him

Twenty years might have robbed her of the cherubic features and chestnut-brown hair of her youth, but the woman peering at Andrew and Peggy in polite confusion was, unmistakably, Lily Woodhouse.

FIFTEEN

Andrew would probably have to credit the wide-ranging spectrum of surprises he'd suffered since entering the Ballroom for giving him the ability to stand perfectly still when faced with someone he'd thought had likely died twenty years earlier.

At that thought, his stomach swooped violently. *Christ*, Lily Woodhouse wasn't actually dead, was she? She looked perfectly alive, if not a bit confused, but Andrew had also met Marnie.

No. No chance. There was absolutely no way that he was currently looking at a ghost.

Was there?

He really missed the days when he wouldn't have needed to even consider the possibility.

'Sorry, can I help you?' the impossible Lily Woodhouse asked courteously. Her voice was dry, and her words faded into a crackle.

Andrew fully deserved the sharp elbow to the ribs he received from Peggy.

'Hi, yes, sorry,' Andrew replied, coughing to clear his throat and his stupor. 'We're looking for Jane Bell. Is she available?'

Lily's demeanour shifted instantly. Really, it was only a marginal narrowing of her eyes, but Andrew took it for the clanging alarm bell it was.

'I'm afraid now isn't a good time,' Lily said, hand already moving towards the door handle again.

Andrew was reaching towards his pocket, ready to actually identify himself, when there was the sound of a door squeaking open at the top of the stairs.

'Who is it, Deb?' A woman called down from the landing before she appeared on the staircase a moment later.

For the second time in under a minute, Andrew was viciously struck by a jolt of disbelief. Even though he'd been anticipating – or at least strongly hoping – that he'd find Beth Nash here, it was still a shock to have the physical proof presented before his eyes.

'Detective Inspector Andrew Joyce, Greater Manchester Police,' he said, keeping his voice quiet so as to not alert anyone on the street behind him.

With a decade of meeting the victims of the most horrific crimes behind him, Andrew knew exactly what genuine terror looked like, and Lily's expression was a flawless example as she made to slam the door in his face.

Andrew was quicker. He threw out his arm to keep the door open. 'We're here because Bill Higson is missing.'

'Missing?' Beth gasped, clutching the bannister tightly.

'Can we come in, Mrs Nash?' Andrew asked quietly, before turning back to the younger woman. 'If you and Ms Woodhouse don't mind, of course.'

The fear on Lily's face drained away, leaving only an expression of pure disbelief as her mouth dropped open.

'Upstairs. Now. All of you,' Beth instructed sharply.

Lily immediately turned away and hurried up the stairs, squeezing past Beth and ducking out of sight when she reached the landing.

'Shut the door, Inspector,' Beth added shortly, before she followed Lily.

Andrew gestured for Peggy to enter the hallway and then pushed the door closed behind them.

They looked at each other at the foot of the stairs, and Andrew wondered if his face held the same measure of sheer astonishment as Peggy's.

He wouldn't bet against it.

They ascended the stairs, enveloped in warmth and the comforting scent of something roasting in an oven. Once they reached the landing, they took the door that Lily and Beth had disappeared through and found themselves in a small, tidy living room.

Andrew had the fleeting realisation that he'd been correct about the television being on as Beth crossed the room to switch it off with a loud click.

There was a Christmas tree in the opposite corner, with a handful of neatly wrapped presents sitting on the carpet beneath it. Framed photographs almost covered one wall, most of them featuring some combination of Beth, Lily, and a pair of children – one boy and one girl – who grew into teenagers and then young adults across the images.

Even though he'd only seen one photograph of a twenty-something Davy Nash, Andrew still could have told you that these were his children. They'd both inherited the same faintly mischievous smile, as well as their father's dark, wavy hair and bright green eyes.

'You might as well sit down,' Beth sighed, moving a stack of fashion and music magazines from the middle of a two-seater sofa, and indicating to Andrew and Peggy that they should take a seat.

Lily perched herself right at the edge of a rocking chair next to the fire, but she looked like she was ready to bolt at even the slightest provocation.

Beth appeared only marginally more settled as she slowly sank into the remaining armchair.

Andrew reached into his pocket for his identification and handed it to Beth before he clasped his hands together and leant forward. He knew that he was going to have to choose his words very carefully.

'Thank you for letting us into your home,' he started. 'As I said, my name's Andrew Joyce. I work with DCI Higson. This is Margaret Jones – *Peggy*; she's a consultant for our department.'

'A consultant?' Beth asked with a small frown.

'That's right,' Andrew confirmed, not wanting to explain any further at this juncture. He was certain that Peggy would be in the same mind as him on that one. They both knew all too well how an explanation of Peggy's presence could entirely derail a conversation, and they really didn't have time for any diversion. 'Peggy brings a unique perspective to our investigations, and she's worked closely with DCI Higson for as long as I have.'

Just as he'd hoped it would, that statement succeeded in reducing Beth's obvious suspicion ever so slightly.

'How did you find us?' Beth sounded genuinely curious. 'I didn't think that even Bill knew where we'd ended up.'

Andrew swallowed down the gasp of surprise that tried to escape at Beth's words: *Bill knew where we'd ended up.* Had Higson really known that Lily was with Beth the entire time? He was going to have to save that question for a more appropriate moment, however, because Beth was still awaiting an answer.

'He didn't,' Andrew confirmed. 'I knew he'd recently been looking into the case file concerning the disappearance of Ms Woodhouse here, along with your husband, Mrs Nash.'

Beth's face crumpled at the mention of Davy, and it took her a couple of seconds to compose herself again. '*Oh.*'

'Then how did you know where we were?' Lily asked, looking no less fearful than she had downstairs. 'We've always been so careful.'

'When we became concerned about DCI Higson's whereabouts yesterday, we visited his house,' Andrew explained, hoping that if he kept his tone as professional and impersonal as possible it might help everyone. 'We spoke to his wife-'

'Annie?' Beth blurted.

Andrew nodded. 'Annie told us about how she and Bill had brought you and your children to the Lake District, and that you sent them a Christmas card the following year to give them your new address.'

Beth looked up at the ceiling, eyes filling with tears. 'I know I wasn't supposed to do that. I'd promised Bill that I wouldn't, but I couldn't bear the thought of losing even more people from my life *before*. I'd always wondered if they received the card, because I never heard back.'

'Annie only briefly saw the card, but yesterday she thought that she'd remembered one line of the address,' Andrew added. 'This morning, we went to Staveshead. We eventually spoke to your old manager at the hotel there, and she told us that she hadn't spoken to you since you left, but she still had a copy of the letter where you'd asked that she forward your final payment to Enid Wetherall in Bowness. We asked around about her, and we were told that Jane Bell was close with Enid before she died.'

'No, that can't be true! Nobody here would talk to you about Enid!' Lily said, suddenly argumentative, voice cracking even more than it had downstairs. 'She promised Beth and I that nobody would ever find us with her looking out for us. When she died, her family turned out to be a bunch of arseholes who just wanted her money, but everyone round here loves Enid, so there's no way one of them would tell two complete strangers anything about her.'

Andrew shook his head. 'Ms Woodhouse, I understand that us arriving here must be a huge shock to you, but I promise you that everything I just said is true.'

'Who did you speak to?' Beth asked, less confrontational but still visibly unsettled that they'd been tracked down from the barest clues possible.

'I spoke to someone in the chocolate shop,' Peggy explained quietly, at which point Andrew realised that he was still holding the chocolate snowflakes. 'She told me that Enid had died, which is how I ended up at St Martin's.'

'That bloody vicar!' Lily hissed, staring at her slippers.

Andrew replayed what Beth had said to him a few moments ago. 'Beth, did you say that you never heard back from the Higsons at all?'

Beth shook her head.

'You haven't seen or spoken to DCI Higson since he dropped you and your children off?'

'Only the once,' Beth replied. 'A month or so after he and Annie brought us up here, he arrived in the middle of the night – scared the living daylights out of me, knocking on the door at almost three in the morning – and he had Lily with him. He begged me to keep her safe until she'd recovered, but not much else. He was in a right state, Inspector. He told me that even Annie didn't even know that he'd brought Lily to me.'

Andrew ran a hand over his chin trying to process what he'd been told, but his brain just kept misfiring when it attempted to reconcile the fact that Higson had somehow located Lily Woodhouse and brought her to *Beth Nash* of all people; the very woman whose husband Lily had apparently been having an affair with.

Beth looked at him shrewdly. 'You didn't know Lily was here, did you?'

Well, there was no point lying about it now. 'No, we didn't.'

'Shit,' Lily hissed, no doubt berating herself for answering the door.

'We only came here because we were hoping to find out if DCI Higson had been in contact with you recently,' Andrew explained to Beth. 'And hoping that you might know *why* he's disappeared while he's been looking into this case. *And* – I'm only telling you this because you'll find out soon enough from the news anyway – because DCI Higson has been named as a suspect in the murder of a former police officer.'

'Who was it?' Beth snapped, sharper than she had been since they'd arrived at her door. 'What was his name?'

'Sean Kelly,' Andrew replied.

Lily let out a startled sob and flinched so violently that Andrew thought she might be about to pitch to the floor.

Beth was on her feet and had her arm around Lily before Andrew could so much as blink again. He cast a quick glance at Peggy, who looked as flummoxed by everything as Andrew felt.

'Anything?' he whispered, taking advantage of the commotion.

Peggy shook her head quickly. It didn't look like Beth Nash was being haunted by her husband then.

'Is this because of me?' Lily asked Beth in a shaky voice.

Andrew cleared his throat as courteously as possible. 'Ms Woodhouse, I can see that this is very difficult for you, but *please*, could you tell us what happened?'

Lily shook her head. 'I don't want to talk about it. I swore I'd never talk about it again.'

The pain in Lily's voice was genuine, and Andrew truly wished that he wouldn't have to push it further, but if he was going to have a hope in hell of working out what was going on with Higson, he needed to understand the sequence of events that had led Beth Nash and Lily Woodhouse to a flat in Bowness.

'I know you don't want to talk about it,' Andrew replied, and he tried to soften his voice the way Peggy had when she'd spoken to the little girl at the school. 'I understand that.'

'No, you don't!' Lily snapped, swiping at her eyes as Beth returned to her seat. 'Nobody can understand what I went through. What *we* went through.'

Andrew nodded slowly, trying to tamp down the frustration that was trying to strangle his words into barbed retorts; it wouldn't be fair to berate Lily for being scared to speak to him. 'You're right, I don't understand what you went through, because Higson never told me. He never told *anyone* about what happened on the night you and Davy Nash disappeared, but now my boss is missing, and I think it has everything to do with that night. Please understand that I need to find him before yet another terrible thing happens.'

'Lil,' Beth said, so quietly that Andrew would have missed it if there'd been any other sound in the room at all. 'I think you should tell them what happened.'

Lily looked at Beth as though she'd committed the cruellest of betrayals.

'I know you're scared, love,' Beth continued. 'So am I, but Bill helped us both so much. He saved your life, Lil, you know he did. And he saved mine; Jules' and Anthony's too.'

Lily's whole body was trembling, and she covered her face with both hands as she took in great gulping breaths.

Andrew shifted his feet, preparing himself to try and convince Lily to speak, but just as he opened his mouth, Peggy brushed his wrist with her little finger, just once. It was the barest of touches, but he heard the message loud and clear anyway: *shut up*.

Lily's hands fell into her lap, and she kept her eyes on them as her fingers curled and uncurled frenetically against her jeans. 'I didn't actually want to be famous.'

Andrew nearly sighed in relief when Lily began speaking, but he held his breath for fear of spooking her back into silence.

'I only went on that stupid show because I knew how much it would piss off my parents,' Lily continued quietly. 'I'd been out in town with some friends and a man from the production came over to us; he said he was scouting for contestants. He asked me if I could sing or dance, and I told him that I couldn't. He said it wouldn't matter much, because I had the face for TV.'

Lily sighed loudly. 'It was stupid, but I was flattered by the attention. My friends convinced me that I should do my party trick for him though; so, I did. I told him to write something down on a piece of paper – anything he wanted – and then put it in his pocket. I told him that I'd be able to tell him what he'd written. He laughed and clearly didn't believe a word I'd said, but he was up for it anyway. By the time I'd 'guessed' correctly four or five times, he told me that if I did that on TV, he was sure I'd be a star.

'So, I went to the audition a week later and they told me then and there that they wanted me on the show. They asked and asked how I was doing it, but I just told them what I always told people when they asked: I had a *gift* for it.'

Peggy twitched beside him, pulling the cuffs of her coat sleeves down over her fingers. Lily's bitter words had obviously touched a nerve.

'When I won, I kept getting invited to parties and things,' Lily added. 'I was out in town all the time, and I thought it was brilliant; my friends loved it too, at first. People wanted to buy us drinks wherever we went – they didn't care that we were all only sixteen and seventeen. God, actually, Liv must've only been fourteen when it started – and one night, we were at the Midland, I think, when we met Jimmy Prentice.'

Lily screwed her eyes shut, and Andrew could see how hard she was digging her fingernails into the flesh of her palms.

'The night we met, he'd have been older than I am now,' Lily's voice shook even more violently. 'I was only seventeen, and too stupid – too *naïve* – to see what he was really like underneath it all.'

'You were still a child, Lily,' Peggy said softly, and Andrew was surprised to hear her speak. She very rarely got involved when Andrew was questioning someone.

He recognised Peggy's words though. She'd cut Andrew off with an almost identical interjection when he'd been explaining what had happened to his brother while still blaming himself for all of it.

Lily glanced over at the sofa in surprise, and it was as though she'd forgotten that she wasn't actually alone. She looked at Peggy searchingly but eventually seemed to accept the comment as acceptable with the smallest tilt of her chin.

'I should still have known better than to get involved with him. The thing was, he knew everybody, and I do mean *everybody*,' Lily continued. 'He told me that he was one of the best detectives in Manchester, and so that meant that important people trusted him to look after them when they were in the city. He'd take me out for dinner with the sort of people that I'd only ever seen in magazines or heard on the radio, and as the summer went on, I stopped bringing my friends along.

'They told me that I shouldn't be carrying on with someone like him, but I thought that they were just jealous of all the things that they didn't get to do, and so I told them as much. I found myself without friends pretty damn quickly which, I realised afterwards, is exactly what he'd wanted; he'd wanted to isolate me from anyone he thought might realise that me being a pretty young thing wasn't at all why he was interested in me. He didn't want anyone who cared about me to actually see the real reason that he wanted to keep me around.'

'Which was what?' Andrew asked.

Lily shot him the barest imitation of a smile, and it looked like it hurt. 'I told you already, Inspector Joyce. I had a *gift*.'

Someone out on Ash Street laughed loudly, and Lily flinched, shrinking back into herself.

Andrew turned his head slightly to give Peggy a meaningful look that he hoped telegraphed that he'd really appreciate her trying out her much more delicate approach here. Peggy looked supremely doubtful, but Andrew took the single slow nod she gave him as she pushed her cuffs back up to her wrists again as silent agreement that she'd at least have a go.

'Lily,' Peggy said gently, 'what did Prentice want you to do?'

'What? Apart from the obvious?' Lily snapped bitterly, but then she took another terribly deep breath and gave Peggy an apologetic quirk of her lips. 'Sorry.'

Peggy earnestly batted the apology away immediately. 'Don't

worry about it.'

'When I first met Prentice – *Jimmy* – he wanted to know about my act on the show. I think, at first, he really was just winding me up. He was always spiteful,' Lily continued after a long moment of loaded silence. 'He told me that he'd seen me on TV, and it had been driving him mad trying to work out how I could get the right answer every single time. He didn't seem very happy when I brushed him off and gave him the usual line, but then he told me that he wanted me to prove it to him, just like that TV man had wanted. So, I did.

'Eventually, months later, when I'd been spending my evenings with nobody but him, he explained to me how he thought I'd been given this gift so that I could do something remarkable with it; something significantly more remarkable than using it to win a tacky TV talent show. He said I'd be able to help people.'

'Help people?' Peggy hadn't raised her voice, but Andrew could hear how her tone had sharpened.

'*Really* help people, he said,' Lily explained, once again flexing her fingers repetitively. 'He said that I could help him put criminals behind bars, you know? He said that all I had to do was come along to some meetings with him and his detective friends and just listen to everything; use my 'little magic trick' to tell him things that these people didn't want him to know about.

'He made it all sound like he was the hero of the piece, right? He'd take me out to dinner, and then we'd end up in some scabby backroom or alleyway somewhere; and afterwards he'd want to know what had been said when he'd been out of earshot, that sort of thing. Or he'd want to know what was going on behind a closed door. Then we'd go out dancing as though none of it had ever happened. I realised quite quickly that all he was doing was looking for blackmail material. Him and his *friends*.'

Andrew didn't think that he'd ever heard someone put so much ire into one word before.

'Sean Kelly and Frank Jackson,' Lily clarified even as her face paled even further. 'In a lot of ways, they were even worse than *he* was. They were always hanging around me if Jimmy left to go and talk to someone, or something like that. Kelly was the worst; he used to look at me and just stare with his awful dead eyes whenever Jimmy wasn't around.

'They all worked together, you know. Apparently, it was this weird department where they weren't supposed to discount weird stuff – like me, I suppose – but all Jimmy and the others seemed to do was drive around in his stupid car, intimidating the sorts of people that everyone else would be intimidated *by*. And I saw all of it; I *helped* them.'

Andrew was very careful not to react in any way to Lily's oblique reference to the Ballroom; he didn't think that just then was the appropriate moment to inform her that he and Peggy were from the very same department that Jimmy Prentice had once been in charge of.

Lily wasn't looking at him anyway. She'd turned away to face Beth and was shaking her head over and over again in denial.

'It's alright,' Beth choked out, holding out her hand for Lily to grasp it tightly. 'You want to talk about it about as much as I want to hear it, but we'll get through it, won't we? We always have.'

Next to Andrew, Peggy made a funny little breathy noise, but before he could ask her what the problem was, Lily started speaking again.

'One night – *that* night – Jimmy said he was taking me to the ballet. He picked me up from the house of this girl I was staying with, and he didn't have Kelly or Jackson with him. I was so relieved about that, and thought that maybe we actually *were* just going out together, you know?

'We drove to the Free Trade Hall and sat together, but he left almost as soon as the show had started – I think he was meeting someone. I didn't seem him again until the end of the interval, and he told me that we were leaving to go to a party.'

'But there was no party?' Andrew prompted when Lily trailed off.

She shook her head again. 'No. We ended up parking near the cathedral and he said we were walking the last bit. He refused to tell me where we were going, and I remember he had his fingers wrapped really tightly around my arm, like he thought I might try and make a break for it if he wasn't actually holding on to me. We were probably walking for less than a minute, and then he stopped outside a sweet shop.'

Andrew recalled that Annie Higson had told him that on the night Davy disappeared, Higson and Chris Benson had been in the Hanging Bridge pub, which was right next to the cathedral. 'Can you remember where the shop was?'

'It was in a little row of shops that ran along the canal side of Deansgate; it was the second shop in from the bridge that crosses over the river,' Lily said, nodding once. 'I can't remember what the bridge is called. Do you know where I mean though? The train station is right in front of you on the other side.'

Andrew tried to visualise the part of the city Lily was referring to. He could pinpoint the cathedral, and Lily was likely talking about Exchange Station, which would still have been operating at the tail end of the sixties. He couldn't for the life of him envisage a row of shops though; he supposed it had been twenty years, and lots of the city's decaying buildings had been demolished in the preceding decade or so. He gave Lily a half nod to let her know that she should keep going with the story.

'It must have been nearly nine o'clock by then, so the shop obviously wasn't open. That wasn't that weird, I suppose, because Jimmy had taken me along to loads of after-hours meetings in all sorts of places. What *was* weird, though, was that there weren't any lights on inside and the place was completely locked up.

'I thought we must be waiting for someone who was turning up late – Jimmy hated it when people were late – but then he just took a key out of his jacket pocket and unlocked the door like he owned the place.'

Lily drew her knees up to her chin, wrapping her arms around her legs as she slid backwards on the rocking chair, steadying herself when the chair momentarily tipped forwards. 'It was so dark in there, but he didn't turn on the light. It was like he knew the shop well enough that he wasn't worried about crashing into anything in the dark. I couldn't see though, and I tripped over something and hit my elbow really hard on the wooden counter at the back. Jimmy got so cross with me for making a racket, and then he dragged me into this little room and closed the door behind us.

'He finally switched a light on, but it was barely bright enough to see anything. He went over to this box, and when he opened it, it was just full of torches. He handed one to me and then took one for himself. I wanted to ask what the hell we needed torches for, but my arm was smarting so much, and he was in such a foul mood as it was, that I just kept my mouth shut.

'In the corner, there were these big sacks, and it was only when Jimmy yelled at me to come and help him move them that I realised they were sandbags. When we eventually got them out of the way, I could see that they were covering a hatch with a big brass ring, you know, like a trap door.'

Andrew didn't have fond memories of the last time he'd had to drop through a trap door – into a gloomy space beneath a stage, where he'd been trying to apprehend a suspect, all while trying not to get himself killed by a spirit who'd had it out for him – and he shuddered at the unwelcome recollection.

'I didn't want to go down there, but I didn't have a choice, did I?' Lily continued, and even though she was looking in Andrew's direction again, her eyes were unfocused, and he knew that she was seeing straight through him and into that sweet shop twenty years earlier. 'There were these really rickety steps, and I was terrified the whole way down that they were rotten enough to collapse beneath me.

'At the bottom, I thought we were just in a cellar at first, but then when we switched on the torches, I realised that it was a much bigger space than that. It was horrible down there; it was warmer than it should have been, and the air was damp. The whole place smelled like something had died and all I knew was that I had to get out of there as quickly as I could.'

Lily shivered violently and buried her head in her knees, muffling her already quiet voice even further. 'He grabbed my arm again and made me walk forwards out of there and into this sort of tunnel. I had to shine the torch in front of me to see where I was going, and I could hear rats running across all the rubbish even when I couldn't see them.

'Jimmy kept going on about how they'd built all of these arches about a hundred years earlier and they'd had little businesses in them, and that you'd even have been able to take a boat down the river before they'd bricked up the exits. He told me that they'd used down there for a massive shelter in the war, but that they'd closed it all up again afterwards.

'We walked for a few minutes but then Jimmy stopped again and told me that we were waiting for Kelly and Jackson to arrive. Maybe I should have just run at that point – being in crowded places with those bastards was terrifying enough, but I didn't even dare think about what might happen when we were entirely out of sight.'

Something cold crawled down Andrew's spine at Lily's words, chilling him entirely and raising the hairs on his arms even beneath three layers of clothing.

'When they arrived a little while later, they both had big duffle bags with them. I didn't know it then, but they were full of tools:

shovels, crowbars, that sort of thing. Kelly was making all these comments about the dress I was wearing, and it wound Jimmy up enough that he gave Kelly a punch right in the face for his troubles.

'It was then that Jimmy told me that they wanted me to find something for them. He wouldn't listen to me when I told them that it didn't work that way.' Lily looked up at them. 'They all just keep shouting at me, calling me all these disgusting names, and they wouldn't believe me when I tried to tell them how it *did* work. They kept just saying it was that I *wouldn't* do it for them, not that I *couldn't*, like I was claiming.

'And then –' Lily blew a harsh breath out between her lips and then suddenly she was looking right at Andrew again, fixing him with an almost challenging stare. 'And then Kelly lunged at me and grabbed me by the neck. He just squeezed harder and harder, even though I could just about hear the other two telling him to stop. I couldn't breathe and-'

Lily sobbed and brought her own hands up to claw at her neck.

'Lily, sweetheart, stop,' Beth said gently but firmly as she once more went and put her arms around Lily, the very picture of motherly concern. Even though there was less than a decade between the two of them, Beth clearly had taken Lily in as though she were her own daughter.

'Why don't I make you both a cup of tea?' Peggy suggested quietly as she rose from the sofa. She barely glanced at Andrew, nor did she wait for a response from anyone else before she left the room without another word.

Andrew was very aware that Davy Nash hadn't yet featured in the story, nor had Higson, but he wasn't going to push Lily to speak more quickly than she was comfortable with. Listening to her reminded him awfully of when Marnie had finally been able to tell them what had happened to her in the moments leading to her death. Even though Lily was living and breathing only feet from him, Andrew still felt like he'd just heard someone describe their own complete destruction.

'Come on, Lil,' Beth whispered into Lily's shoulder, and it was clear that she was crying too. 'Nearly there.'

For a good few minutes, the only sounds were the quiet sniffling from the rocking chair and the occasional quiet clank of something in the kitchen, but eventually Lily gently pushed Beth away from her again.

'I'm alright,' Lily mumbled. She looked at Andrew again, eyes ringed red and swollen. 'Sorry.'

'Don't apologise,' Andrew replied, just as he'd done to Peggy earlier. He shook his head vehemently when Lily looked unconvinced. 'You have nothing to apologise for.'

'I thought I was going to die,' Lily whispered. 'I blacked out, and when I woke up, I was alone; I think they must have thought Kelly had gone too far and actually strangled me to death. I could barely breathe, and I couldn't see a thing, but somehow, I got to my feet and managed to stumble away from where they'd left me. I found the wall with my hands, and it was covered in God knows what, but it gave me a guide even if I didn't know if I was going the right way.

'Eventually, I saw a small light in the distance. I pressed myself against the wall and tried to hide, and it took me a long time to understand that the light wasn't moving. I carried on going, and I saw that it was a torch, lying on the ground like it had been dropped. I picked it up and switched it off – I didn't know if Jimmy or the others were planning on coming back, and I was terrified that someone would realise I was there – and I just kept going. I didn't get very far before that horrible smell from earlier came back, and I thought I might have finally made it to that first space we'd gone into. I thought I heard a bell ringing, you know, chiming the hour – I couldn't have told you what time it was back then, but I know now that it was eleven o'clock. I tried to move faster, hoping that being able to hear the bells meant that the door was open, but then I tripped over something in the dark.'

Beth made a strangled sound and pressed her hand to her mouth and Andrew's heart sank with the prescient knowledge of what Lily was about to say.

'It was Davy.' Lily squeezed her eyes shut and Andrew almost did the same. 'I didn't know that it was him at the time. Despite what the newspapers said about me afterwards, I'd *never* met him, Inspector. We think that he must have seen something happening in the shop and came to investigate. When I fell, he'd made a little sound, so I'd known that I had to look, even if I didn't want to. I switched the torch back on, and it was awful. It was so awful.

'His whole face was covered in blood and there was a shovel on the floor next to him, beside one of those bags they'd had earlier, so it *had* to have been one of those bastards that did it to him.'

Andrew swallowed heavily. 'So, Davy was alive when you found him?'

'Barely,' Lily confirmed, her whole face crumpling around her words. 'I tried to speak to him, to tell him that I was going to try and get some help, but I couldn't get any sound out. He had a jacket on the floor next to him, and there were some keys and money in the pocket, which I left, but there was a card in there too, tucked safely inside, and that's how I knew who he was – David Nash, a constable in the City Police.

'I already knew what Jimmy and the others were like, but I don't think I'd ever imagined that they'd do that to a policeman. I was terrified that nobody would believe me if I managed to get out, so I took Davy's identification and made my way back up those stairs and into the sweet shop. They'd left the hatch open, so I knew that they were going to be back soon enough. The lights were off, but I made it up the stairs and out into the shop. There was nobody there.'

Footsteps drew closer, and Andrew knew that Peggy was on her way back.

'Jimmy had locked the door though,' Lily continued as Peggy paused in the doorway, eyes trained on the carpet. 'It was okay though, I could see headlights up the road, so I thought I'd be able to bang on the window and let someone know I was there. But the car...'

'It was Prentice?' Andrew prompted when Lily trailed off again.

Lily nodded. 'Thank God he had that stupid car, because I recognised it immediately. I couldn't bear the thought of going back down into the Arches, so I took a chance that he wouldn't turn the light on in the shop and I hid behind the counter; I tucked myself right beneath it and prayed to anyone or anything that would listen to me to get me out of there.'

Logically, Andrew knew that Lily had got out of there, but he couldn't ignore the wave of anxiety that washed over him just listening to what had happened.

'I heard the door unlock and the bell ring, and then the three of them came in together. They were arguing, and Jimmy was swearing at Kelly and threatening to kill him later, *after* they'd got rid of their problems.' Lily was trembling again. 'They went back down the stairs and I waited until I thought they were far enough away and then I just ran out of there as quietly as I could. I didn't even dare stop to close the door behind me, and I ran across the road. Maybe I was going to try and get to the cathedral – I don't know, maybe I thought that someone there would protect me – but I didn't get there.

'I'd just reached the other side of the road when this man stopped me and asked me if I was alright. I would have screamed at him if I could have made a sound, but even as I tried to get away from him, he just wanted to calm me down.' Lily swiped at her eyes. 'He looked over the road to where Jimmy's car was parked and he pointed at it, asking me if I knew who the car belonged to. I think that was when he realised that there was blood on my dress, because his whole face changed again, and I would have been terrified if I hadn't just *known* that the expression on his face was for Prentice, not me.

'He told me that his name was Bill.'

And so that was Higson's entrance into Lily's story.

'He asked me if the man who owned the car had hurt me, and I don't even know what I tried to tell him. I remember I just shoved Davy's card at him and tried to make him understand that he needed to get help for him. He looked at it in my hand and it was like he didn't even see it – he just nodded once and then told me that we needed to leave, and that he'd make sure I was safe first, and that he'd come back to help *Davy*. He knew to call him Davy, not David, and maybe that's what told me I should trust him. He gave me his coat.'

Jesus Christ. Andrew couldn't imagine what it must have been like for Higson to have been presented with an impossible choice that night: get this seriously injured, traumatised teenage girl to safety, or leave her behind to go and help his friend.

'He moved us quickly away from the street and then knocked on the door of what turned out to be a pub,' Lily continued. 'The publican answered, and he wasn't happy to see Bill, but then he saw me, and he let us in straight away. Bill made him lock the door and then handed me a notepad and a pencil, and he told me to write down what had happened to Davy and where to find him.

'It took me ages, because my hands were shaking so much, but he never once shouted at me or tried to get me to hurry up. He left when I'd managed to write something legible, and he told the publican not to open the door for anyone until he got back, and to keep an eye on me. He didn't even tell me he was a sergeant in the police until much later; I think he knew that I wouldn't have wanted his help if he had.'

At that point, Peggy soundlessly moved into the room carrying two mugs. She looked completely shellshocked, but given what she'd just heard, Andrew wasn't surprised.

'Sorry,' Peggy said, almost as quietly as Lily had been speaking. 'I didn't know how you liked your tea, but I thought sweet and milky might be best.'

Lily and Beth accepted the mugs with quiet thanks, and Peggy headed back towards Andrew. The look she shot him before she sat down was so full of meaning it was practically a conversation in itself, and Andrew was surprised by how easily he interpreted just what it meant.

With a deep breath, Andrew looked over to Lily and clasped his hands together under his chin, knowing that the inevitable derailment was about to occur after all.

'Ms Woodhouse, you said earlier that Prentice and the others wouldn't believe you when you told them how you just *knew* things,' he said, choosing his words even more carefully than when he'd started this whole interview. 'Do you think you could explain it to me and Peggy?'

Lily looked confused by Andrew's question when they were all aware that she hadn't reached the end of the story yet.

'It's important,' Andrew added. 'I promise I wouldn't have asked if it wasn't.'

Lily dropped her chin to her chest. 'There's no point. You won't believe me, nobody ever does.'

'You'd be surprised,' Andrew replied, and nobody could have been more astonished than he was that he was *inviting* the sort of answer that he wouldn't have even dreamed of entertaining the day he'd arrived on Tib Street, nor for many, *many* days afterwards too.

'My sister told me,' Lily replied and then watched Andrew carefully to gauge his reaction.

Sister. Andrew thought back over that damn file he'd read so many times. 'Your twin sister, Violet. Okay. Tell us more.'

To say that Lily looked entirely stunned by Andrew's response would have been grossly underselling the surprise on her face at the immediate acceptance. Andrew might have looked a bit stunned himself.

'Violet died when we were kids,' Lily added softly. 'How…?'

Andrew turned to face the only person he could trust to stop the derailment from becoming a flaming train wreck. 'Peggy? Why don't you explain?'

SIXTEEN

While Peggy understood Andrew's reasoning for asking her to take over the conversation, and appreciated his obvious show of faith, it still felt a little bit like being thrown under the bus.

Peggy had heard Lily refer to the 'weird' department that Prentice had led in the sixties, but she definitely *hadn't* heard Andrew make it known that he and Peggy now represented the very same place. She was fairly certain that Lily wouldn't take the news well, even if Peggy assured her that the current Ballroom team couldn't possibly be any more different than the men who'd ruined her life.

With Beth and Lily looking at her inquisitively, Peggy settled her hands in her lap and tried not to fidget. 'We have some experience in dealing with the cases that might seem *unusual* to most people. I first came to work with Inspector Joyce and DCI Higson when they were investigating the murder of a young woman; it was a case that had been filed away as unsolved due to a lack of evidence, and so it was passed over to DCI Higson's department to take a look from a different perspective.'

'What sort of perspective?' Beth asked.

'Well…' Peggy paused briefly to collect her thoughts, and to allow herself one second to imagine how she was going to kill Andrew once they got outside. 'I was asked to consult on the case because DCI Higson wanted someone to try and ask the victim what had happened to her.'

Beth looked perplexed, but it wasn't Beth that Peggy was concerned about.

Lily's eyes widened in outrage. 'Are you taking the mick out of me?'

'I assure you that I'm not,' Peggy replied, keeping her voice light and even.

'Yes, you are!' Lily shrieked, waving her arms and splashing tea on the carpet. 'Yes, you are!'

Andrew shifted beside her, and Peggy held her hand up in a silent plea to keep quiet. She didn't need him to jump in now, not when she was perfectly capable of handling the situation, thanks all the same.

'I'm not, Lily,' Peggy argued quietly. 'I would never do that, not only because I know exactly what it's like to have people refuse to believe you about something like this.'

Peggy had the perfect example of 'people' sitting right next to her. Granted, Andrew believed her *now*, but when they'd first met, he'd been the most cynical person she'd ever encountered.

'I can tell you that Violet's worried about you,' Peggy added, as the little girl in question hovered uncertainly in the doorway, her big brown eyes as surprised as they were when Peggy had first spoken to her in the kitchen.

Apparently, that was the wrong thing to say, because Lily leapt to her feet, utterly incensed. 'You can't tell me *anything* about Violet! She left me that night!'

Peggy shook her head. 'She didn't. I swear to you that she didn't. She's still here, even though you can't see her anymore.'

Lily was shaking her head wildly, and Peggy was genuinely concerned that the other woman was going to scarper from the room at any second. Violet looked like she might be having similar thoughts.

'Lily, I can prove it to you,' Peggy said calmly, as though she wasn't at all genuinely concerned that Lily might lunge at her in a burst of rage. 'Ask me something that only Violet would know.'

'No! Stop it!' Lily cried. 'You're lying!'

'She's not,' Andrew said firmly.

'Well, you would say that, wouldn't you!' Lily rounded on Andrew, and Peggy was grateful for the momentary reprieve from Lily's ire.

'Why would you say such a thing?' Beth asked. She spoke quietly, but there was a distinct air of judgement in her eyes.

'Because it's the truth,' Peggy replied simply.

'I don't have to listen to this!' Lily announced, making her way towards the door.

'Peggy!' Andrew's tone was sharpened by desperation.

Peggy looked directly at Violet, who was watching her sister stalk towards where she stood. 'Tell me something only Lily would know.'

Violet looked startled at being addressed again, as though she'd thought that what had happened in the kitchen had been an anomaly.

'Violet, please!' Peggy added, closing her eyes and hoping that she'd get a reply, and that she'd hear it if she did.

When Violet spoke again, it was barely audible. It wasn't as difficult as trying to talk to Rob Joyce, but it wasn't far removed.

'You had a cat called Midnight!' Peggy announced, not feeling as triumphant as she sounded. It wasn't exactly the sibling-guarded secret she'd been hoping for.

Lily didn't pause, and Peggy heard her footsteps on the stairs. This was bad. She shot Violet a look of panic as she rose from the sofa and followed Lily out of the room.

'A couple of days before Violet died, you had a picnic on the beach!' Peggy practically shrieked as Lily reached the front door and began aggressively stuffing her feet into a pair of shoes; she was still clutching her mug tightly in her left hand. 'Violet was annoyed with you because you stole a biscuit from her.'

Lily paused and whipped her head towards where Peggy stood halfway down the steps.

Oh, thank God. Peggy took a deep breath and tried to listen to Violet, hoping that she'd hurry up a bit even as she fully understood that this must be a fairly traumatic event for her too.

'Jammie Dodgers!' Peggy blurted out, holding out her hands towards Lily and begging for just a bit more time. 'You were only allowed them on holidays, and your mum had packed six of them in with the rest of your lunch; one each for her and your dad, and two each for you and Violet. Violet went for a paddle in the sea by herself, and when she came back, you'd eaten the last of her two biscuits. She says she knew it was you, even though you tried to tell her a seagull had taken it.'

Lily reeled backwards as violently as if Peggy had slapped her, and she cracked the back of her head on the door.

'No,' Lily whispered, shaking her head again. 'Someone else told you that.'

'*Who*, Lily?' Peggy asked, whispering herself.

'Someone!' Lily shrieked, pulling on her hair with her free hand as she slid down the door to end up a heap on the welcome mat.

Peggy carefully sat down where she was on the staircase. She looked back up to the landing to see Andrew and Beth watching both her and Lily in concern and tilted her head in a clear request for them to give them both some space, before shifting her focus back to Lily

When she heard them leave, she rested her chin in her hands and just waited.

She wasn't sure how much time passed, but the chink of sky visible through the window above the door had darkened even further by the time Lily raised her head and looked directly at Peggy. Her cheeks were flushed pink even though the rest of her face was a deathly pallor.

'Is Violet still here?' Lily asked quietly.

'She is.'

'Why didn't she want to speak to me anymore after what happened?' Lily asked, and she didn't sound like a woman in her late thirties, nor the teenager she'd been when she'd had her life upended, but like a miserable child. 'Can you ask her that?'

'She can hear you, Lily,' Peggy replied. 'It's just that you can't hear *her* anymore. Violet never left you. She says that she stayed with you when you blacked out, but when you woke up again you kept asking for her to come back, as if she wasn't there at all.'

'Because she wasn't!' Lily choked out.

'She was, Lily.' Peggy closed her eyes and concentrated. 'She said that she was calling out to you, but you didn't seem to be able to hear her anymore. She wants you to know that she never left you.'

'That means that he took her from me as well, doesn't it?' Lily sobbed loudly and buried her head in her knees again.

Peggy thought that punching something might make her feel better, or at least just release some of the anger she could feel curling around her sorrow for Lily and her sister.

'Let me get Beth for you,' she said instead as she stood slowly.

She crept back up the stairs as noiselessly as she could manage, terrified with each step that she'd spook Lily into trying to leave again.

When she looked around the door into the living room it was to find Beth and Andrew talking quietly as they sat together on the sofa.

Andrew glanced over. 'Everything okay?'

Peggy nodded. 'Beth, I think Lily might appreciate seeing you right now.'

As Beth walked past her, she reached out and lightly wrapped her fingers around Peggy's wrist. 'Is Davy here?'

'I'm sorry.'

The flicker of hope in Beth's expression was extinguished immediately, but she still gave Peggy a watery smile and squeezed her arm for a moment before she brushed past her in search of Lily.

Peggy closed her eyes and slowly breathed in and out a few times. She could still just about hear Violet crying quietly on the stairs.

'Peggy?'

Her eyes snapped open to find Andrew standing right in front of her.

'Are you alright?' he asked quietly, concern evident.

Peggy gave him the barest nod of her head and then walked over to the window to look down at the street below, rubbing her arms to stave off a sudden chill. The restaurant across the road had filled up since they'd arrived, full of laughing, smiling patrons sitting only a few feet away, completely unaware of anything going on in this little flat above the chemist.

'Beth told me what happened to Lily after Higson took her to that pub,' Andrew said from somewhere behind her.

Peggy appreciated the shift in topic, content to let someone else talk, and turned round so that he knew he had her attention.

'The pub – the Hanging Bridge, just like Annie remembered, by the way – had been a haunt of Higson's for years, and Beth said that wasn't the first night that he'd turned up after closing time with some poor soul who needed help,' Andrew continued. 'Beth says that Lily doesn't really know what Higson did after he left the pub, but he briefly popped back in not long after he left before disappearing again for hours. He'd found a doctor to check over Lily.'

Peggy frowned. 'Higson found a doctor?'

'Yeah. Sounds like he went and hammered on the door of a retired doctor who owed him a long list of favours and dragged him to Lily, without any specifics, of course,' Andrew replied with a shrug. 'The doctor told Lily that she was lucky that she'd passed out as quickly as she had, otherwise Kelly might have held on longer and done even more damage to her.'

'*Lucky?*' Peggy's stomach churned.

Andrew held up his hands. 'I know.'

Peggy pressed the heels of her hands against her eyes. 'For twenty years Higson's known that Davy was dead, and that Lily was hidden away up here. Why didn't he report what had happened to Lily that night? Or to Davy? He was his *friend*!'

She heard Andrew sigh loudly. 'I don't know that, Peggy. Beth told me that Higson didn't tell her that he was certain Davy was dead until just before he brought her and the kids up here. She had to swear that she'd keep quiet about her husband's death, and I don't think that Higson would have asked her to do something so awful if he didn't have his reasons. As soon as we find him, we'll ask him what those reasons were.'

Peggy dropped her hands. 'After hearing what happened to Lily, are you still certain that Higson didn't kill Sean Kelly in vengeance?'

Andrew nodded slowly. 'Higson's a piece of work when he wants to be, but I can't see him doing something like that, especially not two decades later.'

'Neither can I,' Peggy agreed quietly as she scrubbed her hands over her face. 'Sorry, you were telling me what happened to Lily.'

'Higson took her to his mother's house.'

Peggy's whole body went slack in surprise. 'He did what?'

'He didn't dare take her back to his own house,' Andrew explained. 'Not with Annie and his kids there, and so he took her to his mother's house. Lily stayed there for a couple of months before Higson brought her to Beth.'

Peggy had a whole ream of questions she wanted to ask, but all queries were cut off as Beth and Lily came back into the living room, both looking a bit worse for wear.

Lily shot Peggy a tremulous quirk of her lips as she took up her perch in the rocking chair again. 'Sorry for shouting at you.'

Peggy shook her head and sat down on the sofa.

'Can I ask you why you left Staveshead?' Andrew asked once everyone was resettled. 'It seems like a very tight-knit village; the perfect place to hide in plain sight if you've got the rest of the community on your side.'

Beth knotted her hands together. 'Because one day I was walking up to the shop during my break at the hotel, and I saw Prentice and his wife walking into the pub. I froze right there on the pavement, and I panicked. I thought that he must have found out that Higson had brought me up here, and that he knew where Lily was.

'I ran straight home in a right state, and I told Lily that we needed to get out of there as quickly as we could. It took a few hours for the panic to clear, and when it did, I realised that if Prentice had come looking for us, he wouldn't have brought his wife with him, would he? It was August, and the whole place was jam-packed with tourists, so it was much more likely he was just on holiday. Even still, working in the hotel suddenly felt too dangerous, so I called Judith and told her that the kids were sick. A couple of weeks after that, we just upped and left.'

'And Enid Wetherall?' Andrew asked.

Beth nodded. 'Before all that, we used to come down to Bowness a lot at weekends; it got the kids out of the house and got Lily some air, and one day we got talking to Enid. I don't even know what we talked about that first day, but we stuck to the cover story that Bill had given me: I'd taken the kids to get away from my husband, and Lily was my sister.'

'I still couldn't speak much back then,' Lily piped up quietly. 'Enid was always so kind to me. She was a teacher, you know? She spent ages trying to teach me some sign language so that I could try and communicate when I couldn't use my voice; it gave me a break from needing to write everything down.'

'Just after I saw Prentice, we met Enid for lunch, and she suggested that we all come to Bowness and stay with her until we got settled again,' Beth explained. 'I argued against it at first; I wanted to move away completely, but Enid pointed out that the kids had probably already had enough upheaval in their little lives as it was.'

'Okay,' Andrew replied and then turned to Lily. 'I'm sorry that I need to ask this, Ms Woodhouse, but can you tell me why DCI Higson asked you to keep quiet about the fact that you were neither missing nor dead, and why he thought he needed to get you out of Manchester?'

'He didn't ask me to stay quiet, Inspector,' Lily replied. 'He didn't need to. I don't know what Jimmy and the others thought had happened to me when they realised that I'd disappeared from the Arches. I always just hoped that they thought I'd escaped and then dropped dead somewhere out of sight. If I'd made it known that I was still alive, Jimmy wouldn't have stopped until he'd killed me.'

Peggy swallowed heavily as Violet reappeared beside her sister, her small hand hovering over Lily's shoulder. She looked over at Peggy, obviously trying to tell her something, but the words were completely unintelligible beneath the conversation happening around her.

'You're not going to tell anyone that we're here, are you?' Beth asked, obviously still terrified.

Andrew shook his head. 'Ms Woodhouse, there's one thing I'm still unclear on. Why exactly did Prentice take you down to the Arches that night?'

Peggy watched as Lily looked up at the ceiling, tears brimming over her bottom lashes even as it looked like she wanted to laugh about something. It was an unsettling combination.

Lily looked Andrew dead in the eye and shook her head. 'According to Jimmy, Inspector, we were looking for buried treasure.'

SEVENTEEN

'Treasure?' Lloyd asked for the umpteenth time. He was still so astounded that Andrew wondered if they'd finally found that elusive *thing* that would prove a step too far for even Lloyd's eternal open-mindedness and proclivity for flights of fancy.

'That's what Lily said,' Andrew replied, prodding at the fork on his now empty plate until it was neatly butted up against the knife. 'Apparently some drunk old boy that Prentice had arrested loads of times over the years used to go on about being sure that there was treasure buried beneath the city, in tunnels near Deansgate. I guess, eventually, Prentice must have started believing him.'

'Right...' Lloyd agreed slowly, reaching for yet another spoonful of roast potatoes. 'But...*treasure?*'

'Hey, I'm just repeating what I was told by Lily. Ask Peggy!' Andrew nodded towards the other end of the kitchen table and then frowned.

Peggy had barely touched her dinner, and it was obvious that the shaky quietness that had settled over her as they'd left Ash Street behind them still hadn't lifted. They'd stumbled almost immediately into the others as they'd rounded the corner onto the main road – Jen quickly recounting that their trip to see Pam Moyes had been significantly less fruitful because they'd found her house in complete darkness.

They'd trooped to the car park together to head back to Briersthwaite. Peggy had nudged her brother towards the front passenger seat and tucked herself into the back of the car before Andrew had been able to begin to form a protest.

He'd actually thought it perfectly reasonable that Peggy had wanted some space after the difficulty of her encounter with Lily – and Violet, for that matter – and so he hadn't tried to engage her in conversation in the car.

Even once they'd arrived at St Sunday's, to find the tartan-clad Mrs Laycock in the kitchen, preparing dinner for them all – thankfully sans eligible daughters – Peggy had barely spoken.

There had been a few occasions when Andrew had caught her looking like she was about tell him something important, but each time she'd clammed up and shook her head at herself before giving him an apologetic smile

They'd caught a news bulletin just after they'd got back; Andrew and Jen surreptitiously extricating themselves from Mrs Laycock's increasingly searching questions to switch on the TV in the living room with the volume down as low as they could get it while still being able to hear.

The only real difference between this later bulletin and the one Andrew had seen at lunchtime was that a description of Higson's car had been released to the public that afternoon along with a reminder of the number to call should they spot the car, or the missing man himself.

Andrew's stomach had rolled unpleasantly when the newsreader had then introduced a clip of DCI Richard Chambers giving an update on the investigation. His former boss looked as though he'd aged twenty-years since Andrew had last seen him in person – on the very day that Andrew had announced that he was staying at the Ballroom – and his fingers kept twitching around the paper he was reading his statement from.

Andrew had wondered if Chambers was genuinely distressed at Sean Kelly's death. They'd worked together at the Ballroom, after all, and although Annie Higson had said that Chambers hadn't been respected by the others, that didn't mean that he didn't feel some sort of connection to his former colleague.

Only one message had been left on the answering machine while they'd been in Bowness, and that had been from Annie checking in to say that she still hadn't heard from Bill, but that she'd had her sister, Sarah, call CID to try and find out what was going on. Sarah had apparently spoken to Chambers and told him that Annie was obviously very distressed about the news and so, despite his pressure for her to come in immediately for questioning, she would be coming in when *she* felt up to speaking to anyone outside of the family. Hearing all of this, Andrew had wondered if the reason for Higson and Sarah's rocky relationship might be that they were similarly bullish in their approach to everything and everyone.

Andrew was trying not to be too disheartened that they'd had no new updates from Mike, despite multiple furtive calls from Andrew, and nothing from Marnie at all; it was driving him nuts not knowing who had answered the phone in the Ballroom that afternoon. He had theories, of course, but given that each one was accompanied by varying amounts of trepidation, he'd appreciate some clarity.

As though the universe had heard his pleas, the telephone in the hall chirruped noisily, and Andrew pushed his chair back from the table as though the sound had summoned him. He noticed that Peggy had done the same.

The kitchen door opened, and Mrs Laycock reappeared. Andrew still couldn't understand how or *why* a woman who lived in a house almost as large as St. Sunday's, and whose wrists and fingers were adorned with things that sparkled obnoxiously, had ended up looking after the Swan family whenever they were up in the Lakes, and the house itself whenever they weren't.

It was a mystery that would have to keep for now though, Andrew thought, as Mrs Laycock sought out Peggy with her eyes.

'Lady Margaret, there's a telephone call for you.'

Peggy gave her a small smile, adding a genuine thank you for dinner before she left the kitchen, but Andrew had seen the telltale little flinch that Peggy always gave whenever her title was given a public airing.

'Did you have enough food?' Mrs Laycock asked, even as she

started shovelling more crackling and roasted vegetables onto Lloyd's plate with a beaming smile.

Andrew wondered if this meant that Lloyd had been earmarked for one of the Laycock girls, and so before the same could be attempted with him, he excused himself with a polite thank you and set off after Peggy.

When Andrew stepped out into the hallway, Peggy had her back to him, and she was practically hissing into the phone. 'Marnie, I really need you to calm down!'

Andrew immediately increased the length of his stride in response to the obvious anxiety in her voice.

'What's going on?' he asked as he reached her, and Peggy jumped in surprise.

'Marnie, Andrew's here. Do you want to tell him instead?' Peggy asked, and then immediately winced as Marnie's high-pitched, hysterical response echoed tinnily down the phone line in an obviously negative answer.

Andrew couldn't make out what Marnie was saying but based on the way Peggy's expression morphed from anxiety to outrage, he could easily guess that it wasn't good news.

'Right, but do you know who they were?' Peggy asked and then frowned almost instantly 'Did they have a key? What do you mean you don't know? Did something happen with th– *Well*, I was worried about that when I called earlier. I thought you'd m–'

Peggy's eyes suddenly went wide. '*What?*'

Andrew wasn't sure that he'd ever heard Peggy sound so completely astounded before, which was really saying something considering the things they'd been through together.

'Marnie, how could you?' Peggy asked, and Andrew actually flinched at the cold accusation in her voice.

'What? What is it?' Andrew asked again, concern and frustration at being in the dark mingling together to create a perilous level of anxious irritability.

Peggy ignored him entirely.

'No, I am *not* telling him for you, Marnie!' she snapped instead. 'I'm not your bloody messaging service, and I'm not being your scapegoat for this! No, you're telling him. *Now.*'

Andrew let out a startled huff of breath as Peggy suddenly shoved the phone towards his chest for the second time that day.

'You need to hear this,' she said frostily, and then went to sit at the bottom of the stairs without further explanation.

With what felt like an unreasonable amount of unease, Andrew raised the phone to his ear, while Peggy continued to stare back at him with an inscrutable look in her eyes.

'Marnie?' He cleared his throat. 'Marnie, what's going on?'

Quiet sniffling was the only response he received.

'Tell him, Marnie!' Peggy snapped loudly from the staircase, and Andrew was alarmed to see how agitated she was. It was very rare for Peggy to shout like that, particularly at Marnie, who seemed to have Peggy's almost-endless patience bestowed upon her even more often than Charlie did.

Andrew evidently wasn't the only one who thought this because the kitchen door opened, and Charlie's head appeared. 'Everything alright?'

Andrew waved him away with a pointed look and turned his attention back to the phone, where Marnie had remained stubbornly silent. 'Marnie, come on, I need to know what's going on.'

'You're going to be so pissed at me though,' Marnie replied eventually, and it was probably the most contrite Andrew had ever heard her.

'That doesn't matter,' Andrew replied, already knowing full well that based entirely on Peggy's reaction he was, indeed, going to be pissed at Marnie. 'Can you tell me what's happened?'

Marnie took a deep, unnecessary breath. 'There were people

in the Ballroom earlier.'

'Yeah. When Peggy called.'

'Right,' Marnie replied slowly. 'So, they've completely ransacked the place up here. I hope you didn't have anything you particularly cared about in your desk, because it's either gone, or in bits on the floor now.'

Andrew sighed loudly and pressed a fist to his forehead. 'Okay. What about the archives?'

'All three doors still locked, and nothing touched inside any of them.'

Andrew wouldn't deny that he was pleased to hear that.

'Did they say what they were looking for?' he asked. 'Or mention any names?'

'Not that I heard,' Marnie replied with an odd little lilt to her voice.

'Alright, so talk me through what happened. What did they do when they first came into the Ballroom? How long were they there? Did they mention anything about Higson, or Lily Woodhouse and Davy Nash?' He glanced towards the stairs quickly. 'Anything about Peggy, even in passing?'

'I don't know,' Marnie whispered hollowly. 'I don't know.'

Andrew tried to keep his frustration in check. 'Marnie, I need *anything* you can remember. Anything at all that cou–'

'I wasn't here!' Marnie cried suddenly, and Andrew felt himself go almost cross-eyed in surprise. 'That's what Peggy wants me to tell you!'

'What?'

'Nothing was happening this morning, just like nothing happened last night, and I was bored. I tried to talk to Benson like you said I should, but he never wants to have anything to do with me and I couldn't find him anywhere at all, and I was sad, okay? I could hear bloody Christmas music outside, and it made me *sad*, so I left.'

'You left,' Andrew repeated, still not quite believing that he'd heard her correctly. 'Where did you go? Butterton?'

Peggy gave a derisive snort and Andrew felt unpleasantly like he was caught in the middle of an argument.

'Marnie, where did you go?'

Marnie made a sound that was definitely a poorly stifled sob. 'Strangeways.'

'*What*?' Andrew asked sharply.

'I went to see Rex, alright?' Marnie wept. 'I wanted to talk to him, so I finally did!'

Andrew had the fleeting thought that if he just put the phone down immediately, he might be able to pretend that Marnie hadn't just admitted to speaking to the absolute tosser who was at least partly responsible for her murder – the degree of responsibility Andrew laid upon Hughes was dependent on how generous he was feeling towards that utter bastard on any given day.

'You did what?' he asked eventually, still hoping that Marnie hadn't just admitted to actually speaking to Rex Hughes in a prison full of people. 'Marnie, are you actually completely insane?'

'Don't say things like that to me!' Marnie shrieked, but Andrew could tell that there was already guilt creeping back into her voice. 'Why shouldn't I go and see him? He didn't actually kill me, did he? Athena managed that all by herself!'

'We are not having this argument again!' Andrew snapped. 'You know full well what he did, and just how many people he hurt along the way.'

'It was your idea anyway!'

'What?' Andrew barked. 'How the hell was it *my* idea for you to visit that prick?'

'Stop calling him names!'

'Stop defending him!'

'You're the one who was asking about whether he'd told anyone about Peggy!' Marnie snapped back at him. 'So, I thought I'd ask him. I thought I was helping!'

All of the arguments ready to leave Andrew's mouth promptly disappeared with an almost audible *pop* of dread. 'You spoke to him about Peggy?'

'I thought you'd be pleased to know that he swears he's never told anyone about her being involved!'

'Pleased?' Andrew repeated and he couldn't quite hold in the mocking chuckle. 'You thought I'd be *pleased* that you've been talking to the man who kidnapped the one person who believed in you from the very beginning and nearly got her killed? The same man who was allowed to build a fucking drug empire in *my* city, right under the noses of the very people who were supposed to put scum like him behind bars?'

'Now, that's n-'

'You really thought I'd be pleased about all that, did you, Marnie?' He laughed mirthlessly again. 'So, as you know me so well, do you want to tell me how pleased I am about the fact that the DCI who was in charge of your murder investigation in the first place, mind, and did everything he could to draw any suspicion away from Rex, is the very same DCI heading up the investigation into the murder of an ex-police officer? A murder that Higson supposedly committed this morning.'

'What?' Marnie asked in pure surprise. '*Higson did what?*'

'And how pleased do you think I am about how all of this could have something to do with why Higson has been keeping Peggy away from the Ballroom, which is why I asked *you* – against every ounce of better judgement that I thought I had – to do this one job for me.'

Marnie made a sound of distress and Andrew shook his head, worried that if he actually started yelling, he might not actually be able to stop. 'Do not even think about leaving the Ballroom until tomorrow morning, and if *anything* happens you will call here immediately. We'll be back at Butterton by lunchtime tomorrow and so will you. I mean it, Marnie.'

There was only silence on the other end.

'Marnie.'

'Fine,' she muttered eventually, and the line went dead.

Andrew made himself place the receiver back onto its cradle with the same amount of care as someone handling an unexploded bomb. He slowly turned around, half-expecting Peggy to have a go at him for shouting at Marnie like that, so he was surprised to find that the staircase was empty, and the only other person in the hallway was a terribly uncertain-looking Lloyd.

'You okay, boss?' he asked carefully. 'Charlie took Mrs L out into the garden when the shouting started, and Jen's gone to check on Peggy.'

'And, what? You're here to check on me, is that right?' Andrew barked, still snappish and unbalanced. He held up his hand almost immediately. 'Sorry, Lloyd, that wasn't fair. I'm just being a dickhead.'

'You're alright,' Lloyd replied with a one-shouldered shrug. 'You were right anyway; I did come to check on you. And to bring you this.'

Andrew blinked in surprise as Lloyd handed over a cut-crystal tumbler with a generous measure of something amber sloshing gently inside it.

'We're working,' Andrew replied.

'Yeah, I know.' Lloyd shrugged again and held up a glass of his own. 'Higson would murder us if he didn't think we were doing everything we could to figure out what was going on, because that's what we do. But he'd also murder me for not bringing him a whiskey if he looked like he needed one, because that's also what *I* do. He's not here right now, but you are, and *you're* the one who looks like he really needs a drink, so…'

Andrew sighed loudly, accepting his fate. 'Yeah, alright. Thanks.'

'Come on,' Lloyd added as he started moving towards the kitchen again, 'you can tell us about whatever the hell just happened, and then you can tell us what we need to do next to get everything sorted out, because that's what *you* do, isn't it?'

'You've got that much faith in me?' Andrew raised his eyebrows, a bit surprised at Lloyd's candid show of trust.

Lloyd then turned back to look at him as though he were a complete idiot, which rather ruined the effect of his previous words. 'Course I do.'

* * *

Peggy was well aware that the circumstances of her upbringing would be considered unusual, to say the least, and downright bizarre if she wanted to put a significantly finer point on it.

Yet, despite what she was fairly certain was popular belief by this stage in her life, her early years had been much the same as most childhoods. When she'd been very little, she'd found it easy to get on with anyone she spoke to, discounting the 'friends' that had been pre-selected and thoroughly vetted by her mother, of course, as every single one of those had been an obnoxious disaster.

When she'd been a bit older, and her mother's meddling tendencies had disappeared off into the sunset along with the woman herself, Peggy had been satisfied with her social circle at school; a small, carefully curated set of girls that shared Peggy's twin loves of reading and rock and roll, and couldn't care less about horse riding or the daft boys from the school up the road from their own.

Perhaps her life would have continued in that relatively straightforward vein of contentment if it hadn't been for the Great Indiscretion of 1964 when, as a freshly minted eight-year-old intent to impress his new prep school friends, Charlie had proudly mentioned that his big sister could speak to dead people – a fact that his big sister hadn't even dreamed of sharing with her own friends, mind – and Peggy had found herself dispatched to Switzerland in a very obvious demonstration of 'out of sight, out of mind' by her father. God knows where her mother had been at that stage.

Lausanne had been a terribly lonely place to spend the next six years of her life and so on the day she'd finally returned to Butterton – deemed by her former school as 'finished' as she was ever going to be – she'd decided that maybe throwing herself back into society wouldn't be the worst decision that she could make, and she'd spent two months accepting each and every social invitation that had come her way.

That summer hadn't been too painful in the end, but everything had improved enormously when she'd left Butterton behind her once more and made her way down to London, acceptance letter clutched in her hand out of fear that they might suddenly change their minds about letting her stay otherwise. Her father hadn't been thrilled about her decision to go to university, choosing to inform her – via Timothy, of course – about how terribly concerned he was about women getting *ideas*. In the end, he'd just let it happen; likely because he'd realised that it was more convenient continuing to have neither of his children at home.

Peggy had appreciated the immediate anonymity that came with living in a big city, even if she could have done without the frankly enormous number of ghosts that she'd encountered on a daily basis. At first, she'd found it almost impossible to leave the house, but it had forced her to learn how to focus so that she could go about her life without the fear of being overwhelmed by unwanted voices at any given moment.

Charlie had moved in with her a few years later, under the guise of starting his own university studies, but really just because he didn't fancy the prospect of going home. He'd taken the train straight from Edinburgh to London on the last day of his final term, lugging his school trunk behind him, and for four blissful years they'd conducted their lives with very little interference from their parents. Charlie had quickly become a permanent fixture on the dancefloor at Annabel's, and Peggy had reclaimed the teenage hedonism she'd lost to strict routine in Switzerland through a couple of ill-advised flings – first with a very minor European royal, and then a rugby player who'd apparently been a few years above Charlie at school – and a startling sense of freedom.

It had, of course, all been too perfect to last for long. While William Swan had seemed content enough for Peggy to stay in London until the end of time, Charlie had been summoned back to Butterton the minute he'd graduated.

Charlie had still been young and naïve enough to think that maybe he *could* have a go at behaving a bit more like his father, despite the wild amount of evidence to the contrary, and so he'd agreed to go home after one final summer of liberty. Peggy should have known then that Charlie would realise pretty sharpish upon his return to Cheshire that *no, actually*, he was never going to be like his father, no matter how many lectures he received about what was expected of him.

Peggy had often thought that she should have just stayed in London then, but their mother had recently returned to Butterton to remind everyone in the Cheshire set that she was still the Countess of Acresfield, so Peggy had dutifully packed up her new life and headed home with her brother so that they could face the witch together.

Perhaps going home had been Peggy's biggest mistake.

All of her former friends and acquaintances had, of course, paired up, moved on, and settled themselves into the same well-worn path that their parents and grandparents had followed before them:

Marriage – Kids – Wait impatiently for Daddy to die and then inherit his estate.

And so, Peggy had found herself at the fringes of everything once more. As Charlie had quickly pulled away from any intention of ever learning how to run the estate, Peggy had picked up the slack, learning as she went, because she knew that, at some point, their father would die and she had no intention of letting her mother run the place into the ground, or of letting Charlie ignore it all until it became a problem not just for them personally, but for the people whose livelihoods relied on Butterton functioning properly.

It was a couple of years after that, soon after their mother had taken herself off for another extended tour of the world's cities and the men that ran them, that Peggy had finally given into Charlie's requests to start going out in town with him and his friends again.

Which, of course, is what had eventually led her to Edgar.

There had been so many signs that the whole affair was doomed from the outset, but she'd blithely ignored all of them, right up until the terrible moment when ignorance had been completely removed from the board.

After Peggy's personal life had exploded, Charlie had initially tried to encourage her to think about going back to London, or at least getting out of Cheshire, but she hadn't really seen the point. So, instead, she'd found herself in a sort of parody of those isolated boarding school years, though this time she'd had Charlie and a very, very great – and very, very dead – aunt for company. Peggy had there and then accepted that she would be inexorably linked to Butterton House until the day she died and, knowing her luck, probably even beyond that day, so she might as well stop fighting her fate.

Thus, it had remained like that, until Charlie had opened his big mouth once again and Peggy had found herself being dragged along to the Ballroom, alongside the most cynical man Peggy had ever met, and into the investigation into Marnie's murder.

Marnie, who was more like family to her and Charlie than anyone with the Swan name had ever been (barring Emmeline, of course), but who had also just abandoned their investigation in favour of visiting her scumbag ex-fiancé in jail.

Peggy would never stop feeling awful about how her friend's life had been so brutally cut short, and she could even understand, to an extent, why Marnie was still finding it hard to let go of Rex and everything that he'd meant to her. Peggy's understanding was, of course, always tempered by the fact that Rex had first kidnapped her in an attempt to extort ransom money, and then nearly got her and Andrew killed when that plan had gone awry.

All of that aside, though, Peggy was certain that the real reason Marnie had gone to see Rex was rooted in the fact that she was terrified of what might happen to her if Peggy actually left.

What happens to me when you're not here? is what Marnie had asked her at the Troubadour, and Peggy would be lying if she said that it hadn't been playing on her mind ever since. If Peggy went to New York, she knew that Marnie wouldn't be able to follow her there, not unless Marnie travelled there with her on the plane. But was Marnie attached strongly enough to Butterton, or perhaps to Charlie or the others enough to be totally fine without Peggy's presence for a longer stretch of time? Truth be told, Peggy didn't have the foggiest, and she hated that fact.

The footsteps on the dock behind her weren't a huge surprise when they eventually came, but she still wasn't thrilled to hear them. She really wasn't in the mood for her brother's particular brand of psychoanalysis. 'Not now, alright?'

'I come bearing wine though.'

Peggy turned, startled. 'Jen! Sorry, I was expecting my brother.'

'Mind if I sit?' Jen asked, and when Peggy gestured for her to take a seat, she perched herself just as Peggy had – legs dangling just about the surface of the lake – and put a freshly opened bottle of wine and a couple of glasses on the wooden boards between the two of them.

'Are you not freezing?' Jen pulled her coat more tightly around herself as she eyed Peggy's jumper doubtfully.

Peggy shrugged. 'I'm fine.'

'Alright. Any chance you want to tell me why the Inspector was shouting loud enough to wake the dead then?' Jen asked casually as she poured the wine and handed Peggy a glass. 'If you'll excuse the choice of phrase.'

Peggy sighed. There was no point keeping any of it from Jen, so she haltingly relayed her conversation with Marnie.

'She did what?' Jen's face was set in an expression of pure surprise. 'Jesus, no wonder he kicked off like that. With Chambers leading the investigation, that puts Hughes way too close to the fringes of this. Do you know if Marnie had spoken to him since…?'

As Jen trailed off, Peggy shook her head. 'No. I'm almost certain that she's been to see him without him being aware of it. I think today was the first time she made her presence known.'

'What was she thinking?' Jen took a large sip of her drink. 'Marnie blending into the shadows in the Troubadour is one thing, and I can even understand how she can sit at a table and have a conversation with someone like Fiona as though everything is completely normal; after all, the truth is too bizarre for anyone to even consider, isn't it?'

Peggy understood it too, even if she lived in constant anxiety that Marnie's secret would be discovered.

'But *Strangeways?*' Jen added, shaking her head slowly. 'There's nowhere to hide. How the hell did she manage to speak to Hughes without causing a scene?'

'No idea,' Peggy replied, prodding at a bit of moss by her knee. 'I didn't ask her, and I threw the phone at Andrew before she could try and explain.'

Jen grimaced. 'After everything's that happened, I think that's an understandable reaction.'

'Do you really think that Rex could somehow be mixed up in this?' Peggy asked.

'I don't know,' Jen replied, resettling herself. 'I think the boss just wants to make sure that we've looked into everything. It does seem like it might be sensible to confirm whether Hughes has ever mentioned your name to anyone we'd prefer didn't know a thing about you. Especially now that we're certain that Prentice was using Lily Woodhouse's abilities for his own gain, and that DCI Higson's concern about your involvement with the Ballroom probably stems from that fact. Perhaps somebody said something at Frank Jackson's funeral; something that made Higson think that Prentice might seek to target you if he knew the truth.'

On some level, as much as she didn't like hearing it, Peggy was glad that Jen had voiced that concern aloud. She'd known that Andrew had been silently dancing around it, and the closest he'd come to admitting that concern had been on the phone with Marnie, just before Peggy had decided to take her leave of the situation and head for the lake.

'That possibility doesn't stop me from being able to help,' Peggy muttered eventually.

'And I wouldn't dream of suggesting that it should. Although, I think that it's probably reasonable for us all to be concerned for your safety too. You're as much a part of the team as the rest of us,

Peggy, and we all care about you. Some of us might just handle that concern a bit more *sensitively* than certain other people.' Jen wrinkled her nose and gave Peggy a knowing look, with the identity of 'certain other people' blindingly obvious to the pair of them.

Peggy took another sip of wine, debating whether or not now was a good time to mention the thing she'd failed to disclose to Andrew earlier. The thing that had been needling at her since just before they'd left Beth and Lily's flat.

'What is it?' Jen asked, as good at her job as ever.

Peggy sighed again. 'Violet Woodhouse told me something before we left Bowness. It was almost impossible to hear her, and I didn't want Lily to know that she was speaking to me – she was upset enough as it was – so I couldn't ask her anything specific.'

Jen frowned. 'But, at dinner th-'

'It didn't come up at dinner because I haven't actually told Andrew about it.' Peggy put her glass down and looked out over the water again. 'I don't quite know how to tell him what I think it means.'

Jen didn't say anything in response; she'd let Peggy get to her point in her own time.

'Violet said that Prentice went berserk after Sean Kelly attacked Lily,' Peggy explained eventually, eyes fixed on where the water disappeared into the mist before it reached the opposite shore. 'They really did think he'd killed her, and it was when they were trying to get back out of there that Davy happened upon them. It was Prentice who hit him with the shovel.'

Peggy looked down at her hands, and Jen nudged her gently with her elbow.

'Why didn't you want to mention that?' Jen asked carefully.

Peggy shook her head. 'No, it's something else. I just wanted you to know that's what happened first.'

'Alright…' Jen still looked rightfully confused.

'They realised pretty quickly that they were going to need to get rid of two bodies,' Peggy continued after a long pause. 'They couldn't be certain that Davy hadn't spoken to anyone before he came down to the Arches, so they decided to go and get another car before coming back to take Lily and Davy out to Hulme. Prentice didn't want to use his car.'

Jen closed her eyes as the implication dawned. 'Where all the new houses were being built. *Jesus*, if that's where they buried Davy's body, then he would have only been a few streets away from Beth and the kids.'

'That's still not the bit I'm really worried about.' Peggy's voice was barely above a whisper. 'Prentice didn't want to be involved in the actual disposal part. He told the other two that they should go and wake up Dickie and Chris and get them to help, because they'd keep their mouths shut if they knew what was good for them.'

'Dickie and Chris?' Jen repeated, and from the widening of her eyes, Peggy knew that Jen had reached the same conclusion that she had.

'Violet said she'd been repeating the names for twenty years so she wouldn't forget them, just in case Lily ever managed to speak to her again,' Peggy said, giving Jen a smile that she didn't feel at all. 'Quite clever for a nine-year-old, I thought.'

'Really clever,' Jen agreed, though she looked as unnerved as Peggy felt. 'Did Violet get any other names? Surnames maybe?'

Peggy shook her head. 'No. Dickie has to be Chambers though, right? We know he was at the Ballroom then. But Chris? You don't think that they meant...'

'Benson?' Jen offered quietly when Peggy let the implication die on her lips. 'Is that what you're asking?'

'Yes.'

Jen swore under her breath and dropped her head into her hands.

Peggy knew how mad it sounded, and she'd expected some resistance to the idea – it's why she hadn't wanted to mention it to Andrew without testing the theory a bit more – so she was surprised by Jen's reaction.

'I know you worked with him before Andrew came to the Ballroom,' she added, feeling terrible as Jen looked up at her in utter dismay. 'I know that he was Higson's friend, and he was *Davy's* friend. Chris isn't an uncommon name either, is it? I could be totally wrong, Jen.'

'But you might not be,' Jen argued quietly.

'Do you think there's any chance that Benson might have got himself mixed up with Prentice, somehow?' Peggy asked carefully.

'Honestly? I don't know.' Jen glanced up at the inky sky and took a deep breath before letting it out slowly. 'Higson hid the truth about Lily and Davy for twenty years, so what's to say that Benson didn't have secrets of his own?'

Peggy nodded and looked down at the lake again. That was exactly what she was afraid of.

EIGHTEEN

Andrew hung up on what felt like the hundredth call of the day and tried to stretch out the crick in his neck that had been bothering him since before he'd sat down for dinner. He was tired, he was pissed off with an ever-growing list of people – Marnie and Higson were currently vying for first place – and he really just wanted to go to bed, even though he knew it was unlikely he'd sleep knowing what was coming his way the minute he got home.

He was really hoping that Jen and Peggy had come back in while he'd been on the phone so that he could relay the update he'd finally received from Mike without the need to repeat himself later.

Unfortunately, when he pushed open the kitchen door it was to find the team still two members short and Mrs Laycock's hosting in full swing.

'*Really*, we're more than capable of looking after ourselves,' Charlie was saying, with an obvious edge of desperation to his voice, just as an artfully arranged cheeseboard was placed on the table in front of him. 'You shouldn't have gone to all this trouble. It's far too much!

'Don't be so daft,' Mrs Laycock replied, patting him on the head. 'It's never too much trouble.'

The head patting morphed into a full hair ruffle. Charlie grimaced but sat through it without further comment, displaying the sort of stoicism that suggested that this was far from the first time that this had happened.

As irritable as Andrew was feeling, he couldn't suppress a snort of amusement.

Unfortunately, this drew Mrs Laycock's eyes to the door.

'You must have an awful lot of friends,' she said, eyeing him critically. 'Or is it all business?'

'Pardon?' Andrew blinked in bemusement as he sat down next to Lloyd again.

Mrs Laycock nodded towards the hallway. 'I think you've spent more time on the phone than at the table this evening.'

Andrew was very aware that this sounded like an accusation, and he had to swallow down his natural inclination to ask this woman *who didn't know him at all* to mind her own business. He smiled regretfully instead. 'Unfortunately, work doesn't stop. Not even for weekends.'

'And what exactly is it that you do?' Mrs Laycock asked, and outright accusation had stepped aside for interrogation.

'Oh, Andrew works in the city,' Charlie supplied instantly. 'Very busy, very important, very dull things the rest of don't understand. You know how it is, Mrs L.'

Andrew would have hoped that this would have signified the end of it all, but at Charlie's words, Mrs Laycock's interest seemed only to flourish.

'I see,' she said, tilting her head to the side again. 'You're rather tall, aren't you?'

Lloyd's shoulders were shaking with suppressed laughter beside Andrew.

'I suppose I am,' Andrew muttered eventually, glaring at Charlie, who looked significantly more smug now that Mrs Laycock's attention had been diverted away from him.

Lloyd was still chuckling as he began piling a bit of everything from the cheeseboard onto a small plate.

The back door opened and everyone at the table swivelled towards it in unison.

Jen looked slightly taken aback as she came face-to-face with a wall of curious expressions.

Andrew frowned when Jen closed the door behind her. 'Where's Peggy?'

'Oh, just enjoying the peace and quiet for a bit,' Jen

replied. She widened her eyes for just a second as she looked over at Andrew, letting him know that she was attempting to communicate something. He wasn't sure if he could blame the second definitely-more-than-a-double whiskey he'd had, but he didn't immediately get the message.

Jen's eyes then slid towards Mrs Laycock and back again. Comprehension dawned; she obviously had something to tell them that couldn't be said in front of the housekeeper.

Well,' Andrew announced loudly, clapping his hands together as he rose to his feet, 'I think I'm going to go and get ready to leave in the morning, and then head to bed.'

Lloyd's hand paused over a bunch of grapes, and he frowned as he glanced towards the clock. 'It's only nine-thirty.'

'No, Andrew's right.' Charlie jumped up from his chair, dislodging the hand that had still been resting on his head. 'Early start and all that!'

Lloyd shot Charlie a look so obviously full of utter disbelief that Andrew fleetingly contemplated grabbing him by the scruff of the neck and asking him why he was being so dense.

Thankfully, Andrew's intervention remained unnecessary as Jen clapped her hand on Lloyd's shoulder and squeezed.

'Well, if you're not tired yet, you can sort out the washing up so that Mrs Laycock can get home,' Jen said pointedly.

'Oh, no. I'm very happy to do that,' Mrs Laycock protested.

'He insists, don't you, Lloyd?' Jen replied, smiling around gritted teeth. 'You've done so much for us already, and we really appreciate it.'

'Absolutely,' Charlie added, draping his left arm casually around Mrs Laycock's shoulders and steering her towards the door as he reached out with his right to grab the tartan shawl hanging on the wall hook. 'Thank you for everything, Mrs L.'

'Lovely to meet you!' Jen called as the kitchen door closed.

'That seemed a bit harsh,' Lloyd grumbled, rubbing his shoulder. 'She was really nice.'

'Well, I'm sorry to break up your little holiday and remind you that we're in the middle of a bloody case,' Andrew grumbled, pinching the bridge of his nose as he sank back down into a chair when he heard the front door close.

'Well,' Charlie sighed as he returned, 'Lloyd, she wants to introduce you to Georgina when you're next up, so I thought it best not to mention that you already have a girlfriend. Joycie, I'm afraid the jury's still out for your prospects.'

Andrew lazily shot Charlie the two-fingered salute that comment deserved, too weary to bother snapping at him.

Jen sat opposite Andrew and immediately refilled his empty whiskey tumbler before pouring one for herself.

Andrew blinked himself back to alertness. 'I don't need any more of that.'

Jen said nothing. She poured a generous splash into Lloyd and Charlie's glasses before she looked up and caught Andrew's eye again.

'Oh, Christ, what's happened?' Andrew sighed.

'Is Peg alright?' Charlie asked sharply.

Jen nodded, but she looked profoundly unsettled. 'Peggy's fine. She had a theory she wanted to run past me though, and I think she might be on to something.'

Andrew batted away the bolt of disappointment at not being the person that Peggy had chosen to share her idea with. He decided to blame such an unreasonable thought on the alcohol.

'Right,' Jen began, pursing her lips and looking like she was really trying to work herself up to saying whatever it was that she hadn't yet shared, 'so, you know that Peggy had a very brief interaction with Violet Woodhouse?'

Andrew nodded. God, where was this going? He hoped that Jen wasn't about to announce that Violet had decided to attach herself to Peggy the way that Marnie had.

'Well, Violet shared something else with Peggy before you both left that flat,' Jen explained.

So, that's what all of those aborted little attempts to tell him something had been about. Oddly, knowing that didn't relieve Andrew's flare of annoyance at being kept in the dark about something. 'Right.'

'Based on what Violet said to her, Peggy's fairly certain that Prentice and the others thought Lily was dead when they left her, and that it was Prentice who killed Davy,' Jen continued, drumming her fingers nervously on the tabletop. 'The plan was to bury both bodies in Hulme, but Prentice didn't want to get involved. He told Kelly and Jackson to get two others to help them with it.'

Andrew's exasperation was swiftly replaced by dread. 'Who?'

'Violet said that Prentice called them Dickie and Chris,' Jen replied. 'First names only, I'm afraid.'

'Who are Dickie and Chris?' Charlie asked.

'Well, Dickie is probably Chambers, isn't it?' Jen suggested.

Charlie pointed to Andrew. 'Your old boss?'

Andrew nodded.

'So, who's Chris?' Lloyd asked, wrinkling his nose.

The unspoken suggestion settled heavily in Andrew's stomach as he looked at the serious expression on Jen's face. 'You think they meant Benson?'

'Benson?' Charlie frowned. 'Wasn't he th-'

'*Our* Benson?' Lloyd asked in astonishment, cutting Charlie off. 'No way!'

'Well, we can't know for sure,' Jen said, placating as Lloyd stared at her open-mouthed, 'but we can't rule it out.'

'But he was Higson's friend!' Lloyd argued. He looked to Andrew. 'I know you didn't meet him, boss, but he was a good bloke. He was a good DI to us.'

Andrew held his hands up, not wanting this to descend into an argument. 'Let's just say we need to look into it further, alright? Right now, we've actually got more pressing problems.'

'Like what?' Lloyd asked, still sullen.

'Mike called while you were with Peggy,' Andrew explained to Jen. 'I'd only just got off the phone when you came in.'

'What did he say? Do they have any idea where Higson is?'

Andrew shook his head again. 'According to Mike, they've got nothing on Higson's whereabouts, but Annie's going to get a call from CID tomorrow. Chambers really wants her in. I'll speak to her before we leave in the morning and make sure she's ready for it.'

'Would you mind if I were the one to call her, sir?' Jen asked.

Even though he really, *really* wanted to ask just how and why Jen seemed to know the Higsons so well, Andrew was once again going to have to keep his own questions for later, in favour of answering Jen's. 'Of course I don't mind.'

Jen gave him a small smile of thanks.

'Aside from that, Mike's had the best look around that he could have done without raising suspicion,' Andrew continued. 'As far as he can see, there isn't a single physical record of either Lily Woodhouse or Davy Nash at CID. He found plenty of old, pre-GMP files, so it's not like they chucked all the City Police files when they established the new force, which begs the question of why he can't find anything at all.

'More to the point, though, Fallon's been round asking questions on behalf of Chambers.' Andrew grimaced. 'Mike said Chambers seems unusually agitated.'

'Well, of course he's agitated,' Lloyd said, folding his arms, 'He's been busy framing Higson for murder.'

'We don't quite know that yet, Lloyd,' Andrew replied as diplomatically as he could stand to, even though it sounded like a reasonable theory to him.

Jen looked like she agreed with Lloyd too. 'What's Fallon been asking about?'

'Me.' Andrew pursed his lips in displeasure at his own answer. 'Fallon was asking Mike how long he's known me, and how long we've been friends. Mike told him that he only knows me a bit through football, which Fallon is likely to believe – back when we worked together, he told me to my face more than once that I was an 'unsociable twat'.'

He allowed himself a wry smile when that comment managed to draw a chortle from Lloyd.

'Anyway, Fallon outright asked Mike if he thought it was a bit weird that I'm not at my house the weekend my boss has been accused of murder and apparently gone on the lam,' he added, swiping his palms across the table in front of him. 'Which means that either Chambers genuinely thinks I might somehow be involved because he doesn't actually know what's going on –'

'Or because he's trying to make it *look* like you might be involved as well,' Jen concluded.

'Exactly.'

'Well, what did Mike say to that?' Charlie asked.

Andrew shrugged casually. He knew full well what Mike had told Fallon, and he also knew exactly what the reaction at the kitchen table was going to be when he shared it. 'He just suggested that it was probably reasonable to think that I might be away for the weekend with a girlfriend, and that maybe we hadn't had any reason to be watching the news.'

The amount of effort Jen put in to keeping her expression neutral was commendable, but Lloyd and Charlie had no such compunction.

'And Fallon believed that, did he?' Lloyd grinned, sour mood entirely forgotten.

'Will you be introducing us to this mysterious woman any time soon?' Charlie laughed.

'There's probably still time for you to ask Mrs Laycock if you can borrow one of her daughters!' Lloyd crowed.

Andrew raised his eyebrows and waited for them to stop sniggering. 'Well, whatever story I come up with it better be good, because from what Mike said, it sounds like they're going to pull me into Chester House for questioning before I even get to my front door.'

The effect of those words was instantaneous, and all traces of good humour fled from the room.

'Fuck, mate.' Lloyd shook his head, and then sighed before correcting himself, 'I mean, fuck, *sir*.'

'Plenty of witnesses saw you up here,' Jen said, and even though she sounded perfectly calm she looked as anxious as she had when they they'd first thought Higson had disappeared. 'CID wouldn't be able to place you anywhere near Manchester.'

'Joking aside, Mrs Laycock really will say whatever we need her to say,' Charlie added with a firm nod. 'She's covered me for all sorts of things over the years.'

'Like what?' Lloyd asked, intrigued.

'Don't even think about answering that question while I'm in earshot.' Andrew pressed his fingers to his temples.

'Wasn't planning on it.' Charlie grinned but then grew serious again. 'If CID is looking into where you've been this weekend, Joycie, doesn't that mean that they're probably going to look into Jen and Lloyd as well?'

'Probably,' Andrew agreed. 'If we tell anyone we were all up here, we could lead anyone who might be looking straight to Beth and Lily, particularly if anyone finds out that Higson was in Staveshead on Thursday night. Lloyd, will Fiona cover for you?'

'Course she will.'

'Jen, we might get away with them thinking you're still at your sister's house if we're very careful about how we play things when we get back tomorrow,' Andrew added. 'If anyone tries to claim that you haven't been there all weekend, then they're going to have to admit that they followed you there in the first place, and I don't think they're going to want to do that.'

'They could knock on the door and ask for me,' Jen replied with a wince.

'They could knock on the door and ask for you,' Andrew agreed with a frustrated sigh, knowing that she was correct. 'Let's just hope that they don't, but we'll cross that bridge if we come to it, yeah?'

Jen nodded, pragmatic as always. 'What's the plan then, sir?'

'Well, first, we need to speak to Marnie at Butterton,' Andrew said, and he was expecting the noises of disbelief before they came. 'Yeah, I know, I'm not thrilled about that either right now, but we need her to talk to Benson for us. She said that he was ignoring her today, but I wonder if he'd change his tune if she suggested that we have good reason to think that he may have been as much Prentice's lackey as Chambers was.'

'Sounds a bit risky, doesn't it?' Lloyd asked as he topped another cracker with a chunky wedge of brie. 'Marnie can be a bit…well…'

'Blunt?' Charlie supplied.

'Yeah,' Lloyd agreed. '*Blunt* will do. Is there really nothing we could do to try and sneak Peggy into the Ballroom instead?'

Andrew was shaking his head before Lloyd had finished speaking. 'Even if I thought we could get anywhere near Tib Street without CID breathing down our necks, we can't take Peggy with us. If Chambers or even, somehow, Prentice himself is actually behind all of this and he finds out who our Miss Jones really is…'

He was happy to trail off there; he didn't want to have to say it, and the others understood anyway.

'Peggy still wants to help though,' Jen said eventually. 'You should probably talk this through with her, sir.'

'I will,' Andrew promised. He glanced out the window above the sink, only to see the kitchen scene reflected back at him with no discernible hint of the pitch-dark landscape beyond. 'What's she doing out there anywhere? It's been ages.'

'Enjoying the peace and quiet,' Jen repeated her earlier words as she picked up her glass and drained it, before standing up and rubbing her arms vigorously. 'Right, I'm going to have a shower because I'm still freezing, and then it's bedtime. Lloyd, get on that washing up.'

'Right now?' Lloyd looked outraged as he pointed at his refilled plate.

'Yeah, right now,' Jen confirmed, shaking her head before turning to Andrew. 'What time do you want us ready to leave in the morning, sir?'

Andrew looked down at his watch and sighed, mentally counting down the hours until he'd find himself back in Chester House for the first time since he was sent to Tib Street. 'Everyone's tired, so we can probably stretch it to nine, but no later.'

'Mrs L will be here at seven to make breakfast,' Charlie announced as he started moving plates and cutlery from the table and piling them on the countertop.

'She really doesn't need to come and make us breakfast, Charlie,' Andrew argued.

'Oh, I know,' Charlie replied mildly. 'I told her that but, like I said, she'll be here at seven.'

Andrew shook his head slowly as he pushed his chair back. 'I don't understand you people at all.'

'Nobody does.' Charlie shrugged without the slightest hint of offence.

Jen laughed and bid them all goodnight.

Charlie turned the taps to start filling the sink and rolled up his sleeves. 'Lloyd, you can wash, and I'll dry. Joycie, you can put things away.'

'Actually, I'm going to go and give Peggy an update on the case,' Andrew said.

'Of course you are,' Charlie grumbled.

Andrew rolled his eyes as he went to retrieve his coat and frowned when he realised that Peggy's own coat was still hanging on the hook beside it.

'Yes, well apparently I also need to go and make sure she's not given herself hypothermia,' Andrew added, filling the kettle quickly and switching it on to boil.

'I'm almost certain that I don't need to tell you that she won't appreciate being babied,' Charlie said, dropping cutlery into the sink with wild abandon before folding his arms as he turned to face Andrew expectantly.

Andrew sighed heavily. 'What?'

'Peg likes it up here because it's peaceful in a way that other places aren't,' Charlie said with a shrug. 'No ghosts.'

'No ghosts at all?' Lloyd paused as he trudged towards the sink, wearing the now-familiar expression that said he was being forced to remember that he might not always be as alone as he used to think, but that he still didn't know whether he was amazed or plain terrified about that fact.

Charlie shook his head as he picked up a tea towel. 'Not a one. Literal, or otherwise.'

'Okay,' Andrew said slowly, at a loss for what Charlie was looking for in a response.

'I suppose that's why there's some appeal to the idea of New York.'

Andrew willed the kettle to boil faster as he put teabags in two mugs.

'But New York's full of ghosts,' Lloyd argued, picking up the dish brush. 'We've all seen *Ghostbusters*!'

'Yes, but do you know what New York's *not* full of?' Charlie tilted his head. 'Our father, our mother, *Edgar the Twat*, nor any of the ghosts that come with living in that bloody house. I mean, if it were me, I'd definitely think about staying away from Butterton permanently.'

Was there something wrong with the kettle? It was definitely taking longer to boil than seemed reasonable. Andrew moved closer and stared at the spout just in case it helped speed the process along.

'You think Peggy might stay in New York?' Lloyd asked, and Andrew was pleased to hear that he sounded as disdainful of Charlie's idea as Andrew felt. 'No way, she wouldn't do that! Right, boss?'

Andrew was *not* pleased that Lloyd hadn't noticed that he was actually making a concerted effort to opt out of this discussion.

'I think *Peggy* will decide what she wants to do with her life,' Andrew replied as the kettle finally boiled. He was satisfied with the diplomacy the response was delivered with.

Charlie snorted loudly. 'That's a terrible answer.'

'I'm not sure Peggy would agree that suggesting she has autonomy is a 'terrible answer',' Andrew muttered as he opened the fridge to get the milk. 'And stop gossiping about your sister!'

'Alright, fine,' Charlie held up his hands, shaking his head and waving the tea towel in a parody of capitulation. 'I won't say anything else.'

'Good,' Andrew sighed.

'Except...' Charlie scrunched up his face and held up one hand.

Andrew slammed the milk bottle down on the counter and Lloyd dropped a handful of forks in surprise. '*No.*'

Charlie narrowed his eyes. 'She's already changed her flights *three* times.'

'What?' Andrew asked, before he remembered that he was supposed to be shutting this conversation down, not encouraging it.

'On each of the past three attempts to leave the country – once when we were actually getting in the car to go the airport, by the way – Peggy's changed her mind at the last minute,' Charlie replied quickly, obviously aware that this reprieve would not last long. 'She obviously doesn't want to actually go.'

'Hang on.' Lloyd frowned at Charlie, brandishing a sudsy serving spoon. 'You literally just said that you thought Peggy was going to *stay* in New York, but now you're saying that she doesn't really want to go?'

'What I'm *saying*,' Charlie retorted tersely, 'is that maybe she's not sure that there's any point in staying here, even if she doesn't actually care about going to New York at all.'

'Is this you not gossiping?' Andrew growled as he chucked the teabags in the bin. 'Because you're shit at it.'

Lloyd just frowned harder. 'But I thought that Cohen bloke was in New York? He invited her out there, didn't he?'

'Right, but that's neither here nor there when Peggy's not really all that invested in the person extending the invitation,' Charlie replied, waving his hands.

Andrew really didn't mean to say anything at all, but he hated leaving questions unasked and the words just bubbled out anyway, 'What's that supposed to mean?'

Charlie, the git, grinned infuriatingly. 'Oh, has that got your attention?'

Andrew turned his back on him again and poured a good splash of milk into each of the two mugs before he stomped across the kitchen to put the bottle back in the fridge. He caught Charlie's eyeroll when he stopped to put his coat on.

'Oh, for God's sake, Joycie, they only spent a couple of months together before he went back to America,' Charlie drawled. 'It's all *very casual*, so you can put your mourning shroud back in the wardrobe for now.'

Andrew draped Peggy's coat over his arm and picked up the two mugs. 'Lloyd, door.'

'What? Oh, right!' Lloyd quickly opened the back door once he realised that Andrew had his hands full. 'Christ, that's cold.'

'Be ready to leave by nine,' Andrew snapped without looking back as he headed for the lawn in the chilly darkness. 'Both of you. Otherwise, I'm driving off without you.'

'I think you'll find that's *my* car you're talking about!' Charlie shouted snottily, and it was impossible to miss the snort of amusement that followed that comment.

'Yeah. Well, Peggy has the keys!' Andrew called back. 'And I don't think she'd mind leaving you here either!'

Charlie said something that Andrew was too far away to hear, but Lloyd's raucous laughter burst out into the night before the door was slammed shut with a resounding thud.

'Jesus Christ,' Andrew muttered to himself as he tried to navigate the uneven grass, unsure whether the cursing was aimed at those he'd left behind in the kitchen, or at himself for being idiotic enough to attempt carrying two cups of tea and a coat across unfamiliar terrain at night.

As his eyes adjusted to the darkness, he was able to walk a bit quicker, which still didn't help much in staving off the frigid night air but *did* make him feel better about getting further away from Charlie's self-satisfied comments with each step.

Eventually, he spotted a smudge at the edge of the dock, which became more identifiably Peggy-shaped as he got closer.

'Andrew?' she asked without turning round.

'Good guess,' he replied as he approached her.

'Oh, it wasn't a guess,' she said, and she was definitely laughing at him. 'Even if I hadn't heard you shouting at my brother, you've been swearing since you were halfway down the garden.'

Well, Andrew couldn't argue with that.

'Here,' he said instead as he reached the edge of the dock and held out a mug.

'Hmm?' Peggy turned and looked up at him. 'Oh. Thanks. You didn't have to do that.'

'Peggy, what the hell are you doing out here?' Andrew huffed, sitting down beside her. He didn't dangle his legs over the edge though, because he was genuinely worried that he'd end up with at least his shoes in the water if he did. 'It's bloody freezing.'

'It's alright.' Peggy shrugged with faux nonchalance.

When he passed her coat over, though, she almost ripped it out of his hands.

Andrew laughed disbelievingly. 'I don't believe a word of that, especially coming from the woman I've heard complain about being cold in the height of summer.'

'The height of summer in *Manchester*, Andrew,' Peggy groused, wrapping herself in the coat before she picked up the mug to press it to her lips with a sigh of relief. 'Alright, I was cold. I just didn't want to go back inside.'

Andrew let the quiet settle over him for a minute, curling his fingers around the mug, grateful for the warmth. If he ignored the fact that it was unreasonably nippy, he could really see the appeal of the place.

Eventually though, he had to break the hush. 'So, it sounds like I'm going to have to go to Chester House and speak to Chambers tomorrow.'

'Can't you just tell him to bugger off?' Peggy asked.

Andrew laughed. 'Well, despite how much I would genuinely love to see his face if I did, unfortunately this won't be an optional encounter. From what Mike told me, they'll be waiting for me at the house whenever I get back.'

Peggy swore quietly.

'Yeah, that's about the measure of it.' Andrew squinted, trying, and failing, to see the opposite shore. 'It'll be alright. Charlie's already said that Mrs Laycock will tell anyone who asks that I've been here since Friday night.'

'She will,' Peggy confirmed and then, to his surprise, she giggled.

He looked over in question. 'What?'

'Nothing.' She grinned. 'Only, I hope you realise that if Mrs Laycock has to lie to anyone for you, she *will* expect remuneration in the form of a lovely summer wedding within the next couple of years. I think you'll love having her as a mother-in-law; she's a brilliant cook.'

'Don't even joke about a thing like that,' Andrew replied, with a shiver that was only partially caused by the air temperature.

Peggy turned serious again. 'What about Jen and Lloyd?'

Andrew shook his head. 'Unfortunately, if Chambers knew that we all just happened to be up here this weekend, he might get the *right* idea and think we were up to something.'

'Fair point.'

'So, that means that I need to ask you a big favour.' Andrew winced.

'What is it?'

Andrew stared into his mug. 'I need you to drop me off in Gatley tomorrow and pretend that you've been with me all weekend if anyone asks.'

Peggy frowned. 'I *have* been with you all weekend.'

Andrew looked over at her and his face scrunched up in mortification. 'Not quite what I meant.'

'Oh.' Peggy's eyes widened. '*Oh.*'

'And look, I know that I made a big deal about keeping you out of this whole mess, and that this will mean handing your name to Chambers on a plate,' Andrew continued hurriedly, 'so you can say no. Of course you can say no.'

'Andrew, it's fine.'

'I can't promise that they won't want to speak to you.'

'I'll be fine. I'll just do my best impression of Charlie, and they'll want to be as far away from me as they can get after a minute or so.'

Andrew appreciated Peggy's attempt to make him feel better about what was starting to feel like a more insane situation with every minute that passed but his mood had already swerved towards morose. He sighed loudly. 'Are you really alright?'

'What do you mean?' Peggy tilted her head in confusion at the abrupt shift in topic

'About Marnie.'

'Oh,' Peggy said again, only that time it was a small, lifeless sound.

Andrew immediately felt like an arse for bringing it up.

'She's worried that I'm going to leave her behind,' Peggy said eventually.

That wasn't what Andrew had expected. 'What do you mean?'

Peggy faltered her way through a quick explanation with all the hesitance she usually exhibited when she was required to talk about herself.

'And I don't know what happens to her if I'm not always around,' Peggy concluded. 'It's not like with Emmy – Aunt Emmeline – being part of Butterton.'

'Or like Rob?' Andrew offered quietly.

'Or like Rob.' Peggy's lips quirked in a familiar sad smile before she yawned widely. 'Sorry. That early start is killing me.'

Andrew knew that that this particular conversation was far from over, but he suspected that nothing good would come from continuing it just then. And so, instead, he unfolded his cold limbs and stood up with a yawn of his own.

'Come on,' Andrew sighed, before offering Peggy his hand. 'Time to go in.'

Peggy let him pull her to her feet before handing him her now empty mug so that she could retrieve a wine bottle and two glasses that had been sitting just out of sight.

They slowly headed back towards the house – an easier journey with the warmly lit windows acting as a guide – elbows occasionally colliding as they navigated the uneven ground together.

When they were about halfway up the sloping garden, the kitchen door was suddenly flung open.

'Boss!' Lloyd called. 'Mike's just called back.'

Andrew and Peggy glanced at each other before increasing their speed.

'He had to go almost straight away – Chambers was sending some of them out to follow up a tip – but he thought we needed to know about it,' Lloyd continued, closing the kitchen door again once Peggy and Andrew were inside.

'What is it? Is it Higson?' Andrew asked, pulling his coat off.

Lloyd nodded. 'They've had three separate calls from people who've spotted Higson's car this evening.'

'Anywhere near Tib Street?'

'Nope. The most recent call was from someone who saw the car at a petrol station on the A55,' Lloyd replied. 'Near Chester. It looks like he was heading for North Wales.'

'Wales?' Andrew repeated dumbly. 'Why the hell would he be going to Wales?'

'Not a bloody clue.' Lloyd shrugged. 'Er, sir.'

And that, Andrew supposed, was as good an answer as any he had himself.

NINETEEN

Peggy had always slept well in her bedroom at St Sunday's, so she'd been more than a little bit exasperated to find herself wide awake and staring at the ceiling hours before dawn.

She'd dreamt that she'd been running across the grounds of Butterton House, trying to catch up with the solitary little girl that she'd seen in the playground in Bowness, but no matter how many times Peggy had called out to her, the child had paid her no heed and just kept moving towards the thicket of trees at the edge of the estate's boundary.

Her eyes had snapped open abruptly, and it hadn't taken long for the disappointing certainty that there was no way she was going to drift off again to settle in her bones.

For a couple of hours, she'd just lain there, trying not to think about how she'd told Lily that her sister was still around, but then almost immediately abandoned her with that knowledge but with no way to speak to Violet; or about Marnie's fear of the future and her dependency on Peggy; or about Rex Hughes; or about Andrew's apparently inevitable encounter with Chambers; or about the fact that she was supposed to be 3000 miles away in a week's time.

It hadn't helped that she still felt like she hadn't managed to warm up after her ill-advised outdoors session of the night before.

Eventually she'd crawled out of bed, showered, dressed and headed downstairs to light the fire in the living room.

She'd been staring at the flames with yet another cup of tea in hand, when Mrs Laycock had let herself in at seven to start on breakfast.

Peggy had immediately been shooed back out of the kitchen when she'd offered to help, and Mrs Laycock had given her a look so full of motherly concern that Peggy suspected that she might actually look as terrible as she felt. She'd closed the door to the living room and traipsed back to her armchair with a sigh of deep dissatisfaction.

She'd heard everyone else stumble down the stairs around half-seven, but nobody had bothered Peggy until Andrew, who had obviously been nominated to come and tell her breakfast was ready, quietly knocked on the door just before eight.

By the time everyone was outside on the driveway an hour later, Peggy's head was pounding, and she'd already brushed off multiple concerned inquiries over breakfast, mostly from Lloyd. Charlie probably would have been particularly irritating about it, if he hadn't been wearing his sunglasses inside, which was a clear sign that he and Lloyd had stayed up far too late finishing a bottle of whiskey and therefore wasn't yet in the right frame of mind for critiquing anyone else's life choices.

'Right. Ready?' Andrew asked everyone as Mrs Laycock gave them all one last wave from inside the house and closed the door. Peggy silently shuffled towards the car in response.

'We'll see you at Butterton,' Jen replied with a nod, heading for her own car.

Lloyd, who was delightedly clutching two lemon drizzle cakes and plenty of leftovers courtesy of Mrs Laycock, gave Andrew a quick salute before following Jen.

Charlie was slumped against the Range Rover as Peggy unlocked the boot so that they could throw their bags in.

'Jesus, Peg, you look bloody awful.' He grimaced as he slid his sunglasses down his nose to squint at his sister. Apparently, the hangover had lifted enough for him to become communicative again. 'Were you awake all night?'

Peggy glared at him silently until he slowly raised his hands in a gesture of surrender and crawled into the backseat.

Andrew closed the boot and held out his hand in front of Peggy.

She stared at his palm stupidly. 'What?'

'Can I have the car keys, please?'

'Why?'

Andrew wrinkled his nose. 'I hope you understand that I'm making every attempt to ask with significantly more tact than your idiot brother but, Peggy, *did* you actually sleep last night?'

'Yes,' she replied firmly, and then promptly lost any further argument to a wide yawn.

'How about you take this?' Andrew handed her the large thermos of tea as he simultaneously pulled the car keys from her hand. 'And I'll take these.'

Peggy sighed loudly, but she didn't have the energy to argue with him; even going so far as to not even bother trying to stop him from opening the passenger door for her, or from closing it once she'd climbed in.

With Charlie's loud snoring from the back signalling that he'd opted out of being even remotely helpful, Peggy directed Andrew out of the village, with Jen following closely.

'You should try and sleep,' Andrew suggested when they left Briersthwaite behind them and joined the main road.

'I'm fine,' Peggy replied as she pulled her sleeves down over her hands and then wrapped her arms securely around the flask.

Andrew didn't make any further comment, but he reached over to flip the heating vents so that they were pointing at the passenger seat anyway.

Peggy turned her head to look out of the window as a lazy drizzle speckled the glass and she closed her eyes, trying to settle her thoughts.

When she opened them again, it was to find the landscape both significantly flatter and more familiar.

'Alright?'

Peggy shook her head in an attempt to clear the fog and turned her head at the soft question. 'What?'

Andrew gave her an amused look 'You've been out like a light since before we got anywhere near the M6.'

'I have?' Peggy asked, thoughts sluggish and muddled.

'You didn't even twitch when we stopped for petrol,' Charlie added, far too loudly from behind her. 'Or when I had to retrieve the tea you were selfishly hogging.'

'We're nearly home,' Peggy said as her brain finally began to stagger out of hibernation and she realised that she could see the tall chimneys of Butterton House in the near distance. She caught sight of Jen's car in the wing mirror.

'Are you sure you're alright, Peggy?' Charlie asked with significantly more sympathy than he'd managed back in the Lake District.

'Yes, thank you,' she lied smoothly as her skull throbbed in almost perfect time with her heartbeat.

She pushed her sleeve out of the way so that she could see her watch, and even though she knew how long the journey from Briersthwaite to home should take, she was surprised to find that it was almost noon. She didn't feel rested at all, and it was as though the almost three-hour nap hadn't made so much as the slightest dent in the weariness that she felt she was carrying deep in her bones.

Even though she could only see him out of the corner of her eye, Peggy could tell that Andrew didn't believe her, but she also knew him well enough to know that he wouldn't call her out on her lie when she was obviously trying to divert her brother from the truth.

'Do you think Marnie will actually be here?' Charlie asked as Andrew steered the car through the gates that marked the entrance to Butterton's long driveway.

Peggy's stomach twisted at the thought. She wasn't looking forward to the inevitable explosion if Marnie did actually show up; she already knew what Marnie's arguments were going to be, and she knew just as easily what Andrew would counter each point with. Since the very beginning, Andrew and Marnie had been well-matched when it came to disagreements.

'I do,' Andrew said as the house came into view. 'I trust her to know just how much she buggered up yesterday.'

Peggy wasn't sure what it said about the state of affairs when Andrew had more faith in Marnie than she did.

'Oh fuck!' Charlie yelped suddenly.

'What?' Andrew asked, immediately on high alert. 'What is it?'

Peggy saw the problem just before her brother spoke again and she almost asked Andrew to turn the car around.

'Looks like Father has a visitor,' Charlie snarled, reaching his hand between the two front seats to point at the sleek, silver classic car parked at the bottom of the steps. 'Mother must be going through another Grace Kelly phase if she's driving around in *that*.'

The car wobbled as Andrew's hands slipped on the steering wheel. 'What?'

'She's obviously come cap in hand, looking for something she missed in the divorce settlement,' Charlie replied waspishly.

If Peggy hadn't already been feeling like death warmed up, the thought of her mother – and God forbid, *Edgar* – inside the house would have been enough to drain every drop of blood from her face.

'Peggy, I can turn around and we can come back later,' Andrew said. He sounded calm, but there was a distinct strain to the words.

'No,' she replied quietly. 'We need to get this over with. I'm sure they'll be with Father at the back of the house, so we shouldn't cross paths with anyone.'

'*They?*' Charlie practically shrieked. 'You don't think she'd dare bring *him* here, do you?'

KEIRA WILLIS

Peggy closed her eyes and blew out her breath as slowly as she could stand. 'Andrew, can you please park the car by the garages? Jen can do the same. That should buy us some time before Timothy discovers we're back, if nothing else.'

Andrew did as he was instructed, and Peggy didn't dare look at him for fear of seeing even a hint of pity in his expression.

Peggy climbed out of the car silently, left her luggage in the boot to collect later, and kept her head held as high as possible while she led the way to the house. If she was going to find her mother on the other side of the door, then she wanted to at least look like she couldn't care less, even if her heart was hammering with anxiety.

She took a deep breath before twisting the doorknob and pushing the door open.

Andrew was just behind her as she stepped over the threshold into the blessedly empty entrance hall, and he pressed his finger to his lips as he turned to the others and shut the door behind them with barely a click.

Peggy was well aware of how ridiculous it was that she was sneaking into her house to avoid her parents, even though she hadn't been a teenager in well over fifteen years. Then again, the fact that the four other competent adults behind her knew that sneaking in silently would be better for all of them, perhaps said an awful lot more about how terrible her parents were than anything else.

She eyed the door to the library down the hallway, but decided quickly that it wouldn't necessarily give them enough shelter from any advancing storm that Caroline was probably already brewing in the other wing of the house. Instead, she crept across the hallway and started up the stairs.

Halfway up, she realised that nobody was following her, and so she turned around, confused, to find them standing in an uncertain cluster at the bottom of the stairs.

'Come on,' she hissed, 'She wouldn't dream of coming up here.'

She didn't wait for them but instead tiptoed quickly up the rest of the staircase and crossed the landing towards her bedroom.

Before her fingers had even twitched towards the doorknob, Peggy knew with certainty that Marnie was already waiting for them inside.

Sure enough, Peggy pushed the door open and found Marnie standing by her favoured window, with a concerned Emmeline right beside her. Marnie kept her eyes on her feet as everyone filed in.

'Peg, we could go somewhere else if you want,' Charlie said as he closed the door. Despite his frequent visits, he was well aware that his sister fiercely tried to guard her privacy.

'This is the absolute last place in the house that my mother would ever find herself,' Peggy said, looking around at the collection of awkward individuals arranged in her bedroom, once more wondering how she could possibly be experiencing this situation at this point in her life. 'We should be fine in here. Sit wherever you want.'

To demonstrate her point, Peggy sat on the end of her bed.

Charlie and Lloyd followed suit and sat in the window seat that wasn't currently blocked by Marnie; Jen perched herself on the stool at the dressing table; and Andrew leant against the wall with his arms folded. He was already watching Marnie, obviously just waiting for her to look up and say something.

For a long moment, the only sound that Peggy could hear was Andrew's watch ticking loudly; it reminded her awfully of the very first day that she'd met the majority of the people currently standing in her bedroom, back when she'd been looking for any hint that Marnie had remained in the house where she'd been killed months earlier.

'Marnie?' Andrew prompted eventually, his voice carefully neutral.

Marnie finally raised her head, lips twisted in a way that told Peggy that she hadn't yet decided whether she was going to head into this interaction ready for a fight, or if she would cede immediately.

'Nobody else has been in the Ballroom,' Marnie said eventually. 'There's been two policemen on the door since last night though, so if you had any ideas about heading in today, I'm not sure that's going to happen.'

'Have you managed to speak to Benson?' Andrew asked.

Marnie's calm expression twitched out of place for a second. 'No. Like I said to you yesterday, he always refuses to speak to me. Acts as though I'm not there and then hides himself away somewhere else.'

'Well, I need you to try harder.'

'Try harder?' Marnie raised her eyebrows. 'And how do you expect me to do that? I just told you; he buggers off whenever I'm there, and I don't know how to find him.'

'Well, perhaps he'll be more inclined to talk to you once he hears that we think he might have been complicit in hiding Davy Nash's body twenty years ago,' Andrew shot back.

'He did *what*?' Marnie asked, and righteous indignation fell away immediately. 'How'd you figure that out?'

Andrew looked over to Peggy and raised his eyebrows.

Peggy cleared her throat. 'We found Beth Nash yesterday. Higson didn't just hide Beth up in the Lake District though; he found Lily Woodhouse after she'd been attacked by Sean Kelly, and he took her up there too.'

Marnie's eyes were like saucers. 'She's still alive?'

Peggy nodded. 'She is, and her twin sister, Violet – she died when they were children – has stayed with her. She can't see her anymore though.'

'Can't see her anymore?' Marnie asked slowly.

'She could see her when they were kids,' Lloyd chimed in. 'It's how she used to do the trick that got her on TV.'

'And the trick that nearly got her killed,' Andrew added.

Marnie looked at Peggy for a long moment before she turned back to Andrew. 'But the policeman still somehow ended up dead?'

'Davy Nash was killed by Prentice that same night,' Andrew confirmed. 'According to Violet Woodhouse, they were planning to hide his body in Hulme, and the theory is that the two people drafted into help with that were Chambers and Benson.'

Marnie nodded once. 'Fine. Well, I can try and talk to him again, but he seems to only want to talk to Peggy, doesn't he?'

Peggy was slightly taken aback by the sharpness in Marnie's tone when she said her name.

Jen had a similarly surprised expression on her face, which at least made Peggy feel that she hadn't just imagined it.

'I'm sure he'd speak to you if he knew how important it was, Marnie,' Jen said quietly.

Marnie snorted and shook her head again. 'I doubt it. He probably doesn't appreciate getting the B Team.'

'Marnie,' Andrew warned.

Peggy held her breath as a good old wave of prescience crashed over her head.

'What?' Marnie snapped. She shifted all of her weight to her right foot as she folded her arms and shrugged at Andrew, the very picture of a petulant teenager. 'The only reason you asked me to go to the Ballroom was because you literally had nobody else you could ask!'

Andrew unfolded his own arms and raised his eyebrows. 'I asked you to go to the Ballroom because I thought I could trust you to do as you were told.'

'Trust?' Marnie laughed bitterly. 'You don't trust me at all.'

'Right now, I don't, no,' Andrew replied shortly. 'Because of your behaviour yesterday, we don't actually know what th-'

KEIRA WILLIS

'*My behaviour?*' Marnie interjected angrily. 'Stop talking to me like I'm a child.'

'Maybe I wouldn't need to, if you didn't keep acting like one!'

'Oh, fuck off!' Marnie threw her hands up.

'Marnie,' Peggy tried quietly, very aware of both Emmeline's increasingly uneasy expression and the fact that the air around her felt full of static.

Marnie whirled towards Peggy. 'And don't you start either! You used to be on my side, you know.'

Peggy's head gave a particularly vicious thump, and she pinched the bridge of her nose. 'We're all on the same side, Marnie.'

Marnie laughed derisively. 'You wouldn't have thought so, the way you and him keep having a go at me.'

'Marnie, you were supposed to stay in the Ballroom just in case anyone came snooping around,' Peggy argued before Andrew could interject and inevitably escalate the situation even further. 'You didn't though.'

'I told you why!' Marnie argued. 'I thought you of all people would understand.'

Peggy wrinkled her nose, not quite believing what she was hearing. 'You thought I'd understand why you decided that it would be a good idea to leave the Ballroom to go and visit Rex in prison? Because I genuinely don't understand that, Marnie.'

Marnie pursed her lips. 'Really? You don't understand why I might want to go and see the person I was planning on spending the rest of my life with? At Christmas?'

'Not when we're in the middle of an investigation!' Peggy shook her head in obvious frustration. 'No.'

'You know you're not actually a detective, don't you?'

Peggy chose to ignore that comment, fully aware that Marnie tended to fight dirty when she wasn't getting her own way in a dispute.

Marnie, however, did not appreciate the lack of response, and Peggy saw the exact moment when Marnie, unfortunately, decided that she obviously wasn't fighting dirtily enough.

'It's your bloody fault he's in jail, anyway, isn't it?' Marnie spat, prodding a finger in Peggy's direction.

'Woah, hang on!' Lloyd said, standing up and holding out his hands towards Marnie. 'That's not on, Marnie. Hughes is exactly where he belongs!'

Marnie glared at him. Lloyd swallowed heavily, but he didn't back down.

'Oh my God!' Marnie cried, turning her attention back to Peggy, who was trying to remain impassive in the hope that Marnie would run hot and then burn out quickly. 'Why are you even pretending to care about any of this anyway? We all know you're planning on running away to New York. You don't give a shit about any of us, do you? Jesus, Peggy, you really are a selfish cow, do you know that?'

There was an immediate explosion of sound as everyone else in the room chimed in, but Peggy didn't hear a single word they said. She was focused only on the accusation that Marnie had levelled at her; an accusation that she was absolutely *not* going to let lie.

'Selfish?' In contrast to Marnie's scorching fury, Peggy's voice was deathly cold, but it held enough power to silence the room immediately. '*I'm* selfish? Marnie, we're trying to find Higson and stop anyone else from getting killed, and you're popping off to Strangeways for a chat with Rex, but *I'm* the selfish one?'

Peggy would prefer that she didn't have an audience for this, but Marnie had left her with little choice. She rose to her feet slowly and refused to be cowed, even as the windows rattled in their frames. She'd dealt with Marnie's dramatics before and, if she were completely honest, she thought that she might finally have run out of patience.

Perhaps, honesty was what was needed, even if it was going to hurt both of them.

'Do you want to know what's selfish?' Peggy asked, but held up her hand before Marnie could even think about answering. '*Selfish* is exactly what you've been since the day I met you. Marnie, I am so, so sorry for everything that happened to you because of Rex, and because of Athena – *all of it* – but have you ever stopped to think about the fact that you just moved yourself into this house – *my house* – without a second thought? Or that you constantly expect me to drop whatever I'm doing and *immediately* answer a question, or listen to you talk about Rex, or sympathise with your complaints about whatever it is that you've decided that you're pissed off about on any particular day?'

'That's what friends do!' Marnie argued.

'Not every single hour of every single day, Marnie!' Peggy snapped, and she was vaguely aware that everyone else was looking at her in barely concealed surprise now that she'd raised her voice. 'Not at four in the morning, or when I'm trying to get some work done, or when I just need some bloody peace!'

'Well, I suppose I shouldn't be surprised that you don't know what it means to have friends, should I?' Marnie asked cooly. 'Your entire social circle is a bunch of people you sort of work with, and your brother. Your fiancé left you for your own *mother*, for God's sake. You're literally hiding from your parents right now. You know that none of that is *normal*, don't you?'

'Jesus Christ, you *are* a child!' Peggy growled, balling her fists at her sides.

'Marnie!' Charlie breathed, obviously horrified, but Marnie ignored him as she took another step towards Peggy.

'Well, it's true, isn't it?' Marnie shrugged and she had an awful, malicious smirk on her face. 'God, Peggy, I would *hate* to be you, do you know that? I might be dead, but at least I had a fucking *life*! You've got *nothing*.'

Peggy's hands were shaking. 'That's what you think, is it?'

Marnie nodded with another one of those supercilious smiles.

'Do you want to know what *I* think?' Peggy asked, and she kept her voice as steady as she could.

'Go on.' Marnie rolled her eyes.

'I think that you're terrified that if I leave, you'll just stop existing,' Peggy replied, and she couldn't make herself feel bad about the little flicker of spite when she saw Marnie's face twitch at her words. *Direct hit, Peggy.* 'I think you're terrified that Rex is going to forget about you. I actually think that you're terrified all the time, about *everything.*'

It was Marnie's turn to look taken aback.

'Here's the thing, though,' Peggy continued. 'We're all terrified. Literally, all of us, all of the time, and you'd see that if you just took one second away from thinking that you're the only bloody person on the planet who doesn't know what they're supposed to do next.'

'Oh, you're a psychiatrist now, are you?' Marnie asked snottily, but she'd lost an awful lot of her previous bravado.

Peggy shook her head, taking in a deep breath through her nose to combat the leaden, nauseating weight in the pit of her stomach. 'Look, we all know that you'll do whatever you want, Marnie; you always do, don't you? So, either try to talk to Benson, or don't. I don't really care anymore. You're not actually the centre of the fucking universe, and the rest of us will be just fine working out how to get through all of this without you if we have to.'

With that, Peggy turned away and headed for the door.

'I'll be in the car when you're ready,' she said as she brushed past Andrew, not daring to look up at his expression.

She could feel the strained silence pressing against her back the whole way down the stairs and out through the front door to the drizzly afternoon.

Peggy climbed into the driver's seat of the Range Rover moments later and slammed the door behind her before letting out the shaky breath she'd been holding in since she'd walked out of her bedroom.

'Christ,' she whispered to herself, wrapping her fingers around the steering wheel to steady them. She was more than half-expecting Marnie to come tearing out from the house to shout at her again, and her apprehension didn't diminish one iota even as the seconds ticked by into long minutes that eventually stretched to an almost full half hour.

The rest of her was waiting for the glass in her bedroom windows to blow outwards in a violent shower of deadly shards. Then again, Marnie tended not to do things by degrees, so there was always a possibility that the entirety of Butterton House would be reduced to rubble behind her.

Jesus Christ, how was this her life?

The passenger door opened suddenly, giving her such a fright that she flinched wildly and her elbow collided with the window.

Peggy slumped in relief when she saw that it was neither Marnie, nor her mother – a fleeting, but nightmarish scenario that she hadn't even considered until that moment – but Andrew.

He closed the door with the purposeful care of someone who would have much rather slammed it.

Peggy returned her gaze to the closed garage doors in front of her and turned the key in the ignition.

Andrew sighed quietly. 'Are y-'

Peggy shook her head. 'No.'

She manoeuvred away from the garages and drove back towards the house. Her mother's car was still parked at the bottom of the steps, but even after they passed without incident, Peggy kept her eyes on the rearview mirror until the house was finally lost to the trees when the driveway curled gently past the lake.

There was still a tremor running through Peggy's fingers as the village bled into open fields around them, and she readjusted her grip on the steering wheel in the hope that it would hide the evidence from the keen eyes of her passenger. She doubted she'd managed it, but she appreciated Andrew's continued silence all the same.

'Do you think you'll be at Chester House long?' she asked eventually.

Andrew jolted slightly, obviously surprised at finally being addressed. 'I think that'll depend on what sort of mood Chambers is in, and how willing to believe me he is.'

'He's not going to try and make it look like you're somehow involved in Sean Kelly's death, is he?'

Andrew blew out his breath slowly. 'I have to believe that he wouldn't go that far.'

'That's not the same as *no*.'

'I know, but it's the best I've got right now.' Andrew shrugged apologetically.

Peggy wanted to ask him what they were supposed to do if Chambers *did* go that far, but she knew that Andrew wouldn't have an answer for her; or, at least, not an answer that she'd want to accept.

'I'm going to tell him that I got the bus back to Gatley on Friday, that I briefly went into my house to get sorted, and then came to meet you,' Andrew said, putting an end to any further discussion of it anyway.

Peggy nodded. 'Where did you meet me? And why didn't I come to the house to pick you up?'

'Easy. I met you up by the park,' Andrew replied, 'which is technically true. As for why, it's because we both know that that's where the best chips in Gatley are. We were going to be in the car for a good few hours driving north, so I'd already suggested that I go and order food. That way you could just pull in outside and pick me up.'

'Makes sense,' Peggy agreed. 'And they *are* the best chips in Gatley.'

Andrew grinned but sobered quickly. 'Like I said to Jen, they'll find it difficult to call us out on any of it; they'd have to admit that we were being watched even before Sean Kelly was killed.'

Even so, Peggy didn't like the fact that they were walking into a situation where they seemed to be missing quite a lot of key information. The sign for the Gatley turn off came into view much sooner than she would have liked.

'Look,' Andrew said as Peggy swiped at the indicator, 'you can veto this if you want, but I thought that I'd tell Chambers that you and I first met at the theatre back during *Lady Bancroft* if that's alright with you. I was there for the case, but Chambers can't really question your presence when your family owns the building. It's also likely that someone will know that your brother and Lloyd have been friends for a while, and that only helps our story, I suppose.'

Peggy nodded even as her stomach twisted in displeasure at the thought of that damn theatre.

'Everything else can be the truth with a slight spin on it, alright?' Andrew continued, accepting Peggy's agreement as they neared Acacia Road. 'Places we've been for dinner a good few times, and things like that. If Chambers decides to dig a bit further, enough people have seen me and you together in town.'

'Not much since March though,' Peggy replied, skirting awfully close to an embargoed topic.

'Granted,' Andrew agreed quietly as Peggy turned off the main road. 'Peggy, I can't promise that any of this won't get back to your father.'

'I know,' Peggy sighed as the house came into view. 'I know.'

As she parked the car outside of Andrew's house, Peggy looked up at the front left-hand upstairs window out of habit, but there was no sign of Rob.

'Shit,' Andrew hissed as he released his seatbelt.

'What?' Peggy looked towards where Andrew was subtly pointing at a white Ford Capri further up the road.

'Fallon,' Andrew grumbled, averting his eyes from the other car. 'Well, there goes any chance of a pleasant drive to Chester House. He's going to bloody *love* this.'

He awkwardly reached into his coat pocket and produced a keyring that he then handed to Peggy. 'House keys and my key for the Ballroom. I don't want Fallon to have them for even a second if I can help it. The one with the red sticker is for my front door.'

Peggy took the keyring and quickly concealed it in her own pocket.

'Can you go into the house and see if anyone's obviously tried to get in while we've been away?' Andrew asked. 'If I leave my bag in the boot, you've got the perfect excuse to take it inside. I don't want you to hang around though, Peggy. If Chambers wants anyone to talk to you, it's not happening here.'

'He's seen you,' Peggy muttered as she watched a man wearing an ill-fitting suit and a pugnacious expression climb out of the Capri. He gestured towards the uniformed officer in the passenger seat.

'Alright,' Andrew sighed as he opened the door. 'Let's get this over with.'

'Andrew.' Peggy reached over and grabbed his hand, stopping him from opening the door. 'Be careful. Please.'

Andrew nodded slowly and squeezed her fingers once. 'I will.'

Peggy let go reluctantly and climbed out of the car.

Fallon approached them as Andrew came to stand next to Peggy on the pavement.

'Where've you been, Joyce?' Fallon asked snottily, a wad of chewing gum rolling around in his open mouth as he spoke. 'I thought you'd have come running straight back to us when the news of your scummy boss broke.'

Andrew tensed next to her, and Peggy wrapped her fingers around his wrist as casually as she could manage without drawing Fallon's attention to the silent plea for caution.

'I only saw the news this morning,' Andrew replied, and it was terse, but at least he didn't quite sound like he was only seconds away from launching himself at the other man as Peggy had feared he might.

'Oh, right,' Fallon drawled, before he made the very poor decision to turn his head and leer at Peggy. The yellowed chewing gum squeaked between his teeth and turned Peggy's stomach. '*I see.*'

Peggy channelled every memory of her brother being snotty in Estate meetings and curled her lips in distaste. 'You see *what*, exactly?'

Fallon's face twitched and he turned back to Andrew. 'DCI Chambers wants to speak to you. I'm here to take you in.'

'Now?' Andrew asked, sounding suitably surprised for someone who had actually been expecting this exact outcome.

'Now,' Fallon confirmed smugly. 'So, you need to come with me.'

'What?' Peggy went as wide-eyed as she dared, suspecting that Fallon might not be quite as dense as Andrew had made him out to be in prior diatribes.

'It's alright,' Andrew replied, his focus on Peggy. 'I'll see you for dinner later, yeah?'

'Well, we'll see about that,' Fallon muttered.

Andrew barely suppressed an eyeroll. 'Whatever happens, I'll call you.'

'We'll see about that too,' Fallon added nastily.

Peggy didn't need to feign any of her concern at hearing that. She really hoped that Andrew wasn't underestimating just how precarious his position might be. It was exactly the sort of thing he tended to do.

Andrew shot Fallon a dangerous look and turned his back on him, giving Peggy his full attention.

'It's alright, Peg,' he said with the barest of nods. Then he took a single step forward and enveloped her in a tight embrace.

Peggy blinked in surprise before the realisation that she was probably supposed to reciprocate kicked her brain into gear and she wrapped her own arms around Andrew's back, holding on slightly tighter than she thought she was meant to for the benefit of their fiction.

'If you don't hear from me, be at Bombay Palace at half eight, okay?' Andrew whispered hurriedly beside her ear as he pulled away, lips barely brushing her cheek.

'Alright, put her down,' Fallon sneered and clapped his hand on Andrew's shoulder.

Andrew roughly shrugged him off and gave Peggy one last apologetic quirk of his mouth before he turned and strode towards the Capri with his head held high. As he reached the car, the uniformed officer hopped out quickly and gave Andrew a respectful little nod.

Peggy immediately went to the back of the Range Rover and opened the boot to retrieve Andrew's bag. Looking through the car's interior and out through the windscreen, she caught sight of Fallon staring back at her. Pretending she hadn't noticed, she quickly unzipped the bag and tipped the entire contents out into the boot before fastening it back up. She then took Andrew's keys out of her pocket and located the one with the little red sticker on it and readied it in her hand before closing the boot and carrying the now empty bag towards the house.

Ignoring Fallon completely, she walked up the garden path, making a slight production of switching the arm she was holding the bag in, in the hope that it would help make it look significantly fuller and heavier than it now was.

When she reached the house, she quickly unlocked the door

and placed the backpack on the ground just out of sight in the hallway, before finally turning back to face the road.

Fallon was still standing next to the open driver's door watching her closely. It was unnerving, to say the least, but she kept her eyes focussed on where she could just make out Andrew inside the car. She didn't want to give Fallon the slightest cause to think that she was in any way nervous or had something to hide.

She was just starting to wonder if she should just go into the house and close the door behind her when, suddenly, Fallon looked sharply into the backseat of his car and gestured menacingly with his hand. Peggy assumed that Andrew had said something to cause such a negative reaction, particularly as the uniformed officer seemed to be stifling a laugh with his hand, careful not to let Fallon see.

Eventually, Fallon got behind the wheel of the car and drove far too quickly up Acacia Road, not even bothering to acknowledge Peggy's presence that time.

Andrew gave her a quick wave through the window as the Capri sped by, and Peggy watched after the car long after it had turned onto Altrincham Road and disappeared towards Manchester.

When Peggy finally closed the door heavily behind her, she rested against it as she slowly emptied her lungs in a long, measured exhale. The house didn't look disturbed in any way, but she couldn't be sure until she'd spoken to the one person who'd be able to tell her for certain.

A glance through the open kitchen door at the end of the hall gave her a glimpse of Rob Joyce, who was just about visible as he stood near the window, and she started towards him immediately.

'Hi, Rob,' she greeted him quietly as she approached. 'Sorry, I haven't been around in a while. Things have been a bit…'

She trailed off with a wave of her hand and gave him a small smile, which he returned immediately, breaking her heart a little bit more, just like always.

'Andrew's had to go and deal with something, but he'll be back later.' Peggy leant back against the kitchen counter. 'For now, though, I was hoping that you could answer some questions for me, because your brother might be underestimating just how much trouble we could be in.'

Rob tilted his head to show that he was listening.

Peggy's skull throbbed painfully again, and she had to take a deep breath before she could return all of her attention to Rob.

'Are you alright?' Rob's quiet words were full of static.

'I'm fine.' Peggy forced a smile.

When all Rob did was frown in disbelief, Peggy was hit with the startling realisation that this answer worked about as well on Rob Joyce as it ever did on his brother.

TWENTY

Andrew spent most of the drive to Chester House doing his best to completely ignore anything that Fallon said to him. He disregarded jibes about the Ballroom, about Higson, about Peggy, and about anything Fallon could think of that might needle Andrew into attempting to thump him and thus give him the perfect opportunity to make Andrew's life even more difficult.

Fallon had never been the brightest button, but Andrew still found it disappointing that someone who was *supposedly* at the same level of professional standing as him would resort to such obvious tactics; Andrew would really appreciate greater elegance in any underhanded schemes that were being rolled out to try and trap him.

Pretending that Fallon didn't exist gave Andrew the opportunity to capture the headspace he'd been chasing for days, and he'd stared sightlessly at the passing scenery trying not to think about anything at all for the near half an hour it took to arrive at his old workplace.

When Fallon finally pulled into a space in the carpark, Andrew had to shake himself out of his daze quickly.

He couldn't resist making a show of looking out of the window and raising his eyebrows. 'Do all the DIs have to park this far away from the door these days, or just the shit ones?'

Fallon said nothing, but he practically flung himself out of the car and glared at Andrew. '*Out.*'

Andrew awkwardly unfolded his long legs from the cramped backseat, but he refused to give Fallon the satisfaction of seeing any discomfort on his face as he awkwardly climbed out.

'Tell Chambers that we're here,' Fallon snapped at the uniformed officer.

'Sir,' he replied, but it lacked any real attempt at respect.

Not waiting for Fallon, Andrew strode right past the uniformed officer, and towards the building that had once represented everything that he'd worked so hard for as he tried to keep any hint of trepidation from his face.

He ignored the curious glances from a couple of familiar faces in the lobby, and he was already in the lift with the floor button pressed by the time Fallon caught up with him, just managing to duck in before the doors closed in his face.

Shame. Andrew had been looking forward to arriving at Chambers' door without his escort.

'Not sure why you're looking so smug, mate,' Fallon panted slightly as the lift began to slowly ascend. 'The whole Graveyard's fucked.'

'We prefer not to use that name anymore,' Andrew replied mildly. He had eighteen months' worth of dealing with Charlie Swan behind him, so he wasn't anywhere near as easily riled these days.

For just a second, Andrew wondered if Fallon was going to be the one to actually thump *him*, but blessedly the doors opened, and he took the opportunity to slip out into the corridor before any violence had time to bloom into fruition.

He caught sight of Mike rifling through a stack of paper with a telephone pressed between his chin and shoulder, but they didn't acknowledge each other. In fact, most people avoided meeting his eye as he neared Chambers' office.

Well, it was nice to have it confirmed to Andrew that he was persona non grata these days.

Andrew rapped on Chambers' door before Fallon had caught up with him again.

'Come in,' Chambers called, and Andrew entered, shutting the door quickly behind him.

'Sir,' Andrew greeted his former boss, managing to sound significantly more deferential than he felt.

Fallon burst in a couple of seconds later, red-faced, and Andrew tried very hard not to show any amusement in response to the murderous expression.

'Sit,' Chambers commanded Andrew, before turning to Fallon. 'Out.'

'Out?' Fallon repeated, his surprise evident.

Chambers didn't bother restating his instruction, and instead he uncapped the pen he was holding before returning his full attention to Andrew. 'Joyce, I assume I don't need to tell you why you're here.'

The door closed as Fallon let himself out.

'I saw the news this morning, sir,' Andrew stated carefully. 'I came back to Manchester straight away.'

Chambers narrowed his eyes and looked at him critically. 'And where exactly have you been?'

'The Lake District, sir,' Andrew replied, watching carefully for any particular reaction to the location but seeing none.

'In December?' Chambers asked sceptically as he noted this down.

Here we go. Andrew shrugged nonchalantly. 'My girlfriend's family have a house in Briersthwaite. It's a village on Ullswater.'

'And when exactly did you arrive there?'

'Friday evening.'

'And I suppose your girlfriend will vouch for your presence?'

Andrew tilted his head as though shocked by such a question. 'Why would I need her to vouch for me, sir?'

'Answer the question, Joyce.'

'She can tell you truthfully that I was with her until she dropped me at my house today,' Andrew replied. 'Where, by the way, I was immediately approached by DI Fallon and brought here without explanation.'

'Can anyone else confirm that you were in Briersthwaite?' Chambers asked.

'Am I under suspicion for something?'

'Joyce, can anyone else confirm that you were in Briersthwaite?' Chambers snapped, and there was a hint of strange unease beneath the words.

'Yes, sir,' Andrew replied steadily. 'The housekeeper – Mrs Laycock – can confirm that we arrived on Friday evening and left this morning after breakfast.'

Chambers looked at him as though he'd grown a second head. 'Housekeeper?'

'That's correct,' Andrew replied. 'Sir, I had actually hoped that you'd brought me here to share any information about DCI Higson or his whereabouts that you might now have.'

'Why on earth would you think that?' Chambers asked, putting the pen down. 'You chose to leave CID, Joyce. You are not part of this investigation.'

'Well, I'm here.'

Chambers narrowed his eyes. 'You are *here* so that you have the opportunity to assure me that you are in no way involved in a former police officer's death, unlike your current DCI.'

'You don't really think that Higson killed Sean Kelly, do you?' Andrew asked, and at least some of his disbelief was genuine.

'You are not part of this investigation,' Chambers repeated sternly.

'Higson's not a murderer.'

'You've not known Bill Higson for very long, Joyce.'

'No, but you have,' Andrew argued. 'Will you at least tell me *why* you're so sure he's involved?'

For a long moment, Chambers just stared levelly back at him, and Andrew was braced for a reprimand when his former DCI finally spoke again.

'Kelly identified Higson just before he was killed,' Chambers explained, clasping his hands on top of his notepad.

Andrew's face slackened in shock. Whatever he'd expected Chambers to say, it certainly hadn't been that.

Chambers rubbed his hands over his face, briefly dislodging the spectacles perched on his nose. 'Kelly called 999 to report an intruder in his house. He went on to identify this person as Higson. He was still on the call when he was shot.'

'I thought it was called in when a neighbour heard gunshots,' Andrew said, thinking back to every news report he'd seen over the weekend.

'It *was* called in by a neighbour,' Chambers replied, 'but there was already a unit on the way to Kelly's house.'

'No,' Andrew said, shaking his head. 'I don't believe that Higson would do that.'

'The chain of events isn't up for debate, Joyce,' Chambers snapped, and all previous hints of openness dried up instantly. He tossed the pen and notepad onto the desk in front of Andrew. 'Contact details for your girlfriend and this housekeeper. Now.'

Andrew picked up the pen and scribbled down Peggy's phone number. 'You should warn whoever makes this call that they should be as discreet as possible about the reason they're calling.'

'And why would I need to do that?' Chambers asked, nonplussed.

'Because if Peggy's father gets wind of the fact that his only daughter is having her actions questioned by the police, then I expect he won't be too happy,' Andrew replied. 'I'm fairly certain that the Earl of Acresfield knows the Chief Constable socially.'

Andrew had absolutely no idea if there was any truth to the idea, but he enjoyed the way Chambers' face paled at the idea of the Chief Constable getting involved. More than that, though, if Chambers believed him, it would lend Peggy an extra level of protection. Chambers might be as bent as they came, but he'd always been very careful about presenting a pristine image for the court of public opinion.

'You'll also need to make sure that you address her correctly, especially if the butler answers the phone,' Andrew continued, 'so, that'll be *Lady Margaret Swan*, not Peggy, not Miss Swan. As for the housekeeper, her name is Hilda Laycock, and she lives next door to the Swans' house in Briersthwaite. I don't have her number, but I'm sure you'll be able to get it without too much trouble, *sir.*'

Andrew knew that he was now skirting the very boundary of propriety with a senior officer, but considering that said senior officer was likely involved in concealing Davy Nash's body twenty years prior, not to mention his current connections to undesirable characters in the city, including Rex bloody Hughes, he couldn't bring himself to feel too badly about it.

Chambers snatched the pen and paper back. 'When did you last see Higson?'

'Thursday,' Andrew replied steadily.

'Where?'

'Tib Street.'

'So, you didn't see him at all on Friday?'

Andrew shook his head. 'No, but that's not necessarily unusual. It was Friday, and it's Higson.'

'What case are you currently working on?' Chambers asked, gaze sharpening.

Andrew frowned. 'Why?'

'Joyce, might I remind you that I am currently considering this a casual conversation as a courtesy to the fact that you are a serving officer, but that if you'd prefer to make this entire process more official, I can arrange to have you formally interviewed, with a view to suspension if you continue to deflect my questions.'

Andrew desperately wanted to ask Chambers why he hadn't just suspended him anyway – it wouldn't be that hard to concoct a reason, given the current circumstances, and it would certainly make it a lot harder for Andrew to get any investigating of his own done if that's what Chambers was concerned about – but he thought it might be best not to push his luck any further. Fucking with Fallon was one thing, but Chambers was an entirely different beast.

'Alan Jermyn,' Andrew replied with a practised sigh. 'Reported as a missing person in 1972. We've tracked him down to Spain, and we're expecting his arrival at the airport on Thursday.'

Chambers scrutinised him carefully. 'Anything else?'

'I believe the next case DCI Higson has selected for us is the historical theft of some valuables from a former Lord Mayor.' Andrew kept his face carefully blank.

He left out the part about the missing socks because he was fairly certain that Chambers would genuinely think he was just taking the piss, and he wasn't going to risk suspension for that.

'And that's it?' Chambers asked, eyes narrowed to mere slits behind his glasses.

'That's it,' Andrew lied smoothly.

Chambers sighed loudly, shaking his head, and Andrew wasn't sure what verdict was about to befall him. 'I hope, for your sake, that you are being honest with me, Joyce.'

'Sir,' Andrew replied, which was really neither a confirmation nor a denial, but all that he was willing to offer.

'Stay there,' Chambers instructed as he ripped the page out of his notepad, stood up and opened the door. 'Fallon!'

Andrew curled his fingers against his jeans. Chambers had a whole building of people to dole out tasks to, and he was going to rely on goddamn Fallon to check Andrew's alibi?

'He's just gone downstairs!' someone called back.

Chambers muttered something that Andrew couldn't make out, but it didn't seem particularly complimentary based on tone, and then added, louder, 'Cooke!'

Andrew turned around and watched as Chambers stalked

across the room to speak to someone he didn't recognise. Chambers handed over the paper to the young officer, speaking quickly and gesturing towards his office.

Cooke looked over towards him, a mildly baffled expression on his boyish face, and Andrew gave him a short nod instead of the scowl that he'd have preferred to have bestowed. As Cooke's frown only deepened the more Chambers spoke, Andrew could only assume his instructions regarding contacting Peggy were being relayed.

A minute later, Chambers returned to his office and gestured for Andrew to follow him back out. He led him towards the lift again but paused outside a room just before they reached it.

Chambers opened the door. 'In.'

'In there?' Andrew asked doubtfully, pointing into the small storeroom. 'It's a cupboard.'

'Hopkins, bring that chair here,' Chambers demanded, flapping his hand impatiently.

A few seconds later, an uncomfortable-looking plastic chair was wedged tightly between the shelves and the door had been propped open.

'Now it's a waiting room,' Chambers stated drily. 'Sit there, do not talk to anyone, and do not leave this room until I say so. Do you understand, Joyce?'

Not really, thought Andrew.

'Yes, sir,' is what he said aloud, wearily sinking into the chair under the watchful eye of his former boss. It felt disturbingly like being in trouble at school.

Chambers shook his head and then left him alone.

Andrew folded his arms as he stretched out his legs in front of him, crossing his ankles with a sigh of unhappiness. He then tilted his head back and stared at the yellowed ceiling tiles above him, settling himself in for whatever indeterminate amount of time Chambers deemed appropriate.

Great.

'They found Higson's car in Colwyn Bay a few hours ago.'

Andrew lurched upright in surprise at the sound of Mike Lawson's quiet, hurried voice. Mike was visible in the doorway, but he was turned away from Andrew and for all the world looked like he was engrossed in the open file in his hand.

'What?' Andrew hissed.

'Not now,' Mike muttered before walking away, eyes still on the paperwork.

Andrew leant as far forwards as he could manage without actually standing up and immediately alerting anyone to his movement, hoping that Mike might come back and tell him something else. He just about caught the back of Mike's head as he strolled into an office.

While Andrew appreciated the subtly delivered update from Mike, he actually had a good few hundred follow up questions for him.

The office door remained stubbornly closed though, and it didn't take long for it to become irritatingly clear to Andrew that Mike wasn't coming back any time soon.

He tipped his head back again and closed his eyes in frustration. For now, he was firmly out of the game, and he just had to hope that everyone else – Marnie, in particular – was doing exactly what they'd agreed to do.

When they'd all walked into Butterton House earlier, Andrew had fully been expecting an argument with Marnie. Disagreements had been a cornerstone of their relationship, even back when he'd only had Peggy's word that Marnie existed at all, but he hadn't expected to witness the detonation of the status quo.

Peggy had always made it her business to fight Marnie's corner, even when it had been to her own detriment, and although there had been minor quarrels between the pair of them before, this was the most serious row Andrew had witnessed.

When Peggy had walked out, it had been Charlie who'd spoken first.

'What in Christ's name do you think you're playing at?' he'd demanded. He hadn't raised his voice at all, but Andrew was fairly certain that he'd never heard Charlie sound quite so furious with anyone before.

Marnie had, unsurprisingly, turned on him immediately, but Charlie had shut her down with a single word.

'Why?' Charlie had still been speaking quietly, but from the way Marnie had recoiled you'd have thought he'd have taken a swipe at her. All wind was ripped from the sails of further argument, and she'd deflated before their eyes.

Marnie had wrapped her arms around her stomach, almost bent double as she'd let out a plaintive whine. She'd then slumped to the carpet, drawing her knees to her chin, only moments before she'd begun crying in earnest and buried her face in her hands to stifle the sound.

When Marnie had finally remembered the circumstances of her own murder, she'd been standing right in front of Andrew in the Ballroom, and he'd seen every instant of it play out on her face. He'd never experienced raw grief quite like it, but the events of earlier that afternoon had come close. Standing in Peggy's bedroom, it had felt like Marnie was mourning her death all over again.

Andrew had been furious with her for so many reasons – for leaving the Ballroom the day before, for the way she'd attacked Peggy, for speaking to that arse, Hughes – but he'd also listened to what Peggy had said, not just to Marnie, but to him the night before, and he understood that Marnie was genuinely terrified about her future. It had tempered his anger just enough.

He'd glanced quickly at everyone else to find that they were all looking back at him. A sense of inevitability had settled over him and he'd allowed himself to indulge in one blustery sigh before he'd crossed the room to crouch in front of Marnie.

She'd given no indication that she'd noticed his approach and had just continued to weep into her fingers. Andrew had been on the receiving end of one of Marnie's more dramatic snits in the past, and he had a scar near his right eye to prove it. So, it was with a great deal of apprehension that he'd then quietly called her name.

'What?' Marnie had whimpered pathetically.

Andrew had sighed again, even louder that time, and awkwardly shuffled around until he had been able to sit cross-legged on the floor – something that he really wasn't built for.

'Marnie, I need to understand what's going on with you right now,' Andrew had said.

'You don't care,' Marnie had sniffled, words muffled. 'None of you do. Stop pretending that you're not pissed off with me just so I do what you want.'

'Oh, I *am* pissed off with you,' Andrew had replied evenly. 'Probably more than I ever have been before, but me yelling at you, and you blowing up Peggy's house in retaliation is not really the way I want this to end, so can we just try and keep this civil? I want you to explain to me why you left the Ballroom yesterday.'

Marnie had wrinkled her nose as she'd looked at him. 'You're just trying to sound reasonable because you still want me to talk to Benson, and you don't want to send your precious Peggy in there.'

Andrew had needed to bite the inside of his cheek really hard at that point. 'Marnie, I think you know exactly how unfair you're being right now.'

The murderous glare she'd shot him hadn't filled him with confidence that the tack he'd chosen was the correct one, but he'd barrelled on regardless.

'Don't give me that look,' he'd said. 'You're not stupid, Marnie, and I know that you're aware that everything you just said to Peggy was designed to hurt. The thing is, Peggy's not stupid either – far from it – and she knows exactly what's going on with you. So, if you're so scared of what happens to you if Peggy leaves, why the hell are you saying everything you can possibly think of to make her want to leave?'

For a long moment, Marnie had remained silent as she'd run her fingers lightly over the carpet, leaving darker tracks in the disturbed dark pink fibres. Andrew always needed to take a second to remind himself that, by all usual understanding and technical definition, at least, Marnie was no longer alive whenever she did things like that.

'Because she's going to leave anyway,' Marnie had muttered eventually.

'You don't know that for certain,' Andrew had replied, shaking his head. 'Anyway, she's only planning on going for a few weeks. Nothing will happen to you in that time, Marnie.'

Marnie had looked at him like he was the densest person she'd ever had the misfortune of speaking to. 'Do you really think that if Peggy gets away from all of *this*, that she'll only stay away for a few weeks?'

That was exactly what Andrew had been thinking until Charlie had opened his big mouth in Briersthwaite and listed all the reasons why Peggy would probably be much happier a good few thousand miles away from all of them.

'What if I explain it to her – if I tell her how worried I am – and she decides to stay away anyway?' Marnie had added before Andrew had managed to formulate a response to her first question.

'So, what?' Andrew had tried hard to reign in his disbelief at the conclusion he'd reached. 'If you think that you've *made* her leave, that will somehow make you feel better when it actually happens? Is that it?'

Marnie had appeared instantly caught out. She'd then narrowed her eyes as she pointed a finger at Andrew. 'You don't want her to go either.'

Well, she hadn't been wrong about that, but Andrew had very pointedly not looked at anyone else as he'd sighed in agreement. 'Of course I don't want her to go.'

'Then why haven't you told her that?' Marnie's accusation had been clear and landed as squarely as she'd obviously intended.

Andrew's pride, however, had already taken enough of a beating by that point, and so he couldn't tell Marnie that his own reasoning was eerily similar to hers. Instead, he'd just shrugged and said, 'I don't think any of us should be telling Peggy what to do with her life.'

Marnie had looked as though she were ready to contest that idea with gusto.

'You shouldn't have left the Ballroom yesterday,' Andrew had added, cutting off any tirade before it could get going. 'I was telling the truth when I said that I thought I could trust you to do that, Marnie.'

'Nothing was happening!' Marnie had argued loudly, just like she had on the phone. 'I didn't see how leaving for a couple of hours would be a problem.'

Andrew had swallowed down his irritation again. 'Can you see why it might be a problem now?'

'They just made a mess of the place, and they didn't even get into the archive rooms!' Marnie had snapped. 'I doubt they were even there for very long.'

'You can't know that for sure,' Andrew had replied through gritted teeth.

'Yeah, and you can't know for sure that they *were* there for ages.'

'Which is the entire problem, Marnie, *Jesus*.' Andrew had pressed his fingertips to his forehead at that.

Lloyd, of all people, had taken that as a sign to step in, and Andrew had been too astonished to be immediately thankful for the reprieve. If he'd been expecting support to arrive at any point, he'd have put good money on it being *Jen* who spoke up.

'Marnie, if any of the rest of us had done what you did yesterday, we'd all be expecting a total bollocking from the boss,' Lloyd had said, and he'd actually sounded as annoyed as Andrew felt. 'It's not any different for you.'

'He's right,' Jen had chimed in when Marnie had glared at Lloyd. 'If you get an order, you follow it. If you *don't* follow it, then you need to have a really good reason for making that decision.'

Marnie had raised her eyebrows sceptically. 'Have you forgotten that I'm not actually one of you? I'm not a detective!'

'Neither's Peggy,' Lloyd had argued.

'Yeah, but that's different, isn't it?' Marnie had snarled. 'Peggy gets to help properly.'

'Watching the Ballroom yesterday was your chance to 'help properly',' Lloyd had added mulishly, folding his arms. 'Do you know what the boss would have done to me if I'd buggered off from my post to go and have a chat with Fiona?'

As Lloyd had stared Marnie down, Andrew had been reminded that his DC had three older sisters and was likely very used to being scowled at during heated disagreements.

Marnie had remained silent, pursing her lips.

'He'd have kicked my arse back to Didsbury,' Lloyd had said, before he'd turned to Andrew. 'Wouldn't you, boss?'

Andrew had nodded.

'It's not the same!' Marnie had growled.

'You're right, it's not. What you did was actually worse, and you know it.' Lloyd had stared back unblinkingly.

Marnie had eventually dropped her eyes before she'd returned her attention to Andrew and mumbled unintelligibly.

Andrew had frowned again. 'What?'

'I said I was sorry,' Marnie ground out, and even though she didn't sound particularly apologetic, Andrew was going to take it for the miracle it was anyway.

'Okay,' he'd said simply, hoping that everyone else took that as an instruction to take a step back. They still needed to tread very carefully.

'I hope you're going to apologise to Peggy,' Charlie had added snippily, clearly missing Andrew's silent memo.

Andrew and Marnie had turned twin glowers on him.

'Later,' Andrew had stated firmly, knowing that Peggy would likely not appreciate seeing Marnie just then, but also because he had to get Marnie back onside with the investigation if they had a hope in hell of getting anywhere fast.

'Later,' Marnie had agreed, keeping her ferocious stare trained on Charlie for a few more moments.

Charlie had looked unimpressed, but he'd known better than to push his luck.

'What are we going to do now, sir?' Jen had asked, wisely steering the conversation towards the reason that they were all meeting together in the first place.

It had taken all of Andrew's increasingly limited patience to then stay and work through the finer details of the next steps in the plan, especially when he knew that Peggy was waiting for him in the car.

He had to believe that it had been worth every extra second it had taken to convince Marnie to go back to the Ballroom though, because she really was their only hope of finding out what Benson's connection to all of this was. He'd had to very carefully keep a lid on the many, *many* things he'd still wanted to say to Marnie about her terrible decision to visit Hughes in Strangeways, because it would only have ended in the explosion, both literal and figurative, that he'd been working hard to avoid.

There was going to have to been time for all of that later.

When he'd finally excused himself and traipsed towards the sweeping staircase, all the while listening carefully for interfering butlers and unhinged aristocrats, he'd taken the opportunity to let his eyes sweep around the space he was in.

Halfway along the galleried landing he'd come across a series of portraits that he'd assumed were long-dead members of the Swan family. He'd drawn up short, his mouth open in gormless surprise as he'd stared at the painting of a woman in the middle of the row. The subject of the painting was older and much sterner than Peggy, but they shared similar enough features that the family resemblance was obvious. The painted wisps of fair hair that artfully fell around the face on the canvas were the same as those that framed Peggy's own face.

A surge of icy apprehension had rumbled through Andrew's body and settled somewhere behind his ribcage as he was struck by a memory of arriving at Butterton earlier in the year. He'd been turned away by Timothy on the understanding that neither Swan sibling had been at home, but as Andrew had headed back to his car, he'd seen a flash of blonde hair in an upstairs window. He'd subsequently accused Peggy of hiding from him, but she'd vehemently denied even being there. After everything that had happened at the theatre and in his own house in the days that had followed that evening, Andrew had clean forgotten about it all until he'd found himself on that landing that afternoon, forced to confront the unsettling realisation that perhaps he'd somehow seen another ghost.

Thinking about it again, even miles away in Chester House, caused Andrew to shiver, and his eyes snapped open trying to clear the image from his mind.

He leant forwards trying to see if Mike was around, and as he did so he heard the lift doors slide open.

Thinking it might be Fallon returning, Andrew looked at the

floor, hoping that avoiding any eye contact would also result in avoiding any conversation.

The tips of bright red shoes appeared in the doorway, toes pointed towards him, and Andrew raised his head in confusion.

He immediately jerked backwards in alarm as his eyes landed on the apparition in the doorway.

Black threads of hair edged dark eyes that stood out against ashen, wrinkled skin. The eyes sparkled brighter with what some might have called 'mischief' – but Andrew would deem 'malice' – when cracked lips spread slowly to bare nicotine-stained teeth in a parody of a smile.

Andrew blinked frantically, hoping that this was somehow a hallucination. It *had* to be a hallucination.

'Whatchoo doin' hidin' in a cupboard, Pretty Boy?' A hacking cough closely followed the inquiry.

Sour, smoke-tinged breath fanned over his face and Andrew had to accept that he wasn't seeing things.

'Oh my God,' he groaned as he covered his face with his hands.

Dolly just grinned.

TWENTY-ONE

Nobody had actually spoken directly to Andrew since Dolly had been whisked away from his doorway, but he'd gleaned enough from the comments that had rippled through the floor afterwards that he thought he'd been able to piece together a pretty accurate picture of what had happened anyway.

It sounded as though Higson's car had been parked on the promenade in Colwyn Bay – a place that Andrew vaguely recalled from occasional days out to the seaside when he'd been very small – and it had stuck out like a sore thumb on the otherwise deserted seafront. Just like the Lake District, North Wales in December wasn't exactly a hotbed of tourist activity.

They'd staked out the car, all ready to pounce on an unsuspecting Higson, and had promptly received the fright of their lives when Dolly had appeared next to one of the unmarked cars and knocked on the window asking for a match.

The general consensus appeared to have been that Dolly looked likely to try and curse you at any given moment so, because of that, nobody had wanted to be in a car with her. Apparently, this had resulted in a few feverish rounds of heads or tails to decide who would be given the dubious honour of transporting her back to CID for questioning.

On the drive back to Chester House, Dolly had apparently barely paused for breath – whether through speaking or coughing up a lung, Andrew couldn't be sure – and was happy to tell anyone who'd listen that Higson had agreed to let her borrow his car for the weekend so that she could 'commune with the sea'.

Andrew couldn't help but think that everything about the situation had a distinct air of *Higson* about it.

Half an hour or so after Dolly's dry voice had been muffled

behind Chambers' office door, Andrew heard the lift open again, and Jen walked by a few seconds later.

'Jen!' he called.

Jen backtracked slowly until she saw him. 'Sir?'

Andrew gave her a humourless smile.

'What are you doing in a cupboard?' she hissed, disbelief creasing her forehead.

'Oi!'

Jen whirled around at the shout, and over her shoulder Andrew watched as the detective earlier identified as Cooke hurried over.

'You're not supposed to be talking to anyone, er, *sir*,' Cooke said to Andrew, looking less sure of himself as he grew closer. 'DCI Chambers' orders.'

'Any chance you could tell me why my DI is in there?' Jen asked, eyebrows raised.

'DI Joyce's movements over the weekend are currently being confirmed,' Cooke replied. 'Um. Who are you?'

'DS Cusack,' Jen replied shortly. 'Case Re-examination Unit. I had a message asking me to come in as soon as possible.'

'Oh, er, apologies, ma'am.' Cooke bobbed his head deferentially and Andrew almost laughed when Jen just frowned harder at the other man. 'Detective Constable Cooke.'

'And DI Joyce is in a cupboard because…?' Jen trailed off.

'DCI Chambers' orders,' Cooke repeated. 'If you were to come with me, ma'am, I could confirm your whereabouts as well and let DCI Chambers know that you're here once he's finished with his interview.'

'Dolly,' Andrew supplied for Jen's benefit.

Jen looked over at him in pure surprise. 'What?'

Andrew only nodded. 'Jen, go with DC Cooke here before he has a conniption. I'm sure Chambers won't be long.'

'Sorry, sir,' Jen said to him, 'but aren't we here to find out about what's happening with DCI Higson?'

Jen knew full well why they were there, but as they weren't supposed to have communicated with each at all over the weekend, Andrew offered her a rehearsed shrug instead. 'DCI Chambers wants to ensure that we're not at all involved in this business with Higson.'

Jen did a suitable impression of surprise – Cooke fell for it anyway – as she was shepherded away for a chat.

Andrew glanced at his watch and tapped his thumb impatiently against his lips. He still had a good few hours before he was supposed to meet Peggy, but he wasn't sure whether the surprise appearance of Dolly made it more or less likely that he'd be at Bombay Palace on time.

Every time the lift doors squeaked open, Andrew tensed slightly, but as more time passed with no sign of Lloyd, he relaxed a bit more. If Lloyd wasn't here, that hopefully meant that he and Charlie had got out of Butterton well before Andrew had handed the address and phone number to Chambers, and consequently well before his former boss would have had time to even think about sending a car over that way in case he wanted to keep an eye on Peggy's movements. He hoped that it also meant that they were well on their way to Buxton to update Annie on everything they'd learned in Bowness.

He kept an eye on the other side of the room out of habit, but Jen seemed to answer all of Cooke's questions with the sort of confidence and poise that Andrew had come to expect from her. It wasn't long before Cooke briefly entered Chambers' office before escorting Jen back to where Andrew remained.

'Sir,' Cooke greeted him respectfully, which was somewhat ludicrous when Andrew was sitting on a plastic chair in a cupboard. 'DCI Chambers is still in with, um…'

'Dolly,' Andrew offered wearily.

'Yes, sir. I've spoken to Hilda Laycock, and she confirmed that you and, er, your, um…'

Andrew took pity on him. 'Lady Margaret.'

'Lady Margaret, yeah,' Cooke repeated, still looking unsure. 'That you were both in Briersthwaite from Friday evening until you left this morning. I haven't managed to speak to Lady Margaret yet though, and there was no answer at the number that you gave me.'

Andrew felt his nose twitch, but he schooled the rest of his face into a neutral expression. Peggy not quite being back at home yet was mildly surprising, but not a huge concern as she might well have made a detour on the way back from Gatley. Nobody answering the phone at Butterton at all though was an entirely different matter. Charlie had once explained to him that Timothy could never stand to let a phone call go unanswered, which is why Peggy and Charlie were so quick to pick up the phone if they were expecting a call from anyone they knew. Andrew could only hope that World War Three hadn't broken out between the Earl of Acresfield and his former wife, and that Butterton wasn't currently going up in literal flames.

Chambers' door opened suddenly, and the man himself stalked out of the room. His face hardened even more as he stomped towards where Andrew was rising slowly to his feet.

'Sir, did you find out anything about DCI Higson from Dolly?' Andrew asked, even though he already knew what the answer would be.

'I already told you that you are not part of this investigation, Joyce,' Chambers snapped. 'Cooke tells me that he hasn't yet been able to complete the check on your movements. You may leave, *for now*, but if I have even the slightest reason to believe that you have not been entirely truthful, or if we are unable to confirm your story completely, I will come out and drag you back in here myself. Do I make myself clear?'

'Perfectly, sir,' Andrew replied steadily.

'Sergeant Cusack, I assure you that this warning applies to you as well,' Chambers said, turning his beady eyes on Jen.

'Of course, sir,' Jen replied, and if Andrew didn't know her as well as he did, he wouldn't have been able to find even the slightest hint of insincerity in her agreement.

Chambers seemed satisfied enough. 'You're both dismissed.'

'Sir,' they replied in unison.

Just before Chambers reached his office again, he turned back to them. 'You can take your cleaning lady with you. She was in possession of Higson's car, and we'll be holding onto that.'

Dolly sauntered out of the office carrying her black umbrella in one hand, and a box of Vestas in the other. Her cigarette holder was pinned between the fingers of her right hand, and she waved it airily as she passed Chambers.

'Thanks fer the lights, Dickie,' she croaked, patting him on the chest with her bony fingers. 'I'll be seein' youse.'

Andrew was caught somewhere between wanting to snigger at the deep unease on Chambers' face, and unease of his own at the thought of being trapped in a vehicle with Dolly for any amount of time.

'Come on, Dolly,' Jen said as Dolly walked towards them, 'Let's get you out of here.'

Cooke slowly moved to press himself against the wall to give Dolly plenty of space to get by. She turned her head to leer at him on the way past anyway, and Andrew did actually feel quite sorry for the younger officer.

They reached the lift just as Fallon stepped out of it, stuffing his face with a sandwich.

'Where the fuck do you think you're going?' he asked irately, striding towards Andrew as crumbs flew around him.

'Home,' Andrew replied, making sure to draw himself up to his full height. 'Get out of my way Fallon.'

'Why has Chambers let you go?' Fallon snapped.

'Sorry, Fallon, what's that? Are you questioning your DCI's orders?' Andrew asked loudly, making sure to look around and catch as many eyes as possible.

Andrew would admit that if looks could kill, the expression on Fallon's face would have felled him on the spot. The fury in Fallon's eyes was actually ferocious enough that it knocked Andrew's confidence just off-centre for a split second, leaving behind an unpleasant lick of apprehension.

Dolly took the odd lapse in the conversation as her cue to lean towards Fallon and honest-to-God growl at him before stepping into the lift.

Fallon darted backwards, horror in his expression, and Andrew and Jen hurried after Dolly.

'Christ, what's his problem?' Jen asked, looking at Andrew askance. 'I don't remember him looking quite so murderous last time we met.'

Andrew shook his head. 'He hates it when anyone gets one up on him, that's all.'

'If you say so, sir,' Jen replied hesitantly. 'You alright, Doll?'

'Fine, thanks, Jen love,' Dolly replied as though nothing particularly interesting had happened to her that day. 'Shame I 'ad to come back from the seaside so early though.'

They rode the rest of the way to the ground floor in silence, and nobody spoke again until they were standing beside Jen's car on the far side of the car park. Andrew refused to look up and check if they were being watched; he wouldn't easily be able to see into the building as it was, but he didn't want to give Fallon the satisfaction of thinking that he'd unsettled Andrew in any way.

'Doll, have you spoken to DCI Higson?' Jen asked quietly as Dolly lit another cigarette.

'Not since yesterday, love,' Dolly replied. "E told me to take the car to the seaside.'

'Yesterday?' Andrew asked, breaking his cardinal rule of never addressing Dolly directly.

Dolly looked at him, gaze sharpening as she tilted her head. 'Whassup with yoo?'

'Dolly,' Jen said gently, fully aware that Andrew was not going to answer any such question when it came from Dolly. 'Did you really speak to DCI Higson yesterday?'

"E called me at 'ome, just like 'e did on Friday mornin', and on Thursday too,' Dolly replied with a shrug, still watching Andrew closely. 'Told me to go get 'is car again and drive to the seaside last night.'

'And you just did that?' Andrew asked. 'Without question? Had you heard the news at that point?'

Dolly looked at him as though she'd just deemed Andrew as thick as two short planks, which was, frankly, a bit offensive.

'Do you know where he is, Dolly?' Jen asked, and even she sounded slightly desperate now. 'We really need to find him and make sure he's okay.'

"E didn't say, love, and I didn't ask,' Dolly replied before she then graced both of them with a sharp nod. 'See ye tomorrow.'

Without another word she turned, opened her black umbrella and raised it above her head even though it wasn't so much as spitting. She then strode off across the carpark, heading for God knows where.

Andrew opened his mouth to shout after her, but Jen grabbed his arm briefly and shook her head.

'She'll have told us everything she could,' Jen said. 'Come on, sir, I'll drive you home.'

Andrew didn't have the energy to argue and, to be honest, he was happy to see the back of Dolly and her cryptic comments, so he shook his head and climbed into the passenger seat.

God, he wanted a drink, but he was going to have to settle for a very strong cup of tea once he got home.

'I hope Lloyd and Charlie got to Annie alright,' Jen said after they'd left Chester House behind them.

The concern in Jen's voice was obvious, and Andrew just couldn't let the opportunity to learn something about his enigmatic co-worker – *and friend* – pass by this time. He could probably count on one hand the number of things that Jen had shared about her personal life since they'd met, and he wanted that to change.

He steeled himself as Jen slowed the car down to stop for a red light.

'Jen, how is it that you know the Higsons so well?' he asked, keeping his tone light and inquiring.

Jen's hands twitched on the steering wheel, and she cleared her throat loudly. 'What do you mean, sir? Higson's been my boss for years.'

'Right,' Andrew agreed, 'but when we were in Withington on Friday, Annie called you Jenny more than once. She never tried to call me Andy, or shortened Lloyd's name in any way, so I don't think she's naturally the sort of person who just does that out of habit. You're *Jenny* to her for a reason, and I was hoping that you'd tell me what that reason is.'

Jen glanced at him just before the traffic lights changed, and then she kept her eyes on the road as they set off once more.

Miles passed in silence, and Andrew began to think that maybe he should just tell Jen to forget about it, even if his list of theories was chaotically spiralling and would continue to do so for the foreseeable future.

'I've known them since I was small,' Jen said unexpectedly, when they were well on their way to being back in Gatley. 'My house was in Chorlton, but my sister and I spent more time with our cousins in Withington than we ever did there.'

Andrew could tell that there was a whole other story beneath that simple statement, but he stayed quiet; Jen would share what she wanted to share, and Andrew wasn't going to demand any more from her.

'Long story short, one summer, we got to know the Higson boys,' Jen continued. 'I'd have been about seven, maybe eight, and we were all playing out one day – me, Liz, a handful of cousins - and these two little lads came over and asked if they could join in. John, Higson's youngest, was the same age as Liz, and Lawrie – *Lawrence* – was only a school year younger than me, so they fit right into our little gang. I was always Jenny to my friends back then.'

Jen sighed loudly. 'We all spent that whole summer playing out. I mean, I can't tell you the number of times we had tea together, all us kids crammed around that table in the Higsons' kitchen. The same went for school holidays and weekends for years after that. Annie loved having us all in the house, and our Higson – *Bill* – didn't seem to mind too much as long as we mostly left him be when he first came in from work.

'Then, when I was fourteen, Maria Peat was found strangled in the park where we used to play.' Jen paused and shook her head. 'She was only twelve. We didn't know her, but we kept thinking that we *must* have met her over the years. Her parents said that she was always playing out with her friends, so surely at some point our paths would've crossed, right?'

Andrew knew that he wasn't really expected to answer, but he gave Jen a nod to show that he was listening.

'Anyway, when that happened, loads of the kids we knew weren't allowed out anymore, my cousins included,' Jen continued. 'Nothing really changed for Liz and me, but any time we went to call for Lawrie and John, Annie encouraged us to come in and spend time in their garden rather than heading up to the park.

'It was probably only a couple of weeks after Maria had been killed that Lawrie told us that he'd overheard his dad complaining about the fact that the police weren't getting anywhere with finding out who'd attacked Maria, and how worried he was that there was going to be another dead girl before the year was out.'

They were only a couple of miles from Andrew's house by then, and he'd never wished that he lived further away more than he did in that very moment.

Jen took a deep breath. 'Even longer story short, Lawrie had always wanted to be a policeman just like his dad, and so he suggested that we – him, me, Liz and John – try our hand at finding out what had happened to Maria ourselves. Needless to say, we were kids, and we had no idea just how stupid that was.'

Andrew couldn't remember ever seeing Jen looked ashamed before, but the mortification was plain as day on her face at her admission.

'Liz and John decided quite quickly that the game wasn't for them, but Lawrie and I were planning on going round to Maria's house to speak to her parents,' Jen continued quietly. 'We didn't get that far, because we walked past her mum on the high street one day and Lawrie stopped her. Annie and Bill were so cross with us when they heard what we'd done. Then, Maria's father complained to the police, and Bill got it in the neck because his son was involved.'

The turning for Acacia Road materialised in the distance and Jen slowed the car slightly.

'What we hadn't realised at the time was that there'd been rumours about Maria's dad being a violent man for years,' Jen added. 'Bill's working theory was that Gareth Peat was the one who'd killed Maria, so when he found out that we'd been on our way to the house to speak to the Peats he went absolutely ballistic. He put the fear of God into the pair of us.'

Everyone in the Ballroom had been on the receiving end of Higson's ire at one point or another, and Andrew could easily imagine how intimidating that would have been to two young teenagers.

'A month or so later, they arrested Maria's father when he assaulted someone on the way home from the pub,' Jen explained. 'Turned out he'd done the same to his wife before he'd gone out for the night; it was a miracle that she didn't die. Eventually he admitted to killing Maria too.

'I thought that Annie and Bill wouldn't want Liz and me hanging around with the boys anymore, but Lawrie took the brunt of the blame, and it all seemed to blow over.'

'Seemed to?' Andrew asked as Jen turned the car onto Acacia Road.

Jen parked the car directly outside Andrew's house and switched off the engine before she turned to look at Andrew properly.

'The day Gareth Peats was jailed was horrible,' Jen said, squinting slightly as she shook her head again. 'Loads of his family lived nearby, and they were still trying to claim that the police had forced a false confession out of him. They'd got Maria's mother onside, trying to make out that what had happened to her had been a one-off, and that it had been the stress of his daughter's death that had pushed Peat to assault her. They even got her to say that her injuries hadn't been as bad as people had been making out.'

'But they had been?' Andrew asked carefully, feeling like he was running on borrowed time.

Jen nodded. 'He'd broken her arm in two places, three of her fingers, and her collarbone too. She also had fractured ribs and bruising everywhere, including on her neck.'

'Fucking hell,' Andrew breathed in revulsion.

'Peat was sent to Strangeways anyway, and his brother, Nick, organised a 'wake' for him in a pub for the day after, somewhere on Wilmslow Road. Nobody but the family turned up. Peat wasn't a well-liked man in the first place, so most people were more than happy to see him behind bars, but there were enough of the family that they were likely to make a lot of noise. We'd been warned by Bill and Annie to stay away from the Peats that day, and we had no intention of going anywhere near a single one of them.

'Annie had wanted Lawrie to have piano lessons, and I always used to cycle up to his teacher's house after school on a Tuesday to meet him, and then we'd ride around on our bikes, or go and watch TV at the house if the weather was bad.

'That day, it was raining a bit, and Lawrie had walked to his lesson because one of his wheels had a puncture, and his dad had promised to help him with it once they got to the weekend. So, we set off back towards his house, taking turns pushing my bike. We didn't go down Wilmslow Road like we normally would've done, so it took us longer to get back towards the house. We were nearly there, though, when Nick Peat walked around the corner.'

Jen bowed her head and clenched her hands into fists. 'He knew who Lawrie was. I suppose I mean he knew who his *dad* was. Peat started on Lawrie straight away; calling him and his dad all sorts of things, and then he just *went* for him. Lawrie was a scrawny thirteen-year-old and he just went down straight away. I had this horrible moment where I really thought he was dead, but then he opened his eyes.

'Peat then turned on me. God knows how much he'd had to drink, but I'm still thankful for it every day. I managed to duck out of the way, and then I swung my school bag at him while he was still turning back round. Smacked him square in the face with this horrible, *horrible* sound and then he was on his knees, clutching his face and roaring nonsense.'

Andrew was fairly certain that he was staring at Jen in pure astonishment as she spoke, so he was glad that she still wasn't looking at him.

'I managed to get Lawrie to his feet, though I doubt he could have told me what his own name was just then, and I dragged him up the road and round the corner to his house, shouting my head off for Annie to open the door.' Jen blew out a loud breath. 'Lawrie couldn't stand up by himself and I must have got the whole way there on adrenaline, because as soon as Annie opened the door, Lawrie seemed to get twice as heavy, and we both ended up in a heap on the floor.'

'Jesus, Jen.' Andrew shook his head.

'Yeah,' Jen agreed, giving him a fleeting smile. 'Annie got the doctor round and then called Bill at work. When he came in, I realised that I hadn't actually ever seen Bill Higson angry before that point. All that shouting he'd done at us in the past hadn't been real anger – he'd just been trying to scare the living daylights out of us – but the look on his face when I told him what had happened was the most terrifying thing I'd ever seen. He just went completely blank. I didn't realise at first that he wasn't angry at me or Lawrie, and I sat at that kitchen table and bawled my eyes out, and then Higson just left.'

To Andrew's complete surprise, Jen then laughed softly.

'Higson came back a couple of hours later and told me that Nick Peat had already been picked up and taken into custody,' she said in response to Andrew's raised eyebrows. 'I'd broken his nose with my bag, and when he could see straight enough again, he'd realised that he probably shouldn't have attacked two kids in broad daylight. He'd tried to make a getaway on my bike, which I'd dropped when Lawrie was hit, but he was so hammered after hours in the pub that he'd cycled straight into the side of a stationary bus.

'Higson had brought my bike back to the house, and he promised me that he'd help me fix it that weekend, considering he was already supposed to be sorting Lawrie's tyre out.' Jen smiled again. 'He did as well.'

Andrew genuinely had no idea what the correct response to anything he'd just been told was. He shook his head stupidly at Jen for a long moment.

Her smile dimmed a bit. 'I spent more time in that house than my own for the next few years. That sort of thing tends to bind you together.'

Andrew nodded. 'Do Higson's sons still live nearby? Jesus, I was so focused on Annie that I didn't even think about them. We should probably speak to them, unless you think that Annie...'

Andrew's rambling trailed off when Jen's smile faded entirely.

'Annie will have spoken to both of them, don't worry,' Jen said quietly. 'John lives in Birmingham now. Lawrie's still around here somewhere; Hale, I think.'

'You think?' Andrew asked, even though he could instinctively tell it was a dangerous question. 'Do the Higsons not talk to him much these days?'

Jen's expression did something too complicated for Andrew to understand before settling on something close to uncharacteristic awkwardness. 'Ah. It's actually more that the Higsons don't talk to *me* very much about Lawrie these days.'

She then sighed loudly before adopting an air of false cheer. 'Anyway, Higson encouraged me to apply to join the police when I was old enough, and eventually I ended up on Tib Street as his DC.'

Jen put her hands back on the steering wheel, and Andrew took that to mean that a line had been very firmly drawn beneath this conversation.

Andrew cleared his throat, fighting against the urge to thank Jen for sharing that with him and the even greater longing to ask her just what on earth had happened with Lawrie Higson. He knew her well enough to be certain that she wouldn't appreciate either one of those responses.

'I'm meeting Peggy for dinner later,' he said instead. 'Bombay Palace. Do you want to come? I'd say we're off the hook enough for now.'

Jen shook her head, but gave him a small, grateful smile. He'd definitely given the right sort of answer then.

'Thanks, sir,' she said, 'but I was hoping you'd be alright with me going over to Buxton this evening to bring Annie and Sarah back. I know that Lloyd will have told Annie everything we know so far, but I'd appreciate it if I could make sure that she gets to Chester House alright tomorrow. I'll come straight to the Ballroom afterwards.'

'Of course,' Andrew agreed. 'Call me once you've got Annie home, and I'll let you know if I've heard anything else from Mike, alright?'

'Thanks, sir,' Jen repeated as Andrew reached for the door handle to let himself out. 'I'll speak to you later.'

As Jen drove away, Andrew took a second to look up and down the street. He couldn't see any cars that looked out of place, so he hoped that meant that the surveillance had been called off. Nevertheless, he was still going to keep an eye out until this whole business had been put to bed.

He turned away from his house and walked up the road until he found himself outside the front garden of number seventy-five, with its row of gnomes and small novelty structures that separated the lawn from the pavement.

With a quick glance over his shoulder to check that the coast was clear, he crouched down and pretended to tie his shoelace. As he stood up again, he put his hand out to rest against the top of the little wooden windmill that sat between a pair of gnomes with fishing rods, as though steadying himself.

He pushed harder and the windmill tilted back just enough that he could reach the spare front door key that he'd sellotaped to the base a good eighteen months earlier. He hissed in triumph as he curled his fingers around it and stood up again; he'd been slightly worried that the owner might have seen the key when they'd moved the ornaments to mow the grass. They wouldn't have had a clue what door the key was for, of course, but if it hadn't still been there it would have been deeply inconvenient for Andrew, given that Peggy was in possession of the only other copy.

The road remained deserted as he headed back towards his house, and he once more glanced around in interest; this time wondering where he was going to choose as the next hiding spot for his spare key.

As paranoid as this might have made him seem to anyone else, knowing that there was no way that Fallon or anyone else watching his house over the previous few days would have ever found the key even if they'd searched every inch of Andrew's front garden, filled him with a certainty that he'd made the right choice.

He turned the key in his front door and pushed it open, pleased to be met with complete stillness as he locked himself in.

'Hiya, Rob,' he said quietly, just as he'd taken to doing every time he came home.

As per usual, he was met with only silence, but he was content with the fact his brother would have heard him anyway.

With a sigh of relief, he leant back against the door and ran his hands over his face as he yawned widely. He didn't need to leave for Manchester again for a while, so at least he'd have time for a shower and a change of clothes after his stint in the Chester House cupboard.

A quiet clinking sound caught his ears and Andrew went stock still. His thoughts immediately rocketed towards his mother, but as there hadn't been a hint of Agatha's particularly nasty brand of haunting since March, he was going to have to assume that the intruder was as alive as he was.

He knew that it wasn't Peggy. For a start, there'd been no sign of the Range Rover, but she also would have called out to him as soon as he'd opened the door.

Andrew wouldn't actually have put it past Fallon to get

someone to break in through the back of the house to have a snoop around out of sight of any nosy neighbours, especially if he'd expected Andrew to be tied up at Chester House for a good few more hours.

The hallway was completely devoid of anything that Andrew could brandish menacingly, with only a discarded Yellow Pages coming close to being something useable. He really wished that he hadn't left his umbrella in the boot of the car.

He crept towards the closed kitchen door and pressed his right palm flat against it as he wrapped his left hand around the doorknob. He was just going to have to hope that he could do something with the element of surprise.

Andrew flung himself at the door as he opened it, bursting into the kitchen as ready for a fight as he was ever going to be.

The shock at what greeted him hit hard enough that he almost tripped over his own feet. He had to steady himself against the kitchen counter as he yelped in alarm and stared in witless surprise at the hulking figure casually sitting at his kitchen table.

'Oh, for Christ's sake, Joyce, calm the fuck down.'

TWENTY-TWO

The city centre was much busier than Peggy had anticipated, and it took her a good ten minutes of driving around in circles before a parking space within a reasonable walking distance of Cross Street freed up.

This delay meant that she arrived at the restaurant ten minutes later than she'd hoped. It had, at least, given her plenty of opportunity to keep an eye out for any cars that might have been following her. She was almost certain that she hadn't been tailed by anyone, but she still occasionally glanced in the large windows of the banks and shops that lined the street as she walked, fleetingly wondering at what point she'd become as paranoid as Andrew.

Arun – the manager of Bombay Palace, and eldest son of the owners – was advancing towards her with a beaming smile before she'd even fully opened the door to.

'Princess Peggy!' he greeted her cheerfully, adopting the nickname he'd bestowed on her the first time she'd had dinner there with Andrew. He reached out to warmly clasp one of her hands between both of his. 'We haven't seen you in ages!'

'Hi, Arun.' Peggy smiled at him. 'It's been a while.'

'I thought Mr Joyce was joking when he called earlier and said that you were coming in tonight,' Arun added, gesturing for Peggy's coat. 'We're fully booked, but there's always a table for you two.'

Relief washed over Peggy at Arun's words. She hadn't heard anything from Andrew before she'd left Butterton, and she'd started to worry that he might still be stuck with Chambers. She handed over her coat even though she felt too cold without it.

Raucous laughter burst from the main dining area and Arun winced.

'We've got three Christmas dos in,' he explained, folding Peggy's coat carefully over his arm and signalling for Peggy to follow him, 'so I'm afraid it won't be the quietest. Oh, and Mr Joyce asked me to apologise for being a bit late, but he should be here before nine.'

'Thanks, Arun,' Peggy replied gratefully, trailing after him as he snaked his way through the absolutely packed room, side-stepping discarded wrapping paper and party hats, and squeezing between chairs that were just about far enough apart to allow them through.

When they finally reached the table in the far corner, Peggy took the seat that would give her a good view of the entrance. Andrew would inevitably want to switch places when he arrived, so when she placed her handbag on the floor she pushed it towards the other chair with her foot, ready for later.

'Can I get you anything to drink before Mr Joyce arrives?' Arun asked, his attention drifting slightly towards a particularly rowdy group of men and women even as he lit the candle on Peggy's table.

Peggy shook her head. 'Thanks, Arun, but I'll wait.'

Arun bobbed his head in acceptance, his eyes on where party poppers were now exploding in loud, bright arcs of streamer paper. Peggy could only imagine what the clean-up operation was going to be like when the restaurant closed. 'I'll pop your coat behind the bar. We'll never find it again if it goes in the cloakroom tonight!'

As Arun left with her coat, Peggy slowly scanned the crowded room. She started in surprise when she noticed that she was being waved at by two familiar faces.

From the far side of the table closest to the bar, Fiona and Julie were smiling widely at her. They were both wearing colourful paper crowns and clutching glasses of wine, and Peggy had a vague recollection from the Troubadour of them telling her that their work Christmas party had been planned for that weekend.

She waved weakly back.

Fiona immediately put her glass down and pointed towards Peggy, tilting her head towards the empty chair and then raising her eyebrows in an obvious question.

Oh God, Peggy had so many more things to be concerned about than the inevitable activation of the Fiona-Lloyd gossip machine just then, but *Julie* was there too, and there was a significant chance that this situation was about to be wildly misinterpreted.

Peggy's trepidation was only amplified when a flash of movement at the door caught her eye, and she looked over to where – *of bloody course* – Andrew was on the other side of the melee, standing next to Arun, who was cheerily pointing out where Peggy sat.

She glanced back at Fiona and Julie to see them whispering furiously before, to Peggy's immense surprise, they both grinned at her. Fiona went so far as to give her a double thumbs up while she laughed loudly.

Peggy had to fight the urge to crawl under the table in mortification. She gave them both a quick smile and then took the opportunity to practically hop out of her seat and move towards the empty chair as Andrew approached. He looked slightly dazed, but not particularly distressed, so perhaps the meeting with Chambers hadn't been too unpleasant after all.

'Everything okay?' he asked as he stopped in front of her.

'Fiona and Julie are just over there,' Peggy replied quietly, pointing as discreetly as she could.

Andrew turned his head, and the two women gleefully waved at him. He lifted a hand in casual greeting and then turned back to Peggy, looking more surprised than uneasy.

'They won't hear a single thing we say over that racket,' Andrew said just as a horribly off-key but enthusiastic chorus of

Last Christmas was initiated at another table. He blinked. '*Wow.*'

Peggy frowned as they sat down. 'Go and say hello to Julie if you want. I can order you a drink.'

'Why?' Andrew did look genuinely puzzled by Peggy's suggestion.

'Because...' Peggy trailed off, choosing her words carefully. 'Well, weren't you at the Troubadour, you know, *with* Julie? And, obviously, now you're over here and, *well*, I don't want her to get the wrong idea and th – are you laughing at me?'

Andrew grinned. 'While I'm very thankful for your concern for my reputation, I think if Julie had any interest whatsoever in seeing me again, she probably wouldn't have been all over your brother on the dancefloor on Thursday.'

'*What?*' Peggy asked stupidly.

'For the sake of equality, it's worth noting that he was just as much all over her,' Andrew snorted into his hand as Peggy's eyes widened.

'Oh my God, stop talking immediately,' Peggy whined. 'I did not need that picture.'

'I thought you knew,' Andrew chuckled as he prodded at the candle holder to centre it on the table. 'They weren't exactly subtle about it.'

'Well, I didn't know.' Peggy wrinkled her nose. 'Frankly, I'm disappointed in Julie. I thought she'd have better taste.'

Andrew looked both delighted and deeply amused as Peggy immediately tried to backtrack on any unintentional implication she had just vocalised.

Helpfully, Arun appeared at that moment.

Unhelpfully, he put two filled champagne flutes down on the table with a flourish.

'I didn't order those,' Peggy said defensively.

Arun beamed. 'No, you didn't. On the house. Now, do you want a menu, or shall I just get you your usual?'

'Usual alright with you?' Andrew asked her, and Peggy waved her free hand in agreement while she pressed the fingertips of the other to her forehead in humiliation.

Andrew didn't look any less entertained when Peggy looked up as Arun left. 'I *am* going to advise you not to look over at Fiona and Julie right now,' he whispered with another grin.

'Oh, Jesus Christ,' Peggy groaned loudly.

'Drink up anyway,' Andrew said, tapping his glass against Peggy's. 'Trust me, you're probably going to need it.'

'Why, what's happened?' Peggy's awkwardness was quashed by concern.

Andrew leant his elbows on the table and sighed. 'I'm just trying to work out where the hell I should start.'

The rendition of *Last Christmas* got louder as another section of the table joined in.

'Chambers told me why Higson's their chief suspect,' Andrew said eventually, obviously settling on a course of action. 'Sean Kelly called 999 to report an intruder in his house. He identified Higson as the intruder, and then he was shot.'

'While he was on the phone?'

Andrew nodded. 'He didn't tell me anything more than that, but he made a point to ask me about what cases we're working on.'

Peggy raised her eyebrows.

'Obviously, I didn't tell him anything useful,' Andrew continued. 'He made me wait while he got one of the DCs to check my story. Then, Mike managed to tell me that they'd found Higson's car in North Wales, and they actually brought in the driver while I was there.'

'Not Higson,' Peggy said slowly, 'so *who?*'

'Dolly.'

'Dolly?'

Andrew nodded. 'Chambers let her go pretty quickly. She told me and Jen that Higson called her yesterday and asked her to take the car to the seaside. I think it was Dolly that Higson phoned from the pub in Staveshead as well.'

Peggy blinked in surprise. 'Did Higson tell her where he was when he called yesterday?'

Arun's arrival halted Andrew's explanation, and nothing else was said on the matter as starters were arranged on the table.

When they were alone again, Andrew nudged the onion bhajis closer to Peggy's side of the table as he said, 'I know where Higson is.'

Peggy dropped her fork on her plate in surprise, but the loud clatter was barely heard over the din in the restaurant.

'How could you possibly know that?' Peggy asked in bewilderment.

Andrew pulled his chair closer to the table. 'He was in my kitchen when I got back from Chester House. I think you must have only just missed him.'

If Peggy had been holding anything else, she'd have dropped that too. Empty-handed, she stared at Andrew in astonishment.

'Nearly gave me a heart attack.' Andrew shook his head and picked up a samosa. 'He went straight in with swearing to me that he's never been to Sean Kelly's house, but then he was at great pains to add that I should be assured that he'd have come up with a much more inventive way of killing that 'evil bastard' if he'd ever felt so inclined.'

'Of course he did,' Peggy sighed despairingly, reaching for another onion bhaji.

'Wouldn't tell me where he's been for the past couple of days though, no matter how many times I asked. Instead, he wanted to know what the hell we'd all been doing to clear his name,' Andrew continued just as *Last Christmas* segued – surprisingly – into *La Bamba* behind her, which was as enthusiastic a rendition as it was lyrically butchered. 'He complained that he hadn't been able to get hold of any of us, which is why he'd asked Dolly to shift the car. He didn't seem to think that the fact he'd disappeared without telling anyone what he was up to was a problem.'

Peggy shook her head.

'I told him how we'd gone to his house on Friday and spoken to Annie – he wasn't happy to hear that she'd left Buxton – and how we'd then driven to Staveshead,' Andrew continued. 'A shocked Higson is an amazing sight, by the way. It didn't last long though, and then I got it in the neck for taking the file, reading the file, talking about the file with anyone else, and only *then* did he start in on me about going north without an idea of what I was getting myself into.'

Peggy made a sound of dissent. 'I hope you told him that he'd made enough of a spectacle of himself up there that it took us all of two minutes of arriving at that pub before we found out that he'd been in.'

'Oh, I did,' Andrew agreed, 'and he was pissed about that. But then I told him that we'd found Beth and Lily, and he shut right up. That's when I saw what a *stunned* Higson is like.'

'So, he really didn't know where they'd gone after they left Staveshead?'

Andrew shook his head. 'No. After that, he then got *really* pissed at me for getting you involved in all of it.'

Peggy narrowed her eyes. 'Did you ask him why?'

'I did,' Andrew replied with a slight wince as he leaned in and dropped his voice. 'Annie was right – it *was* Frank Jackson's funeral that set him off. Look, I'll tell you all of that in a minute, but I think you should hear Higson's side of Lily and Davy's story first. Alright?'

'Alright,' Peggy agreed, already steeling herself for being told that Higson had forbidden her from continuing on with the case. She'd had her arguments ready all weekend, so she wasn't going to go down without a fight, but she'd let Andrew relay everything first.

Andrew nodded slowly and he clasped his hands together on the table, settling in for the explanation.

'As we already know, Higson first left the Ballroom because Prentice had been brought in as acting DCI. Prentice didn't want to be there at all. Apparently, he thought it was a dead-end outpost and wanted to go back to investigating serious crimes,' Andrew explained, dropping his eyes to the tablecloth as self-awareness clearly gave him a solid cuff to the back of the head.

'We wouldn't know anyone like that, would we?' Peggy asked wryly, ducking her head until she caught his eye.

Andrew hummed noncommittally. 'Prentice immediately paused any work on reopened cases and then moved Jackson and Kelly in. Benson and Higson were both still there at that point though, apparently, they started looking for an out as soon as it became clear that the focus of the Ballroom had moved towards what Prentice apparently called *informant management*, and what Higson would describe as Prentice cultivating a little mob of his own.

'By that point, Prentice had spent almost twenty years gathering dirt on anyone and everyone he came across. He made it his business to know as much as he could about everyone, which is obviously why he found Lily so useful to him.'

Peggy put down her fork with a sigh, appetite whisked away by the thought of what Lily had gone through at the hands of Prentice and his friends. She curled her fingers towards her palms, and then tucked her hands as far into the long sleeves of her dress as the material would allow.

'He even had something on Higson,' Andrew added as he pursed his lips. 'A few years earlier, when Higson's boys had been very small, and Annie hadn't been working, things were a bit tight. Higson had been out to the scene of an alleged robbery at a corner shop; he gathered pretty quickly that there hadn't been a robbery, and the owner was trying to scam insurance money because they were having a hard time. He didn't give me the full story, but he told me enough that we can be sure that Higson made sure to look the other way that one time, and the Higson boys had a nice Christmas that year.'

Peggy sighed heavily. 'And how did Prentice find out about that?'

'Higson doesn't know,' Andrew replied, shaking his head again, 'but Prentice tried to use it as leverage to get Higson to join his little intimidation team with Kelly and Jackson. Higson refused, and he got himself transferred out of the Ballroom. Prentice seems to have left him alone after that; he obviously assumed that Higson wasn't any real threat to him.'

'Everything alright?' Arun asked as he came to collect their plates. He frowned at Peggy and pointed accusingly at the two onion bhajis languishing on the small platter. 'You haven't finished them.'

Peggy smiled apologetically. 'Sorry, Arun. It's just one of those days.'

'I'll leave them for you,' he replied firmly, nodding furiously as he took everything else away.

Andrew was looking at her with a slight frown as she turned back to him. 'What?'

'You're still cold,' he replied evenly, 'but it's about four-hundred degrees in here. Are you feeling okay?'

Peggy shrugged as nonchalantly as her stiff muscles would allow. 'It's December, Andrew. Everyone's a bit under the weather.'

She could tell that he was about to argue with her, but then Arun reappeared with his younger brother in tow, both laden down with plates and bowls. Apparently Arun had taken the request for the 'usual' and then embellished it.

'Dad's trying out some new things for next year's menu,' Arun offered in explanation. 'So, that one there is a t-'

A crash, followed immediately by a round of clapping and cheering, had them all looking towards Fiona and Julie's side of the room. One of their Midland Bank colleagues was doing a poor job of handling his drink and seemed to have fallen off his chair in fits of laughter.

Arun looked at the ceiling, swearing creatively in a combination of at least two languages before excusing himself and hurrying across the room.

'I feel like we're going to have to leave an enormous tip for him to make up for this,' Peggy said, grimacing as the clapping reached fever pitch when the fallen man was restored to sitting.

'It's going on Charlie's tab anyway.'

Andrew thankfully didn't ask any further questions about Peggy's wellbeing, but he put a spoonful of each one of the steaming-hot dishes on her plate before he started on his own.

'Does Higson's story of what happened that night tally with what Lily told us?' Peggy asked, picking up her fork and giving Andrew a pointed look so that he knew that she was fully aware of what he was up to.

Andrew nodded. 'Everything. Once he'd got Lily settled at the Hanging Bridge he went to the sweet shop. It was midnight by then, and all locked up, but he broke in and followed Lily's instructions until he ended up in the Arches. Davy was gone, but there were signs of a struggle.'

Peggy swallowed heavily. 'I can't imagine what it must have been like to make that choice; getting Lily to safety but knowing that he was probably leaving Davy to die.'

'I know,' Andrew replied solemnly. 'It was an impossible choice, but I think his decision was the only one he could have made in the end.'

Peggy thought that was probably true. 'Would you have done the same?'

Andrew initially looked surprised at the question but then turned more thoughtful. 'Yeah, I'd have done the same. Higson had no idea what he would have walked into if he'd gone down to the Arches then and left Lily to fend for herself. For her sake, he couldn't take have taken that risk. I don't think he's ever stopped feeling guilty about it though.'

'I don't doubt it,' Peggy agreed. 'So, what did Higson do after he left the Arches? You told me that Annie said he didn't go home again until Sunday.'

Andrew put down the chunk of naan he was holding and wiped his hands on a napkin before he clasped his hands on the tabletop again, firmly back in storytelling mode. 'After he summoned the doctor for Lily, he spent the next few hours looking for any signs of Davy, or of Prentice's car, in the area, but when he found nothing, he went back to the Hanging Bridge.

'The publican had put Lily in a room upstairs so that she could try to sleep, telling her to keep the lights off and to stay away from the windows, as per Higson's orders. Higson stayed up for most of the night, just sitting in the bar.

'Around four or so in the morning, someone knocked on the door a couple of times. Higson left it unanswered, but when he heard whoever it was walking away, he took a look out of the window. It was Frank Jackson, and he could see Sean Kelly in the distance. Higson reckons they were looking for anyone who might have seen Lily leaving the Arches.'

Peggy shook her head in despair at the thought. 'They'd have killed her if they'd found her, wouldn't they? Just like that, as though she wasn't worth anything to anybody.'

'That's exactly what they would have done, and Higson knew it,' Andrew continued, looking as disgusted as Peggy felt. 'He left Lily there the next morning once he'd had the doctor back and went into work as though none of it had happened. He knew that if he had the slightest hope of pinning any of what had happened on Prentice, Lily was going to be key; he needed to get her somewhere else and try to bring her round to the idea of helping him make his case.'

'Which never happened.'

'Which never happened,' Andrew confirmed. 'When Higson got in to work, he found out that Benson had called in sick, which apparently wasn't any surprise given the state that Benson had been in when he'd staggered out of the Hanging Bridge the night before.'

Peggy wanted to ask if Higson had known if the 'Chris' that Violet Woodhouse had referred to was indeed Benson, but she knew that Andrew would tell her everything he knew, so she held her question back and had another forkful of rice instead.

'Higson was looking for a good opportunity to get over to Lily and get her out of the city,' Andrew continued. 'Then, just before lunch, Division got a call to say that there'd been an incident at some business down by Central Station which had been flagged as having suspected links to organised crime; it looked like there'd been a break-in overnight. Higson was sent out there, and what should he find discarded at the scene? Davy Nash's warrant card.'

Peggy paused with her glass halfway to her mouth. 'But I thought Lily had given Davy's identification to Higson the night before.'

'She had. Higson still had it in his pocket, but he was also looking at the same identification at a crime scene that Davy couldn't have been at. According to the business owners they'd been there until after two doing their books, so whatever had happened there was well after Lily had already left Davy in the Arches.

'Someone was sent out to call in on Beth Nash, and she confirmed that Davy hadn't come home. Higson told his DCI that he'd been at the Hanging Bridge with Davy and Benson earlier in the evening, and that Davy gone back to Bootle Street to get his keys, but that he hadn't returned to the pub by closing time. Benson came in as soon he'd heard the news, and Higson says that he was distraught at the thought of anything bad happening to Davy.'

Andrew paused the story with a loud sigh and took the opportunity to have some food.

Peggy couldn't quite believe what she was hearing. It was bad enough when it had seemed like Prentice had attacked Davy in the heat of the moment, but *this* showed how calculating he'd been with his intentions to deceive everyone and divert them from the truth after the fact without a shred of remorse.

'Anyway, City Police decided that raising awareness of Davy's disappearance would be the best course of action,' Andrew explained. 'Davy's photo appeared in the papers the next morning, the working theory being peddled was that Davy had perhaps stumbled across a crime in progress and got himself hurt for his troubles. Higson says that he kept pointing out that Davy had promised to return to the pub, so there were *hours* between when he'd seen last him and when he had apparently been near the station after two am.

'Maybe they would have followed up on Higson's point a bit more if Jimmy Prentice hadn't waltzed into A Division on the Saturday morning to explain how he'd been reading the paper that morning over breakfast, and he and his wife had been shocked to see what had happened to Davy Nash. They were particularly shocked because they were entirely convinced that they'd seen Davy at the Free Trade Hall on Thursday evening, where they themselves had been having a night out with friends. Prentice had been at pains to point out that Davy had very loudly been enjoying the company of a young woman at the bar, and she certainly hadn't been the terribly upset wife that had been described in the papers.'

'Why do that?' Peggy asked. 'Why go to the trouble of

making it look like Davy had found himself on the wrong end of organised crime, but then announce that he'd been seen out enjoying himself?'

Andrew grimaced. 'Because Prentice was already thinking two steps ahead. Planting a copy of Davy's warrant card by the station got Davy's name out into the world and then gave Prentice the perfect opportunity to start spinning a story about Davy's conduct. He was laying the groundwork for when Lily would eventually be reported missing. If people thought Davy Nash was some kind of hero, they'd keep looking for him, wouldn't they? They'd want justice for the brave, off-duty police officer and his young family. But, if everyone thought that Davy was a philandering arse who'd got himself involved with a radically minded teenage tearaway and disappeared off into the sunset with her, *well*, they'd be much less concerned about finding him, wouldn't they? Especially if it looked like Davy hadn't been *preventing* a crime that night but instead had possibly been the perpetrator; perhaps stealing cash to fund his and Lily's bid for freedom.'

Peggy could only shake her head again.

'Lily was then reported as missing on Monday,' Andrew continued, 'at which point all the news coverage about Davy took a distinct turn for the worse in tone. All of that, of course, is compounded by the fact that Prentice and his 'witnesses' were all happy to confirm that it was Lily that they'd seen Davy with on Thursday night. On top of that, a scarf identified as Lily's was also apparently found at the scene of the break-in, even though Higson has no memory of seeing any such thing when he'd been sent out there on Friday morning.'

Suddenly, more party poppers exploded loudly behind her, and Peggy clutched a hand to her chest in fright. She swiped at her face, where a stray stand of blue paper streamer had caught in the hair by her left ear. 'Christ.'

Andrew looked over Peggy's shoulder to glare at the table behind them.

Drunken calls of apology were delivered with varying degrees of sincerity, and Andrew shook his head before returning his attention to Peggy.

'Higson had taken Lily to his mother's house on the Sunday, just before he went home to Annie and the boys,' Andrew explained. 'For most of the next week, Higson was worried that Prentice had actually worked out what had happened. He found a couple of opportunities to find Higson and pass on his 'sympathies' for what had happened to Davy, even if Davy was, as he said, 'not the sort of person a DS climbing the ranks at A Division should have been socialising with'.'

'Utter bastard,' Peggy muttered, unable to mute that thought.

Andrew nodded his sincere agreement. 'Next thing, Higson and Benson were called in to explain their association with Davy in more detail. Benson was apparently a complete wreck, concerned that the papers would get wind of his name and paint him as a questionable character, just as they'd done with Davy. Apparently, he'd had a bit of a gambling problem a few years earlier, and he was convinced that if it came out, that would be the end of the road for him at City.

'I asked Higson what he thought about what Violet said. He doesn't believe that 'Chris' could have been Benson. Wouldn't hear a word of it, not when he'd seen the real fear that Benson had shown at the idea of losing his job and his reputation.'

Peggy understood Higson's reasoning, but until they'd actually heard from Benson himself, she was going to reserve her own judgement.

Andrew looked like he might be leaning towards Peggy's train of thought, even if he didn't actually vocalise that fact.

'Higson wasn't fussed about having his own reputation blackened a bit,' Andrew continued, 'but he was worried about

Benson. Then, one day Higson was pulled into his DCI's office, and asked a lot of questions about Annie's association with certain radical student groups.'

'What?' Peggy asked, utterly dumbfounded. '*Annie?*'

'Someone had very carefully made a list of all students Annie had ever meaningfully interacted with at the university and picked out anyone who'd ever been in trouble with the police,' Andrew explained. 'They had a couple on there who were suspected of being members of banned groups, that sort of thing. Higson's DCI suggested that it might be wise for him to really, *really* think back on that last evening with Davy; was Higson certain that Davy hadn't mentioned that he was going to pop into the Free Trade Hall? Hadn't he perhaps told Higson that he was going to meet someone?'

'Higson's DCI did that?' Peggy was horrified.

Andrew shrugged. 'Like Higson said, Prentice had something on everyone, so God knows what he was holding over that man's head. I mean, we now know that even Prentice's *wife* was happy to lie for him, don't we? Knowing that there was now a threat not only to Benson's career, but now, even more worryingly, a threat to Annie and his kids, Higson signed that statement saying that Davy had told him that he was going to meet someone at the Free Trade Hall. *That* was what prompted him to tell Beth the truth about Davy, and to get her and the kids away. Higson knew that Beth would have kept on publicly defending her husband, and he was terrified that Prentice would eventually try and shut her up permanently.'

'Jesus Christ,' Peggy breathed in alarm.

Andrew nodded again. 'Higson's spent twenty years thinking that after that first time he swore never to look the other away again, he'd done just that. He believes that he let Prentice get away with it all.'

'But Higson can't know what Prentice would have done to

Benson or Annie if he'd pushed it,' Peggy argued, mind wheeling with awful scenarios. 'If Lily was refusing to talk, then Higson didn't really have any evidence of what had happened anyway.'

'And he's spent two decades trying to get any of Prentice's 'witnesses' to recant their statements,' Andrew added. 'That's what all those notes were in the file. Remember he'd written 'Bridge' next to Barbara Jackson's name? It wasn't anything to do with the Arches, or the pub; it was that her weekly bridge club met on a Thursday night. She wasn't at the Free Trade Hall; she was fifteen miles away in Lymm Village Hall and Higson knew it.'

'And none of them would change their story?' Peggy asked. 'Even years later?'

'Not one. Apparently, he got close to convincing Frank Jackson's ex-wife to withdraw her statement, but in the end she said it wouldn't be worth it for what she knew Jimmy Prentice would do to her.' Andrew ran a hand through his hair as he sighed again. 'Which, unfortunately, leads me to why all of this is happening now. So, ba-'

'How is everything so far?' Arun asked loudly as he rushed over. 'I'm so sorry about all the noise.'

'It's all great, Arun,' Andrew replied tightly, obviously flustered by the interruption to his explanation. 'Really, tell your dad that the new ones are all winners.'

Arun beamed and turned to look at Peggy expectantly. She glanced at her plate and put the final quarter of the last onion bhaji in her mouth with a cheerful nod.

'All brilliant,' she added when she'd finished chewing.

'I'll leave you to it for now,' Arun said, smile fading as he turned back to survey the chaos around him.

Andrew took a large sip of champagne before he sighed again. 'Right, so, Frank Jackson's funeral back in March. It was the weekend that we were on the *Lady Bancroft* case.'

Peggy's nose twitched as she fought to keep her expression neutral. She'd genuinely hoped to never have to think about that entire debacle again, and yet there it was, cropping up for what felt like the hundredth time that week.

Andrew continued as though he hadn't noticed a thing. 'Frank had had a decent enough career, so all the old boys were expected to go the funeral.'

'Societal expectation doesn't seem like a good enough reason for Higson to go,' Peggy replied huffily.

'It wasn't,' Andrew replied. 'He only went because he wanted to keep his eye on Prentice. Turns out, Jimmy moved to Spain in the early seventies; he lives in the sort of place where his next-door neighbours are likely the same guys he was extorting cash from back before he left the police. Higson didn't like the idea of Prentice and Sean Kelly being back together in Manchester and so he went along to the funeral. Chambers was there too, getting very chummy with his former DCI.

'Prentice struck up a conversation with Higson as though they were old friends. He was asking all about the Ballroom, and how he was surprised to hear that Higson had been transferred back there after he'd seemed so keen to get away.'

'I bet Higson loved that.'

'You can imagine,' Andrew scoffed. 'But do you remember how angry Higson seemed back then? That Monday, after the funeral, I asked him why on earth he'd been into the Ballroom over the weekend, and he nearly took my head off.'

Peggy nodded. She did remember Andrew telling her that back then.

Andrew then seemed to change his mind a few times before he next spoke. 'Do you also remember that someone at the *Evening News* had been tipped off about our investigation, and was going to write an article about GMP detectives chasing ghosts at the theatre?'

The question had been very carefully worded, leaving out any reference to the person who'd done the tipping off, and any mention of the fact that Peggy's own mother had been the one to stop the story from going to print by threatening all and sundry at the paper. Peggy wasn't sure whether she appreciated the effort to spare her any blushes, or if she was pissed off that Andrew had decided that he had to pussyfoot around either topic when talking to her.

In the end she only gave him a single nod.

He cleared his throat. 'I found out about the article because Mike told me about it in the pub that Saturday night. It had already gone round CID earlier that day, which means that Chambers knew about it, along with any other number of people who were at the funeral that afternoon.'

Peggy put her elbows on the table and rested her chin in her hands. She knew what was coming next.

'Prentice asked Higson about his 'little band of ghostbusters', and then he asked about the mysterious Miss Jones that Chambers had just been telling him about.'

Peggy had known what Andrew was going to say, but her elbow still slipped at hearing it confirmed. She shook her head. 'He can't have known it was me. My name isn't connected to anything at the Ballroom.'

'I know,' Andrew said placatingly. 'But, Peggy, I was so focussed on the fact that I was going to come out of that article looking like a complete joke, that it didn't even occur to me to think that it would include *you*. I was worried that your mother would see the article and somehow connect it to you if she saw you at the Court, but I was being too much of a self-involved prick to realise that Miss Jones would be getting a proper mention in print.'

Peggy frowned down at her hands.

'Higson, thankfully, was much more switched on than me,'

Andrew continued, 'and he easily waved away Prentice's questions. Later on that afternoon, though, he heard on the grapevine that Prentice has been making noises about leaving Spain and coming back here permanently. It's getting harder and harder to live the lifestyle he's used to out there when people around him are finally being picked up for decades-old crimes.

'Higson went straight back to the Ballroom and pulled Lily and Davy's case file. Since then, he's been at the witnesses again, telling them that it's been twenty years, and they've all long stopped speaking to Prentice.'

A short burst of *Merry Christmas Everyone* erupted from the intoxicated troubadours at the far table, stealing Peggy's attention for a moment.

'Peggy?'

Peggy looked up, equal measures of surprised and displeased at the level of concern on Andrew's face. 'What?'

'For the past few months, Chambers has been asking Higson about you – well, about Miss Jones – and trying to get any information he can. It hasn't escaped his notice that M. Jones is listed as a consultant in a significant number of our closed cases.

'When Chambers actually sent Fallon to the Ballroom last week, Higson decided that enough was enough and he was going to need to track down Lily and convince her to come forward.'

Andrew gave another one of those blustery sighs, just like he always did when he was about to be terribly earnest.

'Peggy, look,' he continued eventually, 'Annie told us that the idea of any harm coming to you has been keeping Higson awake at night, and I really don't think she was exaggerating.'

Peggy pursed her lips. 'If Higson wants Lily to come forward, it should be to give her and the Nash family the closure that they've been denied for twenty years; it should *not* be because he's worried about me.'

'I think it can be about all of that, Peg,' Andrew replied, and there was just a hint of anger creeping in at the edge of his words. 'Prentice used Lily for his own gain, even when he refused to believe her when she explained how it was all done. And now, two decades later, Chambers has presented Prentice with the idea of someone who seems inexplicably good at *finding things*, right next to a news story about the Ballroom chasing ghosts. He won't have forgotten what Lily told him back then.'

Peggy put her champagne flute down on the table with enough force that the cutlery rattled.

Around them, the party carried on unabated.

'I am not a replacement for Lily,' Peggy snapped. 'She was a child, and she was manipulated and misled by someone that she thought she could trust. Do you and Higson really think that Prentice would come along and tell me to help him, and that I'd do it, just like Lily did?'

Andrew had the gall to look affronted at the suggestion. 'No, Jesus, *obviously* that's not what I meant!'

'You can't possibly think that Prentice is coming back to Manchester, looking to start up again where he left off.' Peggy shook her head vehemently.

'Well, that's exactly what Higson thinks. It won't have escaped anyone's notice that the Ballroom's closure rate is significantly better than it has been in years,' Andrew argued, doing a very poor job of trying to sound like he wasn't annoyed. 'You'd led us to a stash of diamonds the week of Jackson's funeral, so it was entirely possible that someone could assume you'd do that again. That case and all accompanying evidence was sent to CID. Chambers knows that, and he could have easily told Prentice all about it. For God's sake, we know that Chambers followed Prentice around back in the sixties, practically begging for his approval, so what's to stop him trying it again?'

Peggy threw up her hands. 'This is conjecture.'

'It's logical reasoning!'

'Do you know that I have spent *months* thinking that I'd done something wrong, and that's why Higson stopped calling?' Peggy took a deep breath to calm her frustration. 'I drove myself mad thinking of what it could have been. Had I made things too difficult? Had I said the wrong thing? Had I made a mistake? Had I pissed *you* off?'

'*Me?*'

Peggy barrelled on, 'I thought that everything would be fine if we got through this case, and that everything could go back to how it had been before. But now you're telling me, *again*, to stay away.'

'I didn't say that,' Andrew argued.

'You didn't say that *yet*.' Peggy amended with a sigh.

'Look, I'm sure that Higson will manage to convince Lily to come forward now. She's got all of us on her side. We can build a proper case.'

Peggy frowned. 'What did you just say?'

'We can build a proper case?' Andrew repeated hesitantly.

'No, before that. The bit about Higson convincing Lily to talk.'

Andrew twisted his mouth. 'Oh. Right. Higson's on his way to Bowness.'

'Now?' Peggy hissed.

'Now. He dropped me here on the way. No idea where he got the car.'

Peggy pressed her hands to her face. 'Higson – *who is still a suspect in a murder case* – is racing off to the Lake District, to talk to a woman who probably doesn't want to be ambushed twice in as many days, and to ask her to relive the night she was nearly killed, *again*. And you think that's a good idea, do you?'

'No,' Andrew hissed, leaning across the table. 'No, I don't think it's a good idea. I think it's a terrible idea, but it *is* what's happening.'

Peggy folded her arms and leant back in her chair. 'Fine.'

'Fine?' Andrew asked incredulously. Obviously, he'd been waiting for a more drawn-out confrontation.

'Fine,' Peggy repeated. 'If Higson manages to convince Lily to come back to Manchester, I'll stay away from the Ballroom until after we've started building the case, but I want to be in the room when you interview her properly. Violet will be there too, and Lily should know that she has her sister's support, don't you think?'

It felt a bit of a low blow, obliquely referencing Andrew's own need to know that Rob was still around, but Peggy firmly believed in her argument. Lily hadn't gone through the trauma of that evening alone, and Violet hadn't had anyone to speak to for twenty years.

Andrew retreated. 'Fine, I'll tell Higson that's what's happening. For now, you'll probably still need to speak to CID tomorrow to confirm my alibi, but that's it until we know what's happening with Lily. Alright?'

Peggy nodded and stood up, dropping her napkin on the table as she went. 'I'll call you tomorrow then.'

'You're leaving?' Andrew asked in surprise, lurching to his feet.

The group from earlier turned their attention to *Fairytale of New York*, and if Peggy had been in a better mood she'd have been thoroughly amused by the drunken slurring.

Andrew scowled at the performers before turning back to Peggy. 'Peggy, you're still as much a part of the Ballroom as the rest of us. That hasn't changed. We just have to play this really, really carefully.'

'Of course.' Peggy nodded slowly as she took Andrew's keys from her handbag and placed them on the table. 'Goodnight, Andrew.'

Without waiting for a response, she tucked her chair tidily beneath the table and went to grab her coat from behind the bar.

Fiona and Julie were openly gawking at her in surprise as she briskly headed for the exit, so Peggy gave them a fleeting smile and a wave before she pulled open the door and headed out into the night.

The strains of the wine-soaked singing bled through the large windows of the restaurant, following Peggy up the road like a persistent spectre until she turned the corner and the voices faded away to nothing.

Nevertheless, even in the peace and quiet of her own car, that bloody song haunted her the whole way home.

TWENTY-THREE

'You look like you need it.'

Andrew squinted as Lloyd carefully placed the mug on the desk in front of him. The coffee was as dark as tar and the aroma was pungent enough to liberate him from the drowsiness that had been bearing down on his shoulders for hours.

'Christ,' Andrew mumbled. His lips curled in revulsion, but he picked up the coffee and took a sip anyway, immediately burning his tongue.

Wrapping both hands around the mug, Andrew leant back in his chair as Lloyd went to perch on the edge of his own desk. 'When did you get in?'

Lloyd shrugged, pulling his jacket off and chucking it carelessly towards the chair behind him. 'Dunno. Ten minutes ago. Fifteen, maybe. You didn't say anything when I first came up. I thought you might be asleep with your eyes open.'

Andrew shook his head to clear it again. How had he missed the terrible clanking and grating of the door downstairs when Lloyd arrived? Perhaps spending most of the night trying to tidy up the mess that their visitors had left in the Ballroom over the weekend hadn't been his best idea.

'So, what happened yesterday?' Lloyd asked, rubbing his hands together before picking up his own coffee. 'Did you see Chambers?'

Andrew nodded. 'You might want to put your mug down.'

Lloyd complied with a puzzled frown. His expression then morphed from confusion, to surprise, to pure shock, as Andrew explained his stint in Chester House and the visitor that had been awaiting him when he got home.

'How the hell did he get into your house, boss?' Lloyd asked.

Andrew rolled his eyes. 'According to Higson, we're all completely thick if we didn't think that he's had spare keys for all our houses this entire time.'

'But I live in my mum's house!' Lloyd was radiating panic. 'Higson can't just turn up there! My mum would kill him and then kill *me*.'

'I think you're focussing on the wrong thing here,' Andrew sighed loudly. He then proceeded to relay everything that Higson had told him.

'Are you sure that's a good idea, sir?' Lloyd asked, wincing at the thought of Higson speaking to Lily Woodhouse.

Andrew took a deep breath through his nose and let it out slowly. He wasn't having that conversation again. He picked up the well-worn case file from his desk, pulled out the bundled witness statements and threw them towards Lloyd. 'Go through those statements again and find contact details for everyone. If we're going to build a solid case against Prentice, we're going to need as much evidence as we can get.'

'Boss.' Lloyd nodded his agreement, hopping off his desk to walk around to his chair.

'Where the hell is Marnie?' Andrew muttered to himself as he stood up to stretch out his back.

When he'd left Bombay Palace the night before – only after he'd been chastised for letting Peggy leave without giving Arun the chance to say goodbye or to make sure that she'd had some pudding; and only after Fiona and Julie had shot him glances filled with abject disappointment when he'd shuffled from the dining room alone – Andrew had been traipsing to the bus stop when he'd realised that it might just be easier to spend the night in the Ballroom again.

It had already been drizzling by the time he'd stepped out of the restaurant, and it had all felt so grotesquely similar to his miserable life back in March, that when he finally shouldered open the door on Tib Street he was more than mildly anticipating that whatever was resident in the archive room kicking off at his arrival.

Thankfully, his slow trudge up the stairs had been accompanied by nothing more than the familiar creak of floorboards and the distant sound of traffic, and his relief had lasted right up until he'd pushed open the double doors and seen the state that the room had been left in.

Paper and files had littered the floor, and the general detritus usually piled high on Higson's desk was sprinkled around the room like confetti. There'd been matchboxes everywhere, with matches spilling out to mingle with shards of shattered mugs and an unreasonable number of paperclips. Every drawer that hadn't been completely ripped from one of the desks had been pulled wide open, and the small photo frame that Jen kept on her desk lay on the ground with its glass cracked and spidering over the smiling faces of Jen and her nieces.

Andrew had picked up the frame and carefully removed the photograph before any further damage could be done.

Even though he'd tried his best not to think about how he'd had to save one of the few surviving photographs of him and his brother from his mother's wrath earlier that year, he hadn't managed to keep the reminder at bay. He'd still been grimly caught up in the memory when he'd finally dropped onto the shabby blue sofa with a sigh of despair.

'Why are you here?'

He'd successfully held in the squawk of surprise at Marnie's unexpected question, but she'd looked at him with her eyebrows raised in clear judgment. Clearly, she'd still expected him to know when she was going to suddenly materialise in his presence, even though he'd had months of a Marnie-less Ballroom in which to forget that he should expect unannounced visits from her at any and all times of day or night. He *really* should have remembered that he'd ordered her to be there that night.

Once, months and months earlier, Peggy had suggested that maybe Andrew had become more aware of the slight shift in the air that always preceded Marnie's appearance, which was why he was less and less likely to yelp in outrage as time went on. He had, naturally, denied the possibility of any prescient awareness whatsoever and Peggy had, just as naturally, barely restrained from rolling her eyes at him. Marnie had overheard and simply suggested that perhaps Andrew was less of a big baby after a year on Tib Street.

'Well?' Marnie had prompted when Andrew had only continued to look at her in witless surprise. 'You told me to stay here because nobody else would be in. I was downstairs, poking around.'

He'd given himself a mental kick to restart his brain and then presented Marnie with the briefest possible summary of everything that had happened since he'd left Butterton that afternoon.

'Shit,' Marnie had concluded eventually, and Andrew had wholeheartedly agreed.

'Anything from Benson?' he'd asked, too tired for another post-mortem of Higson's story.

'Not a sausage,' Marnie had sighed. 'Hang on, were you planning on sleeping here again?'

'Well, I was, but first we're going to have clean up.'

Marnie had wrinkled her nose immediately. 'No thanks. You said I had to stay in the Ballroom when nobody else was here to keep an eye on things. You're here now, and I have things to do, so I'll see you in the morning.'

She hadn't, of course, waited for any kind of reaction, and had disappeared by the time Andrew had even begun to process what she'd just said.

He'd then spent hours flattening out pieces of screwed up paper, reorganising pots of pens, and a significant amount of time searching for bin bags so that he could throw out all of the rubbish that had once been hiding in the jumbled heaps on

Higson's and Lloyd's desks. He hadn't, of course, dared go anywhere near the cupboard downstairs where Dolly apparently kept her cleaning supplies; this was partly because he suspected that she would *know* if he touched anything that belonged to her, but also because he was half-expecting to find out that she lived in there and he wasn't sure that he could cope with knowing that for certain.

It had been far too close to dawn when Andrew had finally reclined on the sofa. He hadn't been able to doze off for more than twenty minutes or so at a time, brain fizzing and whirring with every single thing that he was trying to avoid thinking about, just like always.

He shook himself out of his reverie and took a large gulp of coffee before sitting down again and looking at the photographs of Lily and Davy staring up at him from the file.

They probably needed to understand what Prentice had been up to since leaving Manchester in 1974, and to do that, Andrew knew that he was going to have to ask Mike to do some covert research for him. He was going to owe him so many pints when all of this was over – a fact that Mike had been keen to reiterate last time they'd spoken.

Andrew grabbed a pen and began jotting down a list of things to get Mike to look into.

For the next hour, the silence in the Ballroom was broken only by occasional short phone calls as Lloyd tried to track down current phone numbers and addresses of everyone in the file.

It was a rare period of peace in a particularly turbulent week, and Andrew would have liked nothing better for it to continue for the rest of the day.

Of course, he should have known that there was no way it would last.

'So, I, er, spoke to Fiona last night,' Lloyd said hesitantly, pen scratching on a notepad.

'Right,' Andrew replied, balefully eyeing his stone-cold coffee and hoping that if he stared at it hard enough it would magically reheat and replenish itself.

'She said that she saw you and Peggy at Bombay Palace.'

'Yes.'

'And she also said that Peggy didn't look very happy at all when she left,' Lloyd added carefully.

Andrew would have no argument with that assessment, but he wasn't in the mood to hear Lloyd's version of whatever story Fiona had regaled him with. 'Witness list, Lloyd.'

Lloyd ducked his head, suitably chastised. 'Got it, boss.'

Andrew looked at his watch. It was well after ten. 'Seriously, *where* is Marnie?'

'Right here,' came Marnie's voice from somewhere behind Andrew.

Lloyd jumped about three feet in the air in surprise, but Andrew had been expecting her that time and only turned his head tiredly.

'Did you tidy this all up by yourself?' she asked in disbelief, sauntering across the room to sit at Higson's exceptionally organised desk.

'It wasn't like I had any offers of help,' Andrew grumbled.

'I told you; I had things to do.' Marnie shrugged.

Andrew wanted to ask her if 'things to do' involved visiting bloody Strangeways again, but he held his tongue. He couldn't afford to risk Marnie having a shitfit and then disappearing into the aether just then, especially when he doubted that Peggy would help track her down if he dared ask.

'I need you to try and speak to Benson again,' Andrew said. 'I know you've said that he's ignoring you, but we need to find out if he knows *anything* that can help us with Prentice.'

Marnie shook her head. 'He won't talk to me, no matter what I say. You need Peggy for this.'

'Well, we don't *have* Peggy for this,' Andrew replied through gritted teeth as he gripped a pen tightly in his fist. 'And we won't have her for anything at all until Prentice isn't a problem anymore.'

'Oh, fine.' Marnie blew out a loud breath – Andrew still found that weird – and propped her feet up on Higson's desk, crossing her ankles neatly. 'Benson? Oi, Benson?'

Andrew was certain that he'd never heard Peggy address a ghost with 'oi' as an opener, but Marnie had always been significantly blunter in the way she dealt with everyone.

Andrew saw Lloyd discreetly checking over both shoulders, obviously concerned that Benson might choose this moment to appear to him for the first time since he'd died a couple of years earlier.

'Nothing,' Marnie said, shrugging at Andrew.

'For fuck's sake,' Andrew hissed, slamming the pen down on his desk before tugging on his hair with a growl of frustration.

'You alright, boss?' Lloyd asked cautiously. 'Do you want another coffee?'

'DI Chris Benson!' Andrew yelled as he got to his feet again, ignoring both Lloyd and the fact that he'd once had to shout for Marnie under very similar circumstances, even though he hadn't believed in ghosts at all back then. 'We need to speak to you. *Now!*'

If Andrew's life was a Saturday morning cartoon, this was the moment a tumbleweed would have blown across the screen in dead silence.

'Benson!' Andrew tried again. 'Don't you want to know what we've heard about you? Don't you have anything you want to say about the fact that we have reason to believe that you might have been involved in hiding Davy Nash's body in Hulme? Or that you lied to Higson about it for twenty years? Or that you were Jimmy Prentice's dogsbody?'

The change in the atmosphere was so immediate that it made Andrew's stomach roll as though he were accelerating down a hill.

Lloyd leapt up from his chair and staggered towards Andrew's desk, obviously taking a safety-in-numbers approach to whatever was going on.

Marnie, similarly, made her way towards the others, and she looked even more perturbed than they did.

'What's going on?' Andrew whispered as his eyes darted around the room.

'I don't know!' Marnie hissed back. 'Maybe you shouldn't have been mardy with the ghost. You've obviously pissed him off!'

'Do you think we should be leaving?' Lloyd murmured. 'I think maybe we should be leaving.'

The double doors burst open and all three of them turned towards them in horror.

'What are youse lot up to now, *eh*?' Dolly croaked. Her eyes were even wilder than usual. 'What're youse gettin' 'im involved for?'

'What?' Andrew asked, baffled, but also horrified that a situation that he'd already thought was fairly terrible had somehow managed to get markedly worse with Dolly's arrival.

Dolly looked Marnie dead in the eye. 'Did *you* call 'im in?'

Marnie shook her head, swallowing heavily. She pointed at Andrew accusingly. 'He did it!'

Dolly frowned. 'Pretty Boy called 'im?'

Andrew shook his head.

'Now, 'ow on God's earth did *you* manage to call 'im 'ere?' Dolly asked, stalking closer to Andrew and peering into his face. 'The creepy girl isn't 'ere. 'As summat 'appened to 'er?'

'No!' Andrew replied firmly. 'We just needed to talk to Benson.'

Dolly frowned and her whole face scrunched like antique parchment. She pointed towards the far side of the room. '*That* ain't Benson.'

'Then who is it?' Andrew asked, despite not being sure that he actually wanted to know the answer.

Dolly looked at him like he was completely stupid again. 'Moses.'

'Moses?' Andrew repeated blankly.

'Like, from the Bible?' Lloyd asked, wide-eyed and alarmed.

Dolly turned her incredulous judgement towards him instead. 'Don't be so thick, lad.'

Unhelpfully, she didn't divulge any further information about the mysterious *Moses*. Instead, she just folded her arms and nodded as though she were listening to something.

Andrew shivered; the air in the Ballroom was definitely more frigid than it had been minutes earlier.

'I can't see anything,' Marnie muttered out of the corner of her mouth. 'I don't know what she's doing.'

Dolly growled. 'Moses ain't 'appy to 'ear what you've 'ad to say about Benson.'

They all looked at Dolly in surprise.

She either didn't notice the glances, or pretended that she couldn't see their shock, because she just went right back to bobbing her head in silent conversation.

'Chris'll be along,' Dolly said, and then gave one sharp nod towards the far wall.

The pressure that had been building around them evaporated as though it had never been there, and Andrew felt oddly weightless.

'What's happening?' Lloyd whispered to Andrew.

Andrew could only shrug helplessly in response.

Dolly shifted so that she could face Marnie directly. 'Youse tell that Benson to listen to ye, girl. I always wondered if 'e were a bit of a bad sort. Look 'im right in the eye and make sure 'e' doesn't lie to youse.'

Andrew looked at Marnie in alarm. Surely, nobody had *ever*

told Dolly that Marnie wasn't just like the rest of them, right?

As though she'd read his mind, Dolly turned her attention back to Andrew and smiled at him with her teeth bared. She then tapped her nose twice with a crooked finger.

'Oh my God, Benson's here!' Marnie declared suddenly. She frowned towards what looked to be an empty patch of air. 'Right, well, whatever. We need you to talk to us now, alright?'

Andrew hated it; he hated that he couldn't see Benson, or hear Benson, or even sense that Benson was there.

'She'll do it, Pretty Boy.' Dolly's voice crackled like kindling. "E's scared of 'er. I can tell.'

'Did you work for Jimmy Prentice?' Marnie asked. Her voice was shaking slightly, but she was standing her ground. 'Did you help him hide Davy's body?'

A few seconds later, Marnie turned towards Andrew, unease clear on her face.

'What? What is it?' Andrew asked, heart sinking at the implication anyway.

Marnie nodded. 'He's really scared. He says that Prentice would've ruined him if he hadn't helped. He doesn't want you to tell Higson about this.'

'I can't keep this from Higson!' Andrew argued. 'Jesus Christ, if lying about it for two decades wasn't enough, how could it *possibly* be a good idea to keep doing it now?'

Marnie looked back towards the wall. 'We have to tell him. We have to let Beth know what happened to her husband. You were *friends*.'

Long moments then passed in silence, Marnie looking agitated while Dolly appeared entirely serene.

'Prentice found out about the gambling four or five years before Davy was killed,' Marnie said quietly. 'He promised to hide it – help out even – as long as he could rely on Benson whenever he called him. Prentice hated the fact that he couldn't get Higson to turn, so having Benson in his pocket soothed the sting of that a bit.'

Andrew's stomach rolled again, though this time with good old-fashioned nausea. Four or five years was a long time to fill with errands for a man like Jimmy Prentice. What the hell had Benson got himself involved in during that time?

He couldn't ask for that information now, though, they didn't have time. It would all have to come later, once they had something definite about Davy's murder.

'He'd only just got home after being at the pub with Higson when Sean Kelly arrived outside,' Marnie continued, and she looked ill. 'Kelly told him that they needed his help to bury a problem, and that Frank Jackson had gone to get Dickie.'

'Does he mean Chambers?' Andrew asked. 'We need to know.'

Marnie nodded and turned back towards Benson.

'Yeah, Dickie Chambers,' Marnie confirmed a moment later.

'Shit,' Andrew hissed. He'd always known that it was going to be Chambers but hearing it out loud still felt like a blow. He had no loyalty to his former boss, but this was an unpleasant reminder that perhaps Andrew's instincts hadn't always been as good as he'd thought.

'Benson says that Chambers wasn't there though,' Marnie added, shaking her head. 'He wasn't at his house, so Jackson met Benson and Kelly out at one of the new housing developments in Hulme. It had all been dug out for foundations, so they just picked a spot and dug a bit deeper.'

'Christ,' Andrew murmured, pressing his fingers to his mouth, and Lloyd sat down heavily on the edge of the desk next to him.

'Benson says that he didn't know it was Davy until Kelly and Jackson carried him over to where they'd dug the grave,' Marnie continued, voice barely above a whisper. 'They'd wrapped him in a sheet of some kind, and it was pure fluke that he got a look at his face.'

Marnie broke off and wrapped her arms tightly around her stomach. Lloyd immediately got to his feet.

'You're alright, Marnie,' he said quietly as he approached her. 'You're doing brilliant. Promise.'

'I'm not good at this. Not like Peggy is,' Marnie whimpered softly. 'She makes people feel better, and she doesn't make them cry. She doesn't start crying herself!'

Andrew had a number of arguments to the contrary for that last allegation – after all, he'd seen Peggy's face when she'd spoken to that little girl in Bowness, and he'd seen the expression that always clouded her features every single time she spoke to Rob – but it wasn't his place to say anything.

Lloyd didn't say anything either; he just put his arm around Marnie's shoulders and squeezed.

Marnie took a few steadying breaths and straightened her spine. 'They all freaked out when Benson recognised Davy, but they decided to go ahead with the plan, thinking that Prentice was going to need them to get rid of any evidence anyway.'

'Can he tell us where Davy is?' Andrew asked, hoping it wouldn't derail everything.

Marnie tilted her head, obviously listening carefully. 'He says he could probably tell you by looking at a map. He remembers that the Hippodrome wasn't too far away.'

Andrew nodded his acceptance. He didn't really want to ask the next question, but he wouldn't be able to live with himself if he didn't, so he turned towards where he thought Benson was and addressed him directly, 'I need you to tell us if you ever spoke to Higson about what happened that night, even vaguely.'

Lloyd looked over immediately, his face creased in disbelief. 'You don't really think Higson's known where Davy's been buried for twenty years do you, boss?'

Andrew held his hands up. 'I have to ask. You know I do.'

Dolly made an indistinct sound beside him and Andrew really hoped it wasn't meant negatively.

'He never said a word,' Marnie confirmed, looking at Andrew seriously. 'He says that he's never breathed a word of it to Higson; not about Davy, and not about anything else he did for Prentice.'

'Do you believe him?' Andrew asked.

Marnie raised her chin slightly, as though in challenge. 'I do.'

If Peggy had told him the same, Andrew knew that he would have trusted her judgement implicitly. He was only the slightest bit surprised to find that he trusted Marnie's conclusion with the same conviction. 'Alright. Okay, so w-'

The shrill ring of the phone on Higson's desk startled them all.

Lloyd was closest so he moved away from Marnie to pick up the receiver. 'Yeah?'

Dolly patted Andrew twice on the arm, slightly harder than could be considered entirely friendly. She then hitched up her voluminous black skirt and left the room without another word, her pointy red shoes tip-tapping on the wooden floor.

Andrew was frozen where he sat, but then he caught Marnie smirking at him in amusement, and he shook himself.

'Come off it, you're terrified of her as well,' Andrew accused as the tension in the room dissipated almost entirely.

Marnie shrugged one shoulder and then gestured towards Benson. 'Do you want me to ask anything else?'

Lloyd put the phone down with a resounding clang. 'That was Charlie, boss.'

Andrew was immediately alert again. 'Why? What's happened?'

'Nothing,' Lloyd replied slowly. 'CID called Butterton this morning and asked Peggy to go to Chester House, so she went over a couple of hours ago. Charlie promised he'd let us know once he got out of an estate meeting, that's all. Are you *sure* you don't want another coffee?'

Andrew ignored Marnie's derisive snort that had clearly been aimed at him, and looked at Lloyd. 'You're going to have to go and speak to Chambers today you know.'

Lloyd made a face. 'I don't think he's all that worried about my involvement, boss.'

Marnie whirled towards Andrew suddenly, eyes darting wildly around the room. 'Something's wrong.'

'What?' Andrew asked. He was utterly bewildered, but that in no way eased the immediate smack of anxiety. Eighteen months on Tib Street had really honed his ability to catastrophise if the occasion called for it.

'Something really bad's happened,' Marnie said, staring at Andrew in alarm.

Andrew found himself striding towards her before he'd given his feet permission to move. 'Marnie, what's going on? Is it Peggy?'

Marnie shook her head. 'No.'

Andrew allowed his shoulders to relax the tiniest amount. 'Marnie, what is it?'

'Oh my God.' Marnie's hands flew to her face. 'It's Rex. I have to go.'

Andrew had barely opened his mouth to ask her what the hell she was talking about, when Marnie simply popped out of existence as though she'd never been there, leaving two baffled detectives – and perhaps the ghost of another – in her wake.

'What does she mean?' Lloyd asked.

Andrew shook his head with a sigh. 'She did this before, back when we were working on *her* case. She had Peggy call me in the middle of the night, panicking that something had happened to Rex. He was fine though.

'Saying that…' he twisted his lips in thought as he trailed off and looked at Lloyd. 'That did look like genuine fear, didn't it?'

Lloyd nodded. 'What should we do?'

'Call Strangeways, just in case.'

'Will do, sir.' Lloyd picked up the phone and Andrew called out the number for the prison to him – a number he hadn't needed since the day he'd walked out of CID, but was burned into his memory from the number of times Chambers had asked him to call to set up meetings with prisoners. These days, Andrew had the unpleasant inkling that the calls he'd made on behalf of his former boss were all part of Chambers' scheme to maintain his network of unsavoury contacts, even when they were behind bars.

Andrew drummed his fingers on his desk and glanced towards the back wall again. 'DI Benson? If you're still here, we'll need to speak to you again once Higson gets back.'

There was no reply of any kind.

Lloyd appeared to be experiencing the same lack of response. He took the phone away from his ear and frowned at it. 'Nobody's answering. Is that weird?'

'It's unusual,' Andrew confirmed. 'Call again. I'll try CID.'

Andrew's call was answered immediately, even as Lloyd's continued to ring out. He hastily identified himself and asked for DC Cooke, the young detective he'd spoken to the day before. He'd have much preferred to ask for Mike, but that didn't seem wise when they were still trying to downplay any association between them.

'DI Joyce?' the hesitant voice at the end of the telephone asked.

'That's right,' Andrew replied. 'Is that Cooke?'

Cooke cleared his throat. 'Yes, sir. Can I help you with something?'

'I hope so. Can you tell me if Jen is there? DS Cusack, I mean,' Andrew replied.

'She's here, sir. She's brought Mrs Higson in to speak to DCI Chambers,' Cooke replied.

'Any chance you could pop her on the phone for me?' Andrew asked, crossing his fingers, only half convinced that Cooke would comply.

'I'm not sure I'm allowed to do that, sir,' Cooke replied. There was a brief pause. '*Am* I allowed to do that?'

'I don't see why not.'

There was the sound of movement and indistinct mumbling for a good few moments.

'Sir?' Jen asked with a reasonable amount of bewilderment. 'What's going on? Has something happened?'

'I was hoping you might know,' Andrew replied. 'Marnie's just had a meltdown, saying that something bad's happened to Rex.'

'Do you think she's telling the truth?' Jen asked carefully.

'Sounded like it. There's no answer at Strangeways though. Any chance there's any interesting chat at CID?' Andrew wasn't holding out much hope, but he didn't know what else to do without actually going to the prison in person, which he was keen to avoid. He bloody hated that place.

'No, nothing,' Jen replied. 'We're just sitting out here waiting for Chambers to call Annie in.'

'Is he still talking to Peggy?' Andrew wasn't thrilled about the thought.

'Peggy?' Jen asked in surprise. 'I didn't even know she was here. We've been waiting for well over an hour, so God knows what he could still be talking to her about.'

Andrew thought about the message Lloyd had relayed from Charlie, and then did the mental calculation of driving time in his head. 'Over an hour?'

'Yeah,' Jen replied slowly. 'Why?'

'Well, if Peggy left Butterton when Charlie said she d-'

'Oh, hang on, sir, sorry!' Jen interrupted. 'Chambers has just come out of his office. He doesn't look happy. He's just gone to talk to a couple of people – oh, Mike's there.'

'Has Peggy come out yet?' Andrew asked.

'No. Chambers closed the door behind him though, so I guess he might be going back in.'

'Shit,' Andrew breathed. What the hell was happening? Chambers couldn't possibly have found anything wrong with Peggy's story.

Could he?

'Wait.' Jen paused for a long moment. 'Chambers is leaving.'

'Leaving?' The question came out loud enough that Lloyd jumped in surprise.

'Leaving and taking people with him,' Jen hissed into the phone. 'Wait. I'm going to find out what's going on.'

Andrew turned to Lloyd as the sounds of shuffling and unintelligible chatter filled his ear. 'Anything?'

'Still nothing, boss,' Lloyd replied. 'Should we be worried?"

'Prisoner disturbance at Strangeways,' Jen suddenly said at full volume again. 'Chambers is taking a team down there. Sounds small, so no tactical response needed. Mike just told me on the way out.'

Andrew had mostly stopped listening after 'Strangeways'; Jesus, had something actually happened to Rex?

'Sir, what do you want me to do?' Jen asked.

Andrew pressed his fingertips against his forehead as his brain whirred. 'Can you go and get Peggy, and tell her that Chambers has left? He's enough of an arse that he'd leave her in there for hours because he knows it would piss *me* off. More importantly, if something's happened to Rex, then we should probably warn Peggy before Marnie turns up shrieking at her; I don't even know if they've spoken since yesterday.'

The current state of Peggy and Marnie's relationship hadn't come up in conversation the night before, and Andrew hadn't wanted to be the one to mention it, fearing that it might have blown up the precarious balance that he and Peggy had found themselves finally staggering back towards over the weekend. An explosion had come anyway, of course.

'I'll be right back,' Jen replied.

Andrew hadn't really intended for Jen to go and get Peggy with such immediacy, but he had no choice but to wait patiently for his sergeant to return as the recognisable sound of the phone being put down on a desk greeted him again.

'Lloyd, where's your car parked?' Andrew asked, reaching for his coat as he kept the phone wedged between his shoulder and his ear.

'Without that bloody van there, I got a space up the end of the road,' Lloyd replied. 'Why?'

'We're going to Strangeways.'

Lloyd looked as thrilled about the concept as Andrew felt.

'Sir!' Jen was back. 'Chambers' office is empty. Peggy's not there.'

Andrew paused in pulling on his coat, one sleeve over his arm and the rest of the material trailing on the floor behind him. 'What?'

'Peggy's not there,' Jen repeated. 'I've just asked Cooke, and he confirmed that he called Butterton earlier. He was under strict instructions from Chambers to get her to come in this morning. Peggy agreed to be in as soon as she could, but she hasn't arrived yet.'

Andrew's aptitude for dreaming up worst case scenarios kicked into action instantly, and he had to smother the intrusive thoughts with as much rationality as he could grasp hold of. 'She's probably stuck in traffic.'

'Right,' Jen agreed doubtfully.

Unless there'd been an utter disaster on the roads, there was no way that it could have taken over two hours for Peggy to get from Butterton to Old Trafford. Andrew glanced at the door, knowing that they needed to get to Strangeways before CID, and that already being in the city centre only gave them a minimal time advantage. Still, he wasn't going anywhere until he'd checked one final thing.

'Jen, I need you to see if Peggy's car is in the car park,' Andrew said as evenly as possible. 'She might have arrived and just be waiting in the car. Oh, and check for the Range Rover, just in case she drove that instead.'

It was testament to whatever concern Jen heard in the request that she didn't reply at all but left immediately.

'Something wrong, boss?' Lloyd asked, shrugging his parka back on.

'I hope not.'

There was the sound of movement on the other end of the call.

'Andrew, love, is that you?' came Annie Higson's voice.

'Er, ma'am, that's a CID phone,' Andrew heard Cooke say with polite panic, 'you're not really supposed to touch it.'

Annie obviously ignored him, because almost immediately she spoke to Andrew again, 'Is something wrong? Jenny's just gone tearing out of here.'

'Not entirely sure, Annie,' Andrew replied tightly. God, they were running out of time. 'Lloyd, go get the car. I'll be out in a minute.'

Lloyd didn't ask any questions. Annie also stayed silent, but, oddly, Andrew appreciated her presence on the call anyway.

'Jenny's back,' Annie announced suddenly. 'Oh dear.'

Andrew didn't like that quiet '*oh dear*' at all.

'Sir, the Range Rover's here,' Jen explained quickly, breathing heavily. 'I couldn't see properly from the window up here, so I ran down to the car park. There's no sign of Peggy though.'

It was as if the dark, stifling atmosphere of earlier had returned to the Ballroom, dialling Andrew's anxiety higher. He held the phone more tightly. 'Jen, send Annie out to your car to wait.

Then I want you to search Chester House for Peggy – she has to be there somewhere. Tell Cooke he's helping you. I want you all back here as soon as you've found her.'

'All of us, sir?' Jen asked, surprised. 'I thought we were keeping Peggy away from the Ballroom.'

'All of you, Jen,' Andrew confirmed firmly. 'I've got to get to Strangeways before Chambers.'

'Sir.' Jen's response was caught between a confirmation and an apprehensive question.

Andrew hung up the phone and tugged his coat on properly, fingers catching in the sleeve in his haste.

The rational part of his mind told him that Peggy was likely just on another floor in Chester House. Rationality, however, wasn't necessarily something that Andrew easily applied to potentially precarious situations involving Peggy at the best of times, so it was right back to imagining the worst.

Peggy would kill him for wasting valuable – *and limited* – time concerning himself with any unsubstantiated concern for her wellbeing when he could be out there, following up on the fact that something had definitely happened in the vicinity of Rex Hughes, if not to the arsehole himself.

That thought spurred him back into action, and he moved quickly to grab everything related to the case from his and Lloyd's desks and unceremoniously shoved it all into his bag.

Andrew permitted himself one last very deep breath through his nose in an attempt to find a single thread of balance to latch onto, before he strode out of the Ballroom and thundered down the stairs as though every ghost he'd ever encountered was right on his heels.

TWENTY-FOUR

'Christ, that was quick for you lot.'

The heavy-set man who'd dismissed their presence entirely until Andrew and Lloyd had waved their identification at him gaped at them in clear surprise.

'We were in the area. DCI Chambers will be here in a bit, so really, we're just here to ask some initial questions,' Andrew replied as pleasantly as he could muster, hoping that they could get a bloody move on. He'd been mentally counting down the scant minutes they had left before a group of CID's finest trooped in, and he figured that they were on borrowed time as it was.

'Bigwigs are in a meeting about it all, so you've got me for now. Al Harrison,' the man added as he pointed at himself. 'Big Al.'

There wasn't a chance that Andrew was going to call him Big Al, but he nodded in what he hoped looked like acceptance anyway, just before Al turned to lead them further into the prison.

It was almost unnervingly quiet compared to Andrew's previous visits. There were far fewer people roaming freely through this part of the building than usual, with most officers and other staff already in their preassigned positions for when a serious incident occurred.

As they walked, Al confirmed that all prisoners were currently secured in their cells, barring the injured party and the alleged perpetrator of the assault, so there wasn't the familiar cacophony of voices and clanging doors streaming out towards the admin area.

They'd yet to confirm the identity of the injured party, or the one who'd done the injuring, for that matter, so Andrew still wasn't sure to what extent, if any, that Rex was mixed up in whatever had taken place.

A sound attempt at festivity had been made, but Andrew wouldn't be fooled. It didn't matter how many Christmas trees had been decorated, or how many miles of colourful paper chains had been strung inside the prison, it couldn't disguise the fact that an undercurrent of volatile tension ran through the very walls of the place these days. Andrew hadn't liked the place much when he'd first been dragged there as a child to visit his father, but after that it hadn't really given him much pause for thought. Since he'd seen the effect the place had on Peggy when she so much as thought about it, however, Andrew had developed a keen dislike for the building.

'So, what actually happened?' Andrew asked as Al led them down another echoey corridor, hopefully buying themselves an extra minute or two before Chambers' arrival.

'Stabbing in the chapel,' Al replied calmly as he opened a door and gestured for Andrew and Lloyd to enter the small office.

'In the *chapel?*' Lloyd asked in surprise.

'Choir practice for the Christmas Eve carol service,' Al explained. 'They're actually half decent this year from what I've heard of them, so this'll probably put a bit of a downer on things.'

'Do you know who was stabbed?' Andrew asked.

Al shook his head with a grimace. 'No, someone'll be along in a minute to tell me though, I'm sure.'

Jesus Christ, they did *not* have time for this. Andrew was going to have to do something.

'Oi. Al!'

They all turned in surprised unison to see a man in a suit hovering in the doorway as though he'd been summoned by Al's words. 'Have you heard yet?'

Al shook his head and then pointed at Andrew and Lloyd. 'No, and the lads are here wanting to know too.'

'Hughes,' the suited man announced, eyes wide with the joy of passing on some hot gossip.

Al jerked his head in question. 'For fuck's sake, Phil. Which Hughes?'

Andrew and Lloyd looked at each other in alarm, already anticipating the answer.

'*The* Hughes,' came the reply. 'Rex Hughes. They've whizzed him over to the Royal Infirmary.'

Al nodded without even a hint of disbelief. 'Nonce. Who had him?'

'Looks like it was that little lad,' Phil added. 'Totney, or Tottenham, or the like.'

'Totness?' Al asked, astonishment now clear as day on his face. 'Didn't think he'd say boo to a goose!'

'Hughes must've really got on his wick then,' Phil replied with a shrug. 'Sounds like it was pretty brutal.'

Andrew held in the torrent of swearing that desperately wanted to escape. 'Any idea why this Totness would attack Hughes?'

'Well, like a said, Hughes is a nonce,' Al replied airily. 'Swanning about all week, singing like he thinks he's Frank fucking Sinatra.'

'It's not just this week though, is it?' Phil grimaced, lips curling in distaste. 'Hughes is always walking round like he's the dog's bollocks.'

'Totness though...' Al said, shaking his head slowly. 'I would've picked out a good few hundred others who'd have gone for Hughes before I even got anywhere near that kid.'

'He probably didn't like Hughes talking to coppers and getting all those extra little privileges he seemed to wangle,' Phil said, sniffing loudly with a derisive glance towards Andrew and Lloyd, like he blamed them personally for Rex's behaviour.

'Who's Hughes been talking to?' Andrew asked, ignoring Phil's disdain.

Phil shrugged. 'No idea. One of your lot yanked him out of

his cell for a meeting at arse o'clock this morning, didn't they? So, whoever that was.'

'Oh, is that right?' Al asked with interest.

'Talk of the town over breakfast, mate.' Phil nodded solemnly.

'You saw who spoke to Hughes?' Andrew asked tersely.

'Yeah.' Phil shrugged.

Al looked at Andrew. 'Not me. I only got in at half eleven, see. Shit timing given what happened five minutes later.'

'Do you have a write up of the meeting?' Andrew asked tightly, marginally concerned that Rex's stabbing wouldn't be the only act of violence to occur within the walls of Strangeways if he didn't get a straight answer sharpish.

Al grimaced. 'Nah. John pissed off home with a dicky stomach as soon as his shift was over. He was in the bogs all morning by the sounds of it – really foul – so I doubt he'll have done his reports yet. If only Totness had gone for Hughes at the beginning of their practice rather than the end, I wouldn't have got in the door, and I'd be at home again by now. John won't be back here until after Christmas now, I reckon.'

Andrew pinched the bridge of his nose.

'Well, we had to sign in, right?' Lloyd asked, evidently aware that his boss was about to lose his temper with the rambling double act. 'So, even if you haven't got the paperwork for the meeting, can't you just tell us who it was that signed in from CID this morning?'

'Can't you just ask them yourselves?' Phil sniggered unhelpfully. 'Or are you two the B team?'

'For fuck's sake, Phil, shut up and go see who it was,' Al directed firmly.

Phil rolled his eyes, but left the room as instructed.

'Sorry about him,' Al sighed gustily. 'There's still no cure for being a dickhead.'

'You're alright,' Lloyd replied.

Andrew thought carefully about his blood pressure.

'You two come across Hughes before?' Al asked conversationally.

'Yeah,' Lloyd announced, far too enthusiastically for Andrew's liking. 'We put him away!'

Al looked down at Lloyd sceptically. 'Oh, right?'

Thankfully, any impending argument was halted by the return of Phil, and his declaration of, 'DCI Chambers.'

'He's here?' Andrew asked, frustrated that they hadn't really got anywhere yet.

'What?' Phil's whole face scrunched up in confusion. 'No. He's the one who had a meeting with Hughes this morning.'

Andrew suddenly felt cold all over.

Chambers had called a clandestine meeting with Hughes that morning and then, only hours later, Hughes was attacked in prison. That was worrying enough, even if Andrew didn't also have to think about the fact that Chambers had also summoned Peggy to Chester House and she was currently nowhere to be found.

Andrew headed for the door without another word, barging through and shouldering Phil out of the way without a second thought.

What the hell was going on?

He strode down the corridor, not entirely sure what his next move would be, and he was only peripherally aware that Lloyd was calling after him.

Andrew rounded the corner and stopped dead; Lloyd walked right into the back of him.

Chambers, head bowed, was marching towards them, unaware of their presence.

Right. Andrew's next move suddenly presented itself in glorious technicolour.

Just as Chambers looked up upon his approach to the corner,

Andrew moved so that he was standing right in front of him.

'Joyce!' Chambers barked in surprise. 'What the hell do you think you're doing here?'

'Where's Peggy?' Andrew snapped, patience wafer thin.

'Who?' Chambers had the nerve to try and look baffled.

'Peggy.' Andrew repeated. 'Margaret Swan.'

Chambers' lips pulled down briefly as he raised his eyebrows. 'Why on God's earth would I know where she is?'

Andrew lurched forwards without a clear plan. Lloyd, sensing danger, grabbed hold of Andrew's sleeve in obvious warning.

'Because you asked her to come into Chester House this morning,' Andrew replied sharply.

Chambers blinked owlishly. 'No, I didn't.'

Even knowing what he was like, Andrew still couldn't believe that Chambers would actually deny that fact to his face. 'Yes, you did. One of your DCs – Cooke – called her this morning, on your instructions, and asked her to come in.'

Andrew shook his head as Chambers just continued to stare at him in feigned puzzlement. 'Why did you visit Rex Hughes this morning? What was so important that you needed to talk to him at dawn? Bit odd he was then stabbed a few hours later, isn't it?'

'What?' The blood drained from Chambers' face. 'I don't know what you're talking about, Joyce.'

Andrew shrugged Lloyd off and turned to him before jerking his thumb in the direction they'd just come from. 'Go and get those two from the office and bring them here now.'

Lloyd hesitated for only a split second before nodding. 'Sir.'

'Why did you visit Rex Hughes this morning?' Andrew asked again. He eyed the far end of the corridor, wondering how long they had before Chambers' entourage lolloped into view.

Chambers' eyes narrowed. 'I don't know what you're playing at, but you are on very, *very* thin ice right now, Joyce.'

'I probably am,' Andrew agreed, 'but so are you, *Dickie*, because we know all about the dirty work that you did for Jimmy Prentice over the years.'

Andrew wasn't particularly concerned that he was embellishing the story slightly – so far, they actually had very little from Benson in the way of specifics, and he'd confirmed that Chambers hadn't actually been involved in burying Davy Nash's body – but any lingering apprehension that he might have had faded away entirely when Chambers took a step backwards in pure shock.

'What are you talking about?' Chambers stammered slightly. 'What has Jimmy Prentice got to do with anything?'

'You tell me.' Andrew knew that all of this might be the most unwise course of action he'd ever taken in his professional life; he also knew that he didn't have a choice.

'I worked with Jimmy Prentice *twenty years ago*, Joyce,' Chambers barked, but he didn't seem as self-assured as he had earlier.

'I know. You were working with him when Lily Woodhouse and Davy Nash disappeared, weren't you?' Andrew raised his eyebrows.

Chambers looked as though he'd been struck. 'I don't know what you're talking about.'

Andrew shook his head slowly. 'You see, you keep saying that, but I'm certain that you know *exactly* what I'm talking about. You know that Jimmy Prentice murdered Davy Nash, and that Sean Kelly attacked Lily.'

Despite all current bravado, Andrew had enough sense to know that it wouldn't be wise to reveal that Lily was alive.

'I also think you know for certain that Higson wasn't anywhere near Sean Kelly's house last Saturday,' Andrew continued. Chambers seemed to have been stunned into silence. 'So, how did it work? Did Prentice call and tell you that he had another mess for you to clean up, just like the old days?'

'I told you!' Chambers argued. 'Kelly identified Higson when he called emergency services.'

'And you believed that, did you?' Andrew asked.

'Why wouldn't I?

Andrew's patience wasn't going to last much longer. 'What were you looking for in the Ballroom on Saturday?'

Chambers looked taken aback. 'Joyce, I've set foot in that godforsaken building on precisely one occasion since I walked out of there in 1974, and that was when I came to try and make you see sense about your declining career prospects.'

The sound of footsteps behind him announced the return of Lloyd, along with Al and Phil.

'What's going on here?' Al asked, looking between Andrew and Chambers warily.

Andrew ignored him and pointed at Phil, then at Chambers. 'This is the man you saw here this morning, right?'

Phil regarded Andrew as though he'd lost the plot. 'No.'

'What?' It was Andrew's turn to blink stupidly.

'That's not the bloke from earlier.' Phil shrugged.

Andrew crooked his finger towards Phil. 'You said DCI Chambers signed in this morning. *That* man there is DCI Chambers.'

'And you said earlier that all coppers look the same to you, so how do you know it's not him?' Lloyd interjected.

Phil looked offended. 'I'm not thick. The guy this morning was a good bit shorter than him there.'

Andrew's stomach clenched unpleasantly. God, was Chambers telling the truth? Could it actually have been Prentice himself who'd have come here to speak to Rex?

'And definitely a good bit younger,' Phil added.

Lloyd threw up his hands. 'But you said DCI Chambers' name was on the log!'

'Well, that's not who was here this morning, alright?' Phil said and then frowned at Andrew. 'Are you okay there, mate? You've gone a bit green.'

Andrew looked at the floor, his eyes darting wildly around as he tried to get his thoughts in order. He needed to *think*. Who would have the balls to come to Strangeways and impersonate Chambers, risking getting caught in the act?

Maybe it didn't have anything to do with balls, though. Maybe this was just arrogance through and through.

Andrew's head snapped up and he glared at Phil again. 'Do you remember anything else about the man this morning? Anything at all?'

At that moment, a handful of Andrew's ex-colleagues from CID came through the door at the far end of the corridor, with Mike Lawson trailing behind them.

Mike gawped in surprise when he saw Andrew and Lloyd standing with Chambers, but Andrew barely noticed.

Phil shrugged again. 'Not really. Bit smarmy, but aren't you all? Oh, I suppose he *was* chewing with his mouth open. That set John's dodgy stomach right back off; he nearly spewed all over the carpet.'

Fingers of icy dread reached out and gripped Andrew tightly, squeezing the air right out of his lungs with a whoosh of horrified astonishment.

'You alright, boss?' Lloyd asked, brows creasing in real concern.

Andrew shook his head silently as everything coalesced into a clear but awful conclusion.

How the bloody hell had he missed *that*?

* * *

'Excuse me, love?'

Peggy squeezed her eyes shut even as she kept her chin to her chest. If she didn't look at the owner of the voice, then they wouldn't know that she could see them, and then they'd just have to leave her alone like the others eventually had, wouldn't they?

When had she sat down? She couldn't remember.

'I really am sorry to disturb you.' The voice was soft and kindly – exactly how Peggy thought a grandmother should probably sound – but still she remained closed off. She knew that she had to ignore them if she had any hope of getting a chance to think straight.

Peggy shook her head minutely, willing them to leave. She immediately regretted the movement when the headache that had ebbed with her stillness made a sudden, vicious resurgence, hammering on every inch of her skull.

'I can see you're upset, sweetheart, and I promise that I wouldn't ask you to move if I really didn't have to.'

Peggy's eyes cracked open, and she squinted up at the owner of the voice – the surprisingly *alive* owner of the voice – who was looking at her in concern.

'Goodness, are you alright?'

The voice belonged to a smartly dressed older woman, wearing a small gold cross on a chain around her neck. Inexplicably, she seemed to be holding a large stack of booklets.

She's not a ghost, Peggy told herself as firmly as she could stand to. Not a ghost, unlike the other hundreds of faces and voices that had approached her since she'd arrived, with miserable entreaties for just a moment of her time – *please, miss, **please*** – or dire warnings for the sanctity of her soul.

She's not a ghost, Peggy told herself again, but she couldn't quite remember why that seemed like it should be terribly important.

'No, do you know what, you stay right there,' the woman added gently. 'Don't mind me. I'll start with the rows at the back. Is there anyone here with you?'

There was an immense pressure building behind Peggy's eyes, and she pinched the bridge of her nose to stave off the pain.

'Poor girl,' the woman said, shaking her head. 'Are you cold? You look cold.'

'What's going on?'

Oh, Peggy realised distantly when that callous, slimy voice reached her ears, *that* was what she'd needed to remember.

She looked up at the woman, blinking hard against the pull of gluey eyelashes.

'Are you with this lass?' the woman asked over Peggy's head, mouth downturned in obvious judgement. 'She doesn't seem well at all.'

'She's just a bit under the weather, you know, like girls tend to get. Not that it's any of your business now, is it, *love*?'

A wave of nausea rushed through Peggy as a clammy hand brushed against the side of her neck on the way to clamping tightly on her shoulder.

The woman looked ready to argue and, *God*, Peggy hoped that she would. That she could do something – anything – that might draw attention to her plight; to telegraph something that could somehow make its way back to anyone who might be able to help.

With a final glance of sympathy, cut through with a glaring streak of worry, and a weak smile directed at Peggy, the woman walked away, booklets in hand.

A weight landed heavily on the chair beside her. 'What the fuck was that about?'

Peggy shook her head as vigorously as she dared. She just needed to be able to think. If she could *think*, she could get herself out of this situation

'You better not have said anything to her. I thought I made it perfectly clear that you were to keep your mouth shut.'

She knew it was a terrible idea, but Peggy still turned her head to give Fallon her best glare.

'Up!' Fallon snapped.

He didn't wait for her to move; he grabbed her arm roughly and tugged Peggy after him as he moved away from the chairs that had been carefully laid out for some sort of service.

Peggy barely had the capacity to wonder if the woman who'd spoken to her only a moment ago was still watching her, or whether she'd permanently turned away in the face of Fallon's aggression.

They moved further into the building, and Peggy tripped more than once on the uneven floor as she was towed along behind Fallon.

Phantom hands reached towards her, stretching from indistinct figures on her left and right in a cathedral almost devoid of living souls; it was as though they all now knew that she was aware of them, no matter how hard she tried to pretend otherwise.

'You better have an idea by the time we get up near the altar,' Fallon growled. His hand was beneath Peggy's coat sleeve, and he curled his fingers around her wrist tightly enough that she knew that there'd be a mark later.

Peggy tried to pull her arm out of his grip, but she was cold enough that all of her muscles felt tight and stiff, making it impossible to do much more than give a feeble tug.

Fallon either didn't notice, or didn't care, and he didn't slow his pace as they approached the choir stalls, storming right through towards the altar. All Peggy could really do was try and keep her balance as they hurried onwards, squinting to shield her eyes from the lights.

When she'd got back to Butterton after leaving Andrew at Bombay Palace, Peggy had gone straight to bed and huddled beneath a bundle of extra blankets, trying to find some warmth even as she'd been fairly certain that she was running a high temperature. Emmeline had hovered around her, only letting her be when she'd finally had to accept that her very great-niece didn't want to talk about her argument with Marnie earlier in the day.

She'd slowly faded away with a sad smile and a promise to check in on Peggy later.

Charlie, however, had been slightly more difficult to dislodge, and even after Peggy had ordered him out of the room, he'd returned to the closed bedroom door multiple times over the following hour or so to plaintively ask if she really was alright or just saying it to get rid of him.

So, when she'd slumped out of the car at Chester House that morning, Peggy had been hoping that Chambers would have simply accepted her story about the weekend with only the bare minimum of follow-up questions and then let her go home to where her duvet and a mug of Lemsip would be waiting.

Why, even after her brother had confirmed that she'd looked about as healthy as she'd felt, hadn't she taken him up on his offer to drive her to CID?

Why did she always need to be so bloody stubborn?

'Right, if it's not back near the tower, it's somewhere up this end,' Fallon snapped at her as they approached the altar, 'so you better fucking tell us where to go.'

'I don't know anything,' Peggy grit out.

Fallon whirled so quickly that Peggy stumbled when her arm was released. She was saved from tumbling to the floor when Fallon roughly grabbed the lapels of her coat in his hands and leaned in close enough that Peggy went cross-eyed.

'You're going to tell us how to get under the cathedral, or nobody will ever find even the smallest fucking trace of you once I'm through with you,' Fallon spat, barely a hint of spearmint left from the hours' old chewing gum.

He then shoved her backwards so violently that Peggy had to frantically reach out behind her to avoid crashing right into one of the carved stone pillars.

'Hey!' The angry hiss came only a second before Fallon himself had his arm grabbed aggressively. 'What do you think you're doing?'

Peggy's stomach rolled when the most forbidding gaze she'd ever encountered swept away from Fallon and landed on where she stood, propped up by the pillar. Fallon was promptly released from the vice grip and Peggy shrank back even further.

Peggy wondered how she'd even believed for a second that the man slowly advancing towards her could be anybody but the same person who'd manipulated a teenage girl for his own gain and dealt the fatal blow to Davy Nash twenty years earlier. She wondered how she could have thought that Fallon had been telling her the truth when he'd introduced her to the man he'd called 'DCI Chambers' in the Chester House carpark; she wondered why she'd believed 'Chambers' when he'd told her that there was a fast-moving situation occurring on Tib Street, and that Andrew might be in some kind of serious trouble.

Peggy would love to be able to blame it all on an elevated temperature and her thoughts moving with all the haste of treacle, but even as unwell as she felt in that moment, she'd still have to admit that she'd heard 'Tib Street', and 'Andrew', and 'trouble', and stopped thinking.

The furious twist to Jimmy Prentice's mouth curved into a predatory smile as he stopped only a couple of feet in front of her.

'Terribly sorry about that,' he said, voice dripping with artificial regret. 'DI Fallon's obviously never been educated in the correct way to treat a woman.'

'Like the way you treated Lily Woodhouse, you mean?' Peggy willed her whole body to stop trembling as she tried to scowl at Prentice.

Astonishingly, Prentice didn't lunge towards her in rage, but instead his eyes twinkled with something that looked disturbingly close to amusement as he grinned at her in surprise.

'Now, how do you know about that little tramp Woodhouse?' Prentice asked conversationally, as though he were merely enquiring about Peggy's day.

'They know what you made her do for you,' Peggy replied slowly, trying to keep her focus as she heard yet another quiet voice trying to get her attention from somewhere over her left shoulder. 'They know what you did to her, and what happened to Davy Nash.'

Even through the haze, Peggy felt a faint jolt of satisfaction when the smirk fell from Prentice's face, to be replaced by true astonishment.

'He's been in and out of here for weeks,' came a sudden whisper, right in Peggy's ear. The voice was breathy and soft, but she could tell nothing else about the owner; without being able to see anything, the voice seemed strangely ageless, and it oscillated between higher pitched tones and a rumbling bass note mid-syllable.

'Always skulking around in the dark, thinking he's invisible,' added the disembodied voice. 'I've seen him though, swearing about all the doors being locked.'

'I asked you a question!' Prentice, having recovered from his shock, barked right in Peggy's face. Beads of spittle hit her cheeks, and she recoiled, pressing her back against the pillar.

Peggy's head throbbed again, and she had to blink even more furiously to get the black spots to clear that time. 'Higson's been onto you for twenty years, and now DI Joyce knows the truth as well.'

Prentice whipped towards Fallon. 'What the fuck is she on about?'

'She's lying,' Fallon said, and it really sounded like he believed that.

'I'm not,' Peggy argued wearily. 'Sean Kelly attacked Lily in the Arches, and then you killed Davy Nash when he came to see what was going on.'

'You can't know that,' Prentice spat. 'You can't possibly know any of th– *oh*.'

Prentice's expression somehow hardened even further as he reached whatever conclusion had just formed in his mind.

'Oh, what?' Fallon asked impatiently.

'Someone's been telling her things,' Prentice replied, before turning back to Peggy. 'Woodhouse would never keep her trap shut when she was alive, so it's no surprise that she still can't shut up. How'd you find her? Hmm?'

Peggy remained silent.

'I do think he might kill you, you know. Seems like the kind of thing he'd do,' the voice chimed in again, and Peggy shuddered at the unpleasant proximity.

Prentice put his hands on Peggy's shoulders and snarled. 'I'm going to give you five minutes to tell me what I need to know, or I'll bash your head in as well.'

It didn't seem like a huge incentive to do as she was told, not when she was fairly certain that Prentice was planning to do exactly that, whether Peggy helped him or not.

He stared at her, unwavering, for a long moment before he stalked back towards Fallon.

Peggy's legs slowly gave way beneath her when Prentice turned away. She slithered to the ground and pulled her knees to her chest. Burying her face in her hands did nothing to block out the mounting chorus of murmuring around her, but at least it meant that she didn't need to look at Prentice.

'What is it that they want you to do?' the voice asked with obvious interest.

'Who are you?' Peggy whispered.

'Oh, so you *are* listening to me,' the voice replied, smirk evident. 'Bit rude to ignore me, wasn't it?'

Peggy swallowed heavily against another rush of queasiness. There were too many voices and *too many faces*, and it felt just like drowning; like she was being pulled down into something shadowy and forbidding. It wasn't like the obvious horrors of somewhere like Strangeways clawing at her very soul but, instead, something even more pervasive and ancient. It felt like the cathedral and all its sanctity had been built exactly where it stood so that it might somehow counteract and contain a wickedness in the very earth beneath its foundations.

She knew that if she submitted to Prentice's demands for her to find a route to the passageways that he was so convinced lay beneath the building she might very well not make it back above ground again.

'Who are you?' Peggy repeated, keeping her voice low enough to avoid either Prentice or Fallon overhearing.

'Now, that doesn't really matter, but how about you can call me Mac,' the voice replied, now sounding bored. 'What I want to know is what they want you to do for them.'

'Why?'

'Because people like you don't normally visit here at all; and people like *them* only come in when it's time to confess their sins and beg for forgiveness because they know that their days are numbered.'

Mac laughed lightly, then added, 'Neither of them really looks to be the confessing sort though, if you know what I mean.'

Peggy pressed her fingertips to her temples and breathed out slowly, trying to find even a pinprick of focus. Now that she was stationary again, she knew that it was going to be her best opportunity to try and reach Marnie once more. She closed her eyes and tried to centre herself.

'What are you doing now?' Mac asked in interest.

Peggy's fragile concentration shattered like glass and any remaining splinters of faith in her ability to get herself out of this mess skittered away until they were firmly out of her reach.

She was out of time, and Marnie was still nowhere to be found.

'Oi, are you alright there?' Mac asked, and perhaps there was finally a hint of concern in there somewhere.

On the very rare occasions that Peggy had allowed her thoughts to wander down particularly macabre pathways in the past, this was not how she'd thought that she'd finally bow out when it was her time to go.

Was this really how it was going to end?

No.

Peggy wasn't sure if the form denial was a voice in her own head, or whether it was uttered by some unidentifiable, external source, but it hammered against her bones with even more brute force than her throbbing headache.

'They want me to tell them how to get into the passages beneath the cathedral,' Peggy found herself muttering to Mac. She pursed her lips and blew gently onto her palms, trying to warm them.

Peggy felt a presence approach her left side, but she didn't quite dare chance a look in case the movement alerted Prentice or Fallon.

'Why do they want to know that?' Mac asked slowly.

The words slowly seeped into Peggy's consciousness, nudging at her rusty thoughts until they uneasily clicked into place. Mac hadn't asked what the hell Peggy was talking about, but instead he'd asked *why* Prentice and Fallon wanted to know about the passageways. Could that mean that Prentice was correct, and that there really was a route down to beneath the cathedral?

Peggy quickly questioned this, and Mac laughed again. There was more recognisable modulation to the voice now, as though the continued interaction with Peggy was slowly but surely improving the connection.

'There's a whole network of them, didn't you know that?' Mac asked. 'They run all under here and up beyond that blue coat school to the north, and down along the river to the south. Everyone who works here denies it any time anyone asks if there's any truth to the rumours, of course. Nasty things, you see, *rumours*.'

Closing her eyes, Peggy tried to situate herself within the geography of the city centre. The blue coat school that Mac mentioned must be what had become the School of Music twenty years or so earlier, but the buildings had stood for hundreds of years before that. She wondered when Mac had last been outside the cathedral.

'You came here with them to find the tunnels, but you weren't actually sure they were here in the first place?' Mac asked when Peggy didn't answer. 'Why would you do that?'

'I'm not here by choice,' Peggy huffed out, feeling even more lightheaded than she had earlier.

Mac hummed, though whether it was a show of sympathy or indifference, Peggy couldn't tell.

'Looks like they're about to come back over,' Mac warned. 'They don't look happy.'

Peggy swallowed her fear and her pride. 'Can you tell me how to get down to the tunnels then?'

'That's not a good idea.'

'Please.' Peggy needed to buy herself some time and she wasn't above begging for help if necessary.

'You won't like it down there,' Mac replied firmly. 'No good will come of it.'

'If you can't help me, I'm dead,' Peggy breathed as footsteps approached.

'It's not actually that bad, if it makes you feel any better,' Mac muttered, and Peggy could hear the shrug even if she couldn't see it. 'Being dead, I mean.'

'Please.'

Without warning, Peggy was roughly hauled to her feet and her eyes snapped open in alarm.

'Well?' Prentice growled.

'The choir stalls,' Mac hissed unexpectedly from behind her. 'Take them back to the choir stalls.'

'Why?' Peggy mumbled.

'Hey!' Prentice shook her violently, and Peggy had to clamp her eyes shut again as the world spun unpleasantly. 'Look at me when I'm fucking talking to you!'

'Choir stalls!' Mac shouted, as if adding volume would somehow help Peggy understand what that was supposed to mean.

'We need to go back that way,' Peggy said eventually, eyes only half open.

Prentice stared at her for a long moment, gaze flickering over her face as he hunted for any hint of deception.

Since she'd first set foot at the Ballroom, Peggy had witnessed Andrew question hundreds of people, but even when he got himself onto his particularly cynical high horse – which was, thankfully, far less often these days – Andrew had never looked at anyone the way Prentice was studying her just then; as though he *wanted* to catch her in a lie, because it would give him the perfect excuse to dole out an appropriate punishment.

'Alright,' Prentice said after a long moment, releasing Peggy's arm. 'Go on then.'

Peggy turned away and took a deep breath to try and steady herself. There was a flicker of movement to her right, but it disappeared almost as soon as she noticed it.

'I told you not to look,' Mac said, and all urgency had dropped away, leaving only that casual tone behind. 'You really won't like what you see.'

On any other day, Peggy might have felt like pushing her luck and taking a peek anyway, but just then Mac was all she had, and that repeated warning was enough for her to train her eyes forward, focussing instead on just putting one foot in front of the other.

She wished that she could just stop shivering, but the trembling was getting worse by the minute. She tucked her hands beneath her arms as she walked, more concerned about trying to stave off the sensation of pins and needles in her fingers than she was about saving herself if she tripped and landed face first on the stone floor.

'When you get to the stalls, you need to go all the way along the back row on the right-hand side,' Mac explained, once more in Peggy's ear. 'There's a door there.'

Peggy squinted towards the carved wood of the medieval quire, wondering what she was supposed to do when she reached it. There was no obvious sign of a door, and even if there was, the wooden stalls had been constructed as a freestanding structure in the middle of the cathedral, so any door would just take you straight back out into an aisle.

For very good reason, there was an awful lot of the *unusual* that Peggy found it easy to believe in, but she couldn't stretch that belief to magic doors, even when her life, quite literally, depended on it.

Peggy stepped up onto the raised platform of the stalls, reaching out to steady herself as she shuffled along the row. She passed the more elaborate seats reserved for higher ranking church officials, and then very quickly reached the dead end at the corner of the stalls. She looked out through the openings that had been carved out to fashion a screen, but she couldn't see any hint of another person in the vicinity, not even the woman from earlier.

'She's fucking leading us on!' snapped Fallon from somewhere behind her.

'Kneel down right where you are,' Mac's voice instructed sharply.

Peggy slowly did as she was told, joints creaking in protest.

'What are you doing?' Prentice hissed, and the hairs on the

back of Peggy's neck leapt upright in terror as he leant down towards her.

'Reach over to the right and in the floor, right by the wall, you'll find a gap, like there was once a knot in the wood,' Mac continued, and Peggy tried to solely focus on the instructions she was being given.

She ran her right hand along the floor until she reached the wall, and then stretched out her fingers, searching for any sign of a knot in the dark wood.

Finally, her index finger caught against something, and she sighed in relief.

'You need to pull up the board,' Mac said, right in Peggy's ear again.

Peggy tried to get as much purchase as possible on the relatively small hollow in the wood, but her arms felt like jelly, and the feeble tug she managed wasn't enough to shift anything.

'Move!' Prentice snarled, running out of patience as he watched Peggy struggle with the board again, obviously understanding what she was trying – and failing – to do.

Peggy crawled forwards out of the way, and by the time she'd managed to turn back around, Prentice had pulled a large board away from the floor; it had been cut to fit the space exactly, and none of the edges had been easily visible when flush with the ground.

'That was always a handy little hiding spot, that one,' Mac announced, and Peggy leant forward to peer down into the gloomy space beneath the quire. With the limited light of the cathedral, it was impossible to really tell what was down there, but it looked to be a space designed to hold a single person as long as they didn't try to stand; it certainly couldn't be described as a passageway.

Prentice snapped his head towards Peggy. 'Are you fucking having me on?'

'Four timbers on the left-hand wall,' Mac said. 'The one furthest from here is hinged at the top. It'll take you down to the passages.'

Peggy relayed this information haltingly, trying to ignore the increasingly murderous expression on Fallon's face, where he was crouched behind Prentice.

'Go on, then,' Prentice gestured first to Peggy and then to the dark compartment.

Peggy shook her head and immediately regretted the movement. 'I won't be able to see anything.'

'Lucky for you, we came prepared,' Prentice sneered, taking a torch out of his jacket pocket and switching it on so that he could point the weak yellow beam down into the dimness, before he turned to Fallon. 'Go and get the bags from the car.'

Peggy looked down into the concealed space with rapidly mounting dread. Her heart was hammering in her ears, and she thought that if she had the energy to do so, she might actually have cried.

'Down!' Prentice yanked Peggy towards the opening, and she knocked her elbow against the edge of the gap hard enough that tears sprang to her eyes.

Climbing into the compartment would have been easier said than done on any normal day, but with Peggy's uncooperative limbs it seemed as though an age passed before she found herself kneeling once more, though this time on a hard, dusty floor.

She awkwardly twisted towards the left-hand wall and found the panel that Mac had indicated.

'Right at the top,' Mac said, and Peggy flinched at how loud the voice suddenly was in the enclosed space.

Peggy reached up and pressed as hard as she could manage, and she was surprised when the bottom of the wide timber swung out towards her without much resistance. She let go and the panel swung back almost flush against the wall once more.

Prentice swore in astonishment and Peggy looked up at him. He'd obviously still been unsure if Peggy was playing games like Fallon had suggested.

'In you go,' Prentice instructed Peggy sharply.

Peggy swallowed hard. An awful voice in her head told her that if she didn't go through the gap in front of her, Prentice would kill her where she knelt, but she knew that by leaving the cathedral she was losing any chance to alert anyone to her plight.

Even if Andrew somehow worked out what Prentice and Fallon were up to, there was no way that he'd be able to find Peggy in a hidden labyrinth beneath the city. After everything they'd been through together, Peggy thought that they might finally have found themselves in an impossible situation.

'In!' Prentice snapped.

Peggy looked up into the cathedral for one more glimpse of the stained-glass window backlit above the altar. She could just about see the grey mizzle of the afternoon beyond, and the hopelessness that had been resting on her shoulders for the past couple of hours sank heavily into her chest.

'You'll come with me?' Peggy mumbled to Mac, hoping she wasn't actually alone.

'No.'

Peggy's heart sank. 'Why not?'

There was a long pause, and Prentice reiterated his blunt instruction for Peggy to get a move on.

'Because,' Mac muttered eventually, 'last time I was down here, things didn't go so well for me.'

For the space of a heartbeat, Peggy was enveloped in a sense of bleak terror that she knew wasn't her own, and she gasped in alarm.

'Go in peace,' Mac whispered, and Peggy thought she felt a brief, gentle pressure on the top of her head as though a hand had been placed there for a moment.

The musty air shifted the slightest amount, and Peggy knew that she was truly on her own.

She reached up and pressed her hands against the wall once again, gracelessly switching her hands over so that she could lift the panel from the bottom once it was far enough away from the wall.

A dull thud next to her pulled her attention away from her task, and she nearly lost her grip on the makeshift door as she looked over to where Prentice had dropped a torch down to her.

Awkwardly crouched beneath the panel as she held it over her head, Peggy stared into the impenetrable blackness in front of her.

She watched in fascinated horror as she breathed out and her breath hung pearly white in the air in front of her.

It felt like a warning.

For just a moment, Peggy thought that she could hear the distant sound of sirens, and her heart lurched with a reignited hope.

'Get the fuck on with it!' Prentice growled.

That brief spark of hope was immediately snuffed out by a ferocious gust of despair.

With a shaky breath, Peggy grasped for the torch beside her and forced herself to stumble into the darkness.

TWENTY-FIVE

'And you really believe that DCI Chambers isn't involved, sir?'

Jen was sitting on the other side of Andrew's desk, apprehension radiating from her in palpable waves.

Andrew could understand all hesitation to believe that Chambers had no part in the current events that were playing out around them, but Jen had asked him multiple variations of this same question in the hours since he'd burst back into the Ballroom with Lloyd, to find both his sergeant and Annie Higson already waiting for them; his answer hadn't changed in that time.

'Sorry, sir,' Jen muttered contritely, correctly interpreting Andrew's weary sigh.

Andrew waved away the apology. 'No, *I'm* sorry.'

No matter how frustrated he was, he knew that none of this was Jen's fault, and he shouldn't be taking his exasperation out on her. Plus, he'd been entirely convinced that Chambers had been behind it all until a few hours earlier, hadn't he? Right up until he'd been slapped in the face by the awful realisation that perhaps Neil Fallon was actually smarter than Andrew had ever given him credit for.

Even when he'd first identified Fallon as the mysterious police officer who'd met with Hughes that morning, Andrew still hadn't quite let himself believe it, and he'd continued to accuse Chambers in front of an encroaching crowd of his former colleagues. It was only when Mike had quietly confirmed to him that Chambers really *had* been at Chester House all night and all morning – just like most of the rest of them had been – that Andrew had let the alternative theory start to sink in.

He'd again asked Chambers if he'd instructed DC Cooke to call Peggy and summon her to Chester House, and Chambers would only confirm that he'd requested that Cooke take Peggy's statement over the phone.

'So, how did Peggy end up at Chester House?' Andrew had snapped. 'Because my sergeant's confirmed that Peggy's car is parked outside.'

'Last night, I asked Fallon to sort it out with Cooke first thing this morning,' Chambers had explained, shaking his head again. 'For Christ's sake, Joyce, what is going on?'

Andrew had stared long and hard at Chambers, searching for any hint of deceit, and eventually he'd had to conclude that his former boss was telling the truth, *and* that Fallon was likely involved in the fact that Peggy hadn't been where they'd expected her to be.

'Why did you send Fallon to have a cloak and dagger chat with Higson on Tib Street last Thursday then? Why have you been sending him to ask questions about our consultant for months?' Andrew had snapped, patience entirely evaporated.

Chambers had only scowled in confusion again. 'I did no such thing! More to the point, why didn't you mention this so-called meeting when you came into Chester House?'

'Didn't seem important at the time,' Andrew had lied.

'I did *not* send Fallon to Tib Street!'

'That's not what I heard,' Andrew had replied evenly.

Chambers' eyes had sharpened instantly. 'What's that supposed to mean? Have you been in contact with Higson?'

'What do you really think happened to Sean Kelly?' Andrew had asked, ignoring Chambers' question entirely.

'Joyce!' Chambers had snapped. 'Have you had contact with DCI Higson that you have been withholding from my investigation?'

'Do you have information about the circumstances of Sean Kelly's murder that you're withholding from *my* investigation?' Andrew had asked with surprising calmness. Apparently, career suicide made him come over all zen.

Lloyd had looked ready to pounce should any of the CID

boys take a swipe at Andrew.

They hadn't taken a swipe, but they'd glanced between their boss and Andrew in obvious unease.

'A word,' Chambers had barked, icy cold, before he'd physically pulled Andrew up the corridor.

'What the hell do you think you're playing at?' Chambers had asked him again when they'd come to a halt.

'Tell me what really happened to Sean Kelly!' Andrew had demanded. 'If you don't, I'm going to make sure that you go down for every single thing you ever did for Jimmy Prentice.'

Chambers' expression had twisted into something queasy, and he'd studied Andrew carefully for a long moment. 'Why are you *still* talking about Jimmy Prentice?'

'Because I think someone opened their big mouth about the Ballroom at Frank Jackson's funeral. In fact, I *know* they did,' Andrew had explained shortly. 'Prentice got wind of it all and was asking Higson questions about us; about our cases, and about our consultant.'

Chambers had looked as though he'd swallowed something particularly sour. 'The mythical M. Jones.'

Andrew had folded his arms. 'Do you know why Prentice was so interested in Lily Woodhouse twenty years ago?'

'There you go again! Mentioning things that have absolutely no bearing on anything currently going on with your unhinged superior officer, and how h-'

'No bearing?' Andrew had snapped. 'Lily Woodhouse has everything to do with this. Prentice's power lay in knowledge, right? He realised that having Lily would make possessing that knowledge even easier.'

'For God's sake, Joyce, she was a self-absorbed teenage girl who loved attention; she wasn't actually psychic!'

Chambers had looked furious once more.

'Oh, I know she wasn't. I'm still almost certain that there's no such thing, but Lily *did* help Prentice find out anything that he needed to know, and it was when she told him that she couldn't help him that Sean Kelly strangled her and left her for dead.'

'Stop repeating this bleeding nonsense!' Chambers had retorted angrily. 'Lily Woodhouse ran off with a policeman who should have known better than to have his head turned by a girl like that.'

'Jesus, you actually believe that, don't you?' Andrew had asked, dazed. It sounded like Benson had been telling the truth when he'd said that Chambers hadn't been involved in hiding Davy's body. Perhaps once Prentice had realised that he'd killed a policeman, he'd kept it on a very need-to-know basis, with Chambers obviously not making the cut. Perhaps it really was just like Annie Higson had told him days earlier: Prentice and the others hadn't seen Chambers as part of their mob, and he'd been no more than a lowly errand boy.

'We have a witness who saw Prentice kill Davy Nash,' Andrew had said quietly, watching Chambers' reaction carefully. 'We have another who can tell us exactly where his body is buried.'

Chambers had started shaking his head, and then he'd just kept on shaking it. For a minute, Andrew had thought that the older man had been stunned into permanent silence.

Eventually, Chambers had glanced at the ground in a show of uncharacteristic hesitation before he'd sniffed loudly and looked back up at Andrew. 'The tape of Sean Kelly's call to the emergency services.'

'What about it?' Andrew had asked when Chambers hadn't immediately added to the explanation.

Chambers had sniffed again. 'There is something *unnatural* about it.'

'What do you mean?' Andrew had really wanted to hurry Chambers along. Up until then, he'd been trying to compartmentalise the various threads to the investigation in an attempt to make sure that he covered everything, but it had been getting more challenging to ignore the fact that he still hadn't known if Jen had located Peggy or not.

'There were some strange pauses,' Chambers had replied tiredly. 'It sounded almost like it had been scripted.'

'You think Kelly was being told what to say?' Andrew had asked, doubtfully. 'Even though he knew he was about to die?'

Chambers pursed his lips. 'I don't believe that Kelly knew he was in real danger. He doesn't sound scared at all on the tape; not until the final few moments.'

'So, you've known that it wasn't Higson since the beginning?' Andrew had snapped accusingly.

'No. I didn't suspect anything differently until I heard the tape.'

'Bullshit! You've known Higson for decades; you know he wouldn't do something like that.'

'Like I told you yesterday, Joyce, you don't know Bill Higson all that well.'

Andrew had shrugged. 'I know him well enough to be certain that he didn't kill Sean Kelly, and I know him well enough to bet that he would have seen exactly what kind of man Jimmy Prentice was and made sure to get as far away from him as he could. I also know him well enough to believe everything he told me about what happened the night Lily and Davy supposedly disappeared.'

Chambers had looked ready to call the CID boys over for assistance, and so Andrew had taken his moment to go for the jugular.

'You see,' he'd said slowly, 'we're quite proud of the work we do at the Ballroom these days. We're going to be pissed if anything happens to our DCI; and if I even *think* that that bastard Fallon has touched so much as a hair on Peggy's head, I will make sure that he never sees the light of day again. And then,

I will come for you, because, for better or for worse, Chris Benson is on *our* side, and he knows everything about you, *sir*.'

At the mention of Benson, Chambers' face had darkened to such a deep red that Andrew had thought that he'd been about to witness the DCI burst a number of blood vessels. 'What is it that you *want*, Joyce?'

'Call off the hunt for Higson; publicly admit that you got it wrong,' Andrew answered without hesitation. 'I want you to find Fallon and put him in an interview room at Chester House and keep him there until I know what the hell he's been up to.'

'I can't just announce that Higson is no longer a person of interest!' Chambers had snarled. 'We have a recording of Sean Kelly identifying him!'

'Which you've admitted is likely scripted,' Andrew had replied, still with unnerving calm. 'Designed to get Higson, and us, out of the way. So, you might also want to send your lot back in to check over the crime scene properly. It's amazing what CID can find when they actually bother to do their job properly.'

At that, Andrew had turned on his heel and walked away, grabbing Lloyd on the way back towards the entrance. He'd known that if he'd stopped moving he might have had to really consider everything he'd just said to his boss.

'Shit, sir,' Lloyd had breathed when they'd climbed back into the car.

'Yeah,' Andrew had agreed, and they'd sped off for a fruitless hour and a half of attempting to get anywhere near Rex Hughes in the Royal Infirmary.

They'd finally admitted defeat when they'd seen neither hide nor hair of Marnie at the hospital either, and they'd returned to the Ballroom with the intention of waiting for Jen, Annie and Peggy.

So, when Andrew had thrown open the double doors to already find Jen and a bleak expression waiting for him, he'd immediately felt like chucking something across the room.

Hours had then passed without word from Chambers, or from anyone else at CID, or even a hint of Marnie, and at some point, in the middle of it all, Andrew had realised that he probably should have called Charlie before they'd reached that point, even if it was the last conversation he'd wanted to have.

Jen had taken the phone away from Andrew while he'd been in the middle of hesitantly dialling Butterton's number and then sent him off to the kitchen to make tea with Annie, promising that she'd make the call instead.

Andrew would have been furious about being babied if he hadn't appreciated it so much.

And so, once Charlie had arrived, they'd sat, all five of them dotted around the room, with only the odd question breaking the strained silence while they'd just waited, and waited, *and waited.*

The stillness was driving Andrew mad, but he knew enough these days to be certain that racing off, utterly harebrained, was likely to result in nothing but trouble, even if was exactly what he wanted to do. Until they had a better idea about whether Fallon was involved – and just what the hell he was involved *in* – they really had nothing to go on.

'Sir,' Jen said again, urgently, pulling him right back to the present, 'do you think we need t–'

Whatever Jen was about to ask was silenced by the sound of the door scraping open downstairs.

Andrew was on his feet and racing across the Ballroom in a flash, with the others right behind him. They were obviously all thinking the same thing: *surely it must be Peggy.*

He ground to a sudden halt at the top of the darkening landing, with the others almost piled up behind him in their haste. Only a miracle kept them all from tumbling down the staircase.

'Alright?' Mike Lawson asked in surprise, pausing lower down on the stairs and looking up at his unexpected audience. 'Your, erm – cleaning lady? – let me in, and then disappeared that way.'

Andrew nodded. 'Come up. Have you heard anything?'

'Yeah, I have,' Mike replied as he walked through the double doors behind the group. He stopped and gawped up at the painted ceiling and the six crystal chandeliers that dominated the space. 'Jesus, what the hell sort of place do you call this?'

Andrew understood Mike's bewilderment, but he didn't have the time nor the patience for it just then. 'Mike, what have you heard?'

Mike shook his head and turned his attention to Andrew. 'Sorry, mate, yeah. Chambers is going to make a statement in a bit; he's announcing that Higson's no longer a person of interest in the investigation.'

Andrew heard Annie sigh in relief from where she sat at her husband's desk.

'That's not an apology,' Andrew replied, gesturing for Mike to take a seat as he returned to his own chair.

'No, it's not,' Mike agreed as he perched next to Charlie on the blue sofa, holding a thin bundle of paper and files on his knees. 'Oh, hiya, you okay?'

Charlie shook his head once and returned to his woeful silence. Andrew understood that too – *he really did* – but he didn't have the time or the patience for that either.

Mike grimaced in apology and turned his attention back to Andrew. 'Chief Constable's threatening Chambers with all sorts of things. They're currently in a meeting about whether it's going to make it all look even more of a fuck up if they announce their new suspect in Higson's place, or if they don't have any suspects at all.'

'Their new suspect,' Andrew repeated slowly.

Mike swallowed heavily. 'Yeah, it looks like you might be right about Fallon's involvement. There might have been a sighting of someone matching his description outside Kelly's house on Saturday morning.'

Andrew had been expecting to hear something to that effect at some point, but he still wasn't prepared for the way that the world seemed to tilt violently at the confirmation anyway. His fingers curled tightly around the heavy, dented stapler that sat on his desk. He kept his eyes fixed on his hand, unwilling to see anyone else's expressions just then. 'What happened?'

'Fallon hasn't shown his face at CID since first thing this morning when he spoke to Cooke,' Mike explained. 'After we got back from Strangeways, and it became clear that Fallon had fucked off somewhere, a unit was sent out to his flat to pick him up, just in case he was there.'

'But he wasn't?' Andrew looked up and saw that Mike looked as grave as he felt.

'No. Considering the circumstances, Chambers told them to go inside,' Mike added. 'It had been cleared out, but there was a packed bag in the kitchen, along with his passport and a one-way plane ticket to boot.'

'Ticket to where?' Lloyd asked.

'Malaga,' Mike confirmed. 'Looks like he's planning to run. His flight's on Christmas Eve.'

Andrew tightened his grip on the stapler. If Fallon needed an exit strategy as permanent as fleeing the country, then he wasn't likely to care about the consequences of his actions, meaning that Peggy could be in far more danger than Andrew had anticipated.

'Do you have any idea where he is now?' Jen asked, the practical one as always.

Mike shook his head. 'No. All units are on the lookout for him, with the understanding that he might not be alone.'

Andrew interpreted that as Mike's way of not wanting to use the term 'hostage situation' anywhere near Charlie.

'There's something else,' Mike added, twisting his lips. 'Now, this isn't confirmed, alright?'

'Alright.'

'Someone *thinks* they saw Fallon driving away from Chester House this morning, but there's some debate over it because it wasn't Fallon's car.'

'What do you mean?' Andrew asked even though a little bird of prescient knowledge had just landed on his shoulder with a noisy suggestion.

'Apparently he drove off in an old, white Jag.'

Realisation dawned, and that was the nail in the coffin for the stapler; it sailed through the air towards the doors and Andrew already had his fists pressed to his eyes by the time it hit the ground with a resounding thump. 'Fuck!'

'A white Jag?' Annie asked from across the room, and she sounded unnerved.

Andrew looked over to her. 'You told us Prentice drove a Jag back in the sixties. Was it a white one?'

Annie nodded as she rose slowly from the sofa. 'He loved that car.'

'Prentice?' Mike asked in surprise. 'The guy you were asking me about the other day? He's supposed to be in Spain!'

Charlie jumped to his feet, pacing in front of the sofa as a string of creative threats erupted from his mouth.

Andrew tried to block everyone else out so that he could concentrate on lining up the events in his head:

Prentice and Fallon working together; Sean Kelly's murder; Higson being framed; Prentice knowing about Miss Jones; Rex Hughes being attacked in Strangeways; Peggy's disappearance.

If Prentice and Fallon were in this together then Andrew had to assume that Rex had told Fallon the truth about Peggy that morning because there was surely no other way he could have found out. But how had Fallon known to ask Hughes in the first place?

'Annie, why don't you and Charlie go and get a coffee?' Jen suggested as Charlie turned and started making his way towards Andrew's desk.

Charlie opened his mouth to argue, but Annie clamped a hand on his arm and steered him out of the room with such speed and tactful sensitivity that Andrew wondered if he really should start believing in magic.

'Is that really Mrs Higson?' Mike asked in poorly concealed amazement.

Andrew's eyes landing on the stack of papers Mike had arrived with. 'Mike, what are those?'

'Oh, shit, sorry, yeah,' Mike said, leaping to his feet and handing everything to Andrew. 'That's everything that was on Fallon's desk. Chambers doesn't know I took it all, but somehow, I thought it would be more useful to you lot.'

Andrew flipped through the stack quickly, eyes widening in surprise as he read the labels. 'These are Ballroom cases.'

'What?' Jen asked as she hurried over to Andrew's desk to see. She frowned as she looked over his shoulder. 'Not just that, sir; they're all Ballroom cases where we've found something valuable. Look, there's that necklace that was stolen from the museum in the thirties, and then the Carmichael case too. Oh, and Arthur Havers' stash of diamonds by the canal!'

Jen was almost entirely correct in her analysis.

'All except this one.' Andrew tapped his finger against the final file, which wasn't technically a Ballroom case, even if they'd been the ones to actually send the perpetrator of the various crimes to jail.

'Rex Hughes?' Jen glanced at Andrew in surprise. 'Do you think Fallon was looking for something before he visited Rex in Strangeways?'

Andrew didn't answer. He opened the file, recognising the

bulk of it as paperwork that had been completed in the very room they were in, and skimmed each page, searching for anything that stood out.

He continued to flick through the pages until he stopped dead in surprise.

'Jesus Christ,' Andrew exhaled as understanding clicked into place. That understanding was followed swiftly by a surge of dread, because he was holding a piece of paper that he'd never seen before; a piece of paper he'd completely neglected to ever be concerned about.

'What is it?' Lloyd asked.

Andrew held up the single page that proved that they hadn't actually been anywhere near as careful as they'd thought. 'Athena Hughes' statement about the car accident from the day before she was arrested for Marnie's murder; the car accident where one Lady Margaret Swan is listed as her passenger.'

Jen pulled the paper from Andrew's grasp as he dropped his head into his hands, fighting the urge to scream.

'Fallon is the one who took Athena's statement,' Jen said slowly. 'He must have recognised Peggy's name when Chambers told him to organise getting her statement.'

The sound of rustling paper was followed quickly by Jen cursing loudly.

'What?' Andrew asked, head snapping back up.

'The next page is the summary of Athena Hughes' full psychiatrist report from before she was transferred,' Jen replied as she passed the paper to Andrew.

Andrew scanned the report quickly. There were numerous perfunctory statements about Athena's belief that she was being haunted by the woman she'd killed, but then, right near the bottom was a neatly typed observation that likely formed the final piece of evidence that had led Fallon to Rex that morning:

Ms Hughes demonstrates a preoccupation with the idea that her brother, Reginald Hughes, also encountered the spirit of Marnie Driscoll; the ferocity of this fixation is surpassed only by Ms Hughes' sustained insistence that a former acquaintance – Peggy Swan – communicated with Ms Driscoll's spirit on multiple occasions.

Fallon – *bloody Fallon* – of all people had worked it out. A man who had never shown a particular aptitude for anything beyond being an obnoxious arse had heard Peggy's name and tied it neatly together with Athena Hughes' ravings about ghosts and a tabloid rag's suppressed story about a ghost-hunting team of detectives.

Higson had mentioned that Fallon had been at Frank Jackson's funeral, but both he and Andrew had been so focussed on believing that *Chambers* was the one still doing Prentice's grunt work, that they hadn't even considered that it could be Fallon acting directly on behalf of Prentice instead.

Andrew wasn't sure if the quiet sound he then heard preceded Marnie's arrival or accompanied it, but the shriek that Mike emitted definitely *followed* the sight of a dead woman materialising in the middle of the Ballroom.

'He told them!' Marnie shrieked at Andrew, unaware that she'd nearly frightened a man to death. 'That utter prick told the police about Peggy!'

Seeing that Jen was dealing with Mike, who by then was hyperventilating on the floor near the sofa, Andrew gave Marnie his full attention.

'Marnie, I need you to calm down,' Andrew said, even as his own tone was far from soothing.

'He told them!' Marnie repeated, no quieter than before. 'Rex told them!'

'We know,' Andrew tried. 'We don't know wh–'

'I asked him when he finally opened his bloody eyes just now, and he said that he knew he'd been attacked because he'd spoken to the police this morning!'

Well, Andrew thought, lips twisting in distaste, Rex Hughes was apparently going to live to see another day after all.

'Marnie, can y-'

'I wanted to warn Peggy, but I can't find her!' Marnie shouted, her tirade unabated. 'Do you know where she is?'

Andrew was fairly certain that he wasn't imagining the slight tremor beneath his feet. 'Marnie!'

The bellow of her name finally seemed to do the trick, and Marnie's mouth snapped closed.

'What the hell is going on?'

Marnie whirled in surprise at the quiet, unfamiliar voice and blinked owlishly down at where Mike was gawping at her.

'Er…' Marnie replied, looking at Andrew in wild panic.

'Don't go anywhere!' he warned her and then turned to his shocked friend. 'Mike, I know that this will be *difficult* to understand at the minute, but I just need you to accept that this is Marnie and leave it at that for now, alright?'

Mike pointed at Marnie and his whole arm was shaking. 'She wasn't there! She came from nowhere!'

Marnie folded her arms. 'Oi, don't point, it's rude.'

Jesus Christ.

'We don't have time for this!' Andrew barked. 'Marnie, what do you mean that you don't know where Peggy is? She's too far away?'

Andrew's mind was already whirring, trying to work out where on earth Fallon and Prentice would be taking Peggy; everything they knew about either of them was centred on Manchester.

'No. I mean, I can't find her at all,' Marnie replied, wide-eyed. 'There's *nothing*.'

Andrew didn't like that answer.

Andrew didn't like that answer at all.

'Maybe she's just really, really out of range,' Lloyd offered, but he sounded unconvinced.

'Right,' Andrew agreed, nodding furiously in the hope that it would make the idea more plausible. 'Right, that'll be it. So, we just to think about where Prentice or Fallon mi-'

'Prentice?' Marnie shrieked in horror. 'How is he involved?'

'I'll tell you in a minute, Marnie,' Jen cut in soothingly. 'For now, I think we just need to focus on finding Peggy a-'

For the second time that hour, Jen was interrupted by the sound of the door grating loudly against the floor downstairs.

'Nobody move!' Andrew barked as everyone except Mike made towards the double doors. He held his hands up placatingly. 'Just wait.'

The doors opened seconds later, and Higson walked in, with a pinched expression on his face, and a cigarette halfway to his lips.

'What in the name of Bert Trautmann is going on in here?' Higson growled and then pointed at Mike. 'And why the Christ is Lawson on the floor?'

Andrew was ready to launch into an explanation, but his own mouth snapped shut when both Lily Woodhouse and Beth Nash walked in.

'Take a seat,' Higson directed the newcomers. 'Wherever you like, though we don't usually loll about on the ground like this tit.'

Mike scrambled to his feet, shooting panicked glances between Marnie and Higson.

Higson looked at Andrew and raised one eyebrow. 'Well?'

'DS Lawson wasn't expecting Marnie's arrival,' Andrew explained diplomatically, not sure he could, *or should*, be any more specific in front of Lily and Beth.

Higson snorted and then looked at Mike. 'You'll be alright in a minute. Get him a whiskey, Parker.'

Lloyd bobbed his head and went straight to the bottom drawer of Higson's desk.

'Bill!'

Higson wheeled around in surprise at Annie's gasp of disbelief when she appeared in the doorway.

To Andrew's astonishment, Higson then immediately rounded on *him*. 'Joyce, why the hell is my wife on Tib Street and not tucked away somewhere safer?'

'You silly git!' Annie berated her husband, although she still wrapped her arms tightly around him. 'Why didn't you tell anyone what was going on?'

'I did!' Higson replied and he glared at Andrew over Annie's shoulder. 'I told that idiot!'

'You told me *bits* of it!' Andrew argued. '*Yesterday!*'

'Beth!' Annie cried in surprise as her eyes finally landed on the woman she hadn't seen in twenty years. She was also doing a fantastic job of not just gawping at Lily. '*How?*'

'For fuck's sake, why is Charlie boy here?' Higson asked as Charlie slouched back into the room clutching a mug.

'Because we don't know where Peggy is right now,' Andrew said, before anyone else could offer up their own more colourful version of that fact. 'And, er, we think that Fallon from CID is working with Prentice.'

'What?' Higson's eyes narrowed dangerously.

Andrew kept his eyes on the ground and raced through the facts as quickly as he could, tripping over his own words in his haste.

When Andrew finished speaking, Higson remained completely silent.

As the silence stretched on, Andrew's eyes seem to raise of their own accord, unable to just await whatever fate was about to befall him.

Higson was entirely expressionless, and his cigarette hung

loosely from his fingers as though he'd completely forgotten that he was holding it. He cleared his throat loudly. 'Joyce, are you trying to tell me that Miss Swan is currently somewhere in the vicinity of Jimmy Prentice?'

'Sir,' Andrew confirmed, swallowing heavily. *Yeah*, he was fucked, and he knew it.

'Joyce,' Higson snarled, 'did you listen to a single bloody thing I said to you yesterday?'

'Bill!' Annie snapped. 'This is *not* Andrew's fault!'

Andrew appreciated the show of support, but he knew that Annie being on his side was only going to piss Higson off even more.

'It's certainly not any more his fault than it is yours!'

Christ, why was *Charlie* getting involved? Though, again, Andrew appreciated the backing, even if it was decidedly less enthusiastic than Annie's.

Higson whipped his head towards Charlie. 'What did you just say to me?'

'I said that this is no more Joycie's fault than it is yours,' Charlie repeated, and he had that awfully belligerent expression that usually meant trouble was on the way for Andrew whenever it was turned on him by either Swan sibling.

Higson looked caught between surprise and fury. He turned and glared at Marnie, seeking a new target. 'Well? Why haven't you found Her Maj yet?'

'I *can't*,' Marnie replied, and her fear was obvious even beneath the sulky attitude.

It was the perfect reminder that they did *not* have time for any of this.

Andrew strode back to his desk and grabbed his coat. 'Lloyd, I need your car.'

'Sure thing, boss.' Lloyd handed over the keys immediately. 'Although, *why?*'

Andrew remembered when he'd fairly recently concluded that racing off, utterly harebrained, was likely to result in nothing but trouble, but he'd take that trouble if it meant that he felt like he was actually doing something useful. 'I need to go and look for Peggy.'

'And how the hell are you going to find her when Driscoll doesn't even know where she is?' Higson snapped, reaching to try and pluck the keys from Andrew's grasp.

'I don't know yet,' Andrew replied, swerving out of the way and heading for the door. 'Jen, chuck me a radio.'

'Cusack, do *not* chuck him a radio!' Higson snapped.

Jen held the radio to her chest, looking between Higson and Andrew, knowing full well that whichever option she picked was going to be seen as a terrible betrayal by the other.

'Er, boss?' Lloyd tried carefully.

'What?' Andrew and Higson responded in unison.

'Er…' Lloyd looked from one to the other. 'Should we not put out an alert for Prentice's car? It doesn't sound like it would be hard to spot, after all.'

'Good idea,' Andrew replied when Higson just continued glaring. He looked over at Lily. 'I'm sorry to ask you this, Ms Woodhouse, but can you tell us anything about the car that will help with a description? Number plate, maybe?'

Lily shook her head. 'All I remember is that it was a white Jag, and he never stopped going on about it. He'd had it for a few years by the time I met him, but I know he'd got it brand new. It wasn't one of the really sporty ones. He used to get the other two to sit in the back.'

'It's probably a Mark 2 then,' Charlie offered with a firm nod. 'Lloyd, if you must, tell them that they're looking for the car that Inspector Morse drives round in, but it's white.'

Lloyd, who apparently had no issue taking instructions from Charlie, nodded and scribbled down the details on a notepad before picking up the phone to call it in.

'The number plate ends in two-three-eight and then a B,' Marnie piped up suddenly.

'What?' Lloyd blinked at her in confusion. 'How do you know that?'

Marnie carefully averted her eyes from Higson. 'Benson just told me. He can't remember the beginning of it.'

'Now why would Benson know that?' Higson snapped.

Marnie looked at him and wrinkled her nose. 'Because he says that he spent enough time driving round after that car, he can still remember the end of the plate.'

Andrew took a furtive step towards the door, watching as the implication of Benson's explanation sank in for his boss.

'What?' Higson barked, turning his glare on Andrew.

'We'll explain.' Andrew gave a single sharp nod and then very quickly looked over at Beth and back again. 'Though perhaps not right now, *sir*.'

The wind in Higson's sails disappeared instantly, but even as he sagged towards Annie, his disbelieving expression remained firmly trained on his DI.

'What the hell is going on?' Mike asked quietly, still white as a sheet.

'Oh my God! Peggy!' Marnie yelped suddenly.

Andrew wasn't proud of the way he whipped around, expecting Peggy to have walked through the door.

She hadn't, of course, but Andrew's hope had been reignited anyway; if Marnie had managed to find Peggy – even briefly – it meant that they still had time.

'She was there, but just for a second,' Marnie hissed, eyes screwed shut in concentration. 'There was so much noise.'

'So, she's somewhere busy?' Andrew asked slowly, looking out at the night sky and wondering where would be particularly active at gone nine o' clock on the Monday before Christmas. 'Like, what? A bar? An event?'

'Not that kind of noise,' Marnie clarified, wincing. 'The sort of noise that Peggy hates.'

'A church?' Andrew asked, heading for the door once more. 'Is that what you mean?'

Marnie shook her head. 'No, it was worse than that.'

'What's worse than a church for Peggy?' Jen asked, frowning.

Strangeways, thought Andrew, but that wasn't going to be the answer. Perhaps he didn't need to go quite that far north. 'The cathedral? Peggy hates driving past it.'

Lily made a terrible sound of pure agony. 'No.'

'We need to get to the cathedral now!' Andrew pulled open the doors and strode out onto the landing

'She's not in the cathedral!' Marnie called after him.

Andrew backtracked and stopped in the doorway. 'What do you mean?'

Marnie grimaced. 'It was noisy, but it was way too dark to be in the cathedral. I couldn't see a thing.'

'So what? Do you think she's in the Arches?' Andrew asked. 'But the sweet shop's long gone. That whole row of buildings was flattened years ago.'

'No,' Lily repeated as she slowly rose to her feet. 'Jimmy went on about how he thought there was a way down to the tunnels through the cathedral, but he didn't know where it was. The sweet shop wasn't just selling Jelly Babies, right, and the owner stored things down in the Arches; things he didn't want anyone to see. Jimmy found out – of course he did – and that's how he ended up with the key. If he hadn't had that key, I think he'd have taken me to the cathedral instead.'

'That stupid bastard really is still looking for buried bloody treasure!' Higson growled, finding his usual gruffness once again as he shrugged off his momentary lapse in self-confidence and stretched back out into the considerable, hulking shape he inhabited when he was particularly pissed off.

Andrew thought back to what Peggy had said to him the night before, when she'd demanded to know if he really thought that if Prentice came along and just *asked* her to help him, that she would. Of course Andrew didn't believe that she would ever do such a thing willingly, which meant that whatever they'd threatened her with had been terrible enough to get her to comply.

'Joyce!' Higson barked.

Andrew flinched. 'What?'

'Stop staring into space like a bloody idiot and get your arse down the stairs!'

'What?' Andrew asked again, as he blinked furiously against the mental whiplash of the situation.

Higson shook his head despairingly. 'We're going to get Her Majesty, and then I'm going to take Jimmy fucking Prentice's head and shove it where the sun doesn't shine. You alright with that?'

Andrew shook himself. 'Yes, sir.'

'Annie, love, I need you to look after Beth and Lily for me,' Higson instructed as he nudged his wife towards the women on the other side of the room. 'Dolly's about, so give her a shout if you need her. I'll be back as soon as I can.'

Higson then pointed between the rest of them. 'You lot, follow me.'

Everyone scrambled to comply as Higson headed for the doors, all of them grabbing coats and car keys on their way.

Jen also made sure to grab a stunned Mike and pilot him out of the room.

'Andrew!'

Annie's shout startled him, and Andrew turned back to look at her as Lloyd squeezed past him and out onto the landing with a bunch of torches in his hands.

'Be careful, love,' Annie said solemnly. 'All of you.'

413

'Joyce!' Higson roared from downstairs.

Andrew gave Annie what he hoped was a reassuring smile, before he bolted from the Ballroom and raced after the others.

TWENTY-SIX

Peggy reached out an arm to steady herself against another wave of dizziness.

The wall felt warmer than she'd expected, but she couldn't tell if that was simply down to the fact that her own fingers were already unreasonably cold. She'd been shivering well before she'd climbed beneath the choir stalls, but by what must have been hours later, her teeth were chattering violently.

'Did anyone tell you that you could stop?' Fallon barked behind her, and Peggy could feel his awful, sour breath on the back of her neck.

Fallon pushed her roughly forwards, just like he had any other time Peggy had needed to pause for a moment to try and collect her thoughts, and she stumbled, palms scraping against the rough walls as she battled to stay standing.

Peggy clamped her lips together as tightly as she could, not wanting to give Fallon the satisfaction of hearing her whimper in pain from either her smarting hands or from the worst headache she'd ever had in her life.

Curling her fingers around the small torch, Peggy continued to take short, careful steps, hoping that if she just kept moving, she could somehow continue to get Prentice and Fallon to believe that she now knew where she was going until she happened across a miracle.

Peggy hadn't had a moment of silence since Fallon had parked the car outside of the cathedral while they'd waited for the building to empty of day-trippers and locals who'd come to see the Nativity. The constant requests for attention above ground level had been exhausting and overwhelming, but the perpetual susurrations in the passages beneath were a hundred times worse; the words were mostly indistinct, but occasionally there would be a torrent of words in languages that Peggy didn't recognise.

The whispering, though, was preferable to the almost constant shrieking and screaming that seemed to come from both above and below her.

When he'd been much, much younger, Charlie had gone through a period of being very into mythology, and he'd always picked out the bloodiest sections of whatever book he'd been reading and then recited them loudly to Peggy – usually when their mother was nearby, so as to try and cause a nervous breakdown – and with every step she took in the murkiness of the passageways, Peggy's imagination ran wild, remembering all the gruesome tales of those who had made the mistake of straying from the main path.

Peggy couldn't work out if thoughts of murderous, mythical creatures were more or less terrifying than the knowledge that even without wings, or fangs, or monsters, abandoned places beneath ground were perfectly capable of killing you in more mundane, but equally unpleasant, ways; like with toxic gases, or suffocation, or a sudden cave-in.

'We're going round in fucking circles!' Fallon snapped, closer to her again.

Peggy found herself turned around before the back of her head collided sharply with the wall behind. Fallon clamped a clammy hand over her mouth and pressed his thumb and forefinger firmly against her cheekbones hard enough that a jagged fingernail caught the delicate skin beneath her left eye.

'She doesn't know where she's going!' Fallon screeched in Peggy's face. 'She's just stringing us along!'

Fallon removed his hand from her jaw, but Peggy didn't have time to even sigh in relief as the same hand then lashed out, landing a vicious slap across her left cheek.

The metallic tang of blood hit Peggy's tongue, and for a horrifying second she thought that Fallon had managed to knock a tooth loose, but then a sharp sting radiated out from the front of her mouth, and she realised that he'd actually split her lip.

Fallon was yanked backwards, disappearing into the gloom in a whirl of scuffling and swearing. It was only when Peggy found the wherewithal to raise her own torch slightly that she saw that Fallon was kneeling, clutching his jaw where Prentice had obviously delivered a painful blow.

'What the fuck do you think you're doing?' Prentice snarled at Fallon. 'You're only here because you convinced me that you could be useful, but if you kill her, how are we going to find what we're looking for?'

Peggy sighed inaudibly in relief; Prentice obviously still believed that Peggy was leading them the correct way, even though she hadn't had a single word of sense from any spirit since Mac had left her in the cathedral, and she still couldn't reach Marnie, no matter how many times she'd tried. She had about as much clue as Prentice did about what was down here, but if he believed in her for a bit longer, then maybe Peggy would be able to engineer a way out.

She'd long had to accept that nobody was coming for her; how could they when they probably didn't even know that she was missing?

Charlie was likely already on his way to Rotters, or the Troubadour, or wherever the hell he was going with Lloyd that evening, and he probably hadn't even noticed that she hadn't come back from her visit to Chester House.

Marnie wasn't currently speaking to her, as far as she was aware, and was unlikely to try and seek her out after their argument the day before.

Emmeline would probably notice, but she'd have nobody to tell if Marnie was absent from Butterton. She could shout at Charlie until the cows came home, but he'd remained blissfully ignorant to his aunt for over thirty years, and that was unlikely to change any time soon.

Which left only Andrew, and he wouldn't have the slightest clue that anything was the matter. Why would he? Given how they'd left things the night before, Peggy doubted that Andrew had even remotely believed her when she'd said that she was going to call him.

Prentice dragged Fallon back to standing, putting an end to Peggy's spiralling thoughts, which was probably for the best.

'That prick Kelly throttled the last little trollop who was supposed to get me to what I wanted, and you saw what happened to him,' Prentice said, and even though he spoke quietly, there would be no question about how dangerous he really was. 'I should've killed him twenty years ago, but I was more forgiving back then. I can drop you just as easily as I did him last week though, so don't for a second think that *you're* in charge here. Got it?'

Fallon nodded, eyes to the ground.

'You killed Sean Kelly?' Peggy asked, voice almost as cracked and dry as Lily's had been in Bowness.

Prentice just laughed and then shrugged. 'Move, or I'll let Fallon have at you.'

Peggy swallowed heavily and turned away. She pressed a hand to the back of her head and winced as her fingers grazed the tender spot where her skull had met the wall.

As she walked, Peggy kept her left hand free, letting her fingers trail along the wall beside her as a better guide than squinting into the murkiness in front of her. The light from her torch had never been particularly strong, but it was weakening further with each minute that passed.

Suddenly, her fingers met only air and Peggy paused. The passageway continued ahead of her, but to the left there was a different path; the air felt colder that way, and Peggy felt certain that she hadn't come across this route before. Just like Fallon, she'd been convinced that they were wandering in circles, and it had been impossible to even attempt to keep track of the way the tunnels twisted and turned around them.

'We need to go left here,' Peggy said, and she took the turn before Fallon could accuse her of any dishonesty.

To her surprise, Prentice and Fallon said nothing, and followed her into the cool dimness. Their footsteps seemed to be louder here, and the jangling of the tools in the large holdalls they were carrying echoed more than earlier.

This tunnel seemed to be turning in a gentle spiral, and after a few minutes, Peggy was certain that they were being led downwards so subtly that it was almost impossible to notice.

The whispering had dropped away to a manageable level, and she'd heard only distant screams since they'd moved onto this new path. Peggy also realised that she'd been wrong when she'd thought she'd been cold in the cathedral. Now, her bones seemed to ache with a deep, unnatural chill and the fear of reprisals that had pushed her to keep walking almost didn't seem like enough of an incentive for her body to keep moving.

As the path unspooled before her, the walls on either side gradually crept closer and closer to each other and the height of the ceiling dropped enough that she had to crouch to avoid cracking her skull open on the exposed stones above her.

Peggy awkwardly pressed through a narrow gap and then stumbled forward in surprise when she found herself in a larger space.

Behind her, Prentice and Fallon were grumbling and swearing as they tried to wriggle through the gap, dragging their holdalls with them.

Peggy turned and her heart leapt with sudden hope; if they couldn't get through the gap – or at least if it significantly slowed them down – Peggy could make a break for it.

She whipped around, trying to ignore the way her legs trembled as she frantically pointed her torch everywhere, desperately searching the dank space for any sign of another exit. There had to be another way out. There *had* to be.

With every unsuccessful pass of the weak beam over the solid walls, Peggy's despair rose higher and higher until she almost sobbed out loud in pure anguish at her conclusion.

She was completely trapped.

Prentice swore loudly and then practically fell into the chamber behind her.

Peggy's chin dropped to her chest in defeat.

It was over.

Prentice swept his own torch around the space and swore again, only this time with a surprising sense of awe in his tone.

Peggy looked up in surprise.

'This is it!' Prentice hissed disbelievingly. 'This is it!'

Peggy wasn't sure what made Prentice seem so certain, but she kept her mouth closed, unwilling to remind him that she was there at all.

Fallon, unfortunately, needed no reminder. He sidled up right next to her and looked around, the disgust on his face bathed in light when Prentice turned towards them.

Peggy watched as Prentice moved slowly through the chamber, stopping when he reached what looked like a rotting piece of wood sticking up from the ground like a marker of some kind.

'Here,' Prentice breathed in awe. 'It's here.'

Fallon, like Peggy, clearly just saw a grotty old bit of timber because he sneered at Prentice in open disdain. 'I don't see anything. There's nothing here.'

'Give her your torch, then get over here and unpack these bags,' Prentice snapped, dropping his holdall on the ground.

Fallon shot Peggy a murderous look before shoving the torch towards her as directed and then stomping furiously towards Prentice.

Peggy had a fleeting wish that she could tell Andrew that

Fallon really was just as petulant as he'd always described him to be – even when faced with a stone-cold murderer – and her chest ached when she swiftly realised that she was never going to get the chance.

The clang of metal-on-metal startled Peggy back to alertness.

Fallon had emptied the first bag of tools onto the dusty floor, and he was readying himself to tip out the second as Prentice shone his torch over the selection of shovels, and crowbars, and all sorts of other tools that Peggy couldn't make out in the weak light.

Peggy held both torches in her left hand so that she could run her right over her face, cooling the inflamed skin of her cheek and lip with her icy fingers.

As the echo faded away, Peggy realised that it was completely silent around her; there were no whispers, nor voices of any kind. Her thoughts, while still significantly slower than she'd like, weren't nearly as sluggish as when she'd been closer to ground level.

Down here might just be far enough away from the shadow of the cathedral and God knows what lurked just beneath it for her to be able to think a bit more clearly.

She took a hesitant step backwards, careful not to make any sound.

When neither Fallon nor Prentice reacted, she took another step, and then another, always making sure to place her heel down without scuffing the ground.

Peggy edged closer and closer to the entrance to the passageway, desperately trying to calculate how quickly she'd need to move if she had any hope of getting through the gap with enough of a head start to be able to at least try and make her escape.

She'd have to worry about how to find her way through the labyrinthine tunnels once she'd got away from Prentice and Fallon.

One thing at a time, Peg.

'Right!' Fallon said suddenly, and his voice was so loud that Peggy recoiled enough in fright that she almost dropped the torches.

Suddenly, Peggy found that Fallon was stalking towards her, with a crowbar raised above his shoulder. She didn't even try to be subtle as she scrabbled backwards in genuine horror.

'No need to keep you around any longer, is there?' Fallon jeered as he stopped only a couple of feet in front of her.

'What the fuck are you doing now?' Prentice screeched, and Fallon turned still brandishing the crowbar.

'We don't need her anymore!' Fallon argued.

'How are we going to get out of here if we don't have her?' Prentice snapped, and Peggy thought that he was going to throw another punch. 'Touch her again and I'll start thinking that I don't need *you* anymore.'

Peggy held her breath, convinced that she was about to witness bloodshed, but slowly Fallon lowered the crowbar as he turned back towards her, eyes narrowed.

'When I'm done with you, that prick Joyce won't even recognise you,' Fallon spat as he lowered his head towards Peggy's face, 'but he'll see it every single time he closes his eyes, and he'll know that it was me that did you in.'

Peggy's stomach turned at Fallon's words, and she knew that this was the final chance she would get.

Before she'd really considered the implications of what she was planning, Peggy used her thumb to spin the large emerald ring on the fourth finger of her right hand around until the jewel sat neatly above her palm. She then swung her hand up towards Fallon with as much weight behind it as she could muster, slamming her palm into his face, just above his left cheekbone. She grimaced when she felt the edges of her ring sink into the meat of his cheek, right beside his eye.

Fallon screeched, stumbling backwards as he clutched a hand to his face, careening into Prentice as he lurched around.

Peggy only just caught a glimpse of blood running down Fallon's face as he pressed a hand over his eye, bellowing in pain and anger, before she turned and desperately squeezed herself back through the gap into the tunnels, unable to hold in a sob as she tried to get her leaden limbs to move faster.

'Marnie!' she yelled with all her might as she thundered away from the chamber. 'Marnie!'

If Fallon caught up with her, there'd be no more chances to escape; she was certain that she'd be dead before she could blink.

Her feet pounded on the ground as she ran, and each turn of the path brought another rush of insistent whispering, pressing down on her from all directions.

A roar of rage tore up the path from behind her and she knew that Fallon was already on her heels.

The twin beams of the torches in her hand were the only guide Peggy had as she heaved her weary body forwards as swiftly as possible, but she knew that if she had any hope of evading Fallon, she was going to have to switch them off.

With a terrified whimper and a desperate plea to anyone who might be listening, Peggy cradled the torches to her chest before switching them off and submitting herself to the darkness.

TWENTY-SEVEN

Andrew kept his eyes on the city around him as they drove towards the cathedral in a car that he was fairly certain didn't actually belong to his boss.

He was in the backseat, sitting right behind Higson, because Jen had refused to let either of them drive, and neither Lloyd, nor Marnie – *thank Christ* – had volunteered for the job. He couldn't keep his hands still, no matter how hard he tried, so one minute his elbow was propped against the window with his chin in his palm, but the next he was tapping out an increasingly frantic rhythm on the closed cover of the ashtray recessed into the door.

Marnie was sitting between Andrew and Lloyd, and she had been nervously chewing on her thumbnail since they'd pulled away from the kerb; it was safe to say that the mood in the car wasn't exactly relaxed.

When they'd all first gathered outside on Tib Street, Andrew had been certain that Higson was about to direct them to the cathedral as fast as possible, splitting themselves between all available cars. So, he'd been surprised when Higson had turned to Mike and told him to go back to Chester House immediately.

Mike had only managed to blink stupidly back at him for a long moment – Andrew knew that he was going to owe the man pints for a *year* to make up for the fright he'd had that night – and so Higson had been forced to turn his attention to Charlie instead.

'Alright, *fine*. Charlie boy, I need *you* to take Lawson to Chester House then, because he'll be a tit and walk himself right under a bus in shock otherwise.'

Charlie had argued against this, of course. He'd wanted to go with the rest of them to find Peggy.

'Not a bloody chance, lad,' Higson had replied firmly. 'You and Lawson need to go to CID and get everyone off their arses and over to that cathedral *now*.'

'Shouldn't we just call it in?' Lloyd had asked.

'No, Parker, we should not!' Higson had snapped. 'Dickie Chambers will do jack shit if he thinks any of this will make him look bad. I don't care if you have to physically drag every single one of them out of the building, alright?'

Charlie hadn't given up without a fight though. 'Now, *really*, I think it would be better for m–'

'I've given you an order, so you can either follow it, or you can get the fuck out of my sight,' Higson had interjected in a terrifyingly calm voice, which had immediately wrong-footed Charlie and stunned him into silence.

'Go with Mike,' Andrew had added. 'Please, Charlie.'

Even with the 'please', Charlie had still clearly considered Andrew's instruction as pure treachery.

'Mate, go,' Lloyd had chimed in. 'The sooner you get to CID, the sooner you can get over to the cathedral, yeah?'

Charlie had scowled, before he'd snapped at Mike to follow him, and only seconds later they'd both sped out of Tib Street in whatever the hell Charlie's latest sports car was.

'Remind me to do him for driving like an arse once this is all sorted,' Higson had muttered, stubbing out his cigarette and reaching for the driver's door of a black Volvo estate that Andrew had never seen before.

'Sir, I think maybe I should drive,' Jen had said, looking between Andrew and Higson, but then she'd just taken the keys anyway and climbed in before either of them could so much as squawk.

Higson had sighed loudly before shambling to the passenger side and looking over at the others on the pavement. 'Well, get in then!'

They'd piled into the car and a loud burst of *I Wish It Could Be Christmas Everyday* had screeched through the speakers when

Jen had switched on the engine. She'd reached for the volume dial quickly, reducing Roy Wood to a mere whisper, but leaving him on as background noise.

'Almost no moon tonight,' Jen had commented, glancing up through the windscreen as they'd turned out of Tib Street.

'It's the winter solstice tomorrow,' Lloyd had chimed in and then, as though he'd needed to explain himself, added, 'Fiona told me the other day.'

Well, that was bloody fitting, wasn't it? All of this happening on the precipice of the longest night of the year. There were many things Andrew didn't put any stock in at all, but at that precise moment, he could easily believe that the universe was fucking with him.

Festive window displays and Christmas trees dotted the short route through the city centre towards the river, and as they got closer to their destination, Andrew's patience for smiling snowmen and beatific angels grew thin enough that he turned away from the window, pressing a hand to his forehead and squeezing his eyes shut.

He was clinging to the fact that they knew where Peggy was, but it wasn't enough to clear away the memory of Lily Woodhouse's story; or negate the fact that Prentice had killed Davy Nash and had him dumped in an unmarked grave; or stop him from recounting the expression of pure venom on Fallon's face the day before. It certainly wasn't enough to erase Andrew's belief knew that he should have done more to ensure that this could never have happened.

'Hey.' Marnie's murmur came a second before Andrew felt cold fingers grasp the hand he'd had resting on his knee.

His eyes opened and he looked at Marnie in surprise.

'It'll be alright,' Marnie said quietly, and Andrew knew that the words were as much for her benefit as they were for his. 'Peggy's clever, and she's probably already halfway to getting herself out of there anyway. We're just the B team, aren't we?'

Andrew didn't say anything, but he didn't pull his hand away either.

As Exchange Station came into view on the other side of the river, Higson flapped a hand towards Jen.

'Park over there,' he instructed gruffly, pointing to the right.

'You don't want to try and get closer to the cathedral?' Jen asked, even though she was already indicating and pulling across the road to park on double yellow lines.

'We're not going to the cathedral,' Higson replied, flinging his door open before the car had stopped.

'What?' Andrew yelped, clambering out of the back just as Higson reached the boot. 'Peggy's there! We need to go to the cathedral!'

'No, we need to go *under* the cathedral, Joyce,' Higson replied as he busied himself with unwrapping something. 'Why go to the bother of breaking into God's house to find a door, when we can try and get in through the closest thing to heaven instead?'

For a second, Andrew wondered if he'd finally been pushed into a breakdown, because no matter how he turned Higson's reply around in his mind he still had no idea what the man was on about, and in the end the only response he could find was, '*What?*'

Higson made a pleased sound and then produced a shotgun from within the dust sheet in his hands.

'Woah! Hang on!' Andrew shouted, waving his arms. 'Where the hell do you think you're going with that?'

Higson tipped the barrels towards the narrow passageway they'd parked in front of. Andrew's eyes followed the gesture and landed on the street sign on the wall – Hanging Bridge.

'Come on!' Higson called as he strode away from the car and into the narrow passage.

'What's going on?' Lloyd asked as Andrew led the others after Higson.

'Christ knows,' Andrew replied.

'Where did he get that shotgun from?' Jen sounded concerned again.

Andrew shook his head. 'The boot.'

'Does it belong to him?' Lloyd's eyebrows shot up.

'Do you think he cares about things like that?' Andrew grimaced as they emerged at the other end of Hanging Bridge and found themselves directly outside the cathedral.

'I thought he just said we weren't going to the cathedral?' Marnie muttered.

Before them, the building loomed up into the night sky, with minimal lighting both inside and out. There was really only just enough illumination to highlight the most noteworthy features, and there wasn't a hint of anything going on inside.

A banner had been strung across the railings near the boundary of the churchyard, advertising a carol service that had apparently happened earlier that evening. One corner was no longer secured and was flapping in the breeze, and the noise was unsettlingly loud in the otherwise still night.

'Joyce, come here!'

Andrew looked back over his shoulder to see Higson leaning against the large wooden door of the building on the very corner of the passageway.

'How's your shoulder these days?' Higson asked casually.

Andrew frowned. Save for the odd twinge that served as a reminder of the damage he'd sustained when he'd been thrown down a staircase by a particularly vicious spirit earlier in the year, it didn't give him much grief. 'It's fine, why?'

'I need you to get this door open,' Higson replied, tilting his head.

'You want me to break in?' Andrew's eyes widened.

Higson pursed his lips, and repeated slowly, 'I need you to get this door open.'

'What is this place?' Andrew asked, making no move towards the door.

'*This* is the place I watched Davy Nash walk out of before he disappeared,' Higson barked, 'and if you fancy seeing her Ladyship again, then you need to open this bloody door now.'

Andrew didn't need to be told again.

He gestured for Higson to get out of the way and shook out his shoulders before landing two solid kicks right above where the door handle was. Then he took a few paces back and, with only the slightest of internal winces, he sprinted towards the door, shoulder first.

The door crashed open, and Andrew stumbled more than he was anticipating when the wood gave way with relative ease.

He threw his arms forward, expecting to land face first on the floor, but found his momentum unexpectedly terminated when he collided with a tall tower of stacked tables.

The tables wobbled precariously before giving way, and Andrew hopped aside to avoid being hit by the furniture as it took out a number of short stools on the way to the ground.

Higson paused next to him and hummed as a stool rolled to a halt at his feet. 'I'd probably have given you a solid eight out of ten for getting the door open, but for that mess I'm dropping you to a four; and that's generous.'

Marnie snorted and looked away.

Andrew grimaced, rubbing his shoulder. 'Why in God's name are we in here?'

'The Hanging Bridge was once the greatest pub in the whole city, for the sole reason that Jimmy Prentice and the twats who idolised him would never set foot in here,' Higson replied gruffly. 'They were too busy in their poncy wine bars every night of the week, except Thursdays, when they'd all go to the Pelican and get chummy with the old bigwigs.'

Lloyd had once told Andrew that Higson wouldn't go to the

Pelican on a Thursday, even if it was the closest decent pub to the Ballroom, and at the time he'd wondered why. Now, though, he understood – twenty years later, Higson was still stalked by the shadow of Jimmy Prentice.

'Used to always sit with Benson in that corner over there.' Higson's expression hardened. 'Wouldn't have bothered if I'd known he was bastard scum like the rest of them.'

Christ, there was going to be a lot to clean up once this was all over.

Andrew thought back to what Higson had said to him outside. 'Are you telling me that this pub is your idea of Heaven on Earth?'

Higson smirked, so at least that awful, desolate expression had been put back in a box for now. 'Through that door at the back there is the way to the cellar.'

'And from there we can definitely get down beneath the cathedral, right?' Andrew asked, following Higson and sweeping his torch around so that he could dodge old furniture and piles of masonry. Based on the dust and grime everywhere, it looked as though the pub might have been in the middle of a renovation but hadn't been touched for years.

'Right,' Higson agreed hesitantly without turning round.

Andrew didn't like the fact that this answer lacked the dead certainty he'd been hoping for. He had the horrible feeling that, despite the bravado, Higson was clutching at straws.

'Sir?' Jen called, and Andrew decided to let Higson's seniority eliminate the need for him to answer; this was currently Higson's show, and Andrew would do as he was told for the time being.

'What?' Higson's voice was muffled as he knelt down to inspect the keyhole of the door. He was trying to turn the key that had been left in there, but the whole thing seemed to have seized.

'Do you think they might be armed?' Jen asked hesitantly.

Higson paused and looked back over at Jen. 'Almost certainly.'

Andrew ran a hand over his face. Somehow, despite all the evidence he held about the way that Jimmy Prentice operated, he hadn't actually let himself think as far as *armed*.

'You lot should probably grab something, just in case,' Higson added as he gestured to the shotgun. 'Right, Driscoll, you're on in a minute. Parker, you can open the door this time.'

'Me?' Lloyd asked, and his eagerness was tinged with only the barest hint of wariness.

'Joyce's face looks like a slapped arse already, and he'll only make another scene,' Higson replied.

Andrew ignored him and turned away to find something that he might be able to use as a weapon if necessary.

'Here you are, sir,' Jen said, appearing from behind another stack of stools and holding out a slightly bowed lump of wood.

'Is this part of a table leg?' Andrew asked suspiciously as he took it from her.

'Yeah. I think it broke off when they all fell over earlier.' Jen sounded faintly amused, but as she hadn't mentioned the fact that the tables had only fallen because Andrew had run into them, he'd let it slide.

'Thanks,' he said, testing the weight of it in his hand. It wasn't bad, actually.

Jen was gripping a short, rusty metal pipe that had obviously snapped off from something larger, leaving a nasty jagged ring on one end.

There was a crash, followed by a whoop from Lloyd, and when Jen and Andrew reached the back of the bar area again, the door was open wide and hanging drunkenly from its hinges.

The doorway opened into a small hallway area, with a handful of doors leading off in different directions, but with no obvious signage on any of them.

'Which way?' Jen asked.

Higson immediately walked to the left and twisted the doorknob. To everyone's surprise, the door opened easily.

The torchlight illuminated a dank narrow staircase, and Andrew's nose wrinkled as a putrid odour rose into the open.

Lloyd wretched and then immediately reached into his coat pocket to pull out a balled-up knitted scarf. He then proceeded to tie the scarf around his mouth and nose.

Andrew would have to admit that he was jealous. He didn't have a scarf, and he'd left his tie somewhere in the Ballroom, so he had to make do with awkwardly pulling his coat collar over his nose while trying not to drop his makeshift bat.

'Right, Joyce, off you pop,' Higson said, standing back and pointing the torchlight down the staircase.

There was no point arguing – and they really didn't have time for it – so Andrew hesitantly put his foot on the top step, checking to make sure that the whole thing was stable, and that he wasn't about to fall down yet another staircase.

Higson would probably think it was bloody hilarious.

When he didn't instantly plunge to his death, Andrew cautiously made his way down step by step. He'd have liked to go more quickly, but a heap of detectives with broken necks wouldn't help Peggy.

'Wait for me at the bottom!' Lloyd's muffled shout came from behind him. 'I need to get a weapon!'

Andrew was going to have to let his DC's enthusiasm slide as well.

The cellar felt oddly warm, and it was clear from the damaged ceiling and the overwhelming scent of decay that the room had experienced a significant flood from above at some point in its history.

'Driscoll!' Higson barked when he reached the bottom of the staircase.

'What?' Marnie asked.

'Any sign of Her Maj?'

Andrew's flicker of hope was extinguished as soon as Marnie shook her head unhappily.

Higson shifted the shotgun to rest against his other shoulder. 'Follow me.'

Marnie did as instructed and trailed after Higson to the other side of the cellar, stopping when they reached what looked like a pile of wooden casks; the timber staves were bowed and rotting, and the metal hoops that had once held them in place had long since given up providing any structure.

Higson spoke too quietly for Andrew to hear, and a few seconds later, Marnie disappeared.

'Where'd she go?' Lloyd asked, voice still muffled as he arrived at Andrew's shoulder. He appeared to be clutching an empty glass bottle.

'What's that?' Andrew asked, gesturing to Lloyd's hand.

'Pernod!' Lloyd replied cheerfully. 'I saw one of the barmaids at the Troubadour smash one of these over some arse's head once, so I know it's a good shout.'

Marnie's reappearance saved Lloyd from hearing what Andrew had to say about that.

'Yeah,' Marnie said to Higson, and Andrew was completely lost, 'but the stairs are gone.'

'Gone?' Higson repeated.

'Gone.'

'You lot, help me move this out of the way,' Higson ordered, pointing towards the disintegrating casks by his feet.

Andrew helped Jen and Lloyd heave the decaying debris across the cellar, all the while pleased that he couldn't really see what he was actually touching; the damp, spongy wood was unpleasant enough without the visual.

Higson kicked the final pieces of twisted metal out of the way to reveal the remains of a trap door. There were chunks of timber missing, and Andrew tried to cast his light through the gaps to see what was below.

Andrew crouched down to pull the handle and the whole door came away from the floor. It held itself together in his hand for just a second, before crumbling into pieces and falling into the space below.

'That drop's easily ten feet – probably closer to twelve,' Andrew said, peering over the edge. The remains of what was once a staircase lay in bits on the dusty floor below, another victim of significant water damage. 'We can go in, but we won't be able to get back out this way.'

'Do you think we need to find another route?' Lloyd asked, grimacing at the distance between the cellar floor and the lower ground.

Marnie's sharp intake of breath had Andrew sweeping the torch towards her.

'What is it?' he asked.

'Peggy's definitely here somewhere,' Marnie whispered quickly, scrunching up her face in concentration, 'but I can't find her. I think something's wrong. Really wrong.'

'What do you mean something's wrong?' Andrew asked, already crawling towards the trapdoor while a whole host of unpleasant possibilities danced across the back of his eyelids as he squinted in the gloom.

Marnie bit her lip and shook her head. 'I don't know.'

'Take these and drop them down to me in a sec?' Andrew handed his torch and bat to Jen. He then lowered himself through the gap, fingers wrapped around the distorted metal edging of the trap door. God, he really was so done with running around *beneath* things.

He squeezed his eyes shut and let go, bracing for impact with the floor, making sure to keep his knees bent and his arms tucked in so that he could roll to the side. It still hurt when he landed in

434

the dust with a solid thump that knocked the breath out of him.

'Sir?' Jen called in alarm, shining her torch right at his eyes. 'Are you alright?'

'Fine,' he grumbled, slowly climbing to his feet once he was sure he was in one piece, and dusting God-knows-what from his coat. 'Torch?'

Jen threw the torch down and he caught it, shining it around where he'd landed. It was a cavernous space with the remains of crates and barrels lined up against one wall; some previous landlord had obviously used this place for extra storage.

On the opposite side of the chamber, a doorway led out to the pitch blackness beyond, and Andrew shivered at the thought.

Jen dropped the table leg down, followed by the pipe she'd found.

'I think she might be getting closer,' Marnie said suddenly from somewhere behind Andrew.

'Lloyd, get down here!' Andrew yelled, looking up at where Lloyd was dithering at the edge of the trapdoor. 'Bend your knees or you'll be on crutches for Christmas.'

Lloyd did as he was told, and a few seconds later he was coughing and spluttering on the ground next to Andrew. 'Ow.'

Jen came immediately after Lloyd had safely caught the Pernod bottle, and despite being shorter than her colleagues, and therefore with further to fall, she still managed a significantly more graceful landing than either of them had done.

'Joyce, catch!'

Andrew looked up just in time to see Higson drop the shotgun. He scrambled forwards in alarm, chucking the table leg away and grabbing the gun before it could hit the ground and risk firing.

When Higson then began awkwardly clambering through the gap, Andrew grimaced in anticipation.

If Andrew told Higson to stay in the cellar he'd never, *ever* hear the end of it and Higson would insist on doing himself a serious injury anyway; but he was equally certain that Annie would murder him if he just watched her husband fall to his death beneath the Hanging Bridge.

All choice was removed when Higson suddenly released his grip and tumbled to the ground with a resounding crash.

'Sir!' Jen yelped, and Andrew was certain that she'd nearly shouted 'Bill' instead.

Higson groaned loudly and flapped an arm around. 'Help me up, you dolts!'

'We need to go,' Marnie whispered urgently to Andrew once Higson was back on his feet, and he certainly didn't need telling twice.

Andrew nodded at Marnie. 'You lead.'

Marnie looked unconvinced but squared her shoulders and strode towards the dark passageway a moment later.

Andrew hurriedly shoved the shotgun at Higson and followed Marnie, resetting his grip on the torch.

Before long, the narrow passage had opened up into another larger space with mossy green walls. Something scuttled along the floor in front of Andrew, and he pointed the light down quickly, only to see a large rat fleeing into the distance.

Marnie stopped dead in the centre of the room and looked up at the ceiling.

'What is it?' Andrew asked warily, drawing his eye back from where the rat had disappeared into a small gap at the base of the wall.

'We're right under part of the cathedral, I can tell,' Marnie said, though she sounded as though she wasn't quite with him. 'It's so loud, it's impossible to hear Peggy.'

'Is there anything – *anyone* – down here you can ask for help?' Andrew let the words fall out of his mouth before he could change his mind about asking such a question.

Marnie shook her head. 'There's nothing down here that could help. It's all either whispering or screaming, and I can only hear a tiny bit of it, while Peggy can hear *all* of it. Plus, I don't think I could even get very far away from you lot if I tried; it's like there's something *wrong* with the whole place.'

Andrew shivered again. He couldn't imagine what being in a place like this must be like for Peggy. They needed to get her away from there as quickly as they could.

'Which way, Marnie?' Andrew gestured at the three different exits.

Marnie looked conflicted. 'I don't know. I don't want to pick the wrong one.'

'I know,' Andrew said with as much patience as he could dredge up. 'I know you don't, but if you *had* to choose one, which one would it be?'

'That one,' Marnie said eventually, pointing towards the right-hand archway.

'Okay.'

Andrew waited for Marnie to lead the way and then they all trooped after her.

'Do you think we should split up, boss?' Lloyd asked, and it sounded like he'd asked the question because he thought he probably should, rather than he believed in the idea.

'No,' Andrew replied, because he didn't like the idea any more than Lloyd seemed to. 'Not yet anyway. Let's stick with Marnie for now.'

Marnie cried out unexpectedly and disappeared in the space of a blink.

'Marnie!' Andrew hissed loudly, picking up his pace even though he had no idea what he was running towards. 'Marnie, what's going on?'

He didn't receive an answer, so he kept running. The torch's beam bounced around wildly as the tunnel curved first to the left, and then the right. They'd only been down there for a short while, and already Andrew was completely disorientated by the whole experience. He had no idea whether they'd doubled back on themselves, or if they were still moving forwards and away from the cathedral.

Abruptly, he stopped dead. Thankfully the others were far enough behind him that they had time to stop before colliding with him.

At first, he wasn't sure why he'd paused, but then he heard a soft sound in the distance. He thought that it sounded like footsteps, but even straining his ears he couldn't be certain.

'I think there's someone up ahead,' he whispered as quietly as he could. 'It might be Peggy.'

'We should switch the torches off, just in case it isn't,' Jen suggested softly.

The lights went out one by one, until finally Andrew switched off his own torch and turned back to the complete blackness. He reached out with his left hand to draw his fingers along the wall as he began walking quickly again, which at least gave him the illusion of having some direction.

He tried to hear a hint of the sound again, but the only noise was Higson's slightly laboured breathing further back in the group.

A sudden burst of commotion echoed through the tunnels from somewhere up ahead, followed immediately by a bellow of pure rage.

Andrew didn't care that he couldn't see even an inch in front of him; he threw one hand out before him, so that he hopefully wouldn't run headlong into a wall, while his free hand dove into his coat pocket to locate the torch again. He was content for the light to draw Prentice and Fallon's attention if it meant that it diverted even a hint of the danger that Peggy was facing towards him instead.

'Peggy!' Marnie shouted in panic from an indeterminable distance away and Andrew ran faster, whipping around another corner just as the unmistakable crack of a gunshot split the air.

TWENTY-EIGHT

The second of paralysis that had come over Andrew ended when Higson shoved him forwards roughly, swearing like a particularly mouthy sailor all the while.

Andrew realised that he'd lost his makeshift bat, but that didn't slow him down one bit as he stumbled onwards and emerged into another space with a vaulted ceiling.

Once again, there were multiple exits leading from the chamber, and Andrew was about to arbitrarily pick one when Marnie suddenly appeared in front of him, grabbed his arm, and yanked him after her as she turned and ran back into the dark.

'Marnie, what's happened?' Andrew asked, uneasy about how silent Marnie was even though she was radiating pure panic.

Andrew was pulled through a sharp left and then he had to quickly hurdle over the knee-height remains of a collapsed wall. He landed clumsily on his ankle, but his hiss of pain was quickly replaced by surprise as he realised that they were running through what seemed to be an old toilet block that had been left to ruin. Chipped and faded tiles covered the walls behind a row of wooden cubicles along one wall, all leading towards a wide staircase that Marnie didn't even slow down for as they approached.

As they ran up the stairs, Andrew glanced up and realised that the architecture here was different than under the pub. The curved brick ceiling was uniform, unlike the larger chambers of the older tunnels, and Andrew just about caught sight of a sign screwed to the wall with instructions for evacuating the air raid shelter should the need arise

They must have reached the Arches.

Andrew swallowed heavily at the thought that this was now all playing out in the same place where Lily had been attacked and

Davy killed twenty years earlier.

God, he *really* hated coincidences.

They barrelled through a door at the top of the steps, and then he was violently pulled to the right before Marnie suddenly stopped and dropped his wrist.

'Go that way!' she hissed. 'I'll go and help Higson!'

Andrew jogged in the direction Marnie had pointed, searching for any clue to where Peggy might be.

Movement caught his eye as he spun around with his torch, but all confidence in thinking that they'd finally found Peggy was ripped away when Andrew's eyes landed on Neil Fallon instead. He was scrabbling around on the floor as though he were searching for something, and he reared back in alarm when the beam of light flashed in his face.

Fallon stared back at Andrew for a long moment. There was a deep gash running down his face, starting just under his left eye, which looked swollen shut.

'Don't fucking move!' Andrew snapped, advancing towards the other man. He wasn't entirely sure what he was going to do when he got there but whatever it was, it wasn't likely to end well for Fallon.

Fallon grabbed what looked like a discarded torch before he turned and hared from the room in the opposite direction.

Andrew bolted after him, but almost immediately screeched to a violent halt when his torchlight caught the tip of a boot off to his right.

He wheeled around in panic, swinging the torch in an arc until it landed on the figure slumped against the wall.

Her head was bowed, and dusty, dishevelled hair fell around her face in complete disarray, but there was no doubt that it was Peggy.

She was frighteningly still, and for one awful, heart-stopping moment, Andrew believed that the gunshot they'd heard must have taken Peggy away from him for good, but then she shifted ever so slightly, and Andrew's lungs emptied entirely in relief.

Andrew hurled himself across the room towards her, just as the others rounded the corner, looking towards him in obvious horror.

'She's alive!' he shouted as he dropped to his knees in front of where Peggy was drooped against the damp brickwork. 'Fallon's gone that way!'

Lloyd and Jen both immediately tore off in the direction Fallon had disappeared. Lloyd had the Pernod bottle raised and ready for action.

'Peg?' Andrew called quietly as he ducked his head to try and see her face properly.

She didn't immediately appear as though she'd been shot, but Andrew couldn't easily shake the fear anyway. He dropped the torch onto his knees to free up both hands, but it bounced off his leg and rolled away, leaving them in darkness.

He swore in exasperation, but before he could move to retrieve the torch, it was picked up by Marnie.

'I'll hold it,' she murmured tremulously, looking at Peggy in alarm as she was once again bathed in the torchlight. 'Is she alright?'

Andrew didn't think he could answer that quite yet.

He reached out and held Peggy's face between his hands, frowning when the tips of his fingers brushed against her temples, and he felt how warm her face was.

'Peg?' he said again, gently tilting her head back.

She made a small sound of protest but one of her eyes cracked open sluggishly.

'Hi,' Andrew said, relief almost overwhelming.

Marnie shifted the torch slightly and Peggy squeezed her eye shut again with a wince when the light hit her.

'I'm sorry,' Marnie said quietly, but it was so full of regret that it was obvious that the apology wasn't just for shining the torch in Peggy's face.

Andrew only vaguely registered that fact, though, because the slight wobble of the torch had been enough to illuminate the multiple scratches on Peggy's face, along with the bruise blossoming on her left cheekbone above a split, swollen lip.

His mind zipped straight to the innumerable ways in which Fallon was going to pay for all of this, because a stint in Strangeways wasn't going to be anywhere near enough to quell Andrew's intensifying desire for a reckoning. He knew that Peggy would likely accuse of him of being a boorish idiot with a hero complex, but he also knew that the others would be entirely on his side.

'Peg, I need you to talk to me.' Andrew carefully moved his hands as he leant back again. 'I need you to tell me if you're hurt.'

Familiar heavy footsteps approached, pausing just behind Andrew's right side.

'Alright?' Higson asked, and all of his usual brusqueness and acerbic teasing had been carefully packed away, leaving only genuine concern behind.

'I don't know yet,' Andrew admitted quietly, looking back over his shoulder.

Higson pursed his lips and nodded. 'Driscoll, come with me.'

Marnie faltered for a moment but then handed Andrew the torch again and trailed after Higson.

Andrew looked down in surprise when he felt ice-cold fingers wrap around his free hand. When he glanced up again, Peggy was looking back at him. Her eyes were glassy and lacked their usual alertness, but at least they were both open.

'How?' Peggy's voice was ragged.

'Marnie, mostly,' Andrew replied, hoping he'd interpreted the question correctly. 'She knew you were somewhere noisier than a church. Peggy, are you hurt?'

Peggy seemed to accept the explanation, but almost instantly looked distressed, ignoring Andrew's question completely. 'It's Fallon and Prentice! They're both here!'

'We know.' Andrew put the torch down carefully and then took Peggy's hands between his, trying to rub some warmth back into them. 'Jen and Lloyd have gone after Fallon, and Higson won't let Prentice get away this time.'

This news only seemed to trouble Peggy further. 'Fallon has a gun. I think Prentice does too.'

Her answer reminded Andrew of the gunshot, and he kicked himself for getting sidetracked. 'Peggy, was it Fallon's gun that went off?'

Peggy nodded once and winced. 'I managed to get away from them, but Fallon came after me even though I'd made sure to take his torch. I thought I'd lost him, but he must have known he'd caught up with me because the gun went off in the dark just back there. I came over here and tried to hide, and then you were here.'

As heat returned to her hands, Peggy seemed to be coming back to herself. There were definitely gaps in her story, though, and Andrew was going to have to try and properly piece it all together with her later. For now, he needed to stick to the basics. 'Were they down here looking for the same thing as before? With Lily?'

'Yes. Prentice thinks I found it for him.'

Andrew's eyes widened. 'You found it?'

'I don't know,' Peggy replied, and she ducked her head again. 'If I did, it's not because I meant to lead them to it. I was just looking for a chance to get away. I'm sorry, I d-'

Peggy stopped talking the instant Andrew awkwardly wrapped his arms around her and pulled her against him, which was exactly what he'd been hoping for.

'Peggy,' he mumbled insistently into her hair, 'you could have handed over every single scrap of stupid, godforsaken treasure that might be down here and I wouldn't be able to care any less about that than I already do.'

Peggy didn't reply, but Andrew knew that she was still going to feel guilty about it.

'The only thing that mattered to any of us was making sure that you were alright,' Andrew added, 'so I'm not going to let you make yourself feel bad for doing everything you could to keep yourself safe. You know, Marnie told me on the way over here that you were going to be well on your way to getting yourself out of this before we turned up, and she was right.'

'I shouldn't have gone with them in the first place,' Peggy mumbled somewhere near Andrew's shoulder. 'Fallon told me that the man who was with him was Chambers.'

Lying bastard, Andrew thought angrily.

'They said there was a problem at the Ballroom,' Peggy continued, 'and that you might be in trouble.'

Andrew's anger sharpened into concentrated wrath hearing that Fallon had weaponised the relationship between Andrew and Peggy, but he crushed it tightly into a box to be dealt with later; he couldn't have Peggy think that any of it was aimed at her.

'Joyce!' Higson call was gruff, but it still lacked any of the expected bite. 'We need to shift.'

Higson was right. Not only did they need to locate Fallon and Prentice, but they needed to get Peggy as far away from the Arches as they could.

Andrew reluctantly let go of Peggy and pulled back so that he could see her face again. 'Are you going to be alright walking?'

Peggy nodded and then hissed sharply with a grimace.

'What is it?' Andrew asked sharply.

'I'm fine,' Peggy replied, slowly trying to stand. 'I already had a headache before I hit my head.'

Andrew's eyes narrowed. 'Where did you hit it?'

'The back. It's fine, Andrew.'

'What did you hit it *on*?'

'The wall.'

Andrew's eye caught on Peggy's split lip again and he had a very good idea of just who had been responsible for her sustaining a head injury on top of everything else.

'I'm really sorry,' Andrew apologised in advance, already moving his fingers towards the back of Peggy's head, checking that it wasn't worse than she was making out.

She winced again when Andrew found the tender spot, and he was just about ready to storm off after Fallon without any backup or even a single ounce of common sense. He wondered if he could get Dolly to hex Fallon for him; he was fairly sure that she liked Peggy enough that she'd do it on her behalf, if not exactly for Andrew himself.

'I'm fine,' Peggy repeated, and it was the steadiest she'd sounded since they'd found her. 'Can you please just help me up?'

Andrew did as he'd been asked.

'If it makes you feel any better,' Peggy added as Andrew let go of her entirely, 'I did manage to hit Fallon with this.'

Peggy held up her right hand and waggled her ring finger slightly so that the emerald glinted in the torchlight.

Andrew would be lying if he said that this piece of information didn't marginally improve his mood.

'Present for you,' Higson said as he walked over and held out his hand towards Andrew.

Andrew looked down to see Higson proffering a small gun towards him. 'Jesus Christ, where the hell were you hiding that?'

Higson rolled his eyes and pointed in the direction Lloyd and Jen had gone. 'It was over there, so I expect it was Fallon's, you nonce. Take it.'

'I'd rather not.'

'Yeah, well I'd rather you had it than he did, so just take the bloody thing.' Higson shoved it into Andrew's hand. He then looked at Peggy. 'You alright, love?'

Peggy blinked a couple of times before she nodded, and Andrew thought she was doing a fairly decent job of pretending that she wasn't flummoxed by Higson calling her 'love' for the first time ever; she was certainly doing a better job than Andrew, who was gawping in astonishment.

'How did you get down here?' Peggy asked eventually, squinting slightly as she shifted her weight from one foot to the other like she was testing her steadiness. 'Did you find the passageway from the cathedral?'

Higson grinned. 'No. We came from much more hallowed ground, didn't we Joyce?'

'We came through the pub.' Andrew explained at Peggy's questioning glance. 'The Hanging Bridge.'

'Right, let's go.' Higson gestured for Peggy and Andrew to follow him as he readjusted the shotgun over his shoulder, giving Andrew no more time to clear up Peggy's confusion.

Andrew looked around. 'Hang on, where's Marnie?'

'She's gone to do a little job for me,' Higson replied. 'She'll be back in a minute.'

'Peggy, I want you to stay behind me, alright,' Andrew said as they reached the passageway leading away from that section of the Arches.

There was no reply and when Andrew looked back in confusion, it was to find that Peggy had stopped, utterly stock still.

'What?' he asked, hurrying back towards her. 'What is it?'

'You said you came in a different way,' Peggy said, terrified eyes on the darkness that Higson was just disappearing into.

'We can't get back out the way we came in,' Andrew explained. 'We have to go that way.'

'I can't,' Peggy said in a small voice. 'I can't go back in there.'

Andrew sighed. He understood as well as he could, but they didn't have an option. 'I'm sorry, Peg, but it's the only way out.'

Peggy looked half-ready to just tell him that she'd stay where she was then, thanks.

'Here, take this,' Andrew said, handing her the torch and readjusting his grip on the bloody gun he was now carrying.

Peggy took the torch and then Andrew linked their free hands together. 'We'll get out of here as quickly as we can, alright?'

'Alright,' Peggy agreed eventually, and without a shred of enthusiasm for the idea.

Once they reached the passageway, Andrew made sure that Peggy was always slightly behind him as they made their way towards where they could see Higson's torch beam flickering in the distance.

Just before they reached Higson, two lights appeared in the murkiness ahead, which seemed to be hurrying towards them. Andrew tensed immediately, ready for whatever fight was coming their way.

To his relief, it was only Jen and Lloyd.

Much less to his relief was what they had to say:

'We lost him,' Lloyd gasped, hunched over and leaning on his knees. He was still holding the Pernod bottle. 'This place is a maze!'

'Peggy!' Jen cried, looking over Andrew's shoulder. 'Are you alright?'

Peggy must have nodded because Jen smiled, demonstrably relieved.

'Where's Marnie?' Lloyd asked, looking around like he might have misplaced her.

'Here,' Marnie announced, appearing behind Higson.

'Well?' Higson asked her.

'I don't know if it's that he can't find his way back to Prentice, or if he's just cutting his losses, but I think Fallon's trying to get out of here,' Marnie reported.

'And Prentice?' Higson asked, lips curling in distaste at the name.

'I *think* I know where he might be, but I can't be sure because there's just so much noise everywhere.'

'Go on then, we'll follow you,' Higson replied gruffly. 'Let me know when you think we're near Prentice. I have a few things I'd like to *say* to him.'

They set off in a clump, moving swiftly with Marnie leading the way.

As they walked, winding their way through the warren of passageways, Andrew noticed that Marnie seemed to emit the faintest glow. He'd never spotted it before – perhaps because he didn't think he'd ever been anywhere that seemed quite as a dark as these tunnels beneath the city – but right then it was so damn obvious that he wondered how it wasn't noticed by everyone Marnie encountered.

Andrew also noticed that Peggy's hand seemed to be getting colder once again, and he could hear little scuffs to her steps; almost like she was stumbling just a little every couple of strides.

Marnie stopped abruptly and turned around to face him. 'Is she alright?'

Andrew shook his head tersely.

'One second,' Marnie said, nodding at Andrew sharply just before she disappeared.

There was a clanging sound from somewhere, but Andrew would be at a loss to tell anyone which direction it came from; he would also be at a loss to tell anyone how the hell they planned on getting out of what seemed to be an increasingly confusing labyrinth. He'd completely lost track of the route they'd taken after the first few turns and couldn't be entirely sure that they hadn't just been wandering in a circle.

'Prentice is that way,' Marnie said upon her return, gesturing to the right with her head. 'The cathedral's right above us, but we're still quite far down. I think this path is a bit like a spiral staircase, but I can't get far enough away from you lot to be sure.'

'Good work, Driscoll.' Higson nodded at her and then faced the others. 'Parker, you and Driscoll are with me. Joyce, Cusack, get up to the cathedral and make sure Lawson and Swan did as they were told. If you meet that twat Fallon on the way, I wouldn't mind if you wanted to give him a thump or two, alright?'

Andrew actually jolted at Higson's words. He was choosing to take *Lloyd and Marnie* to apprehend Prentice?

'Sir,' Jen agreed immediately, obviously seeing no issue with it.

Andrew hesitated, and it must have shown on his face because Higson raised his eyebrows at him.

'Get Her Maj out of here, Joyce,' he stated quietly but firmly. 'I actually have faith that you won't fuck this up. Don't prove me wrong though, or you'll be back in Chester House by morning with all the other useless sods.'

Higson hadn't actually threatened to throw him out of the Ballroom in ages, so it surprised Andrew enough that he could only bob his head dumbly in response.

'Good lad,' Higson said with a nod of approval.

'I don't know where we're supposed to go!' Andrew hissed desperately at Marnie as she began to lead Higson and Lloyd away.

Marnie looked apologetic. 'Just keep following that path and don't turn off it. You might want to run though.'

Andrew wasn't sure if that final comment was to spur him on to get Peggy out of there quickly, or a warning that there was some other awful thing hiding in the dark that he wouldn't want to encounter. These days, it really could be either one.

'Alright,' Andrew sighed, 'let's go.'

'Do you want to lead the way, sir?' Jen asked, stepping out of the way. 'I'll go at the back and keep an eye on things.'

She then nodded her head meaningfully towards Peggy, who seemed to have closed in on herself even further since they'd paused.

Andrew nodded his agreement and then tugged Peggy closer to his side. 'Come on, Peg. We're going to make a run for it, alright?'

Peggy swallowed heavily, and even though she was obviously making a concerted effort to hold the torch still, the light was quivering in time with each shiver that ran through her. 'Alright.'

Based on that shaky agreement, Andrew thought that making any sort of 'run' for it might be no more than wishful thinking.

'Sir?' Jen prompted quietly.

Andrew looked up at the dark ceiling – perhaps seeking some kind of divine intervention, or maybe just bracing himself for anything they might find up there – and breathed out slowly.

Then, with an almost suffocating sense of trepidation, Andrew tightened his grip on Peggy's hand, and they set off towards whatever fresh hell was waiting for them that time.

TWENTY-NINE

For a long time, Peggy was aware of only two things: a distant small bloom of heat in the palm of her left hand, and a cold, deep voice that seemed to be both murmuring directly into her ear and also booming from every direction at once.

Unlike the pleas for help and attention that Peggy was accustomed to, the voice in her ear was hissing and spitting furiously at her. She had a vague awareness that the voice was speaking in Latin, but she didn't need to understand the words individually to be able to comprehend the meaning: Peggy was an aberration, and her presence would not be tolerated any longer.

The harsh litany seemed to summon a suffocating chill behind her ribcage that squeezed harder and harder with every step she took, freezing her limbs and forcing her breath to falter in her lungs.

Another thin, but terribly insistent, thread of a whisper also appealed for her attention, twisting its way between the harsh words and winding around each rasped admonition.

The first voice only grew louder in response to this intrusion, sternly enunciating each word as the tirade became a repeated chant of the same indecipherable phrase, but then the quiet thread spun into a ribbon, tightening around the reprimand as though it were trying to strangle it into submission.

The warmth in her palm spread first to her fingers, and then to the inside of her wrist which lessened the ache in her chest, although this slightly augmented awareness also served to remind her of just how dark it was; dark enough that she couldn't see anything at all through a thick blanket of midnight mist; dark enough that Peggy couldn't make sense of where she was and, despite knowing that she was moving, she couldn't be sure if she was still running away from whatever it was that wanted to pull her beneath, or if she was being dragged back towards it.

The first voice chanted louder, fighting harder against the whisper that was growing increasingly frantic in its unintelligible entreaties.

Her head felt like it was going to split at the seams, and she had just enough capacity to wonder if it might even be a welcome relief if it did.

Without warning, Peggy was suddenly overcome with the terrible sensation of falling from a great height, and her stomach twisted as her heart stuttered in her chest.

A shock of pain radiated through her whole body a split second before her lungs emptied in a rush, leaving only an agonising emptiness behind.

She tried to draw in a breath, but unrelenting hands were clawing at her throat, and she couldn't breathe, and she couldn't see, and she couldn't think, and she couldn't scream and–

'Peggy!'

The insistent whisper became a roar of her name and Peggy blinked in alarm as the chanting ceased immediately, as though the connection had been severed mid-syllable. For a split-second, just as her eyelashes parted, there was a flash of something that was more of a murky dark grey than the desolate blackness she was almost immediately drawn back into.

'Peggy!'

There was that shouting again.

Peggy turned towards the sound, trying to orient herself in the startlingly quiet hollow she'd unexpectedly found herself in. Perhaps if she kept herself small and silent, that first voice wouldn't be able to find her again.

'Peg!'

Peg? Nobody called her Peg, except for Charlie, and that certainly wasn't Charlie shouting at her.

No, that wasn't quite right, was it? *Andrew* called her Peg sometimes – infrequently enough that she still noticed every single time he did it – but why would Andrew be here, in this place of indescribable darkness? This wasn't somewhere that *anyone* should be.

She realised with a desperate urgency that she needed to warn him not to stop here; to implore him to keep running, so that the darkness couldn't creep up and catch him like it had her.

'Peggy.'

The roar had become a whisper again, but it drove a spike of agony through her head, nonetheless. She tried to bring up her hands to press her palms against her eyelids, hoping to relieve the pressure, but she found her arms pinned in place.

Peggy struggled against the unseen bonds, but they just tightened and tightened until Peggy surrendered with a soft whimper of finality, sagging entirely beneath the terrifying understanding that her luck had finally run out.

She felt like she was caught in a storm; the wind whipping at her hair as her body was tossed in every direction with each gust.

Scorching heat suddenly brushed against her forehead, and she sighed at the immediate respite when the band of ice behind her eyes began to rapidly thaw.

A single tear of pure relief escaped the corner of her eye, and then another, blazing fiery trails down her cheeks until saltwater hit her lip and conjured a harsh sting that made her frown in dismay. 'Ow.'

'Peg?'

Peggy blinked sluggishly. That had definitely been her name again, even if it had been less of a word and more of a desperate intake of breath.

She blinked again, and then a few more times for good measure, clearing the dampness from her eyesight and the dread from her thoughts as she did so.

'Peg?'

Peggy finally opened her eyes properly and promptly went cross-eyed.

Andrew's face was very, very close to her own, features distorted by the jaundiced light from the torch that Jen was holding nearby.

'What is it?' Peggy asked as she swallowed heavily, thoroughly confused by the naked distress on the two faces peering at her. 'What's happened? Are you both alright?'

'Are *we* alright?' Jen asked, as though she were shocked by the unreasonable nature of Peggy's enquiry.

'Yes,' Peggy replied slowly, utterly perplexed. '*Are you alright?*'

Andrew wilted with a broken breath, dropping his chin to his chest. Confusingly, that movement jostled Peggy, and it took far longer than it should have done for the realisation to hit that it was because both of Andrew's hands were supporting her head again.

Peggy glanced at Jen questioningly.

Jen somehow looked more upset than she had a moment ago, as she glanced between Peggy and Andrew's bowed head. 'Peggy, we thought...'

'Thought what?' Peggy asked as Jen trailed off.

'Peggy, do you remember what happened?' Jen asked haltingly, not answering Peggy's question. 'Do you know where you are?'

A hint of a memory tiptoed in slowly, nudging its way to the forefront of her mind. Unexpectedly, the hint blossomed into a loud and terrifying summary of the past twelve hours of her life. She could tell that there were gaps in her memories, whether blotted out by fear or fatigue she couldn't be sure, but the scenes that remained played out in a blur, until finally she was left only with a soul-deep exhaustion and the bewildering but undeniable understanding that she'd somehow strayed too close to death.

'Peggy?' Jen prompted gently.

'Um,' Peggy replied, and only then did she really hear how wrecked her voice was. She cleared her throat. 'I think so.'

Peggy shivered as a chill wracked her body, and Andrew's attention snapped back to her immediately, eyes slightly wild.

'What?' he asked urgently. 'What is it?'

Peggy wasn't actually sure what *it* was, but there'd been a shift in the air when she'd spoken, and she just knew that something was heading their way – *her* way, more specifically – and it seemed to be the sort of something that she didn't want to be around to meet.

'We need to leave,' she whispered.

There was a time, not even all that long ago, when Andrew would have scoffed if she'd said something like that, but not anymore. He was moving before she'd even finished speaking.

It was only when Andrew let go of her and made to stand up that Peggy not only realised that she was actually sitting on a cold, dusty floor, but that she also didn't have quite enough energy to get her own legs to do as they were told.

'Come on, up you get,' Andrew said encouragingly when he and Jen reached down to pull Peggy to her feet a moment later.

The world spun as she tried to get her balance, but she managed to successfully stay upright, albeit propped against the wall, when Jen and Andrew took a few steps away.

'Is this how you got into the tunnels, Peggy?' Jen asked a moment later, gesturing to where Andrew was looking through a gap in the wall, slightly further up the path; a gap that Peggy recognised as the hinged wall panel beneath the choir stalls.

'Yes,' she croaked. 'On the other side there's a small space, and then a hatch into the cathedral floor just above it. Most of the doors in the cathedral are locked all the time, so I don't know how we'll be able to get out of the building once we're in there.'

'Did you leave this panel open at all when you came through?' Andrew asked.

'I don't think so,' Peggy replied hesitantly, trying to think back to when she'd first entered the passageway. She closed her eyes and tried to remember it more clearly. 'No. Prentice made sure it was all secured before we left.'

Andrew nodded, though he didn't look particularly happy with her answer as he pulled the panel up to fully expose the small space beyond. 'This wasn't quite closed just now, which means it's likely that Fallon's come back this way. He might still be up there.'

Peggy inched forwards, still leaning against the wall of the passageway for support.

When she was only a few steps from Jen, Peggy stopped suddenly, her eyes blown wide in alarm as a shudder slowly crawled up her spine and settled at the nape of her neck.

There was somebody right behind her.

'Peggy, come on,' Jen said encouragingly. 'We're nearly out.'

Peggy tucked her head right down as she raised her shoulders up to her ears. 'Who is it, Jen?'

'Who's *who*, Peggy?'

'Behind me!' Peggy replied in a desperate whisper. 'Tell me who's behind me!'

Jen shook her head, bewildered. 'Nobody.'

Peggy blinked and the world around her dimmed threateningly.

No, no, no. She didn't want to go back into the dark.

Jen clearly agreed, because Peggy suddenly found herself being yanked forward and bundled towards where Andrew was still holding up the panel.

Peggy was pushed through the gap, and she stumbled into the space beneath the cathedral. Her heart was hammering as her palms hit the opposite wall, and she knew that she needed to get out of there, and that she needed to get Andrew and Jen out of there too, as quickly as she could.

Crouching awkwardly, she reached above her head with her palms flat and tried to push the floor panel loose. It didn't budge.

With a cry of dismay, Peggy balled up her fists and hammered against the wood instead; it rattled, but it still refused to open.

Oh God, what if Fallon had blocked their way out? She doubted that it would have been particularly hard to find something heavy enough to place on the hatch, making it impossible for anyone to open it from the inside.

'I can't get it open!' Peggy cried.

Andrew squeezed through the opening in the wall behind Peggy, completely hunched in the tiny space as he scrambled towards where she was crouched.

'I think he might have jammed the panel to stop us getting out,' Peggy explained frantically as her nails scratched against the wood.

Andrew swore loudly and he reached up to push the ceiling with both hands. The panel lifted ever so slightly, but almost immediately it dropped back down again with a dull thud.

Peggy turned her head frantically towards the sound of heavy footsteps echoing in the passageway they'd just come from, and she grabbed Andrew's arm until he paused in his endeavours. 'Can you hear that?'

Andrew listened carefully for a long moment but then shook his head gravely. 'I can't hear anything, Peg.'

That awful, slinking cold of earlier was sneaking its way back into her bones and with a burst of panic, Peggy reached above her head again and pushed with all her might as Andrew redoubled his efforts to get them out of there.

A terrible scraping sound followed by an ear-splitting *crack* rang out just before the wood panel sprang free with the force of Peggy and Andrew's combined shoves.

'Peggy, go!' Andrew instructed sharply.

Peggy managed to reach out and curl her hands around the

base of one of the carved seats above and tried to scrabble out of the hiding space with Andrew's help.

Suddenly, though, he grasped her sleeve, stopping her, and then held a finger to his lips when she looked down at him in surprise.

'Fallon might be there,' Andrew whispered almost soundlessly. 'Keep your head down.'

Peggy gave one nod and then crawled the rest of the way out of the hole.

This end of the cathedral was dim and shadowy, but the hint of artificial light elsewhere in the city was just visible through the windows; it was such a welcome change from the pitch-black obscurity of the tunnels below them that Peggy could have cried in relief.

She crept forwards, turning back just in time to see Jen coming up through the gap. To the left of the hatch, a heavy wooden lectern edged in some sort of metalwork lay on its side. She'd been correct then; Fallon *had* tried to stop anyone from following him.

Andrew didn't appear immediately behind her. Instead, he passed a couple of darkened torches, a short metal pole and Fallon's gun out to Jen first, before finally levering himself up and out into the cathedral.

With the fallen lectern blocking the other exit, Peggy knew that she was going to have to lead the way out of the stalls, so she turned to face the direction of the altar, slowly crawling forwards as silently as she could.

If Fallon was still there in the building, it would have been impossible for him not to have heard the crash a minute earlier, so all they could do was keep the noise to a minimum and hope that he was hiding himself somewhere else in the cathedral.

After what felt like a lifetime, Peggy reached the end of the wooden stalls, and she'd barely put her palm down on the stone floor when a clock in the distance began chiming the hour.

Peggy shuddered as she thought of how Lily had heard the

bells from the Arches, hoping that it had meant she was on her way to safety. Peggy counted the chimes as she turned to the left, moving slowly and praying that she wasn't leading them all into more trouble.

By the time she reached the narrower aisle, the clock was chiming for the twelfth and final time.

Midnight.

As the last chime faded away to nothing, Peggy realised just how quiet the cathedral was. She hadn't noticed when she'd first come out of the passageway – she'd been too relieved – but now it was clear that there was something amiss. The plaintive voices that had plagued her earlier in the day were silenced, and it felt as though the building itself was holding its breath, just waiting to see what proceedings it was about to bear witness to.

Peggy's arms were shaking beneath her weight, and she had to stop, even if it was only for a minute. She slumped against the stone pillar next to her, and she was so tired that she couldn't fight it when her eyes drifted closed.

A hand clasped her shoulder, and Peggy's eyes snapped open in fright.

'We need to keep moving, Peggy.' Andrew looked deeply apologetic as he shook his head at her. 'Come on.'

Andrew rose to his feet, still keeping his shoulders hunched and his knees bent.

Jen followed suit a moment later, and they both scanned the long aisle warily for any sign that they weren't alone.

Only when he was certain that there was no sign of Fallon, did Andrew reach down for Peggy's hands to help her to her feet. She lolled against his shoulder and Andrew was convinced that she'd be asleep in seconds if they stopped moving.

Even draped in the shadows of the darkened aisle, Peggy looked far too pale, and the minimal light reflecting off the pale stonework lent her an almost ethereal appearance. A chill ran through Andrew at the thought, forcing him to relive the desperate dash from the Arches to the surface, and he had to chase the desperate memory of Peggy going completely limp in his arms from his mind; there would be time enough to torture himself with the recollection of it all later when they were all safe and sound, and as far away from the cathedral as he could get them.

'Sir,' Jen whispered, worry written all over her face as she glanced at Peggy, 'do you think Mike and Charlie managed to get any backup?'

Andrew had been asking himself the same thing since they'd emerged into the cathedral met with only silence. He hadn't been expecting the place swarming with CID officers – he'd known that Chambers would be eager to keep his name and his reputation out of this situation, and that sentiment would have trickled down to others at Chester House – but he'd hoped that in the couple of hours since they'd parted, Mike would have been able to persuade a handful of his colleagues to help out.

At the very least, he'd assumed that Charlie would be able to badger at least *one* person to drive over to the cathedral, if only to take the piss out of the so-called ghostbusting detective.

But there was no sign of anyone, and Andrew could only shake his head in answer to Jen's question. As far as he could tell, they were on their own.

'See over there?' Andrew hissed, gesturing towards the far side of the aisle where a long, semi-open wooden divider spanned the stone columns, creating a sectioned off area that acted as a smaller chapel within the larger space of the cathedral. 'Take Peggy in there, and make sure she's alright. We can't drag her around this whole building looking for a way out.'

Jen nodded her agreement, but it was more tentative than usual. 'What are you going to do, sir?'

'Find a door that isn't locked,' Andrew replied plainly. He didn't want to come across as flippant, but that really was the extent of any plan he had. Once he found a sensible route out, he'd come back to the chapel and direct Jen towards the exit. Then, when he knew that Jen was getting Peggy to safety, Andrew would fight against every bad feeling he had about the idea and head back down into the tunnels to make sure that the others were alright.

'Sir.'

'And take this,' he added, handing over Fallon's gun.

Jen eyed it uneasily, but took it anyway, making sure to pass Andrew the pipe she'd brought from the Hanging Bridge.

'Peg, I need you to go with Jen, alright?' Andrew said, reluctantly loosening his grip on her still icy hands.

Peggy didn't reply as Jen approached, and Andrew got the distinct impression that all of Peggy's remaining concentration was being used to ensure that she stayed standing.

Jen wrapped her free arm around Peggy's shoulders, carefully drawing her away from Andrew, and then with a whispered instruction too quiet for anyone but Peggy to hear, they set off towards the chapel.

Andrew watched as they shuffled down the aisle. Jen's gaze was constantly darting around, looking for even the smallest hint that something wasn't quite right.

He kept an eye on both of them until they rounded the corner into the chapel and then he moved as quickly and soundlessly as he could manage, following a similar path until he passed the chapel entrance and veered to the left, pausing behind one of the columns that lined the larger, central aisle that stretched from the main entrance to the choir stalls, and then to the altar beyond.

Gut feelings usually served Andrew well, and even though he could neither hear nor see anything that seemed out of the ordinary, he didn't believe that Fallon had left the cathedral.

Fallon had scarpered as soon as he'd seen Andrew down in the Arches, which would have given him a decent head start, but who knew how long it would have taken him to find his way back to the cathedral. He'd have then further squandered even more of any advantage he'd had by stopping to obstruct the exit from the tunnels. On top of that, Peggy had explained that most of the doors in the cathedral had been locked earlier in the day, so there weren't actually an enormous number of places to hide in the cavernous space.

All told, Andrew was pretty damn sure that Fallon must be somewhere nearby.

He looked down towards the entrance to the cathedral's tall clock tower, where the only lights that were on in the building shined up from the bottom of the large stained-glass window that was set high in the wall, with its colours shining out into the city beyond. Beneath the window was a set of large wooden doors that had been propped open to afford a perfect view of yet another pair of doors, slightly further away, and down a short run of steps.

It was this second set of doors that Andrew was interested in, because he knew that if he could get them open, then Jen and Peggy would be out onto the street and into the city in seconds.

Andrew grasped the pipe in his hand tightly and stepped out into the much more exposed aisle. He crept towards the tower as swiftly as he dared.

Rows upon rows of folding chairs had been set out, stretching almost the entire way from the tower to the choir stalls, forcing Andrew to keep to the fringes of the aisle.

When he was only a few rows from the back, Andrew's left foot slipped out from under him, and he had to grab one of the metal-framed chairs to steady himself. The clang of the chair legs on the stone floor echoed noisily and Andrew would have shouted in exasperation if it wouldn't have been just another way to give up his location to anyone who might be looking for him.

He glanced down, looking for the reason he'd slipped, and saw what he thought, at first, was a plain piece of folded paper. Upon picking it up and turning it over, Andrew realised that it wasn't a single sheet, but a programme for the carol service that had been held there earlier that evening which, he supposed, also explained the seating arrangement.

All welcome! was printed at the bottom of the front page and Andrew couldn't help but wonder whether the person who'd typed that would have even momentarily considered that their inclusive invitation might be extended to include kidnappers, thieves and rogue detectives.

Andrew put the booklet in his pocket, not wanting Peggy or Jen to slip on it later, before continuing his steady creep towards the tower.

When he passed through the first set of double doors, Andrew sighed in relief. Since he'd clattered into the chairs, he'd been waiting for Fallon to spring out from the shadows. It worried Andrew that Fallon would likely have realised that his chances of fleeing to Spain were dwindling with each passing minute, and that would only heighten his desperation to escape; Andrew knew from experience just how dangerous desperate people could be.

The doors that acted as the final barrier to the outside world were only scant feet away, but as he stood at the top of the steps, his eyes drifted towards the old padlock holding the sliding bolt in place and he grimaced.

Andrew glanced down at the pipe in his hand; a solid swing from it *might* be enough to dislodge it if the lock was decrepit enough or, then again, it might just end badly for Andrew's wrist.

If he were Magnum P.I he'd just go and retrieve the gun from Jen and shoot the lock from the door, but as he was in possession of neither moustache nor particular conviction in his current skill with a firearm, he vetoed that idea immediately. He needed to find something else.

Looking back into the main body of the cathedral, he considered one of the chairs as an option. He could swing one with some heft, but it would probably be too unwieldy if trying to hit something significantly smaller – like the padlock – with any accuracy.

He spun in a slow circle, keeping an eye out for any object in the immediate vicinity that he could use, but the tower was devoid of anything useful. It contained only wall plaques bearing the names of former Lord Mayors and town clerks of both Manchester and Salford on one side, with the opposite wall reserved for bishops and chancellors. His eyes briefly caught on the name of the very Lord Mayor whose missing socks had made some small contribution towards leading Andrew to tiptoeing around Manchester Cathedral in the dead of night, and he couldn't help the small sigh at the absurdity of his own life.

Andrew barely caught the slightest scrabbling sound before an overriding sense of self-preservation kicked in and he threw himself to the ground. He hit the stone in time to feel the rush of air above him when something sliced through the space where he'd been standing only a split-second earlier.

He rolled onto his back to see Fallon spinning away from him, carried off by the momentum of swinging the long brass rod in his hands.

If Andrew stayed in the tower he had nowhere to hide, and the pipe in his hand was too short to be able to take a good swipe at Fallon while the other man still had that damn rod.

Actually, that brass rod was exactly the sort of thing that Andrew had been looking for in his quest for something to break the padlock with. He just needed to find one of his own or figure out how to get that one from Fallon, all without getting his own head caved in in the process.

He sprang to his feet and pelted up the narrow central aisle that had been artificially formed between the rows of chairs, racing towards the choir stalls again.

Andrew was going to add another few pints to his tally for Mike as additional thanks for persuading him to go back to football training once a week. He'd always been a quick runner – certainly quicker than Fallon had ever been – but weekly outings to the park had renewed his ability for bursts of speed, and so he found himself well ahead of Fallon by the time he'd cleared the choir stalls.

He needed to draw Fallon in the opposite direction from Jen and Peggy, so he swung to the right and headed out into the aisle next to the imposing altar.

Lined up together on stone steps beside the altar was a collection of short and heavy-looking brass candlesticks; they were stubbier than Andrew had been hoping for, but they looked weighty enough to be able to exact some damage on the padlock. He concealed Jen's pipe behind a stack of hymn books, before he grabbed the closest candlestick and held it to his chest.

A quick survey of the area revealed another large door in the corner, which Andrew assumed was an alternative exit to the street. This door was without a padlock, but it looked like you'd need a big old key to open it. Given Andrew's string of luck, the key obviously wasn't just sitting in the lock waiting to be turned.

Footsteps behind him alerted him to Fallon's approach and Andrew turned to face him.

'You should have stayed in that fucking tunnel,' Fallon spat as he brandished the rod. 'Now I'm going to have to take your head off.'

Despite everything, Andrew could barely restrain himself from rolling his eyes. 'Jesus Christ, do you honestly think that you're just going to walk out of here?'

It was too dark to see in any detail, but it looked like Peggy had done a real number on the man's face, and Andrew didn't even try to ignore the rush of smug pride he felt at that; not when Fallon deserved everything he'd got.

Fallon's eyes narrowed. 'I'll take your head off, and then I'll start in on her Ladyship. I definitely won't make that quick though.'

The sensible part of Andrew knew that Fallon was needling him, trying to rile him up and increase the chances of him making a mistake that Fallon could then take advantage of. The less sensible part, though – the part that had never taken kindly to threats aimed at people he cared about – was itching to lash out.

He tightened his hands around the candlestick and remained silent.

Fallon was visibly disappointed when Andrew didn't immediately react to his taunt and looked ready to take another swing.

Sensing an opportunity, Andrew suddenly threw the candlestick towards Fallon.

Fallon reacted exactly as Andrew had expected – he dropped the rod in surprise as he brought his arms in protectively to stop the candlestick from smacking him in the face. He yelped in pain as the heavy metal collided with his forearms before it fell to the floor with a deafening clang.

Andrew dived forward and grabbed the fallen brass rod with a sense of victory, preparing to make a sprint for the tower.

He'd only made it a couple of strides when a muffled but distinctive sound brought him to a screeching halt, dread rushing through his veins.

The crack of a shotgun had erupted from beneath them, echoing up through the open hatch in the choir stalls to ring out in the vaulted ceiling of the cathedral.

Fallon seized on Andrew's distraction, grabbing his coat and yanking him backwards until he could throw a punch at his face.

Andrew dodged as best he could with his arm in a vice grip, but Fallon's fist still glanced off his cheekbone even as he managed to avoid getting his nose broken.

He kept his grip on the rod as tight as he could manage, holding onto it even when Fallon let go of his arm and pushed him roughly enough that he tripped backwards over his own feet and landed heavily on the stone floor.

The shock of hitting the ground travelled up his spine and he cried out in surprise.

Fallon reached down to grab the rod, but Andrew heaved it out of the way.

He kicked out with his right foot, hitting Fallon squarely in the shin before he swiped the rod around in a wild arc until it smashed into the side of Fallon's knee with a sickening crunch.

The howl of pain that exploded from Fallon's mouth was teeming with unfiltered fury, and Andrew knew that he was going to have to make his getaway before Fallon had the chance to recover. Desperate people might be dangerous, but desperate people filled with a rage like Fallon's were a whole different story. Thank Christ Fallon didn't have that gun anymore.

Andrew clambered to his feet, bones aching, and the ankle he'd turned down in the tunnels chose that moment to make a renewed effort to remind him that he'd already damaged himself. His face felt like it was on fire, and he'd definitely have a black eye for Christmas – his grandmother was going to be delighted – but he was still standing on his own two feet, and that was going to have to be enough.

As he reached the central aisle, he saw Jen jogging towards him.

'Sir, did you hear that shot?' she asked as she stood on the other side of the chairs.

'Where's Peggy?' Andrew looked over Jen's shoulder but saw

no movement.

'Still in the chapel,' Jen replied. 'She's well hidden.'

Jen's eyes suddenly went wide, and she yelled a warning to Andrew a split-second too late.

Andrew was knocked to the ground, and the rod flew out of his hand, skittering across the floor and between the rows of chairs, clanking as it bounced between the legs, finally coming to rest somewhere beyond Andrew's line of sight.

Fallon grabbed Andrew by the hair and was obviously planning on slamming his face into the stone slab beneath them.

Wheezing loudly, Andrew reared backwards, shaking Fallon off and taking a manic swing with his fist which hit nothing but air.

'Sir!' Jen yelled, pushing her way through the rows of chairs towards him.

'Get that rod!' Andrew yelled to her as Fallon advanced towards him again. 'You need to break the lock on the door!'

Fallon ran full pelt at Andrew, even as every step looked like agony, and threw his arms around him in a brutal rugby tackle that sent both of them careening back into the chairs.

Andrew tumbled, landing painfully on the frame of one chair and cracking the side of his head on another when Fallon landed hard on top of him, knocking the breath right out of him again.

The chairs collapsed in protest against their combined weight and the force of Fallon's attack, and Andrew saw stars when his skull finally made contact with the floor.

For a second Andrew just lay there, too stunned to move, as Fallon scrambled to his feet, and disappeared from view.

Andrew groaned in discomfort as he slowly rolled onto his stomach and tried to push himself to his knees.

Fallon was trying to rip the brass rod from Jen's hands as Andrew sluggishly rose to his feet again.

Jen managed to pull the rod completely out of Fallon's grip, but then Fallon sprang forwards, put his hands around the metal and forced it upwards with ruthless speed until it hit Jen in the throat with a vicious thwack.

She coughed loudly, dropping the bar as she reached up instinctively to protect herself from another attack.

Fallon snatched the rod and swung it towards Jen just as he had at Andrew earlier.

Jen managed to duck by pitching herself to the ground, but she was obviously struggling to breathe normally as she rolled onto her side, clutching at her neck.

Andrew lumbered towards them, and wrapped his hands around Fallon's face from behind, pressing his left hand tightly against what he knew was Fallon's damaged eye.

Fallon roared and tried to shake Andrew off, but Andrew held on more tightly, using his greater height to his advantage.

'Jen, are you alright?' he ground out, looking down at where his sergeant was sucking in great deep breaths.

She held up her hand and nodded, not quite able to answer verbally.

Andrew could really do with Fallon just giving up and he told him as much.

'Fuck off, Joyce!' Fallon roared, and with a renewed strength, he threw his right arm backwards, landing a vicious jab of his elbow in Andrew's stomach.

With a gasp of alarm, Andrew let go as he staggered backwards, bent double in response to the assault.

As he looked down, Andrew's blood ran cold; there, on the ground on the other side of the aisle, towards where Peggy was tucked away in the small chapel, was Fallon's gun. It must have escaped from Jen's pocket when she'd dived to the floor.

Fallon obviously spotted it at the same time, because he turned and gave Andrew another great shove while he was still hunched over.

The force of the push sent Andrew back into the pile of chairs he'd only just managed to haul himself free from and he found himself flat on his back again, staring up at the stone angels that seemed to be mocking him from the highest points of the room.

'Where've you stashed that little bitch?' Fallon snapped. 'Because I'm going to make sure you see me put a bullet in her head before I do you in.'

No, no, no. Andrew struggled to his feet, cursing his stupid long legs as he pulled them from beneath collapsed chairs, feet tangling in bars and folding mechanisms as he kicked them away desperately.

'Fallon!' he shouted as he managed to stand, but the other man ignored him, advancing towards the chapel.

Shit, he must have heard what Jen had said about Peggy being in the chapel and was taking a punt on that being the one she meant.

Andrew staggered towards Jen and reached down to help drag her to her feet.

'Fallon!' Andrew yelled again, moving as quickly as he could towards where Fallon was thudding heavily with an ever-worsening limp.

Fallon burst through the door into the chapel, and Andrew could see him moving through the room methodically, kicking over tables and chairs in his search for Peggy.

'Where is she, Jen?' Andrew asked in mounting terror as Fallon advanced through the room.

'She was right by the door,' Jen managed to croak out roughly.

Peggy must have heard Fallon coming and moved further into the room. There was no way out at the other end of the room – she'd be a sitting duck, and Andrew didn't doubt that Fallon would follow through on his threat.

Fallon approached the altar just as Andrew and Jen reached the door, and he wasted no time in ripping the cloth upwards, obviously assuming – as Andrew had – that Peggy was hiding beneath the draped material.

When there was no sign of Peggy, Andrew let out the breath he was holding.

Fallon turned back towards them, incensed. 'Where the fuck is she?'

A loud, creaking sound startled Andrew enough that he clumsily backed out of the room and limped towards the centre aisle, pulling Jen along with him with her arm draped around his shoulders, only to see Peggy slowly pulling open the large wooden doors in the distance. A tall man was standing beside her, and Andrew had no clue where the hell he'd come from. Had Peggy somehow found someone else in the cathedral? Someone with a key?

Fallon obviously understood that something was happening because Andrew heard heavy, uneven footsteps thundering through the chapel towards the door.

'Run!' Andrew yelled to Peggy and the man beside her as he and Jen stumbled towards the tower. 'Peggy, run!'

Peggy whirled towards him in surprise, and then slow-dawning horror creased her face. 'No!'

Her terrified cry was followed almost immediately by a loud, cracking sound and the heavy thump of a body hitting the ground.

Andrew stared at Peggy for a long moment in pure surprise before he turned slowly to see Fallon face down on the stone floor, and the gun lying far out of reach. Andrew's eyes drifted up again and he blinked owlishly when he found Lloyd grinning at him, the neck of that damn Pernod bottle held in his fist, with the rest of it in shards on the floor around his feet.

'Alright, boss?'

Andrew glanced at Jen, who seemed equally perplexed, and then went right back to gawping at Lloyd.

There was an enormous thud that echoed from the other end of the cathedral, followed by loud – and terribly familiar – swearing.

Higson.

Yet, before the relief of knowing that both Lloyd and Higson had managed to get out of the tunnels could settle over Andrew, a man came running out of the choir stalls, racing towards them with an expression of genuine terror on his face.

It took a good few seconds for Andrew to realise that he had seen the man before, though only ever in twenty-year-old photographs: Jimmy Prentice.

'Excuse me, sir! Sorry!' someone else suddenly yelled from behind Andrew, jostling him slightly as they raced right past him and straight towards the fleeing Prentice.

Andrew's gawping only got worse as he realised that the person who was in the midst of tackling Prentice to the ground right in front of him was DC Cooke from Chester House.

A hand then landed heavily on Andrew's shoulder startling him for the umpteenth time that minute.

'You alright, mate?' Mike asked in concern, before looking over to where Cooke had subdued Prentice. 'Oi, Cooke?'

'Sir?'

'Thursday nights, five-a-side over in Woodhouse Park,' Mike called back. 'I think we could do with you!'

Cooke looked delighted and nodded his agreement.

Andrew wondered if he'd hit his head even harder than he'd realised.

A handful of CID officers he recognised made their way past him into the cathedral, giving him confused nods as they did so.

In the distance, Higson finally made an appearance in the centre aisle. He had one arm crossed over his chest, and Marnie seemed to be propping him up on his other side as well as holding onto that bloody shotgun from earlier.

'Oh, shit, yeah!' Lloyd hissed and hurried over to take Marnie's place.

'What happened?' Andrew asked in alarm as Higson reached him and Jen, and he saw that there was a bloom of red soaking through Higson's shirtsleeve.

Higson looked down at where Fallon was groaning on the floor and smirked, though it looked quite pained. 'Well, it probably wouldn't have done for me to just let Jimmy shoot Parker now, would it?'

Andrew knew that the shock on Jen's face was mirrored on his own.

'Who would've got your breakfast?' Lloyd grinned, obviously supremely unconcerned that his boss was bleeding or that, apparently, he'd almost been shot himself.

Higson thumped Lloyd on the arm with a wince. 'Good lad.'

'Jesus Christ,' Andrew muttered, unable to stop himself.

'Didn't take you for the religious type.' Higson patted down his shirt and then looked annoyed. 'Where's my coat? My fags are in it.'

'Jesus Christ,' Andrew repeated, pressing his hands to his face.

'What the bloody hell is actually going on in here?'

Andrew turned at the crisp, unfamiliar voice and clamped his mouth shut against the string of surprised swearing that tried to escape at the sight.

Standing in the doorway, was the Chief Constable, and to say he looked *pissed* would have been the understatement of the year. He looked so aggravated that his face was almost purple with fury.

In direct contrast, an extremely washed-out, queasy looking Chambers was standing beside him.

Higson nudged Andrew in the ribs. 'Go on, get out of here. If I'd spent most of my day with Jimmy Prentice, I wouldn't want Charlie Boy and Driscoll yapping at me.'

'What?' Andrew asked dumbly.

Higson rolled his eyes.

'Peggy, sir,' Jen explained hoarsely, rubbing at her neck. 'She's just gone outside.'

Andrew looked around at everyone, satisfied that they were all intact enough, though perhaps with a bit too much bleeding, and limping, and bruising between them. Still, at least none of them had ended up in the canal this time.

Andrew gave Higson a respectful nod and squeezed Jen's shoulder before he turned away. He had no intention of interrupting Lloyd's cheerful explanation of the Pernod bottle to DC Cooke as Mike hauled Prentice to his feet.

The Chief Constable strode right past Andrew and towards Higson without a word, but Chambers stood stock still, warily watching Andrew as he approached, as though he thought he might be physically attacked where he stood.

Andrew glared stonily at Chambers as he stalked past, but he didn't stop; he didn't even slow down. Right then, he had far more important things to worry about than his arsehole former boss.

As Andrew stepped outside into the chilly night, he wrapped his coat around his aching limbs and took in the largest breath of crisp air he could manage.

There'd been moments down in the tunnels when he'd genuinely wondered if he'd ever be free of the stale, ancient fug that had seemed to permeate the very walls of the passageways and he knew that it would be a while before he took fresh air for granted again.

He looked around in confusion for a few moments as he saw no sign of either Swan sibling, or Marnie, which didn't tally with Jen or Higson's explanation, but as he took a few steps to the left, he spotted three figures walking slowly around the corner of the cathedral yard's boundary wall.

It took him longer than he'd have liked to persuade his body to move, aching as it did with each step, but eventually Andrew reached the Hanging Bridge pub to find Peggy sitting in the doorway. The door that Andrew had burst through earlier that night was still swung wide open behind her. Marnie and Charlie were standing either side of the door like a pair of mismatched guards, both staring worriedly down at their charge.

'Christ, Joycie, are you alright?' Charlie asked in alarm as Andrew approached.

Andrew waved away his concern. 'Fine, just don't touch me.'

Charlie pulled back the hand he was obviously about to slap Andrew's arm with and gave him a contrite little quirk of his lips.

'Alright?' Marnie asked carefully.

'Alright,' Andrew agreed. He nodded at her seriously. 'You were brilliant.'

Marnie grinned but she couldn't hide the bashful edge to the smile. 'I know. I got to scare the crap out of Prentice and everything. Though, I suppose, you lot weren't bad either.'

Andrew slowly reached out his hand, and Marnie stared at him confused for a long moment before realisation dawned and she clasped her own fingers around Andrew's and gave a single firm shake.

'It's a Christmas miracle,' Peggy muttered, looking up at the pair of them through hooded eyes. There was definitely amusement hiding somewhere beneath all the exhaustion.

Andrew, with obvious difficulty, lowered himself until he was sitting beside Peggy in the doorway. 'Ow.'

Charlie shook his head with a sympathetic wince. 'Right, you're both getting a paramedic each. Come on, Marnie, let's go and flag down an ambulance.'

'That's not how it works,' she replied slowly, but then jogged to catch up with him anyway.

Their arguing disappeared on the wind as they rounded the corner back towards the city centre.

'Do you need to get further away from the cathedral?' Andrew asked quietly, aware of just how close they still were to the building.

'Yes, but everything hurts too much for me to care,' Peggy sighed, dropping her head onto Andrew's shoulder.

Andrew blinked in surprise, before shaking himself and lifting his arm to wrap it around her. 'Christ, you're still freezing!'

'Sorry,' Peggy said, beginning to move away. 'I di-'

'No,' Andrew cut her off, pulling her even closer to his side. 'God, no, that's not what I meant.'

He really didn't want to think about how terrifyingly still Peggy had fallen in the tunnels; or the way that her breath had puffed weakly from her blue-tinged lips; or the way that those breaths had formed icy clouds of pure white that had seemed to suspend themselves in the air; or the way he'd been run through with terror when he'd thought that she'd –

No. He didn't want to think about *any* of it, and the physical proof of the rise and fall of her shoulders beside him made it all easier to forget.

For a long time, they sat together in comfortable silence, and Andrew watched the comings and goings at the cathedral with a detached sort of interest. He didn't know if Peggy had fallen asleep or not, but he'd be perfectly content to sit there on that uncomfortable threshold all night if it meant that she finally had some peace.

Eventually, the Chief Constable strode out of the building and headed for a car parked on the bridge. He glanced up towards where Andrew and Peggy were slumped together and immediately altered his direction to head towards them instead.

Andrew really, *really* hoped that he wasn't expected to stand.

'Very good work, DI Joyce,' the Chief Constable said brusquely. 'Not that I really understand *exactly* what it is that has been going on yet.'

'Sir,' Andrew replied with a very small, deferential nod that he tried not to disturb Peggy with.

'I'll need to speak to you further about all of this, you understand.'

Oh, Andrew understood alright. He could imagine the public relations nightmare that was already on its way. On a personal note, he would be doing everything possible to keep the Ballroom and Peggy out of it.

'You should really think about returning to CID, you know,' the Chief Constable added. 'They could do with someone like you.'

Andrew didn't think that the Chief Constable would like to hear his reply to that suggestion, so he kept it to himself.

The Chief Constable then glanced at Peggy, who appeared to be squinting up at him. He opened his mouth to say something, clearly thought better of getting further involved in whatever the hell was going on and just gave her a short nod, before turning on his heel and returning to his car.

Almost immediately, Chambers exited the cathedral, following the same path as the Chief Constable. He paused when he saw Andrew, but then Higson prodded him in the back with his hand.

'Keep moving, Dickie,' Higson growled loudly. 'Cusack here will give me that shotgun back without question.'

Jen frowned in a way that told Andrew that there was no way Higson was ever seeing that shotgun again, and he almost laughed out loud.

'You two!' Higson called towards the pub, waggling his eyebrows as he pointed between Andrew and Peggy. 'I want you both at Tib Street tomorrow.'

Andrew waved his hand in a show of agreement, just as Charlie and Marnie walked back around the corner only a split second before an ambulance pulled up behind them.

'See!' Charlie grinned triumphantly, hooking his thumb over his shoulder as two perplexed paramedics climbed out and stared at the collection of cars haphazardly parked all over Victoria Street.

'Any chance we could just sneak away in a taxi?' Peggy asked, words slightly slurred as she yawned widely.

Andrew did laugh out loud at that, and he looked over at the motley bunch of people that somehow made up his life these days. 'Sorry, Peg, I think we might be stuck with them.'

THIRTY

Even though he'd only slept for a few scant hours, Andrew felt significantly closer to himself by the time the next morning dawned.

The night before, the paramedics had promptly concluded that Andrew's head had survived its unpleasant meeting with the cathedral floor without concussion, and he'd chosen not to mention the multitudinous other parts of his body that had also collided with multitudinous other things just in case this spurred on a renewed interest in checking him over more thoroughly. He'd known he'd been fine, whereas Peggy had been demonstrably *not*.

She'd been listless and obviously unhappy, and Andrew had hovered silently, keeping his eye on her, until he'd been given his marching orders from the ambulance in stereo by both a paramedic and his own boss. He'd walked as far enough away as it had taken for Higson to stop glaring at him, and then not taken a single additional step.

Higson, meanwhile, had cantankerously refused to consent to anything beyond the cleaning and speedy wrapping of his wound which, to be fair, hadn't really been more than a bad graze that had been aggravated when he'd had to hoist both himself and Jimmy Prentice out of a tunnel that had been designed for people less broad than either of them had ever been.

Despite Higson's gruffness, *he'd* been allowed to loiter by the ambulance, content to remind anyone and everyone that he'd been shot in the name of keeping Lloyd in one piece and therefore could stand wherever the hell he wanted, while the paramedics continued their observations of Peggy and briefly turned their attentions to Jen as well.

Jen had barely let anyone look at her neck, announcing that she was absolutely fine, but she'd promised that she would immediately call someone should she so much as *think* that there was anything wrong.

In the end, the paramedics had concluded that they were more than happy to release the majority of these grumpy messes back into the wild, but that Peggy's very high temperature and obvious signs of concussion were reason enough to whisk her away to hospital, despite her surprisingly vocal protestations.

It had taken Andrew far too long to remember why Peggy might have a particular hatred of hospitals.

Still, he'd been unable to do anything about it. Peggy had scared the living daylights out of him already that night and he couldn't in any good conscience let her leave the cathedral in the care of anyone but medical professionals, no matter how much he wished that he could have whisked her away himself.

Andrew had made sure to quietly recommend to the paramedics that they didn't take Peggy to the Royal Infirmary and had been very forthright about it when they'd tried to protest. He didn't want Peggy in the same building as Rex Hughes for even a second, no matter how good the reason might be, and so he'd held his ground until they agreed to take her elsewhere.

Charlie had clapped Andrew hard on the shoulder with a promise that he'd call him once he had an update, and then he'd driven off after the ambulance with Marnie in the passenger seat.

As the only member of the Ballroom who'd walked, rather than limped, out of the cathedral, Lloyd had been the one to get behind the wheel of the Volvo that definitely didn't belong to Higson and drive them all – Mike included – back to Tib Street.

When they'd parked, Andrew had stopped Lloyd before they'd reached the door and tried to genuinely thank him for saving his life earlier that evening. Andrew was uncomfortably aware that if Lloyd hadn't incapacitated Fallon in the exact moment he had done, then Andrew would likely have a bullet in the back of his skull.

Lloyd had only wrinkled his nose.

'Nah, come off it boss,' he'd replied with a self-conscious shrug as they'd climbed the stairs to the Ballroom, 'you'd have done exactly the same for any of the rest of us. We're a team.'

It hadn't been until he'd heard voices as they'd reached the landing that Andrew had remembered that Annie Higson, along with Beth and Lily, had remained on Tib Street when the rest of them had hared off to Hanging Bridge.

Annie had shrieked, tears springing to her eyes, when she'd heard that her husband had been injured, and she'd thrown her arms around Higson's neck.

On any other day, Andrew knew that Higson would have yelled at the rest of them just for being in the same room as him when he showed any form of affection for another person, but his boss hadn't said anything; he'd just wrapped Annie in a tight embrace and spoken to her in a voice too quiet for the rest of them to hear.

Annie had then immediately pulled Jen (*Jenny!*), Lloyd and Andrew into crushing embraces one-by-one, and Andrew would admit that he'd hugged her back just as hard.

'Where's your Peggy?' she'd asked suddenly as she'd released Andrew, looking around the room, just as she'd done in her kitchen a few days earlier.

'She's just had to pop to the hospital, Annie, love,' Higson had interjected firmly. 'Nothing to worry about; she's just had a bit of a time of it, that's all.'

Andrew hadn't been sure whether the confidence in that response had been for his benefit or for Annie's, but he'd appreciated hearing it anyway.

Lily, unsurprisingly, had been all but inconsolable at the news that they'd finally *got* Jimmy Prentice, and Beth hadn't been far behind her when it came to tears. Annie had dutifully wrapped her arms around both of the women on the blue sofa.

Higson had got a bit grouchier at that point – his arm had obviously been bothering him, no matter what he'd tried to suggest – and so they'd called it a night.

Lloyd had left them with every intention of seeing Fiona, even though it had been nearly three in the morning, and Annie had climbed behind the wheel of the Volvo – not hers either, apparently – to take her husband, Jen, Lily and Beth all back to the Higson house in Withington.

Jen had protested, of course, but Annie would brook no argument, and Andrew had only been able to shrug tiredly as he'd watched his sergeant as she was shepherded into the Volvo with a look of bleak acceptance on her face.

Mike had then driven Andrew back to Gatley, and they'd both been silent for most of the journey.

'Mate…' Mike had started hesitantly when they'd almost reached Acacia Road. 'Do you lot do this sort of thing all the time?'

Andrew had run a weary hand over his face, flinching as he'd grazed his bruised cheekbone. 'Not *all* the time.'

Mike had accepted that with a nod, but he'd obviously been struggling with another question because he'd opened his mouth and closed it again multiple times by the time they'd parked outside Andrew's house.

'What is it?' Andrew had asked, even though he hadn't been at all in the right frame of mind to deal with the hundreds of questions that Mike must have had about the Ballroom.

'It's just…' Mike trailed off. 'Marnie Driscoll?'

'Yeah, I know,' Andrew had replied, because what else could he actually say to that?

What did you say to someone who'd seen a murder victim pop into existence right before their eyes? Christ, that had actually happened to Andrew, and he still couldn't explain any of it to himself even though he'd had eighteen months to try.

At that, Andrew had thanked Mike for the lift and agreed to be right back there on the pavement at eight the next morning so that they could drive back to the Ballroom again. Higson had been very keen to impress upon Mike just how everything that had happened that night was Tib Street business – not CID – and that Mike was part of that business up until such time Higson decided otherwise. Mike had sensibly agreed.

Andrew had slouched into his house and greeted Rob quietly before he'd taken a look at the state of his brand-new coat and concluded that it was going to have to go straight to the dry cleaners in the morning if there was any hope of resurrecting it.

Once he'd set his alarm, he'd then promptly passed out on his bed unable to even think about throwing himself under the shower.

He hadn't moved an inch by the time his alarm clock had startled him back into awareness and he'd hurriedly got himself ready to leave before Mike arrived to pick him up

Despite having still-damp hair, and no coat, Andrew couldn't help the sigh of relief as he climbed into Mike's car. It felt as though a conclusion had finally been reached, although any sense of respite was tempered by the fact that he hadn't heard anything from either Charlie or Marnie about how Peggy had fared.

Mike looked bone-tired, and Andrew realised that he really did owe his friend a significant apology, and an even more significant explanation, and so he tried to provide both to the best of his ability as they drove back into the city centre.

'Prentice was looking for *treasure?*' Mike asked as he turned onto Tib Street.

'As far as I understand it, yeah,' Andrew replied, scanning the street for any sign of a car ridiculous enough to belong to Charlie Swan.

'And Peggy really can speak to dead people?' Mike's expression reminded Andrew of the general mix of excitement and dread that Lloyd always exhibited when it came to the general concept of ghosts.

'She can.'

'Christ.' Mike switched off the engine. 'And you'd rather be here than back in CID?'

Andrew looked up at the decrepit building full of things – and people – that terrified him and shrugged. 'Every day.'

Miked snorted with incredulous amusement as he climbed out of the car. 'Whatever floats your boat, mate.'

Andrew rolled his eyes and led Mike up to the Ballroom.

'Oh, you've finally decided to join us, have you, lads?' Higson boomed as they entered, but there wasn't really any heat to the words.

Andrew headed to sit on the edge of his desk, gratefully taking the black coffee that Lloyd handed to him on the way past. There was no sign of either Swan, and he had to swallow down his disappointment.

'You alright?' he asked Jen instead, who was sitting at her own desk.

'Fine, sir,' she replied, though she looked slightly more shellshocked than Andrew expected. 'You?'

Andrew nodded.

The doors opened again, and Marnie walked in. This unusually understated style of arrival had obviously been employed as a courtesy to Mike, but Andrew still saw the other man's eyes widen in astonishment anyway.

'Peggy only got back from the hospital an hour ago,' Marnie announced to the room, but she kept her eyes on Andrew as she spoke 'They've got her on all sorts of pills and things, but they don't seem too worried about her anymore; she'll be fine as long as she gets a good rest. Charlie's on the warpath, making sure that nobody gets anywhere near her.'

Andrew nodded his thanks.

'Good,' Higson added brusquely.

The doors opened once more to admit Dolly, who waved at Andrew entirely because she knew that it would make him squirm.

Lloyd hopped off his desk and picked up a stash of white and green bakery bags before doing a circuit of the room, dropping off a bacon sandwich to each person, including Dolly. When he reached Marnie, he handed her a bag of Jelly Babies instead. 'So you've got something to hold.'

She grinned at him.

'Lawson, you're first,' Higson proclaimed around a bit of bacon sandwich, and Mike twitched in surprise at being addressed. 'What happened when you and Charlie Boy went to Chester House? I've heard the official version, so now I want yours.'

'Sir,' Mike said, looking like he wasn't sure if he was supposed to stand up or not. In the end, he stayed on the blue sofa but tucked the half-eaten bacon sandwich back into the bag, even though Higson hadn't had a problem talking around his own breakfast.

'When we got there, Chambers had already had an absolute bollocking from the Chief Constable,' Mike said, and then looked at Higson. 'Er…'

'Carry on, mate,' Lloyd piped up. 'The boss doesn't care what you say about any of that lot over at Chester House. No offence.'

Mike waved that comment away, obviously assuming that was the safest response. 'Well, yeah, so Chambers was in the bad books for publicly announcing that DCI Higson had been involved in Sean Kelly's death. Especially when it was pretty damn obvious from the recording that Kelly had been speaking under some form of duress.'

Jen looked over in surprise. 'The Chief Constable had heard the tape? How?'

Mike looked over at Andrew and then grinned at Jen. 'Chambers told Joyce about the recording when we were at Strangeways yesterday; he passed that information on to me and suggested that certain other people might be interested in what was on the tape. It wasn't actually too difficult for me to get my hands on it and get it in front of someone who'd be interested in hearing it. They then got it to the Chief Constable after that.'

Andrew hadn't had a huge amount of faith that Mike would have been able to get the tape quickly enough. It had been an afterthought when he and Lloyd had been heading back to the car after leaving Chambers behind; Andrew had run back into Strangeways to hurriedly leave Mike with the idea in the hope that he'd be able to do *something* with it. When Mike hadn't mentioned the tape upon arrival at Tib Street the night before, Andrew had assumed that he hadn't been successful, and then he'd forgotten all about it anyway when they'd been rushing to locate Peggy.

'Bloody good idea that, boss,' Lloyd said raising his coffee in a toast in Andrew's direction.

'Chambers was pissed,' Mike continued as he relaxed into telling his story, 'so he wasn't delighted when I came in with Charlie. He had no clue who Charlie was, of course, but he tore into him as much as he did to me anyway. Chambers wouldn't listen to a word we said about Prentice being involved; he point-blank refused to accept it, apparently utterly convinced that Prentice has been in Spain this whole time and that Joyce was just utterly deluded about the whole thing. He was perfectly happy for whatever plan the Ballroom had come up with to go to complete shit while he kept his nose out of it. He wouldn't even let us take Cooke, and he thinks Cooke's only good for answering the phone.'

'So, how the hell did you get the Chief Constable to the cathedral?' Lloyd asked.

Marnie, surprisingly, snorted with laughter. 'How do you think?'

Oh, Jesus, Andrew thought, knowing exactly where this explanation was heading. 'Charlie.'

Mike nodded. 'Charlie nicked the phone at the desk downstairs. He made about fifteen phone calls in ten minutes, and by the end of them he had the Chief Constable's home address.'

'Of course he did,' Andrew shook his head.

'He's very persistent.'

'He's a fucking menace, Mike,' Andrew replied wearily, though he was supremely glad about that fact just then.

'So, we went out to Bowdon and Charlie drove right up to the door of this massive house. Then he just leant on the car horn until the Chief came downstairs in his dressing gown. He was really, *really* pissed.' Mike grimaced. 'Nowhere near as pissed as Charlie was, though.'

Jesus, Andrew thought again.

'Lovely,' Higson concluded, wiping ketchup from his beard with his hand. 'Well, that mostly tallies with what our delightful Chief Constable said this morning, though he left out the dressing gown – I'll be sure to bring that up when he calls back with an update on Dickie Chambers. Bastard owes me a good laugh anyway. Do you know, I had to be in here at seven to talk to him, while he was no doubt still tucked up in his cushy bed? Did he seem the type to have a phone right next to the bed, Lawson?'

Mike looked like he didn't know how he was supposed to answer such a question.

'The only saving grace was that it got me out of Annie's hysterical clutches,' Higson continued, looking around for a likely candidate to hand him more breakfast.

Lloyd passed him another bacon sandwich, while Andrew thought it was unlikely that brilliantly practical Annie Higson had been *hysterical* at any point.

'You'd think I'd had my head knocked off with the way she was mithering me,' Higson added, unwrapping the sandwich and taking an enormous bite. 'She called the bloody boys over! John turned up at bleeding five o'clock this morning, and his brother ten minutes later – *mardy arse.*'

At the oblique reference to Lawrie Higson, Andrew's head whipped towards Jen so quickly he nearly overbalanced. Was that what the shellshocked expression had been about?

Jen was pointedly hiding behind her coffee mug and avoiding Andrew's gaze.

Higson apparently wasn't done. 'And the *cheek* the pair of them had, telling m-'

'What happened with Chambers?' Andrew dared to interject, feeling the need to rescue the situation before it descended into further chaos.

'Oh, you'll like this bit,' Higson grinned, turning to him and apparently not taking offence at Andrew's interruption for once. 'Saint Dickie of Glowing Reputations has been suspended, pending a full investigation.'

Andrew's mouth dropped open in surprise. 'Really?'

Higson's grin became a smirk. 'He's offered up his resignation, obviously thinking it'll get him out of this entire shitshow without a mark on him, but somehow I don't think that's going to happen.'

Andrew got the feeling that the 'somehow' might be down to the Ballroom making sure of it.

'Oh, and on the subject of offering things,' Higson continued around another bite of his sandwich, crumbs spraying onto the desk that Andrew had spent ages tidying only the day before. 'I've been offered a lovely little retirement package.'

'What?' Andrew asked dumbly as Lloyd and Jen gasped in alarm. 'You're not taking it, are you?'

On some level, Andrew couldn't believe that he was asking that question with so much trepidation.

Higson snorted loudly. 'What? And leave you lot unattended? I wasn't here for two days and look what shit you got yourselves into.'

Andrew thought that was patently unfair. He folded his arms. 'Did you leave that file out for us to find?'

Higson looked deeply offended. 'I did absolutely no such bloody thing! Your magic cupboard's obviously at work again, Joyce.'

Mike looked over at him questioningly and mouthed 'magic cupboard?'

Andrew ignored him because he was worried that Mike might actually die of fright if he knew some of the other things that had happened in the building of late.

'What's happened with Fallon and Prentice?' Jen asked, sensing everything getting a bit tangential again.

'Well, Fallon is fucked for all of this,' Higson explained mildly. 'The idiot kept records of all of his communication with Prentice, and every payment he'd received for handing over information about our cases. He's been at it since Frank Jackson's funeral, just like we thought. Still seems to think that having 'friends in high places' will save him even after he tried to kill Joyce and Her Maj.'

Andrew shuddered at the reminder.

'Fallon had been paying a few of his little pals in uniform to follow you lot home last week,' Higson added. 'He couldn't be sure that you didn't know anything about Prentice or what had happened with Lily the first-time round, and I think he was hoping that one of you would lead him to Miss Jones eventually. He gave them all up, of course, so I doubt any of those daft pricks will be making it to CID any time soon.'

Andrew shook his head again. It still amazed him that Fallon had managed to show some capacity for planning after all these years.

'As for Jimmy Prentice…' Higson trailed off and clasped his hands together on his desk. He suddenly looked far more dangerous than Andrew had ever seen him before. 'We've got him for Sean Kelly, and Lily's agreed to talk to us, *officially*. She wants to see her parents, and Beth wants her kids and her family to know the truth.'

'Peggy wants to be in the room when we interview Lily,' Andrew piped up, remembering the agreement he'd made in Bombay Palace. 'She thinks it'll be important for Lily to know that she has Violet there. I agree.'

'So do I.' Higson nodded his consent. 'Lily's got enough dirt on Prentice to make sure he never sees the light of day again.'

Higson then cleared his throat and looked each one of his team – including Marnie – right in the eye in full seriousness. 'And we're also going to find Davy, and we're going to give him the funeral that he deserves.'

'Yes, sir,' they chorused in sombre promise. Even Dolly bowed her head.

'Boss?' Lloyd asked, gesturing towards Higson.

'What?'

'Was there actually treasure down there last night?'

Higson shrugged. 'No idea. Jimmy's not as young as he used to be, and when Fallon buggered off, he had nobody to do his grunt work for him; he never did like to get his hands dirty.'

Andrew shook his head. 'Whatever the hell is down there should probably stay buried.'

Lloyd looked over at him. 'What actually happened to you lot in the tunnels, boss?'

Andrew and Jen glanced at each other with deep unhappiness etched on both their faces.

'Something happened to Peggy down there,' Andrew replied

eventually, and he felt the silence around him sharpen with tension. Even Marnie was looking at him like she had no idea what had happened. 'I think we almost lost her.'

That was the closest Andrew was going to get to the truth just then. He wasn't looking forward to being left to his own thoughts about it all later as it was, he certainly didn't want to share any of them publicly.

'Well, I'm sure she'll be right as rain in no time,' Lloyd said with forced cheer. 'Back in the Ballroom.'

Not if she goes to New York, Andrew thought. Not if she realises how much safer she'd be if she just stayed away; not if Andrew asked her to come back to the Ballroom and she said no – If she did, he knew that wouldn't be able to argue with her.

'Oh, what about Hughes?' Mike asked and then tried to backtrack immediately in a panic when he remembered that Marnie was in the room.

Marnie only rolled her eyes at him. 'He'll live.'

'Unfortunately,' Higson muttered, opening and closing his hand in Lloyd's direction until a packet of biscuits was tossed his way.

Andrew was surprised that Marnie didn't even try and rebuke him for such a comment.

'And what about the bloke that stabbed him?' Lloyd asked.

'Fallon had paid him off,' Higson explained, inspecting the Chocolate Hobnob in his hand. 'He'd also promised to get him out of Strangeways early, which will obviously *not* be happening. Hopefully, the lad's at least learned not to put his trust in complete twats. Oi, why have they put chocolate on these now?'

'People like chocolate,' Lloyd replied with a shrug.

Higson made a face but then ate the biscuit in two bites anyway.

Andrew just about caught Mike's look of utter disbelief that this place and these people actually existed; Andrew knew exactly how he felt.

Closing his eyes for a second of peace while he had a large sip of coffee was a mistake, and Andrew probably should have expected the pen that was thrown across the room at him.

'Christ,' he yelped as his eyes snapped open in surprise and he nearly dropped the mug.

'The only person with an excuse to be unconscious right now is Her Ladyship,' Higson grumbled. '*You* can get started on all your paperwork.'

Andrew really wanted to throw the pen back, but he made himself just pick it up and put it on his desk. Higson might be in a more benevolent mood than usual, but he'd still kick Andrew's arse out of the door if he pushed him too far.

Door.

Andrew looked around the room, frowning. 'Did any of you speak to whoever it was that helped Peggy open the door last night?'

'Who?' Higson asked, raising his eyebrows.

'The man,' Andrew explained. 'He must have had the key.'

'What man?' Lloyd asked, looking at Andrew like he thought he'd lost it.

'You probably missed him,' Andrew replied. 'Jen, you know who I mean?'

Jen shook her head slowly. 'Peggy opened that door by herself, sir. I was standing right next to you the whole time.'

'You must have hit your head harder than you thought,' Lloyd offered, even though he sounded unconvinced by his own theory.

Andrew saw Higson smirking at him, and when he looked away, he only made matters ten times worse by catching Dolly's eye instead. She just raised her eyebrows at him and smiled.

'Lawson,' Higson boomed suddenly, cutting Andrew's nervous breakdown short, 'you're alright, but it's time for you to go back to the other arseholes at CID now. I believe this lot is going to fill me in on how they'll be tidying up a fifteen-year-old missing persons case by Thursday night.'

Andrew almost groaned out loud. In the chaos of everything else, he'd completely forgotten about Alan Jermyn, the disappearing exotic animal salesman, who was due to arrive back in Manchester on a Christmas Eve flight.

'Sir,' Mike bobbed his head towards Higson as he walked to the door, before turning back to look over at Andrew. 'Mate, I'll drive you back to Gatley later, yeah? But then you're taking me for at least three pints.'

Andrew couldn't argue with that. He thought he might need at least three pints himself.

THIRTY-ONE

When Peggy had finally limped back into her bedroom after being released from the hospital, moderately concussed and feeling sick to her stomach, a cloudy, insipid dawn had already broken over Butterton, washing everything with an unpleasant yellow tinge.

Charlie had pulled the curtains closed while Peggy had stumbled into her bathroom, wanting more than anything to brush her teeth. She hadn't been able to face the idea of a shower just then, not after hours of doctors and nurses poking and prodding at her face and head, leaving her feeling fragile in a way that she knew she'd resent if she'd had the energy to do so.

When she'd caught sight of her reflection she'd put her toothbrush down in surprise. Her face had been so pale that she'd looked almost bloodless, which had only made the strawberry flush of the bruising on her cheekbone stand out even more prominently than it would have done on any other day. Bolts of black and grey God-knows-what had streaked through her hair, which had already darkened a few shades under layers of subterranean dust and grime. When she'd reached up to run her fingers over the tender spot at the back of her skull, she'd found her hair tangled and matted from a mixture of blood and antiseptic.

She'd prodded at the cut on her lip with her tongue, unable to just leave it be as she'd been instructed by the rotating parade of very concerned doctors who'd suggested to her, at least fifteen times, that she should report the 'obvious assault' to the police; she'd replied, the same number of times, that it was already a police matter. In the end, Charlie had swooped in to handle it all, doling out phone numbers for Higson, for Andrew, and for the bloody Chief Constable of Greater Manchester Police, should anyone at the hospital require any further context.

Peggy had then all but passed out on her bed and stayed there until well after the sun had set once more, with only the vaguest recollection of being woken for another dose of antibiotics and painkillers at some point when it had still been light outside.

It had taken a long time for her lethargic thoughts to arrange themselves into any semblance of order, but when they had, she'd been unreasonably frustrated that nobody had woken her so that she could go to Tib Street as Higson had requested.

Charlie had begun his rebuttal with an air of extreme apology, but as Peggy's frustration had grown so had her brother's snippiness, until he'd eventually snapped and Peggy had witnessed his tearful, halting breakdown about how they'd all been so worried about her when she'd disappeared from Chester House.

Peggy had immediately felt dreadful and climbed down from her high horse without further argument. Without the fog of irritability that had been clutching at her since she'd woken up, Peggy had been able to see that her brother was correct, of course; she really was in no fit state to be on Tib Street. Really, she wasn't even in a fit state to leave her bedroom.

With a meek apology, she'd promptly gone back to bed and slept for another twelve hours.

Wednesday had passed in much the same way, with the dazed monotony of sleep-wake-medicate-sleep broken only by a couple of visits from Charlie, and a brief check-in from a very pinched Aunt Emmeline.

Then, just as Peggy had been settling into bed for the night, Marnie had knocked on her door, unusually hesitant in her approach.

They'd had a frank – *blessedly short* – but draining discussion about their previous argument, and Marnie had explained to Peggy what had happened to Rex in Strangeways on Monday morning.

Up to that point, Peggy had been peripherally aware that something involving Marnie's ex-fiancé had been the tipping point in the Ballroom's investigation, but she hadn't known the intricacies of it until Marnie had laid out the facts with a strange detachment. Peggy had, of course, had plenty of follow-up questions, but she'd remained silent, with neither the energy, nor the desire, to hear the answers in that very moment.

Marnie had also given a recap of the events at the Ballroom the day before, and Peggy was grateful that she'd at least had some representation – she'd be lying if she said that a fear of being sidelined by the team after being the only one to actually be hospitalised hadn't crossed her mind a number of times.

Peggy had also been pleased to hear that Andrew had voiced her wish to be involved when Lily – and therefore, *Violet* – gave her official account of everything that had happened in 1967, just as he'd agreed.

The conversation with Marnie had left Peggy fit for nothing more than another uncharacteristically extended sleep, and the next thing Peggy was aware of was the gently dawning realisation that it was already late morning on Christmas Eve.

She showered and dressed in yet another pair of clean pyjamas. There was no point in digging out actual clothes when she wouldn't be leaving the house any time soon. Furthermore, she had to conserve her flagging energy for Christmas lunch with her father the next day; even a head injury – which had apparently been explained away by Charlie as nothing more than an unfortunate accident – wasn't enough of an excuse to duck out on a protracted, uncomfortable meal with the man.

Peggy glanced in the mirror and grimaced; she looked only marginally better than she had on Tuesday morning and still felt like death warmed up, if not quite like death itself any longer. The ugly bruising had dulled from scarlet to plum, but it looked no less stark against her pallid face.

It didn't escape her notice that she looked like how most people would probably expect a ghost to look, and she shivered at the thought.

Rubbing her arms against the chill that she still hadn't managed to shake, Peggy reached for the cardigan she'd discarded before her shower and pulled it back on, tugging the sleeves down over her fingers. She'd taken her temperature earlier, so she knew that despite feeling cold she was actually still significantly warmer than she was supposed to be.

Peggy couldn't quite face the idea of climbing back into bed and so she perched herself on the window seat and looked glumly out over the grounds and towards the village of Butterton itself. From where she sat, it wasn't at all possible to see Manchester, but she still felt the pull of the Ballroom drawing her away from her bedroom.

When he'd slouched against the back of the ambulance that Peggy had been sitting in, Higson had been at pains to point out that he'd call her as soon as she was able to stay upright under her own steam. Apparently, he'd spent the months when he'd been concerned about Peggy hiding 'the really good stuff' from Andrew and the others, and he was sick to the back teeth of listening to them whinging about being bored. He must have known then that there was no way she'd be making it to Tib Street the following morning, even if she hadn't.

Even though Peggy didn't remember much of what had happened in the passageways beneath the cathedral, she could recall the distressed expressions on Andrew and Jen's faces in startling clarity, and she thought that they might both actually be perfectly content to be bored for a while after recent events.

A small convoy of white vans abruptly appeared on the driveway, meandering past the lake and Peggy frowned at them as they approached the house. What on earth was that about?

Deciding that she didn't actually have the capacity to care just then, she turned away from the window and glanced around her bedroom. Her eyes landed on the box of chocolate snowflakes from Bowness – the ones that she might have bought for Albany – and she lurched slightly at the realisation that she hadn't thought to call him after her ordeal, nor had she once thought about the fact that she was due in New York the following week.

And that, Peggy thought, wasn't really good enough, was it?

Peggy had never been an out of sight, out of mind sort of person, and Albany had done nothing to deserve being no more than an afterthought. Hand on heart, Peggy would be forced to admit that the fact that she hadn't thought about him, even fleetingly, in days probably meant something.

God, she wished she had a cup of tea, just so that she had something to hold in her hands to make her feel slightly less jittery. Plus, in Peggy's experience, the answer to many a question could be found upon staring into a mug for a significant period of time. Instead, she picked up the chocolates and then returned to her previous perch.

Albany was one of the very, very few people who knew what Peggy was capable of, and he'd never doubted her ability, nor made fun of her for it; he'd simply *believed* her and had then asked her out for dinner instead of fleeing in the opposite direction. They hadn't spent a huge amount of time together in the scheme of things, but he'd filled her empty summer days before he'd gone back to New York, and Peggy really had believed that she'd take him up on his invitation to visit.

Now, though, she had an unsurprising, yet still unsettling, reality to contend with: the truth being that when she'd been confronted with her own mortality, there hadn't been even momentary hesitation about the direction in which her thoughts had run, and it hadn't been towards Albany Cohen. Now she had to wonder if she'd simply co-opted the man – entirely without his permission or knowledge – into her efforts to keep her mind off somebody else, simply because it had been *convenient*.

Peggy pressed the tips of her fingers to her forehead and released a gusty sigh of unhappiness, deeply displeased with her own conduct and the utter mess that she'd got herself into through her own poor decisions.

On Monday night, when she'd managed to pull the cathedral doors open, she'd almost fallen to her knees in relief, knowing that she'd cleared the path for Andrew and Jen to get out of there, but then Fallon had pulled a gun on Andrew's back and Peggy had never before experienced terror like she had in that moment.

But it hadn't just been the fear that had blindsided her – it had also been the great wallop of understanding that she might have made a terrible miscalculation in thinking that distancing herself from the Ballroom would, in any discernible way, diminish the feelings that she'd tried so hard to smother before they could further damage one of the most important relationships in her life.

The knock on her bedroom door was welcomed, especially when her visitor was revealed to be Charlie bearing two mugs of tea.

'What are you doing out of bed?' he asked.

At his sister's raised eyebrow, he added with an eyeroll, 'Not that you aren't perfectly capable of making your own decisions, obviously, but you did still have a sky-high temperature last night.'

'I just needed to be up,' Peggy replied, accepting the tea more gratefully than the unsolicited advice.

As Peggy was already sitting in her brother's favoured perch, Charlie took his own mug to the dressing table and sat down on the stool. 'Don't show your face downstairs.'

'I wasn't planning on it, but why not?' Peggy asked, blowing over the rim of her mug.

'Apparently, Father wasn't joking when he said he was hosting a reception tonight. Caterers and party planners everywhere!'

'Really?'

'Yes, *really*, and he'll want to inflict it on you as well if he thinks you're even remotely mobile enough.'

She supposed that would explain the fleet of vans, at least.

'But he hates parties,' Peggy argued, 'and most people, for that matter.'

'Yes, but he loves the fact that he'll be getting one up on *Her*.'

There was no question of to whom Charlie was referring, of course.

'Apparently, she'd booked out half the Midland Hotel for a Christmas party of her own – months and months ago, it seems – and it's why she was here the other day. Here to complain about the fact that she'd just heard about a rather last-minute event that had been announced only last week.'

Peggy had forgotten about all of *that* as well.

Charlie grimaced. 'Turns out, a significant portion of her guest list has defected to the rival party, considering this one's being hosted by the Earl of Acresfield himself, and at Butterton House, no less. Old-fashioned misogyny and avarice at work, of course.'

'Of course,' Peggy sighed, though she couldn't quite bring herself to, in any way, feel sad that someone had found a way to ruin her mother's – and therefore Edgar's – day, no matter the driving force behind it.

'Marnie's determined to come with me to the party,' Charlie added. 'I'm minded to just let it happen, because she'll only make a scene if I don't.'

Peggy hummed in agreement. She certainly didn't have the wherewithal to participate in the inevitable debate that would occur; plus, her relationship with Marnie still felt precarious enough that they could probably both do without any additional antagonism being brought into it for the time being.

Charlie finally caught sight of the chocolates in Peggy's hand.

'If you're thinking of opening those, I wouldn't say no. I tried to nab us a few things from the kitchen, but one of the caterers threatened to slap me if I so much as looked at the fridge for too long. She didn't seem the type to be kidding about such things, either.'

Peggy hesitated, holding the box a bit tighter for a moment.

'Though if you're saving them,' Charlie added, raising his hands in apology.

Taking a deep breath that made her ribs ache, Peggy handed the box to her brother. 'You can have them.'

He eagerly accepted the chocolates with a grin of thanks.

Peggy steeled herself. 'Charlie, I'm not going to New York.'

'Of course you're not,' Charlie replied as though he thought that she was stating the obvious. 'There's not a chance they'd let you on the plane in the state you're in. I'm sure you can always go in January.'

'No,' Peggy corrected as Charlie began tearing into the box. 'I mean I'm not going at all.'

Charlie paused, cellophane crunching noisily as he set the open box down next to his mug. 'Not at all?'

Peggy shook her head, wincing with regret as her skull throbbed. 'No.'

'Dare I ask why?'

'Probably best not to.' Peggy wrinkled her nose.

Charlie shot her a terribly calculating look, picked up his tea and stared at it for a few moments, then put it back down with an audible thud. 'Peg, I hope you haven't made that decision because you think that you need to stay. Look, I know that I haven't exactly been the most encouraging about it all, which, in hindsight, might have been a bit, *well*, selfish.'

Although he hadn't actually said anything of the kind outright to her, Charlie had hinted, more than once, at a completely unfounded concern that Peggy might not come back once she'd experienced a world that wasn't just a constant roundabout of Butterton –Tib Street – Butterton. As Charlie had always had a big mouth, Peggy knew that if he'd thought that there was even a chance that his sister might leave for good, everyone else would also know about it, whether they wanted to or not.

Now that she thought about it, when Marnie had told Peggy that she was worried that she'd fade from existence if Peggy was too far away, that had obviously come from listening to Charlie's scaremongering about Peggy's non-existent emigration plans, rather than based on anything Peggy had said herself.

And while Lloyd's vocal disdain for the idea of the trip likely did stem from his general distaste for any city that wasn't Manchester, rather than it being a case of him spouting propaganda on behalf of Charlie, it had been obvious to Peggy that her brother had already been mouthing off about the upcoming trip on a previous night out, because Lloyd hadn't shown any real surprise when Marnie had imparted the news at the Troubadour, unlike Fiona's squeals of delight.

Come to think of it, Jen hadn't seemed surprised by the news either, had she?

Which meant that Peggy's invitation to New York had been common knowledge outside of just Charlie's regular drinking buddies.

Which *also* meant that Andrew had probably known about it for months before Thursday night, but he'd made absolutely no comment on it, not even in passing.

Which meant *what*?

Peggy shook herself, annoyed that her thoughts had again meandered back to precisely where they weren't supposed to be.

'Peg?' Charlie prompted, and Peggy remembered that she was supposed to have responded to his question.

'No,' she replied firmly. 'I'm staying because I *want* to, not because I think I should.'

Charlie nodded slowly. 'Are you going to go back to the Ballroom?'

'Yes.' There was no hesitation about that answer whatsoever.

Charlie shoved a chocolate snowflake in his mouth with a nod. 'Christ, that's good.'

Peggy snorted in amusement, thinking back to her own – and Andrew's – almost identical reaction to those chocolate truffles in Bowness.

'Look, I know it'll be difficult, but you really do need to tell him,' Charlie sighed eventually, giving Peggy a look full of sympathy.

Peggy's eyes widened in alarm. 'What? Why?'

Charlie frowned. 'You can't just *not* tell him how you feel Peggy. He needs to hear it from you, even though I suspect he's probably expecting it at this stage.'

'Expecting it?' Peggy blinked furiously. He couldn't be *expecting* anything, because he wasn't supposed to *know* anything.

'I mean, I can't imagine he'll be thrilled to hear it, but he'll know it's coming. I mean, it's been obvious to me for ages.'

'How could he possibly know?' Peggy asked before she could stop herself. 'How could *you* possibly know?'

'Peggy, you've been weird about him for *months*,' Charlie continued, apparently unaware that his sister was having a breakdown only a few feet away.

Peggy was going to keel over and die of shame, she really was.

Charlie shrugged again. 'I doubt he really thought he'd be picking you up from the airport next week.'

Airport?

Oh. Peggy cursed her stupid, mangled thoughts.

'You're talking about Albany.' Her mouth had unleashed the words before her sluggish brain could hold them back.

Charlie frowned harder. 'Who else would I be talking about?'

Peggy was saved from answering by another knock at the door, which was followed immediately by Marnie barging in without waiting for a reply.

'Oh, hiya!' she greeted them with the apparent surprise of someone who thought she'd find the room empty, even though she'd have full well known that both Peggy and Charlie were in there before she'd even knocked. 'Did you know that some woman's just arrived with an ice sculpture of our house?'

Charlie and Peggy shared a look of baffled horror; their father had apparently actually lost the plot at last. Admittedly, an ice sculpture was exactly the sort of thing that Caroline would love, and therefore she'd *hate* the fact that she didn't have it herself.

'God, I'd better go and keep an eye on things,' Charlie announced unhappily, picking up his mug again. 'I'll only get it in the neck from bloody Timothy if anything goes wrong before tonight.'

Peggy could only give her brother a half-hearted wave as he left; he'd no doubt be back in an attempt to continue their adjourned conversation before too long, and Peggy was already exhausted from it.

'How are you feeling?' Marnie asked not taking a seat. 'You look like you've got more colour in your cheeks.'

That was demonstrably true, because Peggy could still feel her face burning with embarrassment.

'I'm okay,' she replied. 'Tired.'

'I'm not staying,' Marnie continued quietly. 'You need your sleep, but I just wanted to tell you something before I tell anyone else. I want you to know that I went to see Rex this morning.'

Peggy gripped her mug between both hands.

Marnie shook her head vehemently. 'No, I don't want to talk about that complete arsehole either, but I wanted to tell you that I'm done. Done with him, I mean. I should never have gone to see him – not after everything he did – and I only went today to tell him that, and to let him know what will happen to him if he ever opens his mouth about you, or me, or the Ballroom again.'

Peggy wasn't sure what she should say to any of that. She was certain that Marnie would want to really *talk* about it at some point, but that moment wouldn't – *couldn't* – be yet.

'Anyway, that was all I wanted to say,' Marnie said, not quite looking Peggy in the eye. 'I'll leave you be.'

Without waiting for an answer, Marnie turned to go, but then she paused at the door.

'Actually, there is one more thing,' she said.

'What?' Peggy asked, bracing herself for whatever else could be coming.

Marnie scrunched her face up, clearly wondering how best to continue. 'Back at the cathedral, how did you get the door open?'

Peggy frowned. That wasn't even approaching what Peggy had thought Marnie might say. 'Why?'

'Because there's some debate at the Ballroom about what actually happened,' Marnie replied, and there was obviously something she was keeping to herself.

Peggy sighed and, without any desire to do so whatsoever, thought back to Monday night. 'When Jen ran off to help Andrew, someone came to me and explained how there was an emergency key for each door, and where to find the one in the tower. He helped me.'

'Right,' Marnie replied slowly. 'And was this someone who worked in the cathedral?'

'Something like that.' Peggy thought of how she'd not been thinking straight enough to listen to Mac's repeated warning not to look in his direction as she'd leant back against the open door.

Mac had been wearing robes that might have once been white, but in the dim light of the tower it was clear that they'd been shredded and streaked with blood and dirt; that would have been disturbing enough by itself, but it was when Peggy's gaze had travelled up to his face that she'd recoiled in horror. Multiple lash marks had split the skin on his face from his right temple to the opposite hinge of his jaw, and his right eye had been missing entirely. Beneath his chin, a thick ribbon of burned, red skin had left Peggy in no doubt of what had happened to him even *before* he'd even been allowed to die.

Mac had closed his remaining eye in shame and Peggy had wanted to tell him that she wasn't repulsed by *him*, but by the stark brutality of his death. She hadn't been able to find the words though and he'd only raised his hand towards her in what had been some form of blessing before he'd faded from her sight.

Only seconds later, she'd been faced with the awful realisation that she was about to see Andrew killed right in front of her.

Peggy shivered and wrapped her free arm around her middle, reminding herself that at least that part hadn't come to pass.

'And this man wasn't someone that anyone other than you and I would have seen, right?' Marnie prompted.

'Right,' Peggy confirmed wearily. Where was Marnie going with this?

'Andrew saw him.'

Even if Peggy had been running at full capacity it would have taken her time to process that concise but deeply bewildering statement. As such, she stared at Marnie, completely uncomprehending, as long moments passed.

'Andrew saw him,' Peggy repeated, brain whirring but getting no closer to comprehension.

Marnie nodded. 'Andrew saw him, but nobody else did. Jen had been standing next to him, and she looked at him like she thought he was nuts when he mentioned this man. Lloyd didn't see him either.'

'I don't understand,' Peggy said eventually. 'Andrew can't have seen him.'

A little whisper of a half-forgotten argument from months and months ago skipped into Peggy's mind and landed with an almost audible *thunk*. Back in March, Andrew had accused Peggy of hiding from him at Butterton, when she hadn't even been in the house at the time. Andrew had seen *someone* at the house, but it hadn't been Peggy. They hadn't talked about it after the argument, because by the time they'd had a chance, Peggy had already decided that she was going to make her exit while she'd still possessed even a smidge of remaining grace.

Peggy's eyes widened, because it hadn't just been that one event, had it? Andrew had seen his brother too. Peggy had been standing with him when it had happened, but in the chaos of surviving Agatha Joyce's last stand, she hadn't even thought to question it. As far as she was aware, it hadn't happened since, but she hadn't actually asked him.

'What is it?' Marnie asked, taking a few steps back towards Peggy, worry evident on her face.

Peggy tentatively explained, trying to pick at the threads as she spoke, hoping that an explanation would present itself to her.

It didn't.

Marnie looked just as perturbed as Peggy felt. 'What do you think it means?'

Peggy shook her head helplessly. 'I honestly don't know, but I don't think it can be anything good, do you?'

Marnie's silence was confirmation enough.

Peggy closed her eyes with a deep sigh, put her half-drunk tea on the dressing table, and took herself back to bed to search for the peace that always seemed to elude her when she was awake.

THIRTY-TWO

'You really don't need to stay,' Andrew said as Jen appeared with three cans of Coke. 'It's Christmas Eve, and I know you've got plans.'

Jen shrugged. 'It's fine, sir. It's only early, and you've got plans too.'

For the first time in years, that was actually true. His grandmother has been so thrilled that her grandson had agreed to spend both Christmas Eve and Christmas Day with her and his grandfather that she hadn't even batted an eyelid when Andrew had called from the airport to tell her that he might be a bit late because Alan Jermyn's flight from Alicante had been delayed.

'Don't you worry,' she'd said, with the sounds of industrial levels of kitchen prep occurring in the background, 'it'll keep until you're ready.'

Andrew was even wearing his new coat because he knew how much it would mean to her to see him in it. He'd had to beg for help at six different dry-cleaners in town on Tuesday morning. It had been going so badly that he'd genuinely considered calling Charlie for help, because he seemed the type to have an emergency dry-cleaner in his phonebook, if such a thing existed. He hadn't needed to resort to such tactics in the end, because the kind woman who'd owned his very last hope had taken pity on him almost immediately, and he'd run back into her shop to pick up the coat five minutes before she'd closed that afternoon.

Manchester Airport was in a state of festive chaos around where they stood in Arrivals waiting for Alan Jermyn to appear. His flight had apparently landed fifteen minutes earlier, but there hadn't been a hint of him.

A trio of kids who couldn't have been more than eight or nine kept flying past at varying speeds as they pushed each other around on an empty luggage trolley. The two uniformed officers that Andrew had co-opted from the airport's usual operations as backup in case they needed it were glaring at daggers at the hyper children but had thus far failed to convince them to stop.

'Do we really think this bloke's going to show?' Lloyd asked, taking yet another mince pie out of the box in his hand.

'He bloody well better,' Andrew muttered. He still wasn't a fan of Christmas, but his mood would significantly improve once he wasn't in the airport anymore.

Speakers in the ceiling pinged again to alert everyone to yet another announcement – Andrew was actually baffled by the frequency of them.

'Passengers travelling on British Airways flight BA-five-nine-three to New York, John F. Kennedy Airport, please proceed to gate number seven for immediate boarding.'

Andrew looked up at the departure board and scowled.

'I think I'd find it weird being anywhere but home for Christmas,' Lloyd mused as he watched people approaching the check-in desks, some already dressed for warmer climes in spite of the grey drizzle of Manchester.

Andrew, who'd spent many a Christmas either working or alone in his house, couldn't quite relate.

'Mum would probably kill me if I even suggested it,' Lloyd added with a shudder.

'I hear Annie invited you to spend Christmas with them, sir,' Jen piped up with a grin at Andrew.

'What, really?' Lloyd looked absolutely delighted at the concept.

Annie's call had caught Andrew off guard, which had made him sound so hesitant about his actual plans that she initially hadn't believed a word of it. He'd had to answer a number of fairly involved questions before Annie had been satisfied that he was telling the truth. Part of him was still expecting her to make a surprise call to his grandparents' house, just to check the veracity of his story.

'It must be so weird in that house at Christmas,' Lloyd continued happily. 'Like, can you imagine Higson in one of those little paper party hats? Actually, can you imagine what his *sons* must be like? Do you reckon they're more like Higson or Annie?' Oh, hey, have you ever met them, Jen?'

Jen looked like a deer caught in headlights. 'Yes.'

'What are they like?' Lloyd asked, eyes wide with genuine interest.

'They're fine,' Jen shrugged and then smiled tightly. 'I'm actually popping in to see Annie before I go to my sister's later. Some of us weren't allowed to turn her invitation down.'

Andrew had so many questions, but he couldn't ask a single one of them just then.

Lloyd, thankfully, had already moved on in the conversation. 'You'll come out on Saturday night though, won't you, boss? Charlie'll be out, and Fi's up for it as well. Julie might be there.'

A clump of people streamed through the doors to Arrivals and Andrew once again looked down at the fifteen-year-old photograph of Alan Jermyn in his hand. A mousy, Paul McCartney-esque mullet atop a pair of large square-framed spectacles stared back at him.

Even accounting for the decade and a half in the sun, and the transformation that might bring, none of the travellers who'd emerged looked anywhere near enough like Jermyn to be interesting.

Andrew pursed his lips and rocked back on his heels, remembering that he needed to answer Lloyd's question. 'No, I think I'll pass on this one.'

Lloyd grimaced. 'Is it the Julie thing?'

'What? No, of course not.' Andrew glowered. 'I'd just rather be at home and then sleep for a week.'

'Maybe New Year's then, yeah?' Lloyd suggested and then looked at Jen. 'You too. You never know, Peggy might even be alright enough to come out.'

'If she's alright enough to be out anywhere, Lloyd, then I think she'll be out in New York,' Andrew muttered as the Arrivals door opened again, this time to emit a small group of people who were all staring at the damp, grey outside world in disappointment.

Andrew pinched the bridge of his nose as the luggage trolley whizzed past again. The addition of a small child of about three at the top of the human pyramid that had been constructed on the trolley bed appeared to be the breaking point for the uniforms, and they thundered off after this display of anarchy with a quick promise to Andrew that they'd be right back.

Lloyd was frowning at him.

'Jesus, what now?' Andrew grumbled.

'Well, Peggy's not going to New York, is she?' Lloyd said slowly, looking between Andrew and Jen as though he needed to check that his facts were correct.

'What?' Andrew whirled around.

Lloyd recoiled in surprise. 'That's what Charlie told me!'

'Sir, I think that's Jermyn,' Jen announced suddenly, pointing discreetly to a man with significantly less hair than in the photograph, but still wearing the same glasses.

'Right,' Andrew stowed his breakdown somewhere behind him – he had a bloody job to do. He looked over to where the trolley kids were being soundly told off. 'Well, we've lost our backup.'

'He doesn't look all that dangerous,' Lloyd observed as they began walking towards Jermyn.

Andrew agreed, but that wasn't the point. 'Doesn't mean that he isn't.'

As they approached, Jermyn seemed to twig what was

happening. He made no move to run. He just set down his suitcase and held his hands out, wrists up, as Andrew identified himself.

Jermyn nodded as he gestured with his wrist. 'Fair cop.'

Lloyd frowned in confusion and looked to Andrew, silently asking what he should do.

'That won't be necessary, Mr Jermyn,' Andrew said, motioning for the man to put his hands down. 'Unless you're planning on running or causing a nuisance of yourself on the way to the car, that is.'

Jermyn shook his head. 'Not a chance.'

'Bootle Street then, sir?' Jen asked, taking up position on one side of Jermyn as Lloyd moved to the other.

'Yeah,' Andrew agreed. 'Interview and then we'll go from there.'

'You can carry your own suitcase, mate,' Lloyd told Jermyn as he pointed at the luggage judgementally. 'Does this look like the bloody Midland to you?'

Jermyn bobbed his head in apology, and they walked together to the exit where the GMP-liveried Capri was waiting.

'Get in, Mr Jermyn,' Andrew instructed.

'Bootle Street,' Jen said to the two uniformed officers standing by the car. 'They'll be expecting him, and we'll be along soon.'

'Yes, ma'am,' they chorused, slamming the door behind Jermyn. They then quickly checked the suitcase before stowing it in the boot.

'What did you mean about Peggy not going to New York?' Andrew asked as the car drove away with Jermyn giving them a sad little wave from the backseat. It certainly wasn't the question he'd intended to ask.

'What?' Lloyd looked confused for a second. 'Oh, right, yeah. Well, I called Charlie earlier to see if he wanted to go for a pint, and then he just told me that Peggy's not going to New York.'

'Next week?' Andrew was getting well beyond his better judgement at that stage.

'No, she's not going at all,' Lloyd clarified with a shrug.

Oh, Andrew didn't appreciate the little rush of hope at Lloyd's words. Just because Peggy wasn't imminently leaving, it didn't mean that anything was actually different. It certainly didn't change the fact that Andrew had behaved like an arse earlier in the year, or that Peggy had still let him down gently when she'd realised that he'd overstepped the mark in their relationship just before she'd gone out for dinner with Cohen. It didn't change the fact that nothing good could actually come of him opening his big mouth again and burdening Peggy with his latest inconvenient realisation; the realisation that the months of distance had somehow made things even more difficult.

It would be selfish and arrogant and, *God*, he'd been trying to be less of both of those things.

'Do you want to borrow my car, boss?' Lloyd asked, already holding out his keys.

'Why would I want to borrow your car?' Andrew squinted at the keys and then Lloyd.

'Well, you don't have a car at the minute.'

'We can do the interview, sir,' Jen added nonsensically. 'I don't think it'll take very long.'

Andrew suddenly realised what the other two were suggesting and he opened his mouth to protest.

'Mate,' Lloyd said seriously, slapping Andrew on the arm, and not even pretending that there was anything even remotely professional about this entire production. 'Just take the car.'

Jen, who was apparently a complete traitor after all, just shrugged and said, 'Tell Peggy that I hope she's feeling better.'

Andrew took the keys, avoiding all eye contact before he stalked towards Lloyd's car.

'Oh, boss!' Lloyd called after him. 'Charlie said they were having a little *gathering* at the house tonight.'

Andrew dreaded to think what sort of event Charlie would

term a 'gathering' but he'd committed himself to the idea of leaving already and if he paused to ask any questions, he thought that he might not actually get in the car at all.

He drove away from the terminal more quickly than he should have done, ignoring the amused thumbs up directed towards him as he flew past.

What in Christ's name was he doing?

All he had to do was turn right and he could drive straight into Manchester. He'd be at Bootle Street before Jen and Lloyd got there. Or he could turn right and instead be back in Gatley in ten minutes – it'd serve the other two right, leaving them to interview Jermyn while Andrew strolled off for dinner with his grandparents.

Andrew viciously slapped the indicator and turned left anyway.

It took him twenty-five minutes to arrive at Butterton, and even as he drove through the village – ignoring the fact that he could actually just turn around if he really wanted to – he had absolutely no idea what he was going to do once he got there.

The familiar chimneys of Butterton House rose up into the sky over the village, obvious even in the settling darkness of the evening.

Christmas lights were strung outside nearly every house, giving the whole village the sort of postcard perfection that Andrew had seen in the Lake District over the weekend. He couldn't help scowling at the cheerful groups of revellers heading to the local pub.

It was only when he passed through the gateposts at the end of the driveway that the reality of the situation slapped Andrew firmly on the back of his head. It was only *then* that he realised that he'd found himself at the back of a queue of very slow-moving cars, all heading towards the house.

No. There was. No way he could do it – whatever *it* was.

Andrew glanced in the rearview mirror ready to three-point-turn his way right out of what obviously would have been a catastrophic act of idiocy but he found that his escape route had been blocked by a large fancy car that had joined the line behind him.

Two more cars followed that one.

Right, he thought as they all inched forwards, it would all be fine. He'd just turn around on the grass once the driveway got a bit wider, and then he'd wait for a gap so that he could head back out towards the village.

By the time he reached the lake, Andrew had perfected the entire dressing-down that he would be delivering to his sergeant and his constable the very next time he saw them, and he was more than ready to leave.

But then he made the mistake of glancing at the house, and now that he knew exactly which windows were Peggy's he couldn't help but look in that direction.

Andrew pulled the car onto the grass. He took the keys from the ignition and opened the door, stepping onto the lawn and, no doubt, further invoking the wrath of a groundskeeper somewhere.

He was uncomfortably aware of the perplexed looks he was receiving from guests in their cars as he strode towards the house. He pulled his coast more tightly around himself and turned the collar up to his ears as he kept his head down.

Andrew had always liked a good plan, and it had taken eighteen months on Tib Street for him to understand that you couldn't plan for every eventuality, no matter how hard you tried. Still, he wondered if having no plan at all might just be a step too far for him.

He'd almost reached the gravel in front of the house when Timothy came hurrying towards him with a ridiculously pinched expression on his face.

'Mr Joyce!' Timothy did nothing to mask how livid he was at

Andrew's arrival. 'This is an invitation-only event!'

'I'm not here for your event, Timothy,' Andrew replied, not slowing down as he passed the stunned butler.

'Mr Joyce, is that a *black eye?*' Timothy hissed in horror from behind him.

A number of other suited men were positioned between the cars and the front door, but none of them seemed to have a clue what to do about a gatecrashing pedestrian and seemed minded to just let Andrew carry on about his business.

He hadn't quite made it to the steps when Charlie Swan – in full evening dress, for fuck's sake – sauntered down towards him with an awfully smug grin on his face.

'Joycie!' he crowed. 'I *thought* I heard the sound of Timothy dropping dead from too much judgement. Not that I'm not delighted that you're here to absolutely ruin his Christmas, but I'm fairly certain that you weren't on my father's guest list when I last looked.'

'Yeah, but neither am I,' Marnie announced chirpily, skipping down the steps to join them. She turned to beam unnervingly at the guests ascending towards the door. 'Hiya!'

Christ, Andrew could *not* do this. Not with an audience of these two on top of a whole host of horribly rich people that Peggy probably disliked immensely.

'Lloyd said you were having a *gathering,*' Andrew muttered tightly, feeling terribly self-conscious, 'not whatever the hell this is.'

Charlie rolled his eyes. 'Look, Joycie, as welcome as you are to come in, I sense that you're not actually here for a glass of fizz and inane small talk.'

'No,' Andrew admitted, even if that was already damn obvious.

'I take it that Lloyd also told you that my sister is, in fact, *not* going to New York?' Charlie raised one eyebrow.

'He did.' Andrew tried not to squirm. 'I wanted to see how she was feeling.'

'And you don't have access to a phone?' Marnie asked, smirking as she folded her arms.

Andrew fumbled for an answer.

'Oh, for goodness sake, Joycie, she's winding you up.' Charlie's eyeroll that time was particularly aggravating.

Andrew scowled again.

Charlie sighed loudly. 'Well, did Lloyd tell you that Peg is not going to be rescheduling her flight? That it's all very much over with the American?'

Andrew's nose twitched. 'He didn't quite put it like that.'

'You do realise that Peggy's spending most of her time asleep right now, don't you?' Marnie asked, and the fact that it lacked her usual acidity made Andrew somehow feel dafter than if she'd just outright called him an idiot.

But, *no*, that little fact hadn't actually occurred to Andrew at all. Why couldn't he have just called Peggy like a normal person? A quick phone call just to check that she was alright, and to remind her that there was a whole host of people out there thinking about her.

'Right,' Andrew nodded. 'Look, enjoy your party. Have a good Christmas, alright?'

'Where on earth are you going now?' Charlie exclaimed in bewilderment.

'Home,' Andrew called back, dodging a woman who was dressed suspiciously like a peacock.

'Woah, hang on!'

Marnie zipped after him and grabbed his arm. Apparently holding his hand for moral support on Monday night had really spelled the end for their mutually respected rule that they avoided physical contact at all costs.

'I'm not actually taking the piss,' Marnie added as Charlie joined them. 'I'm just saying that you might want to wait until Peggy's not in her pyjamas with a raging fever before you go professing your undying love.'

Andrew's eyes bugged so much it was almost painful. '*What*? Nobody said a *thing* about love. Jesus Christ, Marnie.'

Marnie took a full step back as though he'd struck her. She then looked at Charlie askance. 'Is he joking?'

She then turned her attention back to Andrew. 'Are you *actually* joking?'

Andrew shook his head. He was done. This had been a terrible idea, even more poorly executed.

Maybe this was a sign – which he didn't believe in – or maybe it was a gut-feeling – which he knew never to doubt – but whatever it was, it was telling him to schlep back to Lloyd's car immediately and to keep his head down.

He held up his hands as he backed away, and whether it was in silent surrender or in defeat, he wasn't sure. He supposed it didn't matter either way because they were the same thing at the end of the day.

Something, though, made him look up and he jolted in surprise when he saw Peggy peering through a gap in her curtains, staring down at him in bewilderment. She was obviously trying to stay hidden from the arriving guests, and her face was half in shadow, but she was still the best thing that Andrew had seen all day.

God, he vaguely remembered being rational once.

He really needed to leave.

Andrew raised his hand and forced a smile onto his face before turning away and walking back towards Lloyd's car with his hands in his pockets and a blinding sense of mortification pinned to his back for all to see.

Marnie caught up with him just as he reached the car and made him swear in alarm when she got into the passenger seat.

'Alright, fine.' Marnie gave a long-suffering sigh. 'I'll give Peggy *one* message for you.'

'I didn't ask you to give her *any* message!' Andrew argued. 'Also, can you get out? I need to get to my grandparents' house.'

Marnie rolled her eyes just as infuriatingly as Charlie had done. 'What do you want me to say to her?'

'Nothing.' Andrew glared.

'Oh, for God's sake, you are *such* an idiot, do you know that?'

Yes, he might well have known that.

He looked back towards the house and thought that he actually shouldn't be a complete arse and leave without saying *something*.

'Just tell her that I came to say Merry Christmas,' he answered eventually, 'and that I'll see her in the Ballroom whenever she's ready.'

'That's it?' Marnie asked flatly, clearly unimpressed.

'Oh, no, hang on,' Andrew added, and Marnie perked up immediately. 'Tell her that Jen says that she hopes she's feeling better.'

Marnie muttered something too quiet for Andrew to hear, but he got the gist based on tone alone and knew that it was in no way flattering. Then she disappeared as though she'd never been there.

Andrew gave it a few minutes for the stragglers at the back of the queue to get out of the way, and then with a blustery sigh he threw the car into reverse and prepared to turn around.

The knock on the driver's window scared the hell out of him and he jumped in fright, his elbow colliding with the horn.

Timothy was glaring at him, lips more tightly pursed than should have been humanly possible.

Andrew rolled down the window. 'Timothy.'

'Mr Joyce,' Timothy replied cooly, holding out something that Andrew couldn't quite make out in the dark of the driveway. 'Lady Margaret has requested that I ensure that you do not leave without this.'

Andrew accepted the small package through the window.

'Good evening, Mr Joyce,' Timothy snapped and then he turned on his perfectly polished heel and headed back towards the house as Andrew rolled the window up.

Switching on the overhead light, Andrew discovered that he was holding a small cellophane bag containing two familiar chocolate truffles, and he found himself grinning at the unexpected present before he caught himself.

He cleared his throat and put the bag carefully in the glovebox.

As he snapped the cover closed, Marnie popped back into existence beside him, and he shrieked in alarm.

'Jesus Christ!' Andrew clutched at his chest.

Marnie grinned. 'Peggy says Merry Christmas too.'

She then raised her eyebrows as though trying to impart something meaningful.

When Andrew only stared at her, Marnie eventually shook her head and disappeared again with a final slur about his intelligence.

Andrew looked back over at the house again. He had no idea if Peggy could see him or not, but he waved in her direction anyway before turning the car around and driving away from Butterton.

Alright, so he'd admit that he hadn't actually really achieved anything, but he still felt a hundred times lighter as he drove back through the village. He even managed not to glare at the latest group entering the pub.

It had been a terrible week, but they'd all survived it relatively intact.

They'd *all* be back in the Ballroom in January, and that would have to be enough for Andrew for now.

Everything else would keep.